P9-DHE-799

PRAISE FOR SUSAN BERNHARD

"*Winter Loon* is a brutal, beautiful coming-of-age story in which a young man who loses everything must return to the landscape of that loss to discover what it all means. Susan Bernhard is a writer of incredible grace and power who employs weather and the natural world to plumb the icy depths of her characters' souls for the warmth of hope, healing, and heart."

—Wiley Cash, *New York Times* bestselling author of *The Last Ballad, A Land More Kind Than Home*, and *This Dark Road to Mercy*

"I lost myself in *Winter Loon*, its rugged heart, its dark secrets, the honesty and vulnerability of its characters. With prose both taut and lush, Susan Bernhard has created the quintessential story of adolescence: raw, tender, and completely spellbinding."

—Mira T. Lee, author of *Everything Here Is Beautiful*

"Wes Ballot is the kind of character I read books hoping to find—imperfect and lovable, haunted yet determined to forge ahead. From the moment I slid out onto the ice with him, *Winter Loon* had me in its grip. A gorgeous novel from a masterful new voice."

—Anna Solomon, author of *Leaving Lucy Pear*

"This is a beauty of a page-turner, dreamy, disquieting, and uncompromising to the end. Against the tide of the wandering heart, the novel tells us, only love can offer us a place to rest—and only if we let it."

—Michelle Hoover, author of *Bottomland* and *The Quickening*

"*Winter Loon* is a stunner. In gorgeous, laconic prose, Susan Bernhard has brought to life an unforgettable character in Wes Ballot, whose coming-of-age is marked as much by his own resilience as it is the tragedy of his circumstances. I read this book late into the night. I bet you will, too."

—Peter Geye, author of *Wintering*

"With stunning prose and unforgettable characters, Bernhard brings us inside the life of a boy struggling to break out of the harrowing cycle of his past. This story is at once heartbreaking and inspiring—for every character determined to hold Wes down comes another with just enough ordinary grace to set him free. And the fine line between despair and redemption Wes walks will keep you holding your breath until the very end. This is a masterful debut."

—Katherine Sherbrooke, author of *Fill the Sky*

"*Winter Loon* seethes with the energy of an adolescent boy trying to figure out how to become a man. Wes Ballot is sixteen, weighed down by loss and secrets, but also uplifted by the joys of falling in love. All the while, Susan Bernhard's muscular writing propels the reader through this striking debut."

—Alexi Zentner, author of *Copperhead* and *The Lobster Kings*

WINTER
LOON

WINTER LOON

A NOVEL

SUSAN BERNHARD

This is a work of fiction. Names, characters, organizations, places, events, and incidents are either products of the author's imagination or are used fictitiously. Any resemblance to actual persons, living or dead, or actual events is purely coincidental.

Published by Little A, New York

www.apub.com

ISBN-13: 9781503902985 (hardcover)
ISBN-10: 1503902986 (hardcover)
ISBN-13: 9781503902978 (paperback)
ISBN-10: 1503902978 (paperback)

Cover design by Faceout Studio, Tim Green
Cover illustrated by Ashley Mackenzie

Printed in the United States of America
First edition

For Mom and Montana

CHAPTER 1

A HAWK BANKED IN THE GRAY DAYBREAK, HEAD HUNCHED, EYES DARTING beneath a cross of wings. Nothing scampered or skittered along the ice, nothing meaty or gamy worth a closer look, nothing with any fight left. All that hawk could have seen was me as I was that morning, a boy only fifteen years old curled up tight as a fiddlehead, ear to the ice, alone on a frozen lake surrounded by remote miles of woods and farmland, a handful of houses sagging in the dark.

I remember watching the hawk disappear, wishing it would swoop down, pluck me up, carry me off in its talons. I cupped my hands over my nose and blew what little steam I had left into them. Pine trees crowded the distant edge of the lake. A black dog barked and bounded back and forth along the unruly shore. From where I lay, I couldn't see the cabin, though in that frozen moment I worried about our cat, Elizabeth, and whether she'd escaped through the open door. I thought to get up, to crawl to safety, but couldn't bring myself to leave. I let my eyes rest again on the craggy spot, dark as spilled ink and barely out of my reach, where the ice had given way and the hungry lake had swallowed my mother whole.

We had been living in a basement apartment beneath the laundromat in town where my mother worked folding clothes, making change, stocking the vending machine, picking lint out of dryers. When the pipes busted and flooded the place, she lost her job and we lost our home in the same night. The drafty cabin on Bright Lake wasn't meant for winter, but we'd been there a week already in that cold heart of January, over ten years ago now.

My father told us the cabin would be temporary, that it beat sleeping in the car. That was a thing we'd done, the three of us sometimes, but more often just my mother and me. My father was something of a welder, I guess, though he seemed to have a hard time holding down a steady job. He worked summers with a traveling carnival or up on the pipeline in Alaska. Other times, he'd take off without explanation, though he'd always go out of his way to remind me that I was to take care of my mother while he was away. I came to resent that relinquishing of power. I had no more control over her than he did.

We arrived at the cabin with only what we needed or could easily rescue. Bedding, winter clothes stuffed into laundry baskets, bargain-bin cross-stitch and latch-hook kits that my mother kept in a plastic bucket, a pair of produce boxes my mother always used for packing. My dad grabbed the wooden crate he kept on a high shelf that held his favorite whittling knife and taxidermy supplies—needles, scissors, wire cutters, borax, cotton batting. He said he'd go back and salvage the rest later. I brought a pile of schoolbooks from the kitchen table, my favorite boots, and little else.

My mother and I watched from the car while my dad patted down the rotted windowsill for the key his friend promised was there. He slouched in the way tall people do, like he was trying to squeeze into a cramped space. When the key dropped into a snowbank, he leaned over from the shoulders like a vulture and plunged his hand over and over, cursing and kicking until he came up with it and held it high, a prize won.

"Oh goody," my mother said. "Grab your things."

The cabin was all but abandoned. White refrigerator, green oven, bare plank floors. A rocking chair by the stone fireplace, a ripped gold-colored couch with sunken cushions against the drafty wall, a table under the window with three mismatched chairs, a sorry-looking white-tail buck trophy hung next to a smallmouth bass, its skin-mounted fins brittle and broken. My father lowered his head sheepishly, like he'd betrayed a solemn blood oath. This was, after all, a hideout for men who left women and children behind. It was no one's home. He defended the cabin against my mother's scornful comments, said we'd have to make do unless she had a better idea. Four cots bunked in the single bedroom were stained with seeped blood and mystery fluids. My mother refused to sleep on them. To be fair, she never did sleep much no matter where we lived. She could curl up on a couch or catnap in front of a fire if we had one. I'd seen her take a pillow and blanket and go to sleep on the kitchen floor between table and cabinets against a radiator that would hiss and bang all night long. Mostly, she said, she wanted to close her eyes last.

My mother didn't like the woods either, didn't trust them. From the moment we stepped foot in the cabin, she was restless and sulky. No television, no neighbors, no jukeboxes or pool tables, no bars that would let a woman bring her child and park him in a corner booth with a pop and a coloring book while she caroused awhile. I'd outgrown that sort of tagging along by then and felt trapped, too, watching her pace the cabin, a panther planning her escape. Darkness settled her down. She would stare out the window at nothing. I caught her performing for her reflection, waning in the simmered light, releasing smoke from a straw-size hole at the corner of her mouth, stroking her own dark hair. Rather than bother turning her head, she would talk to us through that woman on the glass, like that figment was the real her. She'd hear a sound and make goggles of her hands to try to see into the night. Or she'd investigate from the open doorway, letting the built-up heat escape over the threshold, which drove my father crazy since she'd complain again about the cold once the door was closed.

My parents married young—she was seventeen and he was twenty-three. There was a baby, a girl called Daisy, who was born and died that same year. I came along soon after. When I was maybe three years old, my parents divorced. Over the years they'd claim it was the divorce that was the mistake, not the marriage. They reconciled and remarried. I was their ring bearer and remember fishing my mother's own ring—the same one that had left a thin scar on the bridge of my father's nose when she'd wrenched it from her finger and flung it at him a year before—out of my pants pocket, dropping nickels and gum wrappers in the process. My mother had giggled when I tried to put the ring on her finger instead of handing it to my father. "Guess I'm not needed here after all," my father had said.

They no longer tried to shield me from their arguing like they did when I was little, not that I hadn't witnessed their fuck-or-fight love my whole life. They could fight about anything. They fought about money, about jobs, about the men who stared at my mother and the women who sidled up to my father, about what brand of cigarettes to smoke or whether toilet paper was even necessary. As far as they were concerned, I could listen if I wanted. They'd mostly stopped caring what I heard, especially when they were drunk. They had come to use me as judge and witness. "Isn't that right, Wes?" one would say. Or, "Wes was there, weren't you?" For a long time they fought about having another baby, but my father said he could barely afford the family he had. That argument she won. She got pregnant when I was in second grade. Seemed the discussion of more babies ended only after she miscarried.

The drinking and fighting had gotten serious at Bright Lake. There was no sobering up for work because there was no work. The money was running out. That meant no turning drunk afternoons at the bar into lingering nights that hung over through the following morning. They drank at the table instead. They drank instead of eating.

They'd gone into town earlier that night to get supplies and see about the rest of our things. They returned dug in for battle. Cupboard doors slammed, canned goods dropped on the table like bombs from a fuselage.

"Don't be like that, Val," my father said.

My mother clenched and fumed. "Yeah, put this on me. Like always."

He rifled through the grocery bag. "Where'd you set the cigarettes?"

She sidearmed a pack that hit his chin like an uppercut. He bent over, snatched it from the floor, his patience spent. "See what I have to put up with?" He aimed this at me but turned back to her. "So help me God, Val . . ."

"What?" Her arms spread sacrificially as she dared him, practically chest-bumping him though he was so much bigger in every way. "Nothing you can do to me that hasn't been done." She backed off and I backed away.

"I'm gonna—" I gestured with my thumb to the bedroom.

"See, Moss?" my mother said. "See? Wes doesn't even want to be in the same room with you. Say goodbye to your father, Wes. He's leaving again."

"Not right this minute."

"Wait," I said. "What? You promised you'd stay the winter. You said we'd go with you in the spring."

That made my mother laugh hysterically. She'd already poured herself a glass of whiskey. "Oh please. Tell him, Moss. Tell him what you told me."

"Tell me what?"

"You go on now," my father said. "We can talk tomorrow."

So this would be another ugly leaving. When I was younger, I was a miserable snot, kicking and wailing each time he took off, hurling hate on him and my mother both. I missed him terribly while he was gone. He'd come back and they'd try to rebuild on the shifting rubble of their crumbling marriage. When I got older, his leaving became more of a betrayal. That night I was keen to signal my disappointment before slamming the door. "Yeah. Don't bother."

I threw myself onto one of the cots and bent the pillow to muffle my ears against their escalating fight, against words that were all too familiar. The last thing I remember hearing was my father saying he needed air, then the sound of the cabin door slamming shut. I was grateful for the quiet. I wanted to sleep. So when she rousted me later, I protested the way any teenage boy would. I pulled the blanket over my head, trying to shut her out with the cold. She tugged at the bottom of my bedding so hard I sat up, and when I did she lost her balance. Bourbon cascaded from her glass as she landed hind-end on the floor. I was uncovered and she was liquor-soaked and laughing. She righted herself, then kneeled next to me in drunken earnest. "Wes, get up. Come on." She built her words letter by letter out of tongue and breath and teeth and lips. "The loon. Let's go look for the loon."

That was a new thing they'd found to fight about. A hooting sound, a coo at night. My father said it was too late into winter for loons to be so far north, that she was probably hearing a screech owl. "This is an owl," he said, interlacing his fingers, making double doors with his thumbs. He blew into the shed he'd created and baffled out a hollow three-note hoot. "And this," he said, wrapping one hand over the other, "is a loon." The sound floated out more ancient and eerie, a long note that kicked up once, then dropped back down. "See? Owl."

My mother said he was an idiot, that they sounded the same.

"Not that again," I said. "Make Dad go with you. Then maybe you two will stop fighting about it."

The excitement twisted out of her, turned wily, a weasel slinking into a pond. She whipped her head in a side-to-side figure eight. "That. F-f-fuckerrrr's. Gone." She pressed to standing, drained the unspilled drops from the bottom of the glass into her mouth, then stumbled out of the dark bedroom. Firelight seeped across the floor from the dying embers. Elizabeth stood in the doorway, extending her legs in a bored stretch, wondering, I suppose, what foolishness we people were up to now. I heard the clink of bottle to glass as my mother hollered to hurry up.

"I'm not dressed."

"It's not church. Just grab something. Chop, chop," she said, adding a feeble handclap. Outside rushed in when she opened the cabin door. I clambered for the blankets at the foot of the bed, wrapped up, and collapsed against the pillow, aching for sleep. But she'd left the front door open and it banged in the same wind that dropped pine cones and sticks on the lichen-covered roof. I never really considered not following her. We were a pair, my mother and me. I slipped my boots on over my wool socks, my coat over my long underwear, and followed her into the night.

Her dark silhouette staggered down the path, a balancing act, amber liquid wobbling in a glass on one side, her empty hand outstretched on the other. The wind had shifted, swooping down in a wave, warm for winter. The crust of snow was quickly disappearing, leaving mud bogs, pitted ice, fossilized hoof and paw prints. My mother looked west, like she expected to see the wind itself, a hot phantom with black eyes leading its pack down the hilly slope. I caught up with her and saw she was wearing my father's buckskin slippers.

"Mom. Your shoes."

Faint surprise registered on her face, as if someone else had dressed her. "Never mind my feet," she said. "Look."

She used her glass to point at a howling moon, full over a dip in the pines where the lake wound away in the distance. She locked her arm in mine and we stood still there, breathless, silver.

"Man in the moon can see everything," she said. "Every goddamned thing you do." She raised her glass, clucked, and winked a toast skyward, then took another drink. "I fucked this one up good, didn't I, old man?"

"Let's go back," I said, steering her toward the cabin. I was a practiced guide. I could be conspirator, sounding board, an echo, a mirror. Whatever she wanted. I thought I knew when she needed to mother me. "I'm getting cold."

She shook me off, gulped down the whiskey, held the empty glass up, closing one eye. "If I could just stuff him in here . . ." She rested her hand on top of the moon and pressed down. The moon didn't budge. She dropped her arms, then hurled the glass onto the ice. It skipped away, spiraled to a dead stop. She clutched at her head. "Come on, Wes. Take me dancing," she said, grabbing my hand, pulling me toward the ice.

I tried the voice of reason. "I don't think we should. Dad said—"

"Your dad doesn't give two shits about us." She tipped her head to the side. "Come on."

"Did he go into town? Let's wait for him."

Her drunk switch flipped from flirty to angry. "You know what, Wes? You know what you are? You're a party pooper, that's what. I'll go by myself."

Her footing was loose and sloppy as she sidled onto the ice, mocking me, calling me chicken and baby. She told me I was just like my father, no goddamned fun at all. She became tiny in the distance, the off-kilter spindle of a twirling top. "I'm okay," she yelled. "See?" And she jumped up and down, knees together, a toddler in a puddle.

I put my hands around my mouth and hollered for her to stop but she kept at it, testing the ice, proving her point. The shifting ice moaned and twanged, kettledrum then tension wire whiplashing across the lake. And then another sound, a cry—tonal and pitched—a summer sound, one mate calling to the other, *I'm here. Where are you?* What would a loon be doing so far north? My mother whooped, "I told you so," and flapped her arms, spinning her dark hair in the silver moonlight.

I WAS SIX YEARS OLD the first time my father took me to Bright Lake, where his friend—Charlie Something—had this fair-weather cabin good for fishing and hunting weekends, for men, booze, and cards. I was all ribs and freckles and banged-up knees back then, toasted hair poking up off my head in a coarse meringue tangle, my skinny arms crossed hard as I stood on shore, sun beating down on my mottled shoulders, wicked black bugs circling my head. Summer kids had erected a rickety diving board from scrap wood nailed willy-nilly into a scaffolding perched on the end of an old boat dock. Boys in cutoff jeans flailed and jackknifed and cannonballed into the lake while the girls tried not to be impressed.

I was in a standoff with my father. I could jump, he said, but only if I wore one of the bleached life jackets that wintered in a box with spiders and centipedes. I'd refused, thinking if I stood my ground, he'd relent. Instead, he and Charlie sat on the little bluff, drinking beer, watching me watch the other kids. Finally, I couldn't take it anymore and snatched the life jacket off the ground, brushed it off, and strapped it on, glaring the whole time at my father as if he gave a shit whether I jumped or not.

The rungs of the ladder were spread so wide I was knees to chin with each step. My father yelled, "Let's see what you got, Little." He tipped his beer, laughing with the faceless Charlie as I made my way, heel to toe, out to the brink. I stared straight down into the bottomless water, consumed by thoughts of fish with teeth and billowing knots of drowned weeds. The older kids jeered, lolled their heads, rolled their eyes, even pelted me with pebbles. "Go on, Wes," my father said. He was standing now, finishing off his beer, resigning himself, I suppose, to the fact he'd have to come down and coax me off the board or into the water. I steadied myself, unclipped the vest, dropped it onto the dock. *I'll show him,* I thought. He hollered my name, urgent this time, and started down the gravel trail. I took one look at him, plugged my nose, and jumped. I remember the feeling of cutting through the water, of chuting down deep and fast, heavy like a log. I opened my eyes, expecting to be circled by sturgeon and lake trout, serpentine monsters and great schools of fish. Instead, in the murky distance, I saw a diving loon, glistening black, layered in pearls. Its red eye caught mine and saw right through me—every bit of penny candy I'd ever stolen, the times I practiced swearing into the mirror, other six-year-old sins. Floating there between sinking and rising, I thought myself dead and that loon my deliverance. Panicked, I kicked toward sunlight and my father's water-warped face. He pulled me out and up to his chest in a single motion, hugged me good, then gave me a half-hearted licking I knew was mostly for show.

And there I was again, this time in winter, the loon returned for my mother, who stamped and whirled, arms spanned, head thrown back, a summoning dance to some cold god. I could almost see time lagging behind, unable to catch up with the quick work of a thing bound to happen. The ice groaned and gasped, opened its frozen maw in a hibernated yawn. My mother broke through the teeth of ice like she was dropped from the seat of a dunking machine.

The world sped up around me and, forgetting caution, I ran onto the ice. I dropped to my belly and skittered toward her, reaching, begging her to take my hand. Drunk, stubborn, she kept saying no, that she could do it herself. We were frantic and desperate, pleading with each other, yelling over each other. But the more she grasped, the more ice broke off, until peril set in.

"You have to keep trying," I said. "Please."

Her expression calmed, shivers falling from her like shed skin. I peeled my coat off, thinking I'd throw her the sleeve and pull her out.

"You're all white." She huffed out breath in frozen bursts. "Like an angel. Like the moon."

I wrapped one sleeve around my wrist and held the end in my hand. "Grab this!" I tossed the coat and it grazed her fingertips. She didn't even try to reach for it. The elbow of her other arm chipped at the thin ice, like a second hand ticking time away. "Mom!" I pleaded, tossing the coat again and again. "Mom."

"Your dad is going to be p-pissed about his s-slippers," she stammered through chattering teeth.

"I have to go for help then!" I stood, turned my back to her. Where would I go? Not a single light was on. I made for the cabin, calling for help, calling for my father, waiting for a light to flicker on somewhere, for the sound of a voice that was not my own. With her draining strength, she shrieked, begging me not to leave her out there alone. The expanse of ice between us grew and I knew it was too much.

I went back, elbowed my way toward her. The ice shuddered and bent. She shifted her right shoulder and arm toward me, her fingers reaching for mine. We gripped each other's wrists and for a second there, I thought we were saved. I remember the relief of it, the power even. I'd finally done what my father had asked me to do. I let out my held breath and pulled. But she shifted the balance and pulled back with her left shoulder and down with her right hand, which dragged me closer to the hole she was in. She lurched like she was kicking fiercely under the water. I could see it in her eyes, a familiar intent, a thing hungry and alive. She knew she was done for. And right then, like so many other nights when she made me sleep with her or crawled into my little bed with me, she was afraid to be alone. I let out a cry that raced across the lake as we struggled, fisherman and catch.

I yanked free and she dipped below the waterline, then surfaced, sputtering, bluer than before. She seemed to forget what had happened and focused instead on something behind me, riding in on an arc of clouds. "He's coming," she whimpered, reaching for me again though I'd backed farther away. "Please. Don't leave me."

I scooted onto my coat and curled up, never taking my eyes off her. The last thing she said to me, I echoed back to her. She was there, then she was not.

A woman alone in the cabin not far from Charlie Something's had heard a sound that woke her. She'd sat up in bed, pricked her ears, chalked it up to the wind. That's what she told the sheriff. Plus, she said, she wasn't about to go investigating on her own. It was the persistence of the dog that whined to go out in the bare first light of morning, then seeing our cabin door wide open, the thing not right on the lake, that prompted her to call for help. And so I was rescued, though as it came—in the shape of men emerging from the trees, shouting for me to hang on—what I wanted was a do-over. I wanted to see the whole thing again, to rewind, to make it so she wasn't under the ice, so that we were back in the cabin, so that my dad was there, too, so that they were sober and the fire was stoked, so that beans and a ham hock were cooking in an iron pot on the green stove. But my fierce wanting couldn't make it so. All I could do was watch the men as they came for me on ice pink with sunrise. Their pace became more urgent as they got closer, realizing, I guess, that I was a boy, alive and alone. They wore uniforms, hats with earflaps tied on top, black boots, tank-colored jackets with a county sheriff patch in the shape of Minnesota. The tall one dragged a yellow sled behind him. The one who kneeled on the ice next to me was stumpy, with wide-set eyes and a runny nose he wiped with his sleeve. He motioned for the tall one to pass him a blanket.

"Hey, there. Hey," he said, covering my shoulders in dark wool. "It's okay. I'm the sheriff. We're here to help." He patted me all over, up and down, all the way to my socks. "You're dry. You didn't go in?"

I shook my head, my mouth clamped shut with guilt.

"What happened here, son? Why are you out here? Where are your folks?"

I closed my eyes and a span of winged sleep engulfed me. In that brief darkness, she was there again, blue and silver in the moonlight, reaching for me.

"What's your name, son?"

"Wes," I said, sure of little else. "Wes Ballot."

Bits of tobacco caught in the tall man's mustache as he spat on the ice. He crouched next to the sheriff. "Ballot? Your dad Moss Ballot?"

I nodded. "Is he at the cabin?"

The sheriff hesitated, tugged the matted fur on his coat collar. "Let's get him loaded up. Ambulance ought to be here soon. Careful there," he said. "Ice looks thin."

The tall man stood and pulled the sled up next to me, skirting the busted-up ice. "Your dad's back in town. He leave you out here by yourself?"

"My mom."

"What about your mom? Where is she?"

I could feel the truth foaming in the sting beneath my tongue, thickening, lining the inside of my cheeks. "The ice, it took her." Saying the words turned my mouth cold.

"Ah Christ," the tall man said. He unclipped the radio from his belt and turned away.

The sheriff sat back on his boots and pinched the bridge of his thick nose. "What happened out here, son?"

I would spend a good bit of time, years, trying to understand it myself, how I ended up out there, how we got to Bright Lake in the first place, what kind of people I'd sprung from, what kind of person I might be. In the moment, I had no answer. The men maneuvered me onto the padded sled. "You can't leave her here. You have to find her," I begged. They could only apologize, looking at me like men who knew there was nothing they could do.

As our tiny caravan made toward land, the contours of ice creaked and shivered over my tailbone and up my spine. I craned my neck for one last look, but all I could see was empty sky.

CHAPTER 2

At the hospital, doctors pumped me full of warm liquid, checked my toes and fingers for frostbite. Nurses wrapped me in blankets and gave me hot sweet drinks. They told me how lucky I was I didn't freeze to death. But my mother's face, chicory blue, was all I could see. I didn't feel lucky. When they asked me questions, I turned away. What words I had I'd used up.

When my father finally showed, he stood in the doorway, fingers plowing through his brown hair, yanking the roots, knotting the truth into his brain. "Jesus, Wes," he said. "What the hell happened?" He threw his coat in a chair, then laid his sour body across mine. The seeping stink of woodsmoke and booze smothered me. I wanted to latch onto him and throw him off at the same time. He pushed breaths out in quick huffs and his chest heaved against my ribs. He was not one to cry, and made fun of me when I did, but I could tell he was fighting tears. He lifted off me, stubbed his calloused hand from his nose, over the scrub of haywire whiskers around his mouth, down to his neck.

"They tell you about Mom?" The words, tiny and clipped, sniveled out of me.

"They told me."

I could feel my face cinching down as I remembered the unanswered cries for help. "Where were you?"

"I got here as soon as I could."

"No. Last night. You didn't come back."

He dragged a chair across the linoleum floor and sat down. "You try to pull her out?" he asked, changing the subject.

"The ice kept breaking." The tears came then, along with the rest. "She had such a tight hold . . . She almost . . . I almost went in with her."

"What were you two doing out there?"

I started to tell him about the loon, but that wasn't it. Not really. The reason she wanted to go was because she had a wild hair, and the wild hair was because she was drunk, and she was drunk because of him, because you can't really live in a cabin in the winter with no television and no books and three people to play poker and only bourbon for good company without picking a fight to give you something to do.

"How come you won't tell me where you were? You told her you were leaving. Where'd you go?"

My father folded over and made an animal sound. "Got in some trouble. Spent the night in town." He looked up, his eyes bleary and bloodshot.

"What kind of trouble?"

"Jail, okay, Wes? I spent the night in jail. And you spent the night blubbering out there instead of going for help? Why didn't you go for help, huh?"

"She was scared to be alone."

"Well, she sure as fuck's alone now, isn't she?" He stood, walked to the window, stretched spread-eagle, hands against the scratched glass, prepared for frisking. His head dropped. "Fuck," he said, turning to me. "I'm sorry, Little. I didn't mean that. It's not your fault."

"You should have come back."

He scrubbed at his face, removing war paint, the battle lost. "Lots of things I should have done."

We heard familiar voices at the same time—my grandmother, Ruby, cursing in the corridor, demanding attention, and my grandfather, Gip, telling her to quiet down. I could picture them out there, Ruby with her arms folded high on her chest, her dentures clicking as she talked. She would be wearing a housedress, I knew. I'd only ever seen her in that or the high pants and buttoned shirt she wore to the chicken farm where she worked. And Gip, he'd be behind her, his big head tilted forward, eyes canopied under his protruding brow and forehead like a bull ready to charge.

"Great," my father said, pulling a can of Skoal from his back pocket and tucking a dip into his cheek.

"You look like shit, Moss." That was the first thing Ruby said to my father when she walked in. "Suppose it makes sense." My father and Gip shook hands and touched each other awkwardly. Something about that looked false to me, men behaving in a way they thought they ought to, though I knew from experience they were not friends. Ruby headed straight for me. She sat down and put a twitching hand to her chest. Her tired eyes were rubbed red. She reeked of smoke.

"You got big since we seen you last." She looked over her shoulder at my father. "Sheriff said you weren't there even. Just the two of them. That right?"

"I was in town."

Ruby was looking in my direction but her eyes wouldn't focus, not on me, not on anything. "Why on earth you go out there middle of the night like that?" It was like my mother had appeared on the opposite side of the bed, and that's who Ruby was talking to. I closed my eyes and could almost feel my mother's hand, her long fingers on my hair, feel her lifting the cover to climb in next to me.

"You seen her go in?" Ruby asked.

I nodded.

"But you couldn't pull her out, big kid like you?"

The weight of her submerged body pulled on my wrist, my elbow, my shoulder socket, all the spots that connect bone to bone. "No, ma'am."

"Leave him be," my father said. "He's had enough."

"I will talk to my grandson if I goddamned well feel like it. I don't need your permission."

"Lower your voice," Gip said.

"Don't you start in on me now."

Late-day sunlight filtered in through windowpanes crusted white and smeared with fingerprints. The three of them bickered and blamed. I thought about the full white moon, its surface the face of a banished man, who my mother said could see everything. Who was watching over for her now?

"Don't you care at all? They left her out there, you know. She's all by herself." I sat up, heartache doubling me over. "She hates to be alone."

Ruby hung her head. "Ah, Val," she said, her face contorted and wrung. She grabbed my hand and squeezed it hard in the way a person might bite down on a stick to be tough. Her mouth sloped open and a knee-deep cry collapsed out of her.

Gip stared as if he feared her sorrow might be contagious.

"What?" she asked him. "I'm not allowed to cry over our dead daughter? She drowned, Gip. Dead and gone. She's not coming back this time." Ruby let go of the clench she had on my hand and banged the bed rail. "And you," she said, turning on my father, rage folding over grief. "This is all your goddamned fault. Fat lot of good you are. Sheriff told us you were in the drunk tank. I warned her. I told her, 'Nothing good ever gonna come of Moss Ballot.' It was always one thing after another with you. And now look." Ruby cocked her head back and raised her brows, like she was satisfied she'd been right all along.

"What sort of man takes his family out to live in the woods like that, winter and all?" Gip said. "You should have known the ice wasn't safe."

"For shit sake. She did whatever she pleased. Probably did it on purpose. Anyway, Wes was the one was there. Not me." He slapped his bare palm against the doorframe, then spun in a slow circle, his hands woven together on top of his head, elbows bent around his ears.

"Calm down," Gip said. "No one's accusing you of anything. You pull yourself together now. For the boy."

"Good luck with that," Ruby mumbled.

"Fuck you, Ruby," my father said.

They continued like that until the nurse kicked them out, to save me from what she must have thought was an unusual situation brought on by worry and despair. She couldn't know this was common. This was the way my people talked to each other. Ruby pitched a fit, complaining that they'd only just gotten there.

"And you're about to leave," the nurse countered. "The doctor will meet you in the lounge and you all can figure out when our patient here can go home. And you," she said, pointing to my father. "Sheriff's out there and wants to talk."

Ruby picked her purse up off the floor and settled it into the crook of her arm. "We'll be back tomorrow."

"Get some sleep now, Wes," Gip said, like it was possible to ever sleep right again.

My father turned to leave with them. "Dad," I said. "What about Elizabeth? We left the door open."

"Ah shit," he said. "I'll go find her." He stepped up to my bedside and leaned in, one hand in his pocket, one on the pillow next to my head. "Sorry I wasn't there," he whispered. "I am."

The sheriff came in not long after that to check on me one last time. His hat was off, his coat unzipped, his big belly poked out over his stumpy legs. When I was little, maybe five or six, I found a nest full of baby mice, hairless and pink, no bigger than gumdrops. Elizabeth was barely past kitten then but already a good mouser. She'd killed the mother and left it on the doorstep. I'd wanted to help those mice by stomping them right there, but I couldn't bring myself to do it even though I knew they didn't stand a chance. Instead, I tucked them under a leaf and hoped it might be enough shelter from harm. The sheriff, he looked at me the way I suppose I'd looked at those baby mice. He made a show of tucking in my covers, blinked his wide bird eyes, nodded, and walked out.

THE HOSPITAL CORRIDOR WAS DIM at night and hallway traffic limited to nurses and orderlies who came and went, sometimes loitering at the desk to talk.

My eyelids were drape heavy. That one thing my father said was stuck to me, digging in under my skin. He said maybe she did it on purpose. With each thick blink, I drifted back to Bright Lake. Shuffled in with my hospital room, lit blue from the parking lot lights, I saw a firelit cabin, my mother sipping bourbon from a jelly jar, eyelashes brushing her black veil of bangs each time she tipped the glass. Between the muffled beeping of alarms and monitors in other rooms, I heard my parents arguing, lightning and thunder. White blankets and sterile walls became the ice twisting along the serpentine lakeshore. With hushed voices of the staff, my father's voice, his hand on my shoulder.

"Little," he said. "Wake up." I opened my eyes and he was standing over me, his face so close I could smell the chew and black tabs of licorice he kept in his shirt pocket. I could smell the whiskey, too. He still hadn't shaved and wore the same flannel overshirt.

"What time is it?"

He put his finger to his lips and glanced over his shoulder at the door. "Shhh. It's late. I'm not supposed to be here." His eyes drooped. "I went back to the cabin. I got something to ask you."

I hauled myself up to look at him face-to-face. Nothing hurt on me. Not my bones or muscles. But I felt spongy and weak from the inside out.

"Tell me the truth, now. Where is she?" His words came out pasted together.

"Elizabeth? She was in the cabin. Couldn't you find her?"

I'd heard that menace in his voice plenty, when he plunked each word down, saving the heaviest for last. "Not the goddamned cat. The cat's in the truck. Your mother. Where's your mother?"

It was the whiskey, sure, but I'd heard it when he was sober, too. He didn't like to be crossed. My mother knew that as well as anyone. But she never could seem to stop herself. She'd start in on him right when he'd draw a line with her, daring him to do something about it.

"You know where she is" was as much as I could say.

"That's the thing, Wes. No *body*." His eyes flashed, letting me in on the mystery he'd concocted. "Sheriff says wait till spring. 'Course by that time, she'll be long gone, won't she? That was her plan, right? Forget that bullshit about the loon. You can tell me. She was trying to get back at me, wasn't she? Give me a taste of my own medicine. Stick me here with you."

I squeezed my eyes closed and wished my mother had pulled herself out, snuck back to the cabin, changed her clothes, warmed up by the fire. But I knew the truth. At the end, she looked right past me, eyes wide open like she could see heaven. She didn't call to me or her husband. "Mama." That's what she said. And that was the word I echoed back to her. And I cried for my mother in that hospital room, calling to her for help, calling to her though I knew she would not come for me. She'd huffed out one last disbelieving breath and let go. That was that.

"You think I made this up? You think I didn't watch her drown?" I was bolt upright, blood throbbing in my eardrums. Wherever a soul is—in the heart, tendons, the vital organs beneath bones, behind eyes, between the ears—it broke apart in me, splintered, became a thing that longed but did not have.

"Never know. She's a sneaky one." His lips smacked and slobbered against each other. His head wilted, and he let it dangle over the chair back. I figured he was set to sleep off what he'd tied on, but then he towed his head back up and stared past me. "How many times did I tell her? I'd say, 'Don't fuck with the ice, Valerie.' And she was always, 'Don't you tell me what to do.' Blah, blah, blah. The one time, the one time, I'm not there—"

"One time? You always leave." Their fight. It was in my head, but bit by bit. It hadn't made sense, but when did their fights ever make sense? "I'm not deaf. You said 'divorce' and she said, 'Over my dead body.' Guess you got what you wanted."

He sank over the bed rail, his head buried in his arms. "I didn't mean for anyone to get hurt."

"So go, why don't you? See if I care."

"You don't mean that," he said.

But I did. I wanted him to leave and to hold onto me. I wanted him to shut the hell up and to tell me I'd done all I could. I wanted his comfort. I got his pain.

Slouch turned to slump, and he fell asleep in his chair, chin to chest. An orderly found him passed out and tapped him on the shoulder. "Mister. You can't be in here. Mister."

My father startled awake, ready to fight. He looked around the room like he hadn't walked through the door himself. "Dozed off sitting with my son here."

"Mister, you're drunk. Get out of here or I'm calling the police."

He put up his hands in surrender. "No, no. Don't need to make any calls. I'm going." He steadied himself against the bed rail. "I'm sorry, Little. Maybe I was hoping you got it wrong." He pointed his finger at me and narrowed his eyes. "Bet you never saw that loon of hers, though, did you?"

"You want to know where she is? I'll tell you. She's dead and you're as much to blame as me." His eyes creased and he swayed, trailing a stale whiskey plume.

I rolled over and turned my back to him. "Get away from me."

In the half darkness, I fell into a sick, haunted sleep. I woke unrested to a bustle of morning sounds, staff around me. I kept my eyes closed, playing possum so I could hear what they'd say to each other but not to me. I didn't dare squint through my lashes or shudder at their talk, protest. The night nurse spoke in knowing whispers, telling her replacement about my father, stumbling and belligerent, pushing the orderly who escorted him out. She started every sentence with a "well" that turned my broken family into gossip. The two agreed that my father must be devastated, losing his wife, the mother of his child, like that. Not even being able to bury the body. "The body," they said, like that was all my mother was now. A body unrecovered.

"What's he look like, the father?"

"Well, good looking but you can tell he's a drunk. Not worth the time, honey, if that's what you're thinking."

Their voices came up as they went over the clipboard that hung on the end of my bed. I stirred to stop their talk. The new girl, young and stringy with a black mole on her cheek the size of a raisin, introduced herself as Sandy or Cindy and waved to the one whose shift ended, then rolled me over and took my temperature for the umpteenth time, checking the inside of me with a probe that shot me full of shame.

"Doctor says you're going home tomorrow. That's good, huh?" I had spent nights away from my mother, but I'd never known a place called home where she did not live. What was home without her?

Gip and Ruby lived several hours south in a town called Loma. They were not the sort of people to stay overnight in a place, so when they returned to the hospital with my father, they were already worn out from driving back and forth.

My father was freshly showered. He'd changed his clothes but hadn't shaved. "You're looking better. Got more color today."

I could see regret in his forced smile, in the way he made a point to stand up straight and sober. And I felt bad, too, for the way I'd talked to him. I tried to apologize back by nodding in response, tightening up a smile for him. We looked each other in the eye and, in that moment, it seemed all was forgiven between us.

"Nurse said I can leave tomorrow."

"Yeah, Little. I heard that. That's good, right there."

Ruby shook her head and kept her arms crossed as she sat in the only chair. Gip stood in the doorway, still. "So you're feeling better?" he asked.

I shrugged. What was better anyway?

Ruby jabbed my father in the thigh with her elbow. "Go on."

My father rolled his neck until it crackled like sap in a fire. "So, Wes," he said. "Here's the thing."

In the pause before what came next, I went back to him saying maybe my mother was on the run, that she'd crawled away somehow. Could I really recall her going under for good? Hope gathered up in me, a wisp that puts broken things back together.

"Gip and Ruby and me, we got to talking. We think it's better you go stay with them for a bit. Cabin isn't a good place in the winter, and besides, I got something lined up in Montana. Won't make sense you being with me right now."

Ruby chimed in. "You can stay in Valerie's room—your mom's—right in her bed." She said this not knowing I could leap there in my mind, put my mother under the covers, forever shivering and wet.

"But why?" I asked my father. "Is it because of last night? I didn't mean it. I don't want you to go."

"No, Little. It's not that. It's just, I got things to take care of. It's only for a while."

"You can't just up and leave me with them. When will you come get me?"

"Let's take her one step at a time, Wes," Gip said.

That this could be decided while he sobered up, while I slept, that he could ditch me like that. None of it made sense to me. "This is wrong. Don't I get a say? I'll go with you. To Montana."

"You listen now," Ruby said. "You need a roof over your head, square meals. Your dad figures things out, he'll be back for you." They were my mother's people, sure. But I'd spent more time in a car in front of their house than I'd spent inside their house. They could have been anyone. My father was leaving me with strangers.

He stood there, hands in his front pockets up to his wrists. He would not fight for me.

"You'll come back?"

He dipped his head down once. "Yeah, Little. I'll be back. Just you wait." He leaned over and pulled me to him until my head was against his chest. I wished I could climb into his shirt pocket with his licorice tabs. The boozy smell was mostly gone and what was left I tried to source. Shower soap, chewing tobacco, woodsmoke. The final disappearing note held and lingered and drifted off. My mother's lemon perfume.

My last night in the hospital, I made my way to the window. Snow fell again, and I scraped a downward spiral in the buildup of frost, remembering the useless way my mother had clawed at the ice with fingernails chewed to the quick. I looked at the silhouettes leaning against the lamppost below and wondered if maybe my father was down there, holding Elizabeth, stroking her gray fur, scanning the windows for me, planning our escape. But only nurses were there, smoking against the side of the building, their white breath lost in the swirling snow blown up by a passing plow.

CHAPTER 3

I sat in the front seat of the Plymouth between Gip and Ruby on our way to their house in Loma. I'd tried to get in the back seat, but it was piled high with garbage bags, a suitcase, and cardboard boxes I recognized. Happy tomatoes with eyes and arms and legs, tap shoes and top hats, open tooth-free, half-circle mouths. My mother called them her dancing tomatoes. My father and I were never allowed to put anything in the boxes or take anything out. They belonged to her.

"You get all our stuff?"

Ruby told me to never mind, that we'd go through those things later.

My mother said my grandparents never visited us because they were homebodies. She said they drove her nuts as a girl, that she never had privacy because they were always around. Between them in the car, I worried what it would be like for me. Ruby was a tiny woman prone to perturbed sighs. Wrinkles and lines clustered between her eyes and on her forehead and in the puckers around her thin lips. She had graying brown hair that she pulled back in a knot during the day and untied at night. Neither of their faces showed signs of laughter. Gip had spent years laboring at the feedlot and was big as a boulder from his thick neck to his rock-hard beer gut. He'd fought in France during the war and had a bluish divot where a bullet had grazed his right temple. Oiled ringlets of gray hair coiled on top of his head, and his eyes sometimes glassed over like they should have been covered with coins. When I was real little, I'd cowered behind my mother whenever he talked to me. But she warned me off Ruby more. "Watch yourself there, Wes," she'd say. "That one's got fangs."

I could smell lemons even over Gip's tree-shaped air freshener and the cigarette smoke. I twisted around and sniffed for my mother like a hound, expecting to see her in the back seat, smiling her crooked-teeth smile, or fiddling with the silver hoops on her favorite earrings, or folding her hair behind her ears with both hands.

"Sit back down before you make me wreck," Gip said. I tried to scoot closer to Ruby, but she shoved me toward Gip and told me not to crowd her. I sucked myself in. Heat blasted from the vents and Charley Pride was singing "Kiss an Angel Good Morning" on the radio, and all I could think about was my mother under the ice.

"I'm gonna be sick."

"It's that goddamned smell," Ruby said.

Gip cranked the wheel right and the car lurched onto the shoulder. I clambered over Ruby's lap and fell out the door, skinning my chin on the frozen ground. By the time I'd emptied my stomach, I was on my knees, a penitent covered in blood and vomit and gravel. Ruby nudged me aside and got out of the car. I tried to wipe the vomit off my mouth with my shirtsleeve, but the gravel scraped into my cuts, making the pain even worse.

"Hold on now," Ruby said, grabbing something from the back seat. "Get your hands off there before you get an infection." She dabbed at my scrape with one of my mother's white blouses. Drops of blood and dirt dotted the fabric as she turned it over and over. "That ought to about do it." She lifted my throbbing chin, then turned my face from side to side. She softened, allowed me to see her grief. Tears pooled in her eyes but didn't fall. Instead they seemed to recede, like the cascade went down her throat and into her belly. The moment was deep and fleeting and gone.

Gip peered over from the driver's seat. "Can we get back on the road now or we waiting here all afternoon?"

"You done puking or you got more in you?" Ruby asked, stiff again, her guard back up.

"I don't know. I think I'm done."

"Well, let's get going then. Climb back in there."

Ruby got in next to me, pulled the heavy door shut, then opened it right back up.

"Jesus, you stink! Take that shirt off," she said, her hand outstretched. "I mean it."

I didn't want to take off my clothes, no matter how bad they smelled. I'd had enough of baring myself to the cold, and I was already shivering.

"No."

"Take off that shirt, Wes," Gip said. "Do as you're told."

When I pulled the sweatshirt inside out over my head, the smell of my own vomit made me gag again. I swallowed hard, then handed it over. Ruby dropped it on the frozen ground next to my mother's bloodstained blouse. "That wasn't so hard now, was it?" she said. I crossed my arms over my thin undershirt. "And turn up the heat before we freeze to death." We hushed as those words condensed and took shape around us. Ruby went back to staring out the window.

We passed mile after silent mile of barren winter fields and shuttered barns and clumps of white pine. Fence rails pointed us down the road and brief squalls dappled huddled cows white. It was near dark when we passed the municipal tower with the word "Loma" still visible, though the paint had faded over the years. We'd been on the road nearly three hours, and I was ready to put my feet on the ground.

This was the town where my mother grew up, the town we visited when she needed money. That was all it was to me—a town where her parents lived in a cinder block house next to a trailer park on a street called Willow Lane. My mother and I were last there in the summer, when slobbering dogs snapped on the end of chains and kids rode Big Wheels in the street and stared at us when we drove by. Now, the street was empty and dim lights were on in the trailers we passed. We pulled up to the dark house.

Gip made the first move, swatting his big palms on the steering wheel. "Well," he said, and got out of the car. Ruby exited next. They left their doors open, daring me to choose sides.

"You waiting on an invitation? Let's go," said Ruby as she climbed the rickety steps. I slid out the driver's seat, then slammed both car doors shut.

Gip had already gotten himself a beer and was sipping off the foam by the time I walked in. I'd forgotten the bowel smell that lingered in their house, like cabbage and boiled meats. My mother claimed her nose had dulled to it over time. "You learn to put up with a lot in a house like that," she said. I curled my fingers and stroked my empty palms. I felt younger than my age, weak for it, longing for her hand in mine like that.

"Should I grab something out of the car? From the back?"

"We'll get around to that," Ruby said. "I picked up a few things down at the Commodity Center. Toothbrush is in the bathroom. You don't want to end up toothless like me."

Gip sputtered his beer. "You couldn't get him a new toothbrush?"

"What do you take me for, anyway? 'Course I got him a new toothbrush. Jackass." She kicked her shoes off at the door and slid into slippers, all the while shaking her head, looking at me as if I were her ally, like the two of us would form a gang to take on stupid Gip now. "You want to be helpful, you take him on back," she said, gesturing to the hall. "I'll be there in a minute."

My mother's old bedroom. I took slow steps behind Gip, afraid of what I would find there, of falling through the crevice of my own life and winding up in hers. He turned the knob and flipped the switch. The overhead light had a missing bulb so the room was half in shadow.

There was a twin bed with a flowery bedspread, a white dresser with chipped paint, a mismatched side table, faded pink shag carpet. The walls were covered in bird's-eye maple paneling and *Tiger Beat* posters of smiling boys I didn't know.

Ruby came up behind me. Her eyes were raw and pink. "We kept it just the way she liked it."

"No keeping it the same ever brought her back, though, did it?" Gip said. He sat down on the end of the bed and smoothed the bedspread with one hand. "Once she was gone, she was gone. And now she's gone for good."

"There's your things," she said, pointing to a white bag on the bed.

I walked through the doorway, wary of the watchful eyes on me—the long-billed birds in knotted wood, the mysterious smiling boys, the grandparents I barely knew.

"Hold on a second," Ruby said. "I got something for you." She snapped her fingers and pointed at me, then disappeared and came back with a picture frame. She made a fuss out of putting it on top of the dresser. "There," she said. My mother, leaning on a twisted piece of driftwood, barely smiling, her delicate hand posed on her cheek. One more set of eyes.

I CRAWLED INTO BED THAT first night—the bed my mother had slept in, too—and listened to my grandparents fight in their kitchen. Though pots and pans clanked and crashed, I was too frightened to get up for a closer look. But I could imagine them there, circling each other, blue-lit from the stove light. Ruby screeched like a tomcat and Gip slurred back at her in a dulled roar. I pulled the covers over my head, waiting for the fight to fizzle out.

The next morning, I surveyed the front room, half expecting to find chairs tumped over, fist holes in walls. To me, that was the aftermath of a fight. I had witnessed plenty between my parents. Both of them were shovers. When blood was drawn or bruises raised, they could claim it was a doorknob, a stumble and fall, a bash against a coffee table. My mother, being smaller, took the brunt of it. I'd never seen either parent throw a punch, but my mother would throw anything else she could get her hands on. She had good aim, too, or maybe my father was lousy at ducking. But in my grandparents' house, there was no outward sign of fighting at all. Old wedding photos and sad clown pictures still hung cockeyed on the paneled walls. The couch was still ripped but not blood splattered. Gip and Ruby sat at the kitchen table in silence—Gip with his newspaper, Ruby eating a sugar-laced grapefruit, two lit cigarettes dangling in the bean bag ashtray between them. Neither had cuts or broken bones or black eyes. When my parents fought, one of two things usually happened: either my father would be gone, not to return for days or even weeks, or my mother would be wrapped around him, loving on him in a way that made me want to cover my eyes but peep through my fingers. Something about the way they loved each other had always made me feel a little bit dirty.

"Well, look who finally got out of bed," said Ruby.

"Boy just got up, woman. Don't go jumping down his throat."

"No one's jumping down no one's throat. Jesus H. Christ. I'm just remarking it must be nice getting to sleep in, is all. Come sit down and have yourself some breakfast."

I pulled out the vinyl-covered chair and sat down.

Gip folded the paper and pushed back from the table. "I'm working a double. You take that rent check over to Burt. Tell him I'll have the rest by Friday."

"Take it yourself," she said. "I took it last time we were late. It's your turn."

So much went unsaid between them, like words didn't matter when their contempt for each other was clear. Gip snatched the check off the counter. "And find that boy pajamas that fit, will you?" To me he said,

"You'll wear a shirt to the table from now on, you hear?" He grabbed his coat off a hook at the front door and walked out.

"Shut that door!" Ruby shouted after him. "Get up and shut that door," she said to me. I complied.

We sat at the table in awkward silence. Ruby watched me pour cereal, then milk. She watched me sprinkle sugar and take bites like she'd never seen a person eat before. I set the spoon down.

"What? Am I doing something wrong?"

That seemed to break her trance some. "No. No. I'm just looking at you, is all."

I went back to my cereal, but the second I did, she was back at me.

"She must have said something. Val. What'd she say?"

"I told you. She was scared."

"But what did she say? What was the last thing she said?"

She didn't apologize for being reckless or for trying to pull me in with her. She didn't tell me to take care of Dad or Elizabeth. She could have said, "I love you, son." She could have said, "Have a good life. Be a good person." At least she should have pleaded with me to go back to the cabin, to be safe. But she had given me nothing, left me with nothing. And I resented her for it. Resented Ruby like she'd taken something that was rightly mine. The tears started in my chin, shivered up. "She said, 'Mama.'"

Ruby tucked her head down and glowered at me. "You're lying."

"I'm not." I craved for her to slap my face, to hurt me on the outside, to leave some kind of mark to go with the betrayal I felt on the inside.

The chair creaked when she sat back. The burning cigarette and her face turned to ash while I waited for her to say or do something. An image popped into my head of Ruby pulling my mother out, cradling her frozen body, brushing the soaked bangs out of her eyes, kissing her, making her warm again. But I couldn't hold Ruby there. She didn't seem like anyone's mother to me, and I couldn't imagine why mine would waste her last breath that way. Ruby walked her coffee cup to the sink and ran the water. She bowed her head over the basin and let it hang while the water went down the drain. She closed the faucet without washing her dish or even getting her hands wet. "I got work" was all she said.

"You're leaving me alone?"

"You've been alone before. You'll be fine."

"What am I supposed to do all day?"

"I don't know, Wes. What do you usually do? I know Val didn't sit around entertaining you. Just"—she waved her hands around—"play or something."

"I'm fifteen, not four." I propped my head on my hand and spooned the soggy cereal into my mouth.

"This is the way it is," Ruby said to the back of my head. "You got to get used to it now. You got to accept it."

How had I wound up in this house, with these people? My parents had been wiped away, a smudge off glass, and I was to get on with it, to accept it in my open hand like change for a dollar bill. But I couldn't imagine getting past the brokenness I was feeling. I picked at the scrape on my chin until it bled.

I don't know that I had a mission exactly, or even a scavenger's list of items to find, but I began in the kitchen and inventoried every single drawer and cupboard in the house. I was looking for clues—clues about what kind of people my grandparents were, about the way they lived and whether my mother had left parts of herself behind in the rooms of this house. Drawers full of string, dull scissors and wooden spatulas, undeveloped film, pens with names of businesses, receipts and bills and bank statements, some dated years before. I wondered whether my mother had made the peg-loom potholders when she was a girl, weaved colorful nylon over metal teeth, whether she had wrapped them in tissue, given them as a gift. I found where they kept their cartons of cigarettes and bottles of whiskey, the Green Stamps, cans of peas, powdered milk, and Campbell's soup.

In the living room, I sat in each seat on the olive-colored davenport and in both of the ragged tweedy recliners and ran my hands across the stubbly fibers, cranking the footrest up and down. There was a radio on top of the television console so I turned it on, hoping it would fill the quiet and keep me company. I looked more closely at what I figured was Gip and Ruby's wedding picture. Ruby, girl size and rail thin, barely came up to Gip's shoulder, but she was tucked tightly there, invisible arms intertwined behind stiff backs. She held a bouquet of flowers upside down at her side. Gip wore a pinstriped suit, Ruby a dress but no veil. They both were bent toward the camera, as if the photographer was on his knees in front of them. Neither was smiling, though I could just barely see Ruby's splayed teeth—her real ones before she got dentures.

I touched every knickknack—the porcelain cow with the blue bonnet, the sad clown with flowers pressed hopefully upward on thin bronze wires, a wooden sea turtle, its flipper reduced to a tattered stump—wondering how long they'd been on that dusty shelf and whether my mother had cared about any of them or anything else in that house.

The medicine cabinet in the bathroom was filled with prescription bottles, tubes of ichthammol ointment and toothpaste, denture polish and hemorrhoid cream. I opened the bottles and smelled the pills. The rubber dropper on the tincture of merthiolate flaked and cracked as I twisted off the lid. I dabbed it on an old scar on my knee until the whole thing was stained bright red. A phantom sting coursed to the bone, and I thought of my father blowing on the fresh gash as he applied the medicine. "Tiger blood," he'd said. "For brave boys."

Time has numbed the ache of that moment, but I remember feeling the loss of them, both at once. It ran deep in me, through that scar and into my veins and right up to my mouth, so that when I spotted the familiar green Nyquil bottle behind the toilet brush, I reached for it, remembering how many times my mother gave it to me before bed, sick or not, to make me sleep. I took a swig and coolness lifted off my tongue, tiny moths taking flight. I felt the menthol spill into emptied-out nooks around my heart. I took another drink and brought the bottle with me to the kitchen.

I slathered a piece of white bread with butter and sugar, then went back to that wedding picture. Those people, though decades younger, bore some resemblance to my grandparents. But something in the picture, if only around the edges—a possibility—didn't last in the real world. If there had been love between them, as the neglected snapshot hanging there seemed to imply, it was gone like the rent money, the better job, gone like their dead daughter.

I would come to know the cold of my grandparents' house and felt it that first day. I turned up the thermostat until I heard the click and smelled dusty heat from the baseboards. When I returned to the bathroom, my intention was to put the medicine bottle back under the sink. But I was so cold.

The room was dim and dinky, one bare bulb lit, the other burned out. The tub was surrounded by a striped shower curtain that hung from an aluminum bar suspended from the ceiling. The tile, the tub, the sink, all of it had once been white. But a yellow and gray layer of age and grime had built up that the dim light couldn't disguise. I leaned over the tub and plugged the rust-stained drain, careful not to touch my bare stomach on the chipped porcelain. The pipes clanged as water, hot as I could stand it, gushed into the tub. I took another swig and climbed in, letting the water scald every inch of me until only my head was dry. I took the bar of soap from the wire dish in the corner and rubbed my skin until I could hardly feel it anymore. Then my pink body disappeared in the murk of bathwater. My father had told me that if you put a frog in a pot of water and boil it, the frog won't jump out. "It'll sit in that pot and stare at you while you cook it alive," he'd said. But if you tried to put a frog in a pot of boiling water, he'd jump right out to save his own skin. I couldn't save my mother. Could I save myself?

The word wrung out of my tongue and took the shape of a question behind my teeth. Carefully, I let it escape my lips on a tiny bubble. "Mom?" It came out again, wet and choked and pleading. "Mama." And finally, one last time, the life sucked out of it. I slipped below the surface and let the soap sting my eyes and fill my mouth. I stayed under as long as my lungs would allow, then came up for air because I could.

Hazy, boiled, and medicine drunk, I crawled back into my mother's bed. Ruby found me there, hours later. She poked at my shoulder. "You got to be kidding me. Up. Now." Had I forgotten to drain the tub, turn off the water? Was she looking for the medicine bottle I'd emptied and kicked under the bed? I found her in the kitchen, hands on the high waistband of her work pants. I'd spilled sugar on the floor and left the bread and butter out on the counter. She reached up to me and whacked the back of my head with a wooden spoon. "I've been wringing chicken necks all day long, and this is what I come home to? You will pull your weight around here, Wes. You hear me?"

"Yes, ma'am," I said.

"Lucky for you it's winter or the place'd be crawling with ants. Now, clean up after yourself," she said. "I got to go get changed. I smell like the chicken coop."

CHAPTER 4

THE SECOND NIGHT, I HAD A HORRIBLE DREAM. MY EYES WERE POPPED open but I was crouched in complete darkness, and all sounds were muffled like the cotton-stuffed quiet of hands cupping ears. At first, I thought I was dead, but then I realized I was alive but in a grocery box, the flaps taped closed. When I opened my mouth to scream, water cascaded over my lips, filling the box, rising over my ankles. I woke in my mother's bed, drenched in sweat. I'd been afraid to even ask about the things from the back seat. I had no idea what had been salvaged from all that had been lost.

Ruby was in the kitchen, cranking a hunk of roast through the meat grinder. "What do you mean 'your stuff'?"

"The stuff from the cabin. From town. Our stuff. It was in the back seat."

She jammed the ends of celery into the grinder to follow the wormy ribbons into the bowl. "You got your box. The clothes and such. Gip saw to that."

"I mean the other stuff. Mom's things."

"Gip took most of it to the Commodity Center yesterday. What would you want with that old stuff anyhow?"

"Did you at least go through it? Did you even look at it?"

"Filled with bad memories." She crammed an onion into the metal cone and wiped her eyes.

"Not for me, it wasn't. That wasn't yours to decide. So what belongs to me, huh? I lose everything, is that it?"

"You watch your tone with me, you hear? Gip thought it best we be rid of the lot." She unclamped the grinder from the countertop and dropped it into the sink. "Plenty of her crap still in that bedroom, you want to get all sentimental about it."

The fumes from the onion were getting to me now, and I pinched my nose as I inched closer, like I was moving in on a rattler. "Don't you miss her?"

She wiped her hands on the apron she'd tied around her ribcage. "Can't miss something you never really had. I don't think she liked me much." She stared out the kitchen window like she was looking at something other than the propane tank behind the trailer next door. "Get out of here now," she said, returning to the kitchen, the gray sink water, the chipped countertop and worn linoleum floor. "You're on my nerves."

I rifled through the trash barrels alongside the shed next to the house. Nothing in there but food scraps and household waste. When Gip came home from work, I asked him the same thing I'd asked Ruby.

"What the Commodity Center didn't want, I threw away there."

"What about photo albums? What about her sewing projects? I can't believe you'd just throw it all away."

He cranked the recliner back. The rank smell from his stiff socks filled the room. "I have about had it with this. First Ruby and now you. She's gone and so is all that shit, you hear? And that's all it was. Pile of shit not worth a plug nickel. You got any more thoughts on the matter, you keep them to yourself."

"So that's it? If you can't pawn it, you got no use for it. I get it."

Gip snapped open his newspaper. He cleared his throat and swallowed hard enough I could hear the glob pass—his answer for me.

ALL WINTER LONG, I HOLED up in my mother's bedroom staring at the walls, listening to scratched 45s on her old record player, waiting for my father to materialize from a promise. I found magazines stuffed under the bed, sweatshirts still in the dresser, even outfits hanging in the closet. I wasn't sure how to carve out a space for myself in a room that didn't belong to me.

I decided no one would notice if I emptied one drawer for myself. This began the process of dividing up the space in the back bedroom between my dead mother and me. I'd look at her picture and have one-sided conversations, so much so I thought I was going nuts. "I'll take this one drawer and this side of the closet, and you keep these drawers and this section here." No matter how much I encroached, there was just the one bed, and that I shared with her ghost.

For the most part, my grandparents and I stayed out of each other's way, though I watched them for signs of the grief that revisited me each morning when I would wake up confused, not certain where I was, a teenage version of my mother staring at me. I would right myself on the earth first, then in the house, in the room and bed, then finally back out to a world where my mother no longer lived. I kept wondering if it was that same grief that was keeping my father away. I suppose I let myself imagine that his heart had grown fond of her in death and that he blamed me for taking away another chance to get it right. And so I began most days as I had that morning on the ice, curled up in disbelief, wondering how this thing had happened and who could explain it to me.

Ruby enrolled me at the local high school and forced me back, though I told her it was a waste of time since I would only have to leave again once my father returned. I knew how to be the new kid. Stay quiet. Watch where you're going in the hall. Spot the boss and either be his friend or steer clear. Don't raise your hand. Sit near the door to be first out of the classroom. Don't eat at the table where most of the kids wear glasses. Better to eat in a bathroom stall than to risk eating alone. Watch out for friendly girls until you know which ones you can trust.

Boys in Loma called the pretty girls "foxes," and one pretty girl in particular, Kathryn Rook, took a shine to me. I'd never had much chance to get into trouble with girls up to that point. We never stayed in one place long enough, plus I'd always been kind of a grubby kid. My pants never fit me quite right—they were either too short or too big around. I remember a girl who held her nose when I walked into a classroom. I was in maybe the third or fourth grade. Once I started growing taller, started taking after my father, I became more aware of myself and made an effort to keep clean and to wear clothes that fit. By that winter, my legs were long and my shoulders were square but meatless. My wavy hair had grown out, which made it swoop over my ears at odd angles. Though I would sometimes see my father in the shadows when I looked in a mirror, mostly, as I came into my own, I deemed myself not half-bad.

This Kathryn was blond and curvier than the other girls, plump even, though it looked good on her. Her top lip curled under when she smiled, which made her look a little more like a rabbit than a fox. In science class she sat behind me, and I could feel her eyes stroking my back. She sat on the other side of the aisle in study hall, her left palm resting on her cheekbone or temple so her head was cocked just right to stare at me. I'd try to stretch out and look uninterested, but the restless part of me wanted to know what was on her mind. Despite my wariness of the girl, I found myself looking back.

She caught me at my locker, planting herself like a point guard, so when I turned around with my bag lunch, I couldn't get away. She bothered to introduce herself, though we both knew I knew her name. A girl like Kathryn had a way of making herself known. She was always smiling, never alone. Never a hair out of place, lips always glossed. Her clothes were neat, and before she ever spoke a word to me, I imagined her underpants matched her bra.

"You're new. My dad says you're living with your grandparents over there on Willow Lane. He said . . ." Her confidence seemed to falter as she searched for the right words. "He said your mom, well, that she maybe died. Is that true?"

I looked for a way to squeeze past her, but she shifted her hips to tell me I needed to answer. I cleared my throat and nodded. Maybe a month or more had passed, but the cold was fresh on my skin. I rubbed my arm for warmth.

"Well, I'm sure sorry about that, Wes. It is Wes, isn't it? My dad says he knew your mother. That they went to high school together. He works at the bank, you know." She took a step closer to me, and I had nowhere to go except against the locker. I closed the door and leaned back. "No," she said. "Of course you wouldn't know that. The bank, they own your grandparents' house. You guys pay rent to my father. Well, to the bank, not him. But he is in charge of that sort of thing. Anyway, I'm sorry. Listen to me rambling on." She rolled away and hooked her thumbs in the back pockets of her jeans, then twisted her whole body in the direction of the cafeteria. "Any time, you can eat with us, okay, Wes? Ballot, right? Not Furniss, like your grandparents?"

"Right."

She said my name twice, first and last—Wes Ballot, Wes Ballot—like she was pulling a dress down her hips, as if my name needed to fit over her teeth. "I like that." She made a two-step turn and bounded off to catch up with a group of girls who'd been watching from a safe distance.

She made it easy to fall in with her. When she asked if I wanted to go to the movies with her and her friends, I told her plain I didn't have money. She paid my way. I tagged along with them to the Canoe Café and ate plates of greasy french fries dipped in ketchup. She indulged her sweet tooth with cola and chocolate syrup mixed together, dipping her finger in the froth and licking it off, which seemed to be for my benefit. The seat in the booth next to her she saved for me, pushing her friends to the other side. Her warm thigh would press against mine, and she would laugh and grab my arm or rest her head on my shoulder for the shortest time. It embarrassed me that her touches reminded me of my mother's, especially since I was stirred by her. I ached for closeness, for the pressure of a body against mine. It could have been anyone. But it wasn't. It was this girl, clean and pretty. Her clothes were new, her makeup careful. From her talk, I knew she was fatter than she would have liked, but I liked it plenty. That's what she was to me—plenty. I wanted what she had and what she offered. I didn't think much about what she wanted from me.

On the day I worked up the nerve to put my arm along the back of the bench, behind her yellow hair, to reach across in front of her to dip my fry in her ketchup, her friends stiffened, and I thought I'd made a mistake, had gone too far. I sat back, took my arm away. A broad man in a watch-plaid overcoat was looking straight at us through the plate glass window. His head was round and his top lip was cinched up. He put his hand on his brow to block the afternoon glare. Kathryn smiled at him and waved, her straight fingers bowing over and over at him. The man backtracked toward the café door. Kathryn slid out of the booth and grabbed my hand to pull me out with her. She didn't let go when I stood up next to her. "Here comes your landlord, Wes. Look alive."

Burt Rook took three great strides and was at the booth. "Girls," he said to Kathryn's friends, who perched on the edge of their Naugahyde seat, birds on a power line.

Kathryn swung my arm like we were on a walk in the park. "Hi, Daddy," she said. "This is Wes. You know, the one living with his grandparents."

His eyes were fixed on Kathryn's hand around mine, and for a second there I thought he might be set to blow. But his fluster dampened, and he held out his hand to me. "Burt Rook, Kathryn's father."

"Yes, sir," I said, wrenching my sweating palm free of Kathryn's grip. "Wes. Wes Ballot."

"I knew your mother some. Sad story. Tragic," he said, shaking both my hand and his head.

"Yes, sir."

Kathryn's friends slurped the dregs from their milkshakes, eyes peeled on this encounter. I glanced down at my old boots, my oil-stained jeans, and plain shirt. Burt Rook didn't want me around his daughter. It was in his voice and in the way he surveyed me.

"I do business with your grandparents." He rolled his eyes from side to side. I could see he'd blanked on their names. "Furniss," he said, like he'd looked up the name in the phone book. "Gip and Ruby. Ballot your father's name?"

I figured it was probably all he could do to keep himself from tossing me out with the trash. I was guilty by my association with people whose names he barely knew. My mother hadn't died from something respectable or tragic like cancer. In families like mine, mothers die young of their own mistakes and fathers run off like cowards, and lowlife boys like me are left with the likes of Gip and Ruby, who don't matter a lick to people like Burt Rook. A length of embarrassment ran through me. Another "yes, sir" was all I could muster.

"And he's?"

What could I say? I had no answer to that question. There'd been no letters, no phone calls. Nothing. "Working in Montana. Be out here for me come spring."

I believe Burt Rook relaxed on that bit of news that this boy his daughter seemed keen on would not be around much longer. "That right," he said. "Well, then." He turned his attention back to his daughter, telling her she had to be home soon, that her mother was expecting her.

"I'm out of money, Daddy," Kathryn said, her hand out.

He gave me a look that said he could see my cash balance on the sleeve of my shirt. He pulled a bulging wallet from his back pocket and peeled out a ten-dollar bill. He scowled at the plate of half-eaten french fries, the puddle of grease, the smear of ketchup. "No more fries," he said to Kathryn. "I thought your mother talked to you about that."

Kathryn flushed, pulled the hem of her tight top down to meet her jeans, and snatched the bill from her father's hand. A how-dare-you, well-you-had-it-coming look passed between them.

"Girls," he said. And to me, "Ballot."

CHAPTER 5

SPRING TRICKLED DOWN THE FOOTHILLS WITH THE MELTING SNOW. Even lifeless Loma turned green. I walked from town along the railroad tracks, my jacket unzipped to the mild weather. I'd been growing antsy as the temperature ticked up, knowing my time in my grandparents' house was coming to an end. I'd distracted myself with the liberties Kathryn allowed me to take—a handful of breast in the darkness of the theater, a rub along her crotch under the cover of a table, a mouthful of sugar-coated tongue. The want of her was a lump of clay lodged in my groin, taking shape on its own. It bothered me that it didn't include her face or her voice in my ear, but that didn't stop me, which bothered me, too.

I hopped off the rail and cut through backyards to the house. From the corner, I could see the sheriff's truck parked out front. My thoughts sank right to my father. Maybe he'd been locked up again. Or worse. I imagined him on the lam, getting cornered, putting up a fight, barricading himself in a farmhouse, taking hostages. At least that would explain why, in three months, he hadn't returned for me.

They were in the kitchen, Gip with his back to the door, Ruby at the table, the sheriff next to her, his brown Stetson in his hand. All eyes turned to me when the metal door slapped shut. "It's my dad, isn't it?" The sheriff started to say something, but Gip cut him off.

"They found your mom out there at Bright Lake, Wes."

A cruel glimmer leapt inside me. I could see her clawing her way out just like he said she might, exhausted and cold, searching for her family. "She alive?"

"Is she alive? Don't be stupid," Ruby said. She rose and her cigarette quaked between her yellow fingers. The chair pushed away from her, the unstoppered legs scraping the linoleum. "She's been under that ice since January. How you think she'd have lived through that? Jesus H. Christ." She shook her head at me. A snake of ash dropped to the floor.

"No call to be cruel, Ruby. The boy's been through plenty," the sheriff said. "Their medical examiner said you all can make arrangements, for the transfer and whatnot. You call Pete down there at the funeral parlor. He knows what to do."

"I want to see her then," I said, though what I pictured was my father's kicked-off slippers sunk to the lake bottom.

"She ain't fit to be seen no more, son."

"How do you even know it's her? Maybe it's somebody else." Again, she was there, reaching for me, trying to pull me in. *Is this what it felt like for her?* I wondered. Futile grasping for a frayed line that would keep the near dead from dying?

"Just how many people you think drown out Bright Lake last winter, Wes?" Ruby asked. "She come up. It's her." She shooed me with a wrist flick. "I don't need this bullshit from you. Go back outside and let us talk to the sheriff."

What was worse than dead that they were hiding from me? "I want to stay and hear the sheriff out."

"Maybe we want some privacy, you ever think of that?" Gip said. "Get. And close that door behind you."

I stood on the curb and threw rocks into the street and tried not to think of my mother as a body. I thought instead about her smile, the way her little teeth up top jutted out, sometimes peeking out over her lips. I thought about her flowered halter tops that she made herself out of scrap fabrics she bought by the pound. I remembered watching her cut her own dark bangs in the mirror, careful to make the blunt line straight. I was about to be swallowed up by those memories when the sheriff came out. He put his hat on and hiked up his pants.

"Sheriff, you know anything at all about my dad?"

He looked back at the house, checking, it seemed to me, to see if Ruby or Gip had followed him to the door and were listening there. "I don't think you have to worry about him anymore."

"I'm not worrying, Sheriff. I want to know when he's coming back, is all."

I read something, a wariness on his face, around the squint in his eyes, the way he scratched the side of his head and glanced again at the house. I looked at the revolver on his belt.

"You'll be alright here with your grandparents. You keep your head down. Don't go looking for trouble."

My grandparents left soon after, headed for the funeral home. Ruby told me to stay put, that I'd only get in the way. Her overcoat was loose, and she seemed even smaller than usual. She followed Gip to the car like a scolded toddler, arms crossed, brows knit. Gip hunkered behind the wheel, rubbed his nose with his wristbone. They sat there, the two of them, not looking at each other or at me, long enough for me to guess they could stay like that forever, not starting the car, not coming back into the house, just staring over the dash at the nothingness of a dirt road. I retreated into the house.

The manila envelope was in the trash can, bent in half, stained by fresh coffee grounds poured in on top of it. There was a sticker on the outside printed with the word "Ballot." My father. I pulled it out, careful not to brush any grounds onto the floor. What were they hiding from me? What trouble was he in now?

The car door slammed, and I heard Gip tell Ruby to get the checkbook, too. I tucked the envelope inside my jacket and pushed out the front door as she was coming in. "Forgot my pocketbook," she said. "Where are you off to in such a hurry?"

"Need some air," I said. "Going for a walk."

I skirted the side of the house to avoid conversation with Gip, then tramped back along the rails until I reached the abandoned spud house I'd found weeks before. It was a squat shack with wood steps leading down into the hole where root vegetables had once been cellared. I pushed the crooked door open.

The air inside was damp and wormy. Light came in through a chimney vent, enough to shed a column on the envelope. I undid the clasp and braced myself for the information I knew was there that would tell me all about my father. Instead I found photographs. Up until then, I hadn't let myself imagine how cruel thawing out might be, what might have picked away at my mother or seeped into the open spots of her previously frozen self. But there she was. Her hair was broken off, but her silver hoops were still in her ears. Her skin was black blotched and dimpled, her mouth rigged open like she had one more thing to tell me. I shoved the pictures back in the envelope. The air in the spud cellar went from mineral earth to stinking corpse, and I stumbled out into the light, depositing myself on the old steps so that only my head was aboveground, unburied. Everything was springing to life around me, but those cold pictures I held in my hand told a different story. Lilac buds were popping out on branches, crocuses were poking up through the green-brown grass. Even bloated bodies bubbled to the surface in a thaw.

The sun went down, dinnertime passed, and I sat there, that envelope in my hand. This was what my father left me with. I wanted none of it. I considered packing up and leaving. I could go find him if he wouldn't come for me. What if I headed west, to Montana, just as he headed east for me? If we passed each other going in opposite directions, what then? I had to go back to the only place I knew my father would look for me. And I kept those gruesome pictures. I could have left them in the spud cellar, thrown them in a barrel somewhere like my grandparents had done. But I couldn't abandon her again, no matter how ugly she was, how dead. And I didn't want her calling to me if I left her behind.

Gip and Ruby were glued to the evening news when I walked through the door. I figured I'd be in the soup for missing dinner, but they barely said a word. Instead, they were staring at images on the television of a Korean airliner, askew on what looked like a frozen lake. I sat down on the couch and listened with them as the reporter talked about how the Russians had fired on it and how that plane—tons of metal and people and paper and fuel—had made an emergency landing on an iced-over lake near Scandinavia. Two people were killed, over a hundred survived. Gip said it out loud, but I don't think he even heard his own voice. It was more like our collective thoughts drifted out of him. "How you figure a big heavy plane like that doesn't break through, but a skinny girl . . . ?"

And Ruby replied, "Because God doesn't give a shit about us, that's why."

"You think God let her die?" I asked.

"God wasn't there, Wes." She said it without looking away from the television. She twisted her head to me for the length of two short words. "You were."

The reporter moved to the next story.

My mother was thirty-three years old when they put her in a box and put the box in the back of a long black car that we followed to the cemetery.

I'd asked my grandparents if they could get a hold of my father, if they had a number or anything to let him know his wife, my mother, was being buried that day. They shook me off, said they hadn't heard a thing. I scanned the paltry crowd anyway, knowing he would show, knowing he could not let me go through this alone. But the funeral home sat out only three chairs for family. A few other folks were at the graveside, mostly people who worked with Gip down at the feedlot or drank with him when he tended bar at the taproom. There were ladies from the Catholic church who Ruby told me later went to every funeral. I wasn't surprised somehow to see Kathryn there with her father and a woman I guessed must be her mother. Burt Rook stood tall, his arms behind his back. Kathryn's mother's blond hair was shellacked with hairspray that glittered in the sun. They looked shiny and new, polished, clean. Their presence felt like charity. Kathryn smiled weakly and waved at me. I closed my eyes, hoping she and her family and everyone else would disappear. I wanted to put the months into reverse, to reel them in like a bad cast.

Gip nudged me. "Open your eyes, goddamn it," he hissed. He was fidgety in his ill-fitting brown suit, too short in the legs so that when he sat, I could see his ankles and calves, strangely blue, hairless, and smooth. That morning I had seen him near naked, hollering at Ruby to help him find a shirt to wear with the suit. His big belly protruded over his threadbare shorts. His whole gut was blanketed in gray curls save for the long scar along his side, where I guessed his appendix had been removed. In the end, he dressed himself and Ruby had complained about his scuffed white shoes, but he'd said it was all he had. She wore a shapeless black dress, thick as a horse blanket, droopy black stockings, and shoes so big she looked like a girl playing dress up.

I sat between them in a borrowed suit, my hands tucked between my legs, while the preacher talked about evil valleys, ashes, and dust. It hit me there like a single thunderclap. It was not a nightmare. It was all true. I had buried my mother once in ice and I was burying her again, this time in dirt. She would not come back. Then the preacher started in about the resurrection and the life, and at that moment, I wished the ground wasn't quite so soft because what was in those pictures was in that box, and I was afraid it would come back out and pull me in with it. I rose with my grandparents as the gravediggers, solemn but bored, uncinched the straps that held the box in place. I closed my eyes tight and apologized to God then for not pulling her out, for letting her drown while I got away, for not wanting her dead body back.

I'd been trying hard not to cry, not to speak, but what everyone there at the grave heard were the words I bleated to God: "I'm sorry. I'm sorry. I'm sorry." The preacher put his arm around me. He said, "God told Job: Brace yourself like a man." He pulled me tight to him, the way a father would, as they lowered my mother into the ground.

The gatherers fell away with brief nods. Kathryn came up to me, hugged me, kissed my blotched cheek. She gave her condolences like a mockingbird, saying what she'd seen on television maybe or read in a book. "I wish I'd known her," she added. What I would have given to punch her in the mouth right then, to make her hurt because I was hurt. I saw through her act. People like the Rooks didn't know grief. Watching Burt Rook take my grandfather's hand, give a proper nod to my grandmother, seeing two perfectly matched pathetic mother-daughter smiles, the falseness of it all, made it seem like I was the butt of a long, cruel con. The fresh soil said otherwise.

Gip wandered off and ended up on a bench near the road, childless, looking older by a generation. I stayed next to the mounding dirt, next to Ruby, who hadn't budged. I wondered if we might stay the whole day, if the sun might sink on us there. "You think we ought to go?" I tried to whisper, to be reverent, not knowing whether I could use my regular voice.

"My God," said Ruby. "My God."

"It's okay. We can stay. I don't mind."

"Don't you be nice to me. I can't take it," she said, shaking her head slowly, keeping time to a sad song only she could hear.

THE CHURCH LADIES CAME BY with a ham after Gip had changed and left for the feed store. I sat down on the sofa, still wearing my good pants. Ruby kept on her black dress but switched into pink house scuffs. She turned on the television, but instead of sinking into her recliner, she came and sat next to me, so close I could smell must from her dress and scalp. "I'm watching my programs now," she said. And we sat there, the two of us, watching television until Gip came home. Then we all ate the ham.

CHAPTER 6

Without fail, when Gip was out at night, he came home drunk. If Ruby had fallen asleep watching Johnny Carson, she would yell at him over the white noise of the television station signed off for the night. Other times, I'd wake to stumbling grunts in the darkness, urine hitting toilet water, odious sighs as his bladder relieved and his prostate unburdened. On the worst nights, I stood my pillow on its side and sunk in, hoping to muffle the limp rutting that seeped through the walls from their bedroom to mine.

On occasion, he'd open the door to my bedroom after I turned out the light to sleep. Mostly he would loom backlit in the doorway, though twice he'd sat on the end of the bed, not speaking at all. I felt bad for him, missing his daughter that way. Still, though, I didn't utter a word, preferring to fake sleep and hope the moment would pass unmarked. He brought the feed store home on his skin and, had it not been for the mix with cigarettes and alcohol, it might have smelled natural and good, a bale of hay or a full grain silo. But with his bad habits layered on top, his smell was suffocating and foreign. The smell of him is what woke me in that week after the funeral, images from the envelope still fresh in my mind, dirt fresh on her grave. He lifted the blankets and lay down in the bed next to me, shifting me off balance. I wanted to tell him to get away but I didn't know how. All I could manage was a shriveled whimper as I willed Gip away, willed myself to disintegrate.

His big paw was on my shoulder in the next motion. He flung his leg over me and pinned me down.

In my ear, he whispered my mother's name, pulled me closer to him than I'd ever been. I felt him rise and harden against my backside. I squirmed to get away. "Gip. It's me. It's Wes."

He stood more surely than I would have thought possible, and I scooted against the wall. I could just make out that he was staring at me like I was the one who didn't belong. He came at me quickly, one knee on the bed, one foot on the floor. The bridge of his thumb and forefinger pressed against my throat, sticking me to the wall like a trophy buck. He watched me squirm and struggle to breathe, then dropped his hand. He retreated to the end of the bed, his back to me, saying my mother's name over and over, asking her ghost where she'd gone. I waited with him for the answer.

Though cowardice and fear gripped me, fantasies of murder, of cords and wires, of kicking and pummeling stoked my boiling blood, sickening me even more. Finally, wordless and spent, he walked back out. I jumped up quick, slammed the door, pressed my body against it. I felt like I'd let go of a live wire, fear and anger vibrating through me, skin to marrow. His hands were off my neck, but I felt stuck anyway, a bug on a pin. I tried to fight my imagination—Gip's shadow in the doorway, the girl who used to sleep in my bed—but those ugly pictures cropped back up like weeds. How many nights had she been trespassed upon, in that same bed with the yellow-and-pink bedspread that suited her, not me? What lurked in that room that drew him in?

There was a time before—before my mother died, before she and my father screamed at each other constantly and slammed doors and furniture at night—when my mother would tuck me in, kiss and hug me, and say, "You're my favorite boy in the world, Wes Ballot." Now, I slept in her old bed, under a quilt that still smelled faintly of her, in a room covered in posters with quarter-fold creases slicing through faces of teen idols I didn't recognize. Those smiling boys with white teeth and clean hair didn't seem to care that the girl who used to sleep in my bed was gone.

I waited until I could hear asphyxial gasps and exhales snoring through the thin walls. Then I gathered the last of her clothes out of her side of the closet and out of the only drawer I'd given her in the dresser we shared. I pulled the posters of the watching boys down off the wall and crumpled them in wads, tossing the works onto the bedspread. Could I ward off evil by removing the temptation of her entirely? I lay down on the floor and pulled all that was under the bed out—sweatshirts and empty shoeboxes, magazines, lipstick, a leather knife sheath, and candy wrappers. I found the empty medicine bottle and tossed it on the pile and reached deeper, making sure the last remnants of her were out from under me. I heard a heavy clank and figured the 1x4 board that kept the mattress on the metal frame had fallen. I stretched my arm under the bed, feeling in the dark for what had dropped.

My hand grazed cool steel and knuckles on horn. I closed my fingers and sat back in the cubby between my bed and the wall, quieted by my find. Moonlight came in through the window, glinting off the blade as I turned the knife over in my hand. The elk-antler handle was smooth and the nodules worn. The blade curved in an upward sweep, good for unzipping an animal, good for skinning. I held still, trying to sense whether that knife's rightful owner—whoever that might be—was standing over my shoulder. I dared to glance. I was alone. I shifted it from hand to hand, feeling its weight and balance in my palm.

I rubbed the blade with my fingertips and ran it against my palm, conjuring a fearsome genie emerging in a wisp to grant dark wishes I harbored. I set the knife down next to the picture of my mother and stared at her from the stripped bed.

We called it spooning, what she did, wrapping herself around me, all arms and legs. My dad would say, "Stop humping him, for shit sake. You'll smother him," which only made her nuzzle more. I can honestly say I hadn't quite outgrown her affection. But almost. I do remember feeling the greater need shift from me to her. I'd taken already to denying her access to me—rejecting her attempts to hold my hand, turning my cheek to her when what she wanted was a kiss on the lips. My father called me a mama's boy and he was right about that. His coming and going didn't help, not for me or her. It was only my dwindling adolescence that disrupted the team we were, that and her dying. Now what solace I could take in the memory of her loving on me was blackened by my grandfather and what I gleaned in his intent.

She was staring back at me, that girl she was before there was me or my father or the sister, Daisy, I never met. That was the only picture I had of her, that and the ones shoved in the golden envelope. I dug those other ones out from the back of a drawer and without looking at them again threw them on the pile, bundled it all with the bedspread, opened the window, and shoved the works into the night. I put on a sweatshirt and jeans, snapped the sheathed knife onto my belt loop, then climbed out the window. If I'd been seen, someone would have thought I'd robbed the place and was making my escape, dragging my loot behind me down the railroad tracks.

There were no cars on the road, no lights on in houses or stores. It was too early for the early shift, too late for the late. In the morning gloom, I found a dumpster and discarded what remained of that girl in the picture and the sad images of what had become of her. I unsheathed the knife and pressed the point against my wrist, testing whether I could sacrifice myself right there. To be anywhere else. To be with her. And I let Gip sneak back into my thoughts, his want of her. What was I, anyway? Their blood ran through me—loser, liar, thief, cheat, brute, drunk, creep. Was there good at all? My neck still hurt from where Gip had pinned me. That stuck feeling, that flailing, caught. I let out a roar that shook my arms and my head free. I let the knife drop. What I wanted was to not crawl back in through the window I'd left open, to not be where I was, to not have my mother dead, my father gone, my drunk grandfather lurking in the dark. What option did I have? Go to Kathryn? Beg the Rooks to take me in off the street? Fat chance.

I pulled the bedspread back out of the dumpster and wrapped myself up in her for a while more, trying to find a hint of lemon from that girl long gone, though I must have known it was no use. And in that blossoming spring, I fell asleep alone on gravel and cold ground. I woke with the store manager's boot nudging my ribs. I was told to get. I left the bedspread in a heap on the ground and went back to the only home I had. But I was not about to settle in. I took the knife, for defense, to help bide the time until my father came for me like he said he would.

I lifted the window quietly and pushed aside the curtain. Ruby was there, on the end of the bare mattress. Her voice was tight, grimaced. "What have you done?"

My foot caught up on the sill and I tripped into the room, quickly righting myself to stand against the wall. "I couldn't take it."

"Take what?" She looked around the room stripped clean of my mother. "What was to take? You couldn't leave it be? I left it be fifteen years, longer even. You couldn't leave it be for a few months?"

"You're one to talk. It took you two days, two days! You threw everything that belonged to me away, and you left me in here with everything that belonged to her." I sank to the floor and let my head fall between my knees. Did the dust in that left-be room contain fragments of her skin? Were the bitten fingernails tangled in the shag rug hers or mine? I'd never thought to ask why Gip and Ruby hadn't done anything to change that room, hadn't taken down the posters or thrown out the ratty teddy bears. It was a room stuck in place, a boot in a bog.

"Why didn't you ever clean this room out, Ruby?"

The rattle of her stilled and she let her eyes drift to some middle space, out of focus. Her voice simmered and she mostly whispered, "Thought she might come back someday."

I pressed my head against the wall and looked around the wrecked and empty room. Scraps of paper and scotch tape dangled from the maple birds on the paneling. She'd up and left. Just as sure as Ruby had left everything the same, my mother had rejected it all. What had she even bothered to pack if so much of her things were left behind? "Why do you think she left?"

Ruby put her hand to her mouth, dragged her jutting finger bones back and forth across her lips. "Well, there was the baby." In her voice, I could hear the effort she was making to keep from breaking down.

"Daisy," I said.

Ruby raised her brows, resting her eyes on that truth with a nod. "She'd taken up with your dad. Nothing but a carny, that Moss Ballot. Couldn't believe she'd gotten herself pregnant that way. I told her . . ." Ruby shook her head, twisting her jaw to tap her teeth together. "Told her she didn't have to have a baby, didn't have to keep it. She was so pigheaded. No diploma even. Nothing at all."

"I thought Daisy came after she and Dad were married."

"Don't mean she wasn't made before. About the second Val could, she hitched herself to Moss, screaming at me, trying to tell me everything I'd done wrong." Ruby put her hand up. "I didn't want to hear it. I'd done my best and I figured she'd be back, figured Moss would leave her once the baby came. Thought I'd get a chance to do better. But I never did."

"They never told me what happened to Daisy."

"Died in her crib, they said. I never even got to see her. No picture. Nothing. They were living in Eau Claire. Your mom said we weren't welcome. She was already pregnant with you by that time. You'd a been Irish twins, you and that girl."

"Daisy," I said.

"Why she chose that name . . ." She tapped her teeth again, as if she were sending a message in code.

"What's wrong with it?"

"Awfully fresh, is all. For a girl like Val, getting pregnant, running off."

The image of Gip crawling into the twin bed where Ruby sat cropped back up. I could imagine my mother desperate to get out of this house, desperate to get away from whatever was happening here, desperate for something clean.

"I threw it all in a dumpster, down by the market."

Ruby pushed on her knees to standing. Her robe fell open, revealing a threadbare nightgown with missing buttons, her deflated chest. "Doesn't matter anymore. What's done's done."

When I stood, my shirt bunched, revealing the knife at my waistband. I pulled my sweatshirt over it as Ruby eyeballed me and her lower lids drew up. She took a step toward me like she might not be able to stop herself from reaching for it. "What you got there?"

"Nothing," I said. I turned my back to her but prepared to fight, to lay claim to this one thing. When I looked again she was in the doorway. All she said was that I was late for school. Her eyes were filled with suspicion and fever, as if I were hiding a ransom from her.

I replaced the discarded bedding with mismatched sheets and an old wool blanket I found in the hall closet. It stunk of first aid and something animal, and I hoped the smell of it would ward Gip off like a rope of garlic or twig of wolfsbane. The knife I slid into a slot along the wall, the point in the bed rail. I would spend sleepless nights on my side with my back to the wall so he couldn't sneak up on me and often woke on my stomach with my arm tucked along the mattress, my fingers grazing the antler tang.

For his part, Gip said only one thing. At the dinner table that night, he pointed to the thumbprint welt he left on my neck. Through a mouthful of meatloaf, he said, "Got a girl, I see."

I didn't want him to speak to me, to even look at me. "What?"

"Your neck there. Got a love bite. Tell me it's that Rook girl chewing on you."

Ruby glanced up from her plate. "Don't look like love to me."

The look he gave me, what was it? He was telling me that he remembered and that I had best forget. He popped out his shoulders, made himself big and me small. I wish now that I had stood up to him, called him on it right there, made him say in front of me and Ruby and God that he had been in that back bedroom time and again. But that's not what I did. Instead, my hand went to my neck as if it were my problem, not his. Shame wormed up from the chair and took me over, entering me in the most primal of spots. I could feel it tighten and coil inside, a thing that should not be disturbed. I withered from the weight of it. Gip saw me give in, and I suppose he thought his secret would be kept.

"What a thing that would be, huh? Our grandson sticking it to that girl. Bet Burt Rook would love that."

"You're a pig," Ruby said. She didn't say it in a way that sounded angry or disgusted. It was simply a fact stated.

Gip shrugged and turned his attention back to his meal. I excused myself while my grandparents shoveled food into their open mouths, eating as if the hungry were at the door.

CHAPTER 7

Spring turned to summer, and there was still no sign of my father. School let out, and Gip got me signed on as a fourth hand at a farm outside of town, changing irrigation pipes and doing odd jobs. I was happy for the work and to stay out of the house, away from Gip and his dirty mind and dirty mouth, away from Ruby, who seemed to be drying up before my eyes.

Kathryn got her driver's license and a shiny yellow car to go with it. She and I had an unspoken agreement that she would not come into my house and I would not invite her in. She told me early on that her father didn't approve but that she'd do what she wanted, to hell with him. I can't say she made much of an effort to go unseen.

Gip was all for me hanging around with Kathryn Rook. That alone should have put me off her. Any time he saw her leaning against her car in front of the house, waiting for me to come out, he'd say something lewd, even if Ruby was within earshot, about the way her lucky shorts rode up between her legs or how the gold cross on the chain she wore pointed to the promised land. Was he trying to goad me into a fight or make some kind of point? He would double pump his fist into the palm of his hand and tell me to go on and have fun. Walking out of their sad house, getting into Kathryn's clean car, and driving away made me feel better than the both of them.

The Fullerton dairy was a big operation with 150 cows, give or take. They had almost three hundred farm and pasture acres for crops and grazing, a brick-red hip-roof barn for heifers and calves and winter hay, and a metal equipment shed for machinery, tools, and tack. Another lower barn had a milking parlor attached. Next to that, two concrete stave silos, a chicken coop, and an old open-front loafing shed. Four of us—me, Drew Fullerton, Bull Hightower, and Lester Two Kills—worked for Drew's uncle, who owned the place. All four of Drew's cousins had gone off to Vietnam, but only most of one came back. That one, Roger, spent his time indoors. Drew said he'd lost one leg and all his marbles over there and couldn't take being outside. Drew was a quiet kid my age and mostly kept his head down, though his favorite thing to whisper was "motherfucker." The first time Kathryn drove up in her new car, it was "motherfucker" in admiration. When he stepped in cow shit, "motherfucker." I'd heard it so much from him, it got me thinking about the word in its parts, which brought up other stuff for me I didn't like to think about. I'd asked him once to find a new word. "Yeah, alright, motherfucker," he'd said with a grin.

Lester and Bull were both Indians, pals, it was clear from my first day. Lester was a year older than me and Drew, Bull a year older still. Lester I knew of from school, where he was a star basketball player and notorious loudmouth. He was tall and angled and wore his hair over his ears. His lips were flat and his mouth wide, especially when he smiled, which was often and ear to ear. Bull was shorter than me, but his chest was planked and broad. He could carry more weight than any of us, but we did most of the heavy lifting anyway since he was, for the most part, in charge of our crew. We did what he said.

It was a busy place that summer, us boys doing what we were told, changing pipes, readying the cows for milking, managing the hayrick. When the alfalfa was ready, we made hay—cutting, raking, drying, baling, and bucking. I was green compared with the others. I had to learn about farm machines and equipment, operation, and repairs, though

Bull and Lester would never let me or Drew drive. In between, I lazed with the others, smoking cigarettes and bullshitting on the flatbeds. I bulked up that summer and grew like grass. My father would be impressed when he returned.

Kathryn would sometimes stop by when I got off work, a cold six-pack under the front seat of her car. I got plenty of ribbing from the guys about her. "Lucky motherfucker," Drew said. They'd follow me out of the barn like a pack of curs. Lester would throw his arm around my shoulder like we were old buddies. "Hey there, Money," he'd say to Kathryn. "How about the three of us drive around, get in some trouble together. You must have a friend for old Lester."

Kathryn would be polite, but I could see in her narrowed eyes that she didn't like the way he looked at her or talked to her. "Party of two," she'd say, or something like that, to let Lester know she wasn't about to double date with him.

Bull was the one who would pull Lester back. "Come on, big mouth. Take a hint. That girl and hers aren't interested in you." And Lester would come back with something directed at me, about how our peckers compared, if that was what she was after, or how neither one of us was worth a damn, so it couldn't be that.

I'd throw my bike into the trunk of her car and go park with her on some back road, under some tree. It didn't matter where.

Everything about Kathryn I wanted and resented. She was full in every way. Her hair, her belly, the gas tank in her daddy's car. She had big ideas in her full head about going away to an eastern college, of traveling to places I'd never even known to dream about. "You're so small town," she'd say when I confessed my ignorance, as if she was something else entirely in puny Loma. We had moved quickly from kissing to groping in the spring. That summer, we moved from the front to the back seat. Then came the day she started undoing the button on my fly. "I'm Catholic," she said, unzipping, forcing her way down my underwear. I wallowed in the sin of her hand and tongue, probed her with longing fingers, blamed her for making me want more of her, when in truth I knew I didn't care about her the way I should. Then there was that mouthwatering giggle of hers—I'd heard a sound like that before, coming from women my father called lizards, from behind a locked door when I'd been shut out.

WHEN I WAS SEVEN YEARS old, my father took me away from my mother. We were living in Wisconsin at the time in a tiny white house behind an antique doll and train shop. Every wall in every room was papered with the same pink flowers bunched in the same bouquets. It had one bedroom my parents shared, a bathroom, and one room with appliances, a table and chairs, and a foldout couch where I slept.

The woman who'd lived there before us made beads for necklaces out of rose petals. They were marble size and still had a chalky rose scent, suitable for an old lady or a casket lining. I'd collected a handful that had gotten stuck in the cracks of the couch and kicked behind radiators. I was rolling one on the kitchen table, watching it wobble between my open palms, when my dad told my mom he was leaving for the summer.

She picked up a pair of underwear off the floor, mine, held them up, and scowled at me. I knew the face was for my father. "Who leaves a wife and kid and goes to work for a carnival?"

"I can't find anything here."

"Can't or won't?" She threw the underwear at my feet. I slid them against the wall with my heel.

"You promised me. You said we'd move to California. Live by the ocean. I'm still here in Wisconsin. Wisconsin, Moss. Working at a bar. I'm a barmaid." She stormed over to me and grabbed the underwear again, this time throwing them into the bedroom. "Goddamn it, Wes."

He stood up, my big father, and went to the front window. He pushed back the frilly curtain with the coffee mug he held in his machine-worn hands. The gray mist of a rainy day seemed to pass through him into the room.

"What do you want me to do?" he said to the outside. Then he turned to my mother. "You say you want to leave, but you always have an excuse. Let's make this time for real. You save a little, I'll save a little, and we'll get out of here next summer. Find a place out in Oregon maybe, or Washington. You'd like it out there, Wes," he said. "Salmon big as goats."

"Stop giving him ideas. How am I supposed to take care of him by myself? Just leave him? I can't do that every night."

He cocked his head and stared her down.

The bead clattered across the table between my hands like a duckling crossing a road. I scooped it up, then launched it again, in time with their quarrel.

She slammed her hand down between my palms and cupped the bead. "Stop it with the beads, will you?" She chucked it at my forehead and it bounced to the floor.

I pocketed the bead and leaned back in the chair.

He dropped the curtain and sat down across from me, sizing me up like I was the fish. He could keep me or throw me back.

"I'll take him."

The night before we left, I slept in the sag between them. In the morning, I gave my mother the handful of rose petal beads, which she held to her nose as we pulled away.

We hooked up with his crew in Sheridan, a cowboy town at the base of the Bighorn Mountains, snarling peaks that gnashed out of the ground. It was a man by the name of Topeka who'd helped my father get on the crew and who my father had greeted with a wide-open bear hug the day we joined up. "This guy here," Topeka had said, grabbing my father's shoulder when he introduced me. Topeka right away told my father about a mutual friend named Paul who got his arm ripped off in some gruesome accident on a ride called the Zipper.

"That Paulie was dumb as a box of hammers. Not your dad, though. Only limb he's like to lose is his pecker, ain't that right, Ballot? Stick that pecker of yours in the wrong damn slot and that thing might get chewed right off."

"I'll keep that in mind," my father said.

Topeka was the first person I'd ever seen with a tattoo on his face. It was a bony hand reaching up out of his shirt with fingers poised to rip his eyes out of his head. He said it was to remind him of someone he once knew who might be trying to reach out to him from the grave. "Keeps me on my toes, kid."

"Did you kill that sumbitch?" I asked, trying my hardest to curse like the rest of them.

Topeka lifted his porkpie hat and rubbed his shaved head. "Let's say he and I had a difference of opinion and leave it at that."

"You wanna give me that hat?" I asked.

"Nope, kid. This hat belongs to me."

IT WAS THRILLING, DRIVING ALL night and waking up on the seat of the stock truck, Elizabeth curled up next to me. My father would go to town first thing—that was his routine—and get coffee at a local diner. He said it gave him a feel for the place, what kind of people might show up on the midway. He said you could know a town, take its measure, by the six a.m. folks. He'd return full of coffee and breakfast, ready to work. Usually he'd bring me a fist-size muffin or bacon biscuits. For

Elizabeth, he brought coffee creamers, mostly, I think, because he knew how much I liked watching her lick from the tiny cups, her wisp of a tongue flicking to get the last drops.

Carnival life was like living at the playground where the ice cream truck was always parked. I was free to wander as long as I didn't leave the fairgrounds. I never got bored of the rides and novelty tents or eating corn dogs and candied apples. When I wasn't taking tickets for my dad, I helped keep the crew dogs off the midway, reset burst balloons, or duped marks for Topeka's flat store that he ran behind the Fun House. "Jesus, even the kid can do it!" he'd say when I miraculously was able to locate the ball under the shell to win ten dollars, which I later returned to him for a five.

But one thing did scare me, and it was the Barbosa Wandering Freak Show—a collection of misfits who circled the midway hawking the chance to take a picture with a freak for fifty cents. One spectacularly fat lady with red hair and thick freckles all over her face took a shine to me early on. This woman, Delilah, she looked like a bullfrog in a party dress and she terrified me. She had a sidekick, a tiny man with long blond hair called Sampson, who she treated like a pet. Whenever she saw me, she'd grab me and pull me so close I could feel her giant bosom resting on my head and the flab of her lumpy arms on the back of my neck. Her teeth barely broke the gum. She used to tell me how sweet I was, that I was "like sugar, so fine," she'd say. Sampson seemed to like me less and stood by silently watching this display, his pudgy arms folded against his chest.

One afternoon, green-black clouds cropped up in the western reaches of the prairie where we'd set up, rolling over the shelterbelt toward the midway like a tar carpet. The wind bent back the wheat, and the carnival crew scrambled to get booths shut tight before the storm hit. I stood next to the Tilt-A-Whirl and up comes fat Delilah. "You'd best run for cover," she warned me, "or you're like to melt." I couldn't move, thinking about that wicked witch I'd seen turn into nothing when the water hit her. I put my hands on my head and stood there, hoping against the rain.

She stared at me with her mushroom face, then waddled off, yelling, "Moss! Hey, Moss! Your boy's 'bout to get drown out here. You best fetch 'im." The sky cracked open and I got doused. Along comes my dad, running toward me. He was so tall and had that wicked smile, and to remember it I realize that he was probably just a little older then than I am now. "Hey, Little. You're soaked through." He scooped me up and stuck me under his arm like a sack of flour and carried me back to our trailer.

A dark-skinned woman was there, bobby-pinning loose strands into her hive of hair. Elizabeth was up on the table next to her, batting away at a dead sparrow my father had stuffed and tied to a string for her to play with. He jerked his head toward the door and the woman got up in no hurry. "I can take a hint," she said, scratching the cat between the ears with her long painted nail. "Oh, and Moss, x-y-z." He looked down and pulled up his zipper, then tossed a towel over my head. His big hands tousled my head and ears, muffling anything he might have said to her, blinding me to any look he might have given her.

I'D SEEN WOMEN LIKE THAT one before. My father called them lizards, women who wore short skirts and tight tops and waved back at the dirty men. The story goes that they'd get with some guy, then follow the show around from town to town until he got tired of them or they got bored or someone got beat up. They'd wiggle their asses at my dad, even with me standing there. Sometimes, he'd lean over the high rail and talk to them or give them rides for free if they asked nice. One time, he sent me off to find Topeka when a woman with a gap between her two front teeth showed up. I went back to our trailer when the gates closed, but the door was locked. I banged on it until a light flickered on. I heard a woman's laughter, followed by shushing noises, then my father's voice. "I'm feeling sick, Little. You go sleep at Topeka's tonight." The light went out and the laughter came on again. I scuffed the dirt and sulked away. Next day, my dad acted like nothing happened, just asked if I had fun sleeping over at Topeka's, like that had been the plan all along. That woman showed up in the next town driving a crumpled bronze Firebird. I saw my father talking to her, but he didn't look happy to see her.

"That looks like the same one was back in that last place," I'd said.

"Girl had the wrong idea about me, Little. I had to tell her what was what."

"She a lizard?" I'd asked.

"Suppose she is, yes."

He was sitting on the steps of the trailer while I kicked hay into piles, careful not to tangle my foot around the thick black electric cords that wound around behind the rigging. "That how you met Mom? She a lizard?"

His eyes got wide and he smiled and rubbed his forehead. "Your mother is no lizard. Lizards eventually scurry off. No, your mother is a whole different breed of cat," he said, which at the time made no sense to me. "Don't make mention of lizards to her, understood?"

She showed up not long after my father got rid of that lizard, summoned by him or of her own free will, I don't recall now. She said she'd been on the road all night in the borrowed mustard-colored Vega so she could meet up with us and take me back to Wisconsin with her. I made a fuss about going back, but in a truth I never shared with my father, I was ready to be done with the show. The moving around was hard on me in a way I didn't expect or even understand at the time. I was happy to be at the next place, wherever it was, but not happy to go. I liked watching the show come together, but the dismantling and load out unsettled me. I would often hide in the trailer with Elizabeth so I wouldn't have to help or even watch the breakdown.

I spent one more night banished to Topeka's trailer. The next morning, my parents kissed each other long and deep, my mother with her arms clasped behind my father's head, his hands on her backside, which he swatted when she turned to the car. We left him there with Elizabeth and the trailers, the cotton candy, the greasy food and oily rides, the loud music, and the lizards.

CHAPTER 8

In early July, insects hatched and swarmed, an annual rite of summer in Loma. Black flies in particular were drawn to me, leaving behind red-hot dot-to-dot patterns on the back of my neck. No amount of slapping kept them away. In fact, I think they waited for me to slap blood to the surface of my skin, then came back for more. The bugs I couldn't keep away. My father was another story.

I tried to pin his continued absence on grief, not neglect. The longer he stayed gone, the more he grew in favor in my head as I imagined him, not in Montana but up in Alaska, working day and night to make money for the two of us. I daydreamed about being able to go with him when I turned eighteen, which didn't seem so far off anymore. What I couldn't understand was why he hadn't been in touch at all. No cards or letters, no phone calls. It was like he'd dropped off the face of the earth. And I imagined it that way when I was low, that the earth had swallowed my mother and rejected my father. I didn't know what it would do with me.

Gip tended bar a couple nights a week at the taproom, and when he wasn't behind the bar, he was in front of it. He and Ruby had been haranguing each other nonstop since spring. I owed the increase in animosity to them burying their daughter, having seen those pictures, wishing, like I did, that they could unsee them. For my part, I could hardly look at him without thinking about his coming into my mother's bedroom. As much as I didn't want to imagine the worst, I found myself more and more recasting her as a girl my own age who'd been hurt, obscenely so, by her own father. Being in the same house with him felt like I was betraying her all over again.

Summer heat brought everyone outdoors, Ruby included. The house was stifling, and she would often sit in the evening shade of the front landing, a can of beer in one hand, her other bellowing the button placket of her loose blouse. She was not one for undergarments, so whatever bustline she'd once had lay down against her ribcage, flat as kneaded dough.

With Gip gone, I would sit with her sometimes, carefully asking questions about that girl my mother was. She would turn the question around and end up talking about her own miserable upbringing, her own mother who ran out and left her to be raised by her hillbilly father and three older brothers, how she ran out on them herself when she was still a teenager, left for Virginia, she said. When I asked her where she was from, she said only that she came from the hard part.

One of those nights, I took that knife out from the bed frame and grabbed a piece of wood, thinking maybe I could try my hand at whittling, though I knew the blade was all wrong for that. I sat down on the front steps and out comes Ruby, fanning herself, complaining about the heat. She unfolded an aluminum lawn chair. "Shit," she said. "I forgot my matches. Go in and get them for me, will you?"

I stood, set the knife and wood down where I'd been sitting. Ruby stiffened and paled. "Where'd that come from?" She was looking at the knife.

I hesitated, considering my options. "It belonged to my dad."

She kept her eye on it like it was a coiled snake. "Did it, now."

She'd seen the knife before. I'd made a mistake. "Yeah, I think maybe Mom gave it to him, though."

"Is that right? Is that what you think? That she gave him that knife?" She turned her attention to me. "What would you say if I told you that knife belonged to me? That it went missing years ago. And now suddenly it shows up right back here. You mean to tell me you had that with you the whole time, out there at the lake, then in the hospital?"

"It was with our things."

"Your things? So your daddy and Gip packed up all your crap and one or the other of them threw that knife into the box with your clothes. Neither one of those two cocksuckers thought to keep it for themselves? They give it to you without a word. That your story now?"

I sheathed the knife and put it in my back pocket, hoping I could lay claim to it just like that. I kicked the deformed wood into the street. "I'll go get you those matches."

"Yeah, you do that."

—

I TURNED SIXTEEN YEARS OLD the day Bull Hightower was struck by lightning. We were in a rush to make hay ahead of forecast rain, which would ruin the crop if we didn't get it in. The air was green and sweet with the scent of manure and cut alfalfa. Drew drove the baler along the windrows, and Bull the truck that pulled the hay skid. Lester and I took turns, one bucking bales from the field onto the hay wagon while the other stacked.

The sky turned plum and thunder rumbled in the distance as we got the last of it into the barn. While Lester and I pitched the bales off the wagon, Bull and Drew ran out to help his uncle bring the last few heifers in from the pasture. We could hear their shouts and whistles and claps, the yipping of Drew's dog, Tadpole, over the mounting thunder. The crack almost knocked me off my feet. Lester and I cursed in unison, then raced from the barn. Drew and his uncle were running back to the pasture while a group of heifers crowded their heads together in the barnyard, their chestnut eyes rolling in the whites like biddies gossiping at a fence. Bull was staggering in the field, taking a step, dropping to a knee, trying to get up again. A cow was down next to him.

"Get those cows in. I'll bring Bull's truck around," Lester yelled. I smacked the heifers to herd them into the barn, then ran to open the pasture gate. Lester pulled the two-toned Ford around the side of the barn. I jumped in the back, banging my head against the cab window. I righted myself only to get dropped again when Lester slid to a stop. Drew and his uncle lifted Bull up by the armpits. I hurtled out the back and opened the cab door. The smell of smoked meat hung in the air as Drew and his uncle slid Bull across the bench seat. He slumped next to Lester, who kept saying it was going to be okay as if he needed to reassure the both of them. Drew's uncle grabbed a dirty horse blanket from behind the seat and wrapped it around Bull. I got a closer look at the electrocuted cow, smoldering next to a burned patch of grass. A whole side of it was blackened and singed down to open flesh.

"You boys get him to the hospital. Drew, get in there next to him and keep him warm. He's in shock. I'll call ahead to let them know you're coming, and I'll call Mona and Troy. Lester, put the hammer down, you hear? Ballot, you jump in the back and go with them. I'll take care of the cows and meet you down there."

I vaulted into the back of the truck and Lester took off, black mud spitting behind and all around us. The rain turned to hail by the time we hit pavement. It was five miles into town and the hailstones got bigger with each mile. I got as flat as I could against the cab and put my arms over my head. The hail felt like frozen buckshot against my bare arms, and I figured I was bound to watch another person die.

I was soaked and battered by the time Lester got to the hospital. I ran in before the truck even came to a stop, yelling for help the whole way. Orderlies were ready and wheeled a gurney up to the truck and lifted Bull onto it. He blinked his eyes like the light was too bright. His plaid shirt had fallen open, and welts like cigarette burns pocked his chest where the superheated metal snaps had seared his flesh. His jeans were burned along the seam and the toe of one of his boots was blown clean through. I half expected his black hair to be frazzled and wiry, but it lay flat against the white of the hospital sheet. They whisked him into the hospital, leaving me, Lester, and Drew standing in the steady rain.

Drew chewed the calloused skin on his thumb, spitting it onto the ground. I hung my head and shoved my hands into my pockets. "The fuck," Lester said. He covered his mouth, like he was keeping the disbelief in. He took a faded blue bandana out of his back pocket, rolled it, and tied it around his forehead. The three of us stood for a second longer, staring at the door, wondering whether Bull would come back out of the hospital alive. "Fuck," Lester said again, then turned toward the truck. "I'll park and see you guys in there."

We'd settled into seats in the waiting room when Drew's uncle pushed through the door. He was soaking wet and covered in mud and manure. Troy Hightower, Bull's father, was right behind him, followed by a woman wearing jeans and a man's shirt, a dark braid dropped in a single rope down her back. I assumed she was Bull's mother. With them was a girl I'd never seen before.

"Who's the girl?" I whispered to Drew.

"Beats me."

Lester stood to meet them and we followed, heads down, hands in our pockets. Troy was a big man with square shoulders, the kind of man they put in cigarette commercials. He ran the machine shop at the high school and wore a Western shirt with pearl snaps, cowboy boots, and jeans every day. His silver hair was pulled back in a ponytail that looked coarse and bristled like a paintbrush. The way he went to Lester—both hands up, then on Lester's chest, then his shoulders, a single beat in each spot, then a palm on Lester's face—said these two men knew each other, that there would be no apologies or blame, that there wouldn't be a scene like there was that previous winter when it was me in the hospital bed. Ruby scoffed at men with long hair, calling them savages or sissies depending on whether they were Indian or not. I wondered what she would make of Troy Hightower and the silent way he and Lester acknowledged the bad place Bull was in.

Lester turned to me and Drew. "You guys know Drew, right? And this is Wes."

I raised my hand, then felt stupid, like I'd mocked them with the "how" gesture we did when we were kids playing cowboys and Indians, when we would run around a field whooping and tapping our hands to our mouths. I tried to cover and quickly extended it instead. "Ballot," I said. "Wes Ballot."

Troy's hand was big around mine. I could feel the roughness of his palm and watched his branchlike fingers wrap and grip my hand. "Glad to meet you. Wish it was under better circumstances."

The woman next to Troy touched Drew's shoulder and put her hand out to me. "Mona. Bull's stepmother." As we shook hands, I glanced at the girl. She caught my eye out the corner of hers, then let them sink, like she was reviewing a checklist. Based on the blankness of her expression and the way she blinked to move her gaze, I guessed I did not tick any boxes. I smiled weakly and let Mona's hand drop when she turned to Drew.

"Drew, how's your mom?"

"Ah, she's good. I'll tell her you asked after her."

I wish there was a snapshot of that moment, of Drew and his uncle, a couple of hayseed farmers, nervously shifting from one mud-caked foot to the other, of Mona and Troy Hightower clutching each other, concern burrowing into the dark lines of their faces, of Lester Two Kills, puffing up his chest, retelling the story of our drive through the hail, of this girl, who turned out to be Mona's niece, Jolene Oliver, who had only just come back to live in Loma, and of me, gaped and breathless, struck, not able to stop staring at Jolene, at her one exposed shoulder, brown and polished, at the way her lips moved while she listened to Lester, at the pink nail on her ring finger that traced the toffee-colored crescent moon scar on her cheekbone. I have looked at that picture in my head going on a dozen years. I would like to hold that picture in my hand.

"Forget it, motherfucker," Drew whispered. "No chance in hell."

The doctor was out before Lester stopped talking. Bull would be fine. He was lucky the cow had taken the direct hit instead of him. There was plenty of sighing and nervous laughter, some introductions all around, head nods, back slaps, ball caps removed, brows wiped. Drew's uncle said Bull was welcome to come back when he was ready and that they'd be taking off, him and Drew—"leave you folks to it." Lester was friends with the Hightowers, with Bull. He would stand at Bull's bedside, josh with him about the lightning bolt. I was in the gap, nothing to any of them. Lester half rescued me. "Wait around and I can drop you home later," he offered. I was about to accept when Drew's uncle countered. "You folks got enough to worry about. We can take him."

I clamped my mouth shut and nodded a thanks, then stole one more look at this Jolene, trying to catch her eye. She looked at me openly, nothing sly about it, no intention, holding me there before closing her eyes longer than a blink and redirecting her attention to the door.

—

THE SUN CAME OUT AND a rainbow arced like a doorway, seeing the storm clouds out. The brick buildings and sidewalks, the cars and lawns, everything was saturated with rain and color. Even the air, cool now, was fragrant as tea. I rode in the bed of the Fullertons' truck, my back against the cab, watching where I'd been disappear down the road. I ripped a hunk of pemmican off with my teeth, figuring I could probably ride for ages like that—carefree, hopeful, a feeling so new I wanted to parade it like an expensive suit. I was glad to be alive, glad to not have been struck by lightning, glad Bull wasn't dead. Fountains of oily puddle water splashed in our wake and that girl popped into my head, her silence, her drape of black hair, straight and heavy, weighing her head down so it cocked away from the parted side. Would it feel like tassels between my fingers, like some sort of fabric if I could hold a fistful? I rapped on the window of the farm truck. Drew slid the window open.

"This is good," I said. "I'll walk from here."

I hopped over the edge when the truck pulled over. The Fullertons pulled away, and I got the quick sensation that I was a hitcher getting dropped off in a new town, one with some possibility after all.

Kathryn was at the house when I got there. She was leaning against the car, her blue blouse inching up over her belly. Her hair was pulled along the side of her head in a ponytail that ambled over her splotchy shoulder where a sunburn had peeled to an indifferent tan. She put on a fake pout and crossed her arms when she saw me walking up. "Where have you been?" She'd gone out to the farm looking for me after the storm let up, figuring I'd take a ride home from her. When I wasn't there, she called the house. When I didn't answer, she came over. She said she'd laid on the horn as usual to get me to come out.

"Ruby or Gip in there?" I asked.

"Well, I didn't go to the door, Wes, if that's what you're asking. But no one came out so I guess not. Their car's not here, anyway."

I had Jolene on my mind but what was stirring elsewhere felt less specific. I thought about telling Kathryn it was my birthday, curious what gift she might give me, whether she'd come into the tenants' house if it was empty. I was looking at her but thinking of this other girl I knew not one lick about, who stared me down without a hint of interest, without cracking a smile, blank and smooth and unreadable. Kathryn's face registered a bouquet of emotions, each of them suddenly plastic.

"Bull Hightower got struck by lightning," I said. "We had to take him to the hospital."

"The Indian? Aren't there two of them?" she asked.

I didn't know what she even meant by that. "Yeah, Kathryn, he's Indian, and yes, I work with two Indians, him and Lester, and yes, only one of them was hit by lightning."

"You don't have to be snotty about it," she said. "I was just asking."

"Well, anyway, he's going to be okay. He was bringing in some heifers and one next to him was killed."

Kathryn tented her hands over her mouth and nose, breathing deep and dramatic. "Oh, that poor cow! Mr. Fullerton must have been so upset."

"No, well, I think he was more worried about Bull. Glad he was safe and all," I said, put off she might start comparing the value of an Indian against the value of a cow.

"Well, yeah, I mean. Of course." All concern fell off her and she perked right up. "So, you wanna go do something?"

"It's been a long day and I'm beat. Rain check, okay?"

A storm of emotions passed over her face. "Suit yourself."

By the time Ruby got home, she'd already heard about the lightning strike, knew it was "some Indian" who got hit. She took off her work shoes at the door. "You near it at all?" she asked. "Feel the charge?"

"No, I was in the barn. I heard it crack, though. Felt like a giant hammer came down."

She dropped the mail on the table and plunked down in a chair to look through it. My grandparents had kept the same post office box since they'd moved to Loma. Ruby had the only key. She didn't like the way the postman came right up to the door of a person's house, "like a Peeping Tom," she said. "Bad enough they can look through the mail. Don't need them looking through the window, too."

I watched for an odd size as she fanned out the envelopes, hoping my father had sent a card for my birthday. "Anything for me?" It was there, that hopefulness in my voice. I wished I hadn't said anything, hadn't called attention to myself in that way. If they were going to forget my birthday, I'd rather they did it outright and not have to backpedal and try to make something out of nothing.

She gave me a curious look, like it was strange that I should ask such a thing, strange that I would think anyone at all would have anything to send to me. But if there was even an inkling that this was anything other than an ordinary day, she didn't let on. She stacked the mail back up and slid it to me. "See for yourself," she said.

Bills. Overdue notices. Flyers. There was nothing for me. Could endless daylight in Alaska make one day blend into the next until a person could be blinded in some way, completely lose track of time, lose track of what was important?

The storm had cooled the air some and Gip stayed home that night. I spent my birthday in the living room watching the television with my grandparents, fans rattling in the windows, moths thick around the streetlights, thoughts of a mysterious girl pushing out the fact that I still had not heard one word from my father.

CHAPTER 9

That fall after my mother collected me from the carnival, my father didn't return as planned. I could feel her waiting for him to show up, to call. She started leaving notes on the table when we went out, explaining where we were—grocery store, gas station, bowling alley. When we came back to darkness, to emptiness, she'd crumple the note with both hands. Certain tire sounds on the road and she'd pick her head up, turn to the front door. I'd watch for the knob to turn, let myself imagine throwing myself at him or holding back to make him feel bad. When whatever teasing sound it was passed, we'd go back to what we were doing. We'd learned not to look at each other because hope is fertile and multiplies into disappointment.

Then he was back.

"Son of a bitch," my mother said. His duffel bag was by the door. The note was still on the table, but scrawled beneath my mother's printing was my father's. *Home. Where are you? Went down to the Signal.*

I picked up Elizabeth and hoisted her to my shoulder so I could breathe my relief into her fur.

My mother slapped the note with her palm. She put her hands on her hips.

"Put those groceries away," she said to me.

I set Elizabeth down again so I could grab the bags we'd left by the door.

"No," she snapped. "To hell with him. Let's put them back in the car."

"Why?"

"Let's see how he likes it." She unzipped his duffel bag and dumped the contents on the floor. From a squat, she rifled through what she found there, sniffing shirts, turning out pockets.

"Thinks he can just waltz back in here and have us waiting for him, he's got another think coming."

"But we *were* waiting for him."

She kicked his things out of the way, tangling a grease-stained shirt around her ankle. She unwound it and threw it with the rest. "Wes," she said. "You need to learn to keep your mouth shut."

She went into the bedroom and switched on a light. I could hear drawers being opened and shut, the sliding closet door chugging against the loose rail, my mother mumbling and cursing to herself. She dropped the full duffel next to the door and stomped into the dark kitchen. Elizabeth was rubbing up against my legs, begging for the food. We'd been waiting on a paycheck to shop and Elizabeth seemed as eager as I was for something fresh. "Move, cat," I said, nudging her away with my foot. She padded into the pile of clothes on the floor, working a spot with her paws. The smell of him mingled with the lingering floral of rose beads, and I wanted to do what the cat was doing and bury my face in his man smell—sweat salt and chew, hangover on flannel, the fust of unwashed hair.

My mother was wearing a black sweater and dark pants. Only her white face, hot with anger, was caught in the cold light when she opened the refrigerator door. She bent down and took out the rest of the beer. She stormed past me, snatching her car keys and the note from the table.

"And get Elizabeth," she said to me.

We spent that night bundled up together in the car on a dirt road not far from town. I'd asked her why we couldn't go home. Her hand was over her mouth, her head turned from me. She only shook her head. I ate Wonder Bread and let Elizabeth lick cat food off my finger so she wouldn't cut herself on the jagged edges of the can I'd jimmied open. My mother drank the beers until she complained they were making her cold. She got out of the car, squatted to pee in the berm. We fell asleep propped up against each other. By morning we could see our breath. Frost had built up on the windshield. Elizabeth was mewing and fussy, needing a litter box.

The car started on the second try, and we drove to a playground so the cat could claw around and do her business in the sand.

"Am I going to school?" We were at a stop sign, and I could see that other kids were making their way in that direction. A car behind us honked. My mother gave the finger without turning around and waited to go, waited some more until the horn blared again.

"We're playing hooky."

We drove to the next town over—so no one would recognize us, she said, as if we were on the run, as if my father was in hot pursuit. She pulled into a grocery store parking lot. "Let's go in and get warm," she said. "I got no money for gas." I made a towel nest for Elizabeth and followed my mother into the store. We took our time, going up and down each aisle, filling our cart full of wishful things—cereal boxes and bags of cookies, canned fruits and scarlet-colored jugs filled with juice. My mother pretended to be organized, and we made a game out of packing the cart like a moving box. "Get me something thin and about this size," she said, measuring out dimensions with her hands. I searched the store for the item that would fit neatly into the empty space, eager to keep her happy enough to go home.

At the deli counter, she made up a story about her daughter, Daisy, who was at school—"this one's sick," she said of me. Daisy and I would need sandwiches the next day, she said, and how very much kids these days ate, she said. The clerk sliced off bits of ham and cheese for us, and we devoured it, though we tried not to behave like the animals we were. At the bakery, she said my birthday was in a few days and asked if I could taste some cake before we decided which one we would get for my big party. She went on about all my friends and how she and Daisy were planning the party, how we would have balloons and toys and a piñata shaped like a tiger. "We should name that tiger 'Moss,' shouldn't we, Wes?" she asked me, smiling broadly, sickeningly, at the clerk. My mother promised she would be back the next day to pick up the cake.

We ate the deli ham in the aisles and stashed the white waxed paper behind the toilet tissue. After she crammed a few items into her coat pockets and purse—beef jerky, peanuts, bags of M&Ms, a bottle of Nyquil—we abandoned the cart in the frozen food aisle. When we got out to the car, she burst out laughing and I did, too. How funny it was to make them go through all that work when we had no money at all.

But that night we did have money enough for a motel room. Through the plate glass window, I watched her negotiate with the serpent of a man behind the counter. She leaned and popped her hip, pointed to me, the boy she'd told to look helpless. I put on the big sad eyes of late-night commercials—children with no food, dogs with no home. She nibbled her thumbnail, rubbing the rough of it against her lips, looked back at me. I tried to imagine the bargain she was driving, the wheedling. My father said she was an expert at "jewing people down," a born dealmaker. The man behind the counter was long and slick. His wily neck jutted and collapsed back on itself. Finally, he nodded and she came back out to the car, spinning the key around on the plastic fob.

The room was small, mildewed. A painting hung cockeyed above the one sunken bed, a failing ship in a stormy sea. My mother switched on the television, which flickered to life. We both plunked down, bouncing on the end of the bed. She leaned over, switched the channel until she was satisfied, then sat back. I got up to go to the bathroom. I fought and lost the urge to check behind the torn blue plastic curtain that circled the tub. What or who I thought would be there, I don't know, but I yanked it back, thinking at least the element of surprise would be on my side. My mother yelled to me through the closed door.

"I gotta go out," she said. "I'll bring back food. You stay here."

I closed the blinds to keep bogeymen from spying on me through the plate glass window. There was a phone on the nightstand, and I rested my hand on it, thinking I could call the house, explain to my father she was mad at him, tell him he really ought to come get us. I wanted to go home. I wanted to be with both of them.

—

"C'mon, Wes. Wake up," she said, kissing me all over my face. Her breath was god-awful and I dove under the pillow.

"What took you so long?" I asked. I'd waited and waited, watching daylight turn from sundown to darkness, until I'd given in to sleep, curled up with Elizabeth for comfort. She hugged on me like I wasn't a living thing, squeezing me until I had to cry uncle.

"There's burgers in the bag," she said, pointing to a greasy sack next to the television. "I have to take a shower."

—

We watched television, me in my pajamas, my mother in her T-shirt and panties, her hair twisted up in a towel. We ate bags of vending machine chips and the takeout burgers. She smoked one cigarette after the next and drank whiskey from a plastic cup, getting up to peek through the blinds from time to time.

She tucked me in when I couldn't keep my eyes open anymore, but the television she left on. I woke to the sound of her talking, and I wondered if I had in fact called my father because I could hear her swearing at him. But when I opened my eyes, I could see the person she was talking to was in the mirror. She was practicing the biting words she would put on him and the faces she would make. "Who does that?" she hissed. "I should have ended you." It scared me to watch her, scared me to see how angry she was, to see her wrestling with this phantom.

I sat up, rubbed my eyes, stretched long, like a cat in the sun, to get her attention.

"Oh, baby," she said, her voice now sweet, the venom vanished. "Mama wake you up? I'm sorry. I'm sorry."

She scooted me over, put my head down in her lap so she could soothe me. I remember the feeling of my cheek against the flesh of her thigh, the feeling of her hand on my head, her fingers in my hair.

"Maybe we should keep going, the two of us. Just keep going." Her voice wandered on a journey of its own, and I went with it, closing my eyes. "I could bleach your hair. He wouldn't look for a little blond boy, would he? Go see the ocean, Hollywood. Where else could we go? Should have been just the three of us—you, me, and Daisy. That would have been better. Way better than this." I let her take me there, the two of us plus the mirage of that lost baby whose face I only knew in my imagination. I fell asleep again to her whispering that I would have been a fine little brother and we would have been a family, the three of us, without my father to ruin everything.

She was sitting on the bed the next morning, already dressed. Her hands were in her lap, her back was stiff. She stared at the door as if she expected someone to kick it in. When I stirred, she didn't turn, though I could tell she'd registered my waking.

"Rise and shine," she said, without even looking at me.

I glanced at the telephone, thinking one more time I ought to call my father, not sure when I'd get the chance again.

"We're going home."

He wasn't there. His things were still strewn in the empty living room. My mother gave the pile a good kick, like it was a man down on his knees. She went straight for the cabinet and the bottle she kept there.

"What?" she said, licking her lips after the first sip.

I shrugged, careful, knowing it wasn't quite over yet.

"Go do something, why don't you? Get out of my hair. I'll make you a potpie in a bit."

I picked up Elizabeth and stroked her, trying to concentrate on her trembling purr, her twitching ears. I found one of her toys, a feather dangling from a stick, and flicked it for her, but she seemed more interested in her favorite spot in the sun on the back of the couch beneath the window. I followed her there and put my nose to the glass. I could smell the dust and limescale. Housefly carcasses were strewn along the sill, black legs up, crooked and stiff. I flipped them over with my fingertips. One was barely alive, no longer able to fly. It walked like a drunk, flinging itself at the window as if it could see salvation out of reach. "You're dumb," I whispered to it. "You got wings. You should have used them."

Sometime that afternoon, I heard the familiar rumble of his truck and ran to the door.

"Dad's here!"

She pushed herself up from the table and pushed me away from the door.

"Stay here," she said.

From the doorway, I saw him get out of the truck, a big homecoming-king smile on his face. It faded as my mother approached him. She pushed his chest with both hands. "Where you been?"

"Me?" he said. "Where have you been? I've been looking all over for you." He leaned in, then stood back up. "You're drunk."

"The fuck I am."

"You stink, Val."

"And here I thought you wanted to kiss me." She dipped her head and threw her arms around his neck.

"Let's get you back into the house."

"Oh yeah, let's go in the house, Moss. You been gone so long." She practically sang the words, drawing each one out. "Bet it's been ages since you got laid. You must be stiff as hell."

She released her hands and pranced around him, laughing, though the sound was forced and menacing. "Poor, poor Moss Ballot. Hasn't gotten his wood trimmed in ages. Get out of my way!" She pushed him again, then pulled open the truck door.

"You get back in the house, Wes," she said. "Me and your daddy got business to attend to here." She fell back on the seat and hoisted her spread legs up in the air.

He grabbed her ankle and pulled her out of the truck. She resisted, screaming and hitting at his arm. Her head thudded against the chrome stepside, and she landed on her back. She scrambled to her feet, yelling, calling him a son of a bitch and more, then ran past him, past me, into the house. She came right back out in a huff and began tossing his things over the railing and into the street, evicting him and his belongings piece by piece.

I could go live with him and Elizabeth, I thought. We'd travel around with the carnival and I'd eat cotton candy for breakfast and corn dogs for dinner. I asked him with my eyes and she saw me.

"Don't you get any big ideas, now. Mom needs you here. And you," she said, pointing at my father. "You try to take him and I'm calling the cops, Moss. I swear."

"Go on, Little," he said to me. "I'll be back soon. After she cools off."

I climbed halfway up the stairs. What they were saying I couldn't hear anymore. My mother was waving her arms this way and that, a weather vane in a windstorm. It was like watching a movie, and I thought they might kiss and then he would be home for good. But he got real close to her, reared up, then grabbed her by the neck. I screamed for him to stop and started back down the stairs, but they both told me to stay where I was. My father backed away again. I could see in the fading light that my mother was smiling. He reached behind the seat and pulled out something made of sticks and string and handed it to my mother. She held it at arm's length and laughed and flung it into the road. He squared off at her like a boxer, like he was going to hit her good. I screamed, and it was like we were right next to each other, the way he could see me. He went limp, and I knew he was leaving me again. A short rope pulled in my stomach, the fibers tugged with each step he took away from me. I picked up Elizabeth and ran after him.

"Little, you stay here," he said to me when I caught up with him.

"Don't go," I said. "Please."

"Watch over your mom and Elizabeth for me."

I buried my face in the cat's coat, dousing her with tears. "No, you take her. She loves you most," I said, pushing the cat into his arms.

He knelt down next to me and touched the side of my face. "I'll take good care of her, I promise."

I raised my hand and held it weakly next to my face, and he did the same. He got into the blue pickup truck, plunked Elizabeth down on the seat next to him, and drove off.

In the morning, I saw the remnants of the thing my mother threw into the street—tangled fishing line, busted branches, and dead songbirds squashed in the road, their cotton stuffing waving gently in the breeze.

He was back a week later. I came home from school and there he was, sitting on the couch like he'd never left. Elizabeth wove herself around my ankles, letting me know she was happy to see me, too. He smiled and whistled and told me how much he'd missed me all summer, said how I was growing faster than corn. When my mother got home, she threw her arms and legs around him like he was a soldier come home from the war. She sat on his lap while we ate supper, feeding him with her fingers, which he sucked clean. He stood behind her at the sink, one arm wrapped low around her waist, one high. I had to look away when I started thinking where his hands might be. I turned the television up loud when her giggles turned hoarse. A dish fell to the floor and I startled, thinking a fight would break out next. But instead she swept by me, him in pursuit, and the two of them went into the bedroom and closed the door.

CHAPTER 10

Lester drove a midnight-blue Impala that he'd mostly rebuilt with Bull's help. The inside was torn up, but he'd splurged on a high-gloss paint job. He used the bandana he kept in his back pocket to buff off fingerprints and bug smudges. Lester said he was in love with that car and would screw it if he could figure out how. I bummed a ride with him to go check on Bull and maybe catch a glimpse of that Jolene, who I hadn't seen since my birthday but couldn't get off my mind.

The doctor had insisted Bull take it easy for a couple of weeks, which kept him off the farm. But other than a persistent ringing in his ears that drove him half-nuts, Bull's only other side effect from the lightning strike was that he swore off beef. Lester said he reminded Bull that the cow was a dairy cow and that he'd be more justified in not drinking milk or eating cheese, but Bull said to honor the dead cow he'd never eat beef again. Lester being Lester grabbed a greasy sack full of hamburgers from the taproom on our way over.

Lester talked about the Hightowers like they were family to him. I thought I'd have to get cagey to pump him for information about Jolene, but she was all that mouth runner wanted to talk about. From him I learned that Jolene was a year older than me, that Mona's sister Trudy was Jolene's mother, that Trudy had hung herself—"booze, drugs, sex . . . you name it," Lester had said—that there was no father, never had been, that Jolene was a "wildcat." An image of Lester and Jolene popped into my head, the two of them scratching and clawing at each other.

We rode with the windows down, and I put my arm out, tapped the roof with my fingertips, tried to pretend I wasn't hanging on every word. "Trudy never could keep her shit together much," Lester said. "Mona and Troy about half raised her and Jolene. Trudy would come around, say she was going straight or something, mooch off them for a while, then pack Jolene off. The two of them were around a lot a few years ago. Shit, she was ugly then. Big forehead, messed-up teeth, flat as a board." Lester panted, his head jostling from side to side like a big dumb dog. He kept rhythm with the radio and drummed his leg and the dashboard. He pounded my chest with his palm. "But damned if that didn't wear off, am I right?" I rolled my eyes, tried to sell him on me not noticing. Lester laughed and punched me in the arm. Lester was the happiest guy I ever knew.

The Hightower house was a rundown ramshackle, its blistered brown paint peeling like a sunburn. The front-door screen had a dog-shaped hole in the bottom. Mismatched lawn chairs and tires turned to flower gardens littered the side yard. I imagined it was that house where kids gathered to run through sprinklers on hot days, where kick the can games ended at night. I loved it the moment I saw it. I had never been in an Indian's house before, and the conditioning I'd gotten my whole life—to be wary, suspect—put me on edge. I didn't know whether I would be welcomed or turned out. I felt the white on my skin like dried paste.

"Ballot," Lester said. He was holding the door open for me with his foot. I realized I'd stopped in the middle of the sidewalk. "You going to stand there or you coming in?"

"Yeah. Yeah." I loped up the steps, trying to assure myself it was no big deal that I was there.

Bull was sitting on the couch, a mixing bowl full of milk and cereal in his lap. Lester plopped down next to him. "You lazy, you know that, brother?"

"Watch it, man," Bull said. "You'll spill my milk."

"Me and Ballot working our asses off out there. You sitting here watching cartoons. Makes me hungry. We brought burgers," he said. The paper sack was almost soaked through.

"I told you, no more cows, man."

"They're for me and Ballot."

The room was cramped with worn furniture. Cushioned love seats were arranged with little rhyme or reason, a long davenport was against the wall. Wooden chairs, some painted, others not, were wedged in anywhere they'd almost fit. One television was on, another right next to it was not. Random pictures hung loosely on plywood paneled walls—snowcapped peaks, rivers, glossy teepees surrounded by Indians on horseback next to framed school pictures, metal peacocks. I stood, surveying the whole room, imagining it filled with Indians, a council of sorts, old ones, young ones, headdresses, war paint.

"Ballot, would you sit down, please?" Bull gestured at any number of open seats. "The fuck are you looking at, anyway?"

Lester tossed one of the hamburgers to me, nearly grazing Bull's crooked nose. Juice dripped down out the sides of his mouth as he taunted Bull with his relish-soaked hamburger. I was careful not to make too big of a mess of myself in case Jolene happened to make an appearance. Bull eyed the burgers but stuck with his cereal, telling us again what it felt like to have lightning in his body, about the smell of the cow's sizzling hide.

Jolene walked into the room, and I jumped up. My hamburger slid out of the bun, toppling mustard over ketchup over relish down the front of my shirt and onto the floor. Behind Jolene, a floppy-eared hound lumbered into the room and headed straight for me. I took a step back and knocked a chair over. The dog devoured the burger in a gulp, then the bun I dropped trying to right the chair in another. Jolene whistled a high chirp through her teeth. The dog looked over his jutting shoulder at her, frisked my crotch for another burger, then returned to the girl, licking his dangling jowls. Jolene scratched his head like she was scouring a pan. "You big dumb nut, Sparky," she said. Her voice. Bristly, but smooth and loose. She wore a short sundress with thin straps over the shoulders, muscular legs bare to her toes. Lester and Bull were practically in tears laughing at the whole scene. I was paralyzed. I thought of Bull's lightning strike, whether it felt like what was coursing through my veins. The smile slid from her face. "You got something," she said, dull as can be, tapping her own breastbone with her middle finger.

I looked down, shamed by the stoplight of condiments smearing my white T-shirt. When I looked up, she was gone.

The whole of me drooped and wilted, hope dead on a bent stem.

Bull and Lester, shoulder to shoulder now, moping eyes fawning at me with mock concern. "Oh, Ballot," Lester said, his voice singsongy. "You poor, poor son of a bitch."

Bull chimed in. "Yeah, Ballot, that shit is never ever gonna happen. You go back to your little blondie to get laid."

I sat back down and grabbed the greasy bag from Lester. "Don't know what you two assholes are talking about," I said. "Dog ruined my fucking shirt, is all."

"Sure, Ballot," Bull said. He pushed the empty bowl of cereal away. "Fuck it. Give me one of those burgers. Smells too good."

The playground was in the center of town, across the street from the Elks Lodge where Kathryn's father routinely stopped for a drink after work. I think she liked to meet me there in hopes he'd see us and she could get a rise out of him. She was late, so I stretched out on the splintered seesaw plank, lit a cigarette I'd bummed off Drew, traced the pattern the oak leaves made against the blue sky. I closed my eyes and thought about Jolene Oliver, the way my feet felt pinned to the ground when I saw her, like being in the same room with her somehow added to my atomic weight.

A shadow passed over the pink screen of my closed eyes. I sniffed the summer air for Kathryn's baby powder perfume. When I opened my eyes, there was Jolene, looking at me like she was examining something left for dead.

"You can't do that by yourself, you know," she said to me.

I sat up, shielding my eyes with my hand, shifting so her head would block the sun.

"What?"

"Seesaw. Teeter-totter. It's a two-person thing." She nudged me with her foot. "Spin around. I'll go to the other side. I want the one with the handle anyway."

She was in the way, so I couldn't avoid getting up right next to her. I'd grown in those months in Loma and was pushing six feet. I was tempted to measure her off with my hand, or to put my arm around her dark shoulder. I struggled to keep my hands to myself, and my sweaty thoughts from puncturing the moment. I moved to take a drag off my cigarette, but she tweezed it out of my fingers, dropped it, then ground it out with the toe of her shoe. "And stop smoking," she said. "It's disgusting."

I was too shocked to do much of anything other than stare at the swirl mark her shoe had made in the dirt. Had I daydreamed her there?

"You look like you were the one struck by lightning. Stop staring." She went around and balanced the board on the metal bar. "Go on." She looked at me like no one ever didn't do what she told them to do.

I rolled my eyes, swung my leg over, and tried to keep my wits about me. "This is stupid."

She pushed up with the toes of her red sneakers. She wore cutoff jean shorts and a tight yellow tank top, no bra. I took her in while she was suspended up high, the glimpse of navel, the bead and string bracelets around her wrist, the shape of her breasts. Her fingers, nails polished pink, clutched the handle between her legs underhand like a bull rider. I caught myself staring at her crotch.

"Let me down! God, do you really not know how to do this?"

I pushed my bent legs straight, and she came back down. She splayed her feet out in front of her and leaned back. I was stuck up.

"How do you like it?" She smiled at me then, a funny, crooked, closed-mouth sideways smile that I would later try to imitate in the mirror. It was like she could see something in me that I didn't know about, and I wanted to try on that expression so I could know it, too. Mercifully, she didn't leave me up there and, despite how idiotic I felt, we fell into an easy up-and-down rhythm.

"Bull said your mother died. Mine, too. Hung herself." She said it matter-of-fact, without a hint of embarrassment over the scandal of it all.

"I heard. Lester told me."

"What happened to your mom?"

The scenery changed behind her with the motion, from sky to earth and back again. I felt weak and dizzy, like I was time traveling to be there with her. I had to warm up the next word in my mouth so it wouldn't crack out. "Drowned. If it makes you feel any better."

"Why would that make me feel better?"

"No, I mean. Guess we're in the same boat, is all." There was something about the restful look in her eyes, the tilt of her head, the way she sat up straight on that board, not slouched, that told me we might not be all that alike.

She was up in the air when the impatient honking sunk in. I saw the yellow car and panicked. The seesaw and Jolene hit the ground in an abrupt thud. I nearly went to her, to dust her off, to take hold of her. I could picture it, the two of us, hands locked, running down the street, laughing, checking over our shoulders only once, then never looking back again.

"I've got to go," I said. "Sorry."

She stood up, the crooked smile gone, and brushed playground dirt off her back pockets.

"See you around?" I said it hopefully, asking her a real question, asking her to see me. Her answer was in the twitch of her eyebrow, the lingering blink, the shoulder shrug that seemed to shiver up her cheek and land on that scar.

—

"JUST SOME GIRL," I TOLD Kathryn, playing the scene off. "Bull Hightower's cousin."

"Is she retarded?"

"Why would you say a thing like that? Of course she's not."

"Well, why else would a boy in his right mind play like that unless it was to humor some retard? Lots of Indians are slow, you know."

"She's not slow. She was there, is all. We talked about Bull."

Kathryn turned into a dirt pullout under a grove of maple trees past the golf course and cut the engine. She scooted along the seat closer to me. "Well, you ought not make a habit of hanging out there, then. She's probably trouble." She straddled me and I circled my arms around her hips, pulling her closer. I felt the weight of her, the flesh, and closed my eyes. Her mouth was on mine, swallowing and probing. I kept my dark focus on the girl I'd left up in the air, black hair against blue sky.

CHAPTER 11

My mind wandered to Jolene, natural as a leaf floats to the ground. Would her skin be taut and leathery or soft like felt on an antler? Would she smell good behind her ears, like a poultice of soap and honey? I'd catch bits about her once Bull returned to work and he and Lester got to talking, but nothing they shared was as rich as my imagination. Then there was Kathryn, who continued to please and pester me at the same time. Lester was as relentless as a dripping faucet about Kathryn, convinced I was putting the blocks to her, mangling the bird-in-the-hand metaphor by trying to substitute pussy. He was almost as bad as Gip, who leered at me when I came in from a night out with her. One time he even went so far as to sniff the air when I walked by him. "You smell like snatch," he said.

It was nearing the end of summer and I was sick of all of them—sick of the farm, the endless cycle of work there, the heat and the bugs, the stink of manure and milk souring in the sun. Sick of Bull and Lester and their endless bullshit, sick of Kathryn and her neediness and her mouth, sick of Ruby, who lurked around me like a coyote, waiting for me to flounder so she could pick at my bones. And I was sick to death of myself and the lather I'd worked myself into over Jolene, constantly trying to find reason and chance to casually pass the Hightower house, hoping to catch another glimpse of a girl who lived completely in my head, so worked up over the fantasy I'd go right to Kathryn and start all over again. I thought my days in Loma must be numbered, but the longer I stayed, the less likely it seemed I could ever leave.

—

She had seen me. More than that, she'd watched me for days on end, passing her house, sometimes on foot, other times on bicycle, sometimes behind the wheel of Ruby's clunker. And when she was good and ready—because that's how Jolene Oliver worked, on her own time—she stepped off the porch and stopped me.

I'd spotted her by the time it was too late to divert or retreat, so I kept walking, examining my fingernails, listening to my shoes slap the hot concrete. She was sitting on her porch behind the rail on my right so I glanced left, wishing I had a watch I could check to show her I had someplace to be, that this was a shortcut to get me straight to where I was needed. When I was lined up with the front walk of the Hightowers' house, I dared a look. She was at the landing, one leg out to the side, hands on her cocked hips.

I smiled, tight-lipped, weak. My guts and brains dropped into my pants.

"Wanna come in?" she asked.

I stopped, scratched my head, did a poor job of faking surprise. "Oh. What?"

"Do you want to come into the house?" She bobbed her head with each word, like I might need to read her lips.

"Uh, sure," I said. I don't know why I did it, but I looked around, like someone might be watching me, like what I was doing was somehow wrong.

"Worried you'll get caught?"

"Caught? Caught by who?"

The look she gave me was complete, an x-ray of my emotions, my biology, my potential. In that silent exchange, I came to believe she understood everything that there was to know about me. I was drawn to her by a terrestrial force I had no power to resist.

The spot Bull had occupied on the couch was empty, which was a relief to me. I wasn't ready to have him see my intentions, which felt embossed on my face. Chaos rose in some other room, thrilled screaming of children. I heard a rush of feet, then a little girl in a flowered dress shot out from a long hallway. She stopped in her tracks and stuck her tongue out at me. I threw my suspicion back at her with a squint.

"Who's the white boy?" she asked Jolene, her eyes glued to me.

"Get lost," Jolene said. She flicked her away with her wrist like she was shooing a fly. The little girl stood firm. "I mean it, Mariah. Scram."

I got one more fresh face. Then the chanting began: "Jolene and a white boy sitting in a tree, k-i-s-s-i-n-g." Jolene lunged at her and she took off, smooching sounds trailing down the hallway.

"Forget her," Jolene said, grabbing me by the arm to lead me into the kitchen. Mona was sitting at the square table, an assortment of needles and thread and a bowl full of tiny colored beads in front of her, the telephone wedged between her ear and shoulder.

She looked up at the two of us. "I'll talk to you later," she said, standing to hang up the receiver on the wall-mounted base. Jolene dropped my arm, and I touched it without thinking, rubbing the spot she'd been pulling on. "You remember Wes, right? Works with Bull?"

"Sure," Mona said. She wore a man's T-shirt with a howling wolf on it. Her long braid rested on her shoulder. "You're looking for Bull? He's not here."

Jolene answered while she rifled through the whitewashed pine cupboards. "Wes is here with me." She said it as if we'd made a plan, like we were to be friends. "You want a peanut butter jelly sandwich?"

I was looking for signs that I wasn't welcome in that warm kitchen. White curtains spotted with red strawberries fluttered and sucked at the screen in the open window. The sun was behind the house and the kitchen was in shadow. The dog, Sparky, was panting under the table, not interested in me or my crotch this time. I felt the urge to vow that my intentions were good, that I could not possibly harm this girl, if that's what her aunt feared might happen. All of me was foreign yet I wanted more than anything to sit down at that table, maybe even lay my head on my arms and rest. "Sure," I said to Jolene. I turned to Mona. "That is, if you don't mind."

"Not one bit," she said, pushing a chair out for me. "Have a seat."

Mona picked up tiny beads with the end of a long needle, then wove them between threads strung on a wooden loom. "I remember her, you know," said Mona. "Your mom. She was a few years younger than me in school."

I shifted my feet a little and kept my head down, not sure what else to say.

"How's it going over there with Gip and Ruby? Been a long time since they had a kid in the house."

"Quit with the third degree, already," Jolene said. "Sit down, will you?" She pushed on my shoulder, put the plate on the table. "Here's your sandwich." She shifted her attention back to Mona. "You making more bracelets?"

"Oh, you know me," Mona said. "I was talking to Dot. We have to run our hands while we run our mouths."

I tried to keep up with the dueling conversation and eat the sandwich at the same time so as not to appear ungrateful. I choked down the bite in my mouth. "It's okay," I said to Mona. "With Gip and Ruby."

"They know you're here?" Mona asked. The sound in her voice made me think she probably knew a little about them.

I was content there in that jam-scented kitchen, content with my discomfort, content to have those two sets of brown eyes staring at me. I took another bite of the sandwich and sipped milk from a glass jar with little orange flowers painted on it. I didn't want to go back to that other kitchen just yet.

"They don't pay much mind to what I do."

She nodded, satisfied enough, I figured. "Well, glad to have you then."

"You about done?" Jolene asked as I took another bite of sandwich.

"Give him a chance," Mona said. "You're so impatient."

Jolene rolled her eyes at the both of us, then snatched my sandwich away midbite and dropped it on the plate. "Oh, just leave that." I gulped from the glass of milk to help wash the peanut butter down as she grabbed hold of my arm again. "Let's go," she said and pulled me into the dining room.

I'd barely swallowed the last bite before the little girl in the flowered dress ran up to me in terror, circled my legs like a barrel racer, and peered through my knees. "He comin' to git me!" she screamed. "Hide me!"

I crouched to make a better shield of myself. "I'll protect you," I said, with all the bravery I could muster. A black-haired boy wearing a leather vest, white underpants, and nothing else but a plastic holster belted around his waist came squealing into the room. He brandished a toy pistol.

"Where's that varmint? She stoled my gold!"

Jolene pried the little girl off my legs. "Here she is, prospector! Here's your thief!"

The little girl kicked and wiggled until Jolene let her go. She stood in front of me, the pistol pointing into the base of her spine, scorn pouting out her squinted eyes. "You said you'd protect me. You're a liar." The accusation stung, salt in a fresh wound.

"I'm sorry," I said, and meant it.

"He gonna string me up now, and it's all your fault."

Jolene's hand shot up like she might slap the girl's face. She caught herself and let it drop. "You and George go on now. We don't want to play with you two. Go on," she said.

"Fine," the little girl said. "I don't trust him anyhow." She laced her hands behind her head and turned stoically. The underpantsed prospector led her back down the hall.

I'd flinched at the "string me up" remark and wondered if that's what made Jolene want to raise her hand to the child. Me, I wanted to put my arms around Jolene and make promises to protect her from all manner of hurts, whether sticks, stones, or harmful words.

Jolene let out a puff of air. "They're so stupid sometimes. Come upstairs. I wanna show you something." We climbed the back stairs through the middle of the house into an open room Jolene shared with Mariah. Under the eaves on either side was a bed, one with a blue quilt and the other with yellow.

"Tidy," I said.

"Yeah. Rules, you know. Mona says we have to make our beds every day."

Jolene opened a door in the far corner, despite the handwritten sign declaring the room off-limits to girls. "This is Bull's room."

The room was at the front of the house, A-framed, a single window with a bed beneath it. "He can climb right out and sit on the porch roof," Jolene said. I'm sure my mouth was hanging open. It was a life-size diorama of a boy's room, and I'd never seen anything like it. It even smelled like a clubhouse, though I couldn't tell where that smell was coming from—the poster of Steve McQueen on a motorcycle? The plum-colored satin blankets that shone like Ali's boxing shorts? The gold trophies of athletes frozen midpass, midshot, midswing? Or was it coming from the car magazines and wadded-up clothes that littered the floor? I wanted to go in and inspect it all. I'd never in my life lived anywhere long enough to accumulate an identity in the room where I slept. A younger Bull and Lester stood next to another basketball player in one of the pictures on the wall.

"That's Bull and Lester, right?" I asked.

"Yeah," Jolene said. "The other guy's my uncle Thomas. He used to live here, but he got married and moved to South Dakota. My mom, Trudy, she and Mona were sisters. Thomas is their little brother. They all had the same mother, my grandmother. She died a few years back.

And Bull, he's Troy's son but from a different woman, not Mona—long story. Mariah belongs to Mona and Troy. That naked little bugger downstairs is George. He's Mona's friend's little kid. Mona watches him sometimes."

"Jesus," I said.

"Tell me about it. Anyway," she said, closing the door to the boy's room, "that's not what I wanted to show you."

A denim curtain hung on a thin pole in the doorway of a closet in the corner of the room. She pushed the curtain aside and glanced over her shoulder. "Just follow me, okay?" she said and got down on her hands and knees.

The bare soles of Jolene's feet disappeared when the curtain fell back in place. No rustles or bumps, no noises at all. She was gone and there I stood, motionless, wondering what cavity had swallowed her, wondering for a brief moment what might ice over her, to seal her away from me. I pressed my hand against the curtain, testing the force field for tingling or teeth. Her head popped out below me, and I stumbled back.

"You're a jumpy one," she said. "So? Are you coming or what?"

I crouched onto my hands and knees and inched toward her. I knew I was being stupid, thinking about my mother and that other gap in the world, of falling through or being pulled down. I rubbed the floorboards with my thumbs. When I lifted my head, my face was up close to the pockets of Jolene's cutoffs as I crawled behind her. I could smell some sweet part of her drifting over me, and I let myself be led. An assortment of coats and tablecloths and ladies' dresses swept over our backs as we made our way to the corner. Jolene pushed on the wall with her hip and a section of particleboard collapsed, revealing a narrow void, black as pitch.

"Bull and Thomas hide girlie magazines in here," Jolene said. "Don't touch the pink stuff. There's glass in it and it'll make your hand itch."

We crawled over the baseboard and into the darkness. The click and light came at once. Jolene held a flashlight up to her chin, which exposed the beams and roofing nails and cotton candy insulation. Her nostrils were lit like a torch.

"You scared?"

"No," I said, trying to sound convincing. My clammy palm landed on an open page of a dog-eared magazine. I peeled it away, leaving a moist print on a naked boob. The woman in the picture, bone thin with dark hair and long bangs, reminded me so much of my mother, I had to take another look. She would sometimes come home late at night and strip down to her underwear about the second she walked through the door, like she'd rolled in something awful and had to get the whole works into the wash. Then she'd slip into a flimsy T-shirt and hug me close to her, the way a kid might hug a teddy bear.

Jolene slapped the magazine closed. "Would you forget about that, please? Here," she said, handing me the flashlight. "Hold this."

I tried to imagine what she might have for me. I knew what Kathryn would do in that darkness and will admit to wanting it from Jolene—to see her ribs and navel, her breasts that were smaller than Kathryn's. I wanted her hands on me, linked around my neck, gripping me. But I also wanted out of there, to be in the open, no walls, and no more darkness. I thought about Mona downstairs in the kitchen, the little kids running around, clueless to what might go down in the closet above them. I thought of saying to Jolene, *You know, we don't have to do anything. We can hold hands or drive around or talk or something.* I held the flashlight and my breath still. She dragged a box along the floor, removed the lid, and lifted out a wooden board and a small pegged paddle.

"It's a Ouija board. You can use it to talk to dead people. I found it in the neighbor's trash and brought it here. I know it's silly. I mean, spirits don't live in a game board, but I think we should try anyhow," Jolene said. "I can't do it myself. You need two people." She hesitated and knotted her lips. "I think we should try to talk to our moms."

"What, like a séance?" I asked. I was glad to be sitting, since the whole of me grew weak and limp. I'd seen what happens to the dead.

I easily conjured my ghostly mother, watered down and fed upon, dog-paddling to the surface in the stifling closet air, and Jolene's, too, drugged and dangling from the darkness overhead, her feet grazing our backs. And because I'd never seen even a photograph of her, I could only picture Jolene there, her face blank, neck broken. I shook my head, too quickly I imagine. I tried to sum up all my feelings, my regret for crawling in there in the first place, my wish for something from Jolene I couldn't name, my fear that you can't open up a portal to the dead without getting more than you bargained for.

—

WE SETTLED OURSELVES CROSS-LEGGED, FLASHLIGHT propped against a hunk of insulation so that a beam of light lit the board between us and little else. The wooden paddle—called a planchette, Jolene told me—was oblong, almost heart shaped, with a round hole at the tip. The words "Mystifying Oracle" were painted on it in the black lettering of a snake-oil salesman. "Put your fingers on it, lightly, like this," Jolene said. I obeyed. The board itself had the alphabet in two rows of letters in arcs. The words "Yes" and "No" were in opposite corners, and the word "Goodbye" was at the bottom, as if all that was left unsaid could be answered that way. "So I think we should just ask questions. You want to start?"

"Jolene, I—"

"I'll go. It's okay. Don't be scared."

"I'm not—"

"Shhh. It's okay." She took a deep breath and closed her eyes, like she was channeling some mystic in a movie. "Is there a ghost in this closet?" Jolene asked in a spooky, melodic voice. Nothing happened.

"I said, is there a ghost here?"

The paddle glided across the board, our fingers along for the ride.

Yes, the board said.

"Are you Wes's mom? What's your mom's name again?"

I barely wanted to say it. "Valerie."

The paddle swung around and landed right back where it started. Jolene looked at me and flared her eyes and clenched her teeth so the tendons in her neck stuck out. A lump lodged in my throat.

"Valerie, is my mom with you? Is Trudy with you?" Another yes from the wooden board.

"They're both here . . ." Jolene whispered.

"I don't think I like this."

"Go on. Ask."

Where would I start? *Are you still cold? Are you in heaven? Why did you leave me? Where is my father? Is he dead with you? Were you trying to break the ice? Did you try to pull me in with you? And Gip and that knife under your bed?* I was frozen. I pulled my fingers from the planchette like it was smoldering coal.

"Don't, Wes." Jolene's voice was quiet and pleading. "Don't break it."

I let my eyes rest on hers as my fingers touched back down. She blinked hard, then asked the ghost her question. "Why did you do it?"

I wanted to come up with a short answer, one that I could guide the paddle toward, that would give this girl the peace she wanted. I couldn't think of a thing. The planchette didn't move. She repeated the question, and when there was still no answer, she shouted it. I had to counter the pressure she put on the paddle with pressure of my own, like the teeter-totter in the park. I did not want her to fly off, to crash down. "Do you hate me? Is that why?" Jolene's voice was quiet again, and I could feel the tension rest on my fingertips as they glided along the board to the corner. *No.*

"I have to stop," she said. "I feel sick."

She backed out of the light and fumbled toward the opening. Her breathing was startled and damp with sobs. I grabbed for the flashlight, upsetting the board. I crawled away, but my knee wobbled and I felt something snap. I knew instantly I'd busted the planchette. I pushed a scratchy ladies' coat off the top of my head. Jolene was sitting in the closet doorframe, the denim curtain bunched against her back. I held out the broken paddle. "I'm sorry," I said. "I smashed it."

She knelt beside me and took it from my hand delicately, like it was a wounded animal, like she might check it for a mother's heartbeat. Her smile consoled me, but as she threw the paddle back into the crawl space she lingered a moment, as if she was hoping the call she'd made might get reconnected.

We scooted into daylight, into the tidy room Jolene shared with her little cousin. If our mothers' ghosts were still lurking in the crawl space, whispering about us, we could not hear them. Jolene drew her knees up to her chest and rested her head on her arms. Our shoulders, arms, hips were touching. I put my fists to my mouth like I was preparing to make a birdcall and blew my last frightened breaths into my palms.

"I don't know if it was an accident, my mother drowning like that." My thumbs were on my lips as I spoke and the words muffled in the hollow of my hands. "We thought we heard a loon. She was jumping on the ice, flapping her arms."

Jolene lifted her head and let it bump against the wall. "Mine was gone three days. I don't know where she was between then and when they found her. She left me at her boyfriend's place. No note. Just . . ." She opened her hands like she was setting a bird free. "Mona said she took her weakness with her. Left her strength behind for me."

I put my head back, too, and closed my eyes. Sleep was there, and I feared I could doze right off. I allowed myself to glance at her. Her eyes were closed and restful, black lashes hovering above the moon-shaped scar on her cheek. I turned back, closed my eyes again, and was surprised to feel the sweep of her hair on my arm, her head soft on my shoulder. Her bent legs collapsed against mine, and she curled toward me, quiet as a cat. I let my hand drift across her knees and pulled her closer, careful not to crush another thing, careful to let her know I wanted her right where she was and that I would not move until she was ready.

CHAPTER 12

I knew Bull might find out and not like it at all, but the day after our failed attempt at summoning dead mothers, I called the Fullertons, told them I was sick, then talked Jolene into going down to the river with me. Kathryn was out of my hair, away on some sort of vacation with her family, and the sense of doom that I'd felt the whole time I'd been in Loma—over six months—was lifting. It was mid-August, and suddenly I wished summer could go on forever.

We rode bicycles down Main Street and climbed the hills to the old highway. We took our time, riding side by side, riding without hands for as long as we could. Magpies swooped along the hayfields, raising a stink when we pedaled past. We turned onto a dirt road and got off our bikes to walk them over the cattle guard. I was already sweaty, and I could taste field dust when I sniffled. I second-guessed my decision to bother with a shower.

"C'mon, moo with me," Jolene said. She laid down her bike and went over to the rail fence, mooing her head off.

I stayed with my bike in the road. "Moo."

"That's no moo, Wes! For Pete's sake!" She mooed again.

"Those cows look concerned," I said. The three closest to us had stopped eating grass and looked our way.

"They're cows, not bulls. They won't charge us or something. Now, let one rip or we're never gonna get to the river."

I dropped my bike and stood next to her on the fence rail. The sweet smell of manure and hay filled the air. I breathed it in, threw back my head, and bellowed out a moo. "There," I said. The cows dropped their heads to the grass again.

"Good," said Jolene, as she jumped down from the rail and headed back to the bikes. "Tired of waiting for you." Hands on my head, I watched the back pockets of her jeans ticktock as she walked away from me.

—

AT THE END OF THE road, we leaned our bikes against a tree and headed down the trail that ran alongside a marsh. Red-winged blackbirds perched on cattails, their reedy calls seasoning the dry air. Other kids had already staked out spots between low shrubs on the rocky shore. Two shirtless boys, cigarettes pursed in their lips, were busy on the opposite bank securing a rope onto the iron bridge supports while girls in bikini tops rubbed oil on their bronzed bellies.

Jolene and I stopped a ways upriver on the edge of what we generously considered a beach. She pulled a striped sheet out of her bag and whipped it like she was driving a team of mules. It fluttered neatly over the ground, and we stayed the edges with larger river rocks before sitting down. The river was running fast and shallow after a hot summer. Dragonflies flitted in stitched circles along the surface. Beneath the bridge, the swift water gelled over a deep pool.

The sleeves of my old T-shirt rode well up my arm, exposing a hard line where summer met my natural pale color. "Let's see what we can do about fixing your tan there, redneck. Take off your shirt. I'll put some oil on your back."

I pulled my shirt over my head in a single motion and rolled over onto my stomach. I examined the pebbles and turned my head to watch Jolene's hands digging in her bag. She pulled out a bottle of baby oil and straddled my back. I registered the weight of her there on my tailbone and thought of what little was between us. She must have held the bottle high, since the oil dribbled one excruciating drop after the next.

"You're taking long enough."

She swirled her thumbs and fingers around my shoulders and back like she was finger painting.

"I'm serious," I said. "I can't breathe."

"Fine," she said, and climbed off me. "You want me to do your stomach, too?"

My boner was boring a hole in the river bottom. Nothing could have made me turn over right then. "Maybe later," I said, thinking softer thoughts.

Jolene shrugged me off and rambled on about school and teachers and girl stuff while my eyes surveyed the length of her leg, the long scratches darkened by healing, the way she propped herself up on locked arms and tilted her head back, twitching the tail of her braid over her spine. She went quiet and I did, too, happy to doze listening to the clack of aspen leaves, the laughter echoing from beneath the bridge, until my back sizzled like pork rinds in a fryer. Pebbles crunched next to me when she got up. I rolled over and watched as she stooped for flat stones to skip into the eddy. My gaze drifted from the bright string bow in the middle of her brown back to the dangerous curves leading down to the waistband of her cutoff shorts. She'd taken her braid out, and her hair fell in heavy waves on her shoulders. She turned to look at me, and I will swear it was in slow motion.

Everything in front of me shifted and tossed like trinkets in a kaleidoscope—the pink bikini top, the white frays of denim brushing her thighs, the tawny crescent moon and the starstruck eyes. I could see bits of the river, the stands of birches, kids swinging from the rope. But more than anything, there was her. She unbuttoned her shorts, let them drop on the stones. She flexed fierce like a bodybuilder, laughed at herself. How I wanted to be strong like her. For her. To this day, I can't be at the river bottom and not think of how we became bound by love and loss there. The particular smell—the decay of wet things, fish and moss, that heady pine-and-honey stink of cottonwood resin, the river disappearing and remaking itself in the current—it's the stuff of memory. I am soaked in it.

She summoned me. I was at once powerless and powerful. "C'mon, sleepy! Let's jump in."

—

THE COOL SLIME ON THE river rocks slipped between my toes as we gingerly waded into the cold water. We let the current carry us downstream. Beneath the bridge we hooted and hollered so our voices would ring hollow off the riverbanks. The boys beneath the bridge watched us float by from their rock perches.

I was a graceless swimmer, I knew, but I was strong and capable. Jolene, on the other hand, swam like she'd sprouted a tail, a trout effortlessly dissecting the currents. We took turns dunking each other and, underwater, I caught fleeting glimpses of her brown legs kicking in the green river, bits of algae and fish scales swirling around her like tiny water fairies. Tinfoil rays of sunshine shimmered on the submerged rocks. I had no winter thoughts. I was anointed in summer water. In that moment, I was all for rivers and swimming with Jolene. I could have floated all the way to the Pacific Ocean.

We watched from downstream as one of the boys scrambled up the rock embankment. He had the rope in his hand as he pitched backward, kicked up both feet, his backside for a moment barely missing the ground. Then he swung far out over the river and, at the last minute, he surged upward, let go of the rope, and plunged into the deep water.

I watched Jolene watch him, her eyes calculating the angles. She made for the shore and ran back upstream. "Dare you!" she said. I followed her wet path and jumped back in behind her as she powered her way across the current before wading out under the bridge on the opposite side.

The boys were older than us, with scruffy beards and lean bodies. The rope was secured next to them on a rock. It was only then that I realized one of the bikinied girls was a friend of Kathryn's.

"You mind?" Jolene asked.

One of the boys handed her the twisted rope. "All yours," he said. He passed a lighter-weight and longer rope to me. "You have to hold this so we can get the big rope back."

"Guess this means I'm going first," she said.

"You want me to go? I can."

"Not my first rodeo, Wes." She hiked her hands way up on the rope, pulled herself back like an acorn in a slingshot, then picked up her feet with little hesitation and launched. At the top of the arc, she let go of the rope and grabbed her own bent knee instead, jackknifing cleanly into the water below.

"Whoa," one of the boys said.

Kathryn's friend scoffed. "Big deal."

"How was it?" I yelled to Jolene, ignoring the friend's glare.

"Cold!" she yelled back, her voice in stereo beneath the bridge. "Cool."

I reeled in the big rope and was surprised by how heavy it was, by how much I had to counterbalance it to keep it from swinging out on its own. I gripped it tight and felt its frayed threads scratching my hand. The river seemed a long way down from the top of the embankment. Kathryn's friend whispered to another girl. The two of them snickered in my direction.

"Don't forget to let go," Jolene yelled.

"Helpful. Really."

"Go on," she said, treading water in the pool. "Don't be a chicken."

I reached up as high as I could, took a deep breath, and pulled up my feet. In a moment, I was a human wrecking ball, angling over the river toward the center of memory—my own defiant jump into Bright Lake, my mother above ice, then below. A split second of flagging courage and I scotched my entry. Instead of elegantly puncturing the water, I let go on the backswing and tumbled into the current off balance and backward, a boulder in a landslide. The river rushed up my nose and I swallowed a mouthful, the mineral cold ache of it heavy in my chest but earthy and clean on my lips. I kicked for the surface, snorted out my nose, alive, and shook my head like a dog after a cloudburst.

The boys were scrambling feet first, hands dragging down the rocky slope. The drag line and thick rope were both twisting above me. Shouts—"Grab her! Grab her!" and "Shit!"—ricocheted off the cement pilings. And then I saw it. Jolene's head bobbing lifeless out of the pool and into the current. I swam hard, as hard as I could, while the other boys ran along the shore to head her off. Those two other boys and me, we got to her about the same time. Her eyes were closed, and from what I could tell, she wasn't breathing. All I could think was that it was me that killed her, and those words came out of my mouth as I laid her across my stomach and backstroked frantically to shore, my arm beneath hers and over her lifeless body.

We got her up the riverbank, and one of the boys rolled her onto her side and pounded on her back. I dropped down next to her, calling her name. Someone screamed something about mouth-to-mouth. A wave pulsed from her stomach and Jolene clenched, spewing a convulsive stream of river water onto the rocks caked with dried moss. I peeled wet hair out of her eyes and rubbed her back. She coughed up a few more times, on her knees now, before sitting back down.

"I'm so sorry. I'm so sorry," I said, not able to stop repeating my apology.

"God. I told you to let go," she said, smirking.

Grab hold. Hang on. Let go. Pull. Yank free. "I know. I guess I panicked. Are you okay?"

She rolled her head and nodded with a faint smile, and I hugged her as hard as I had swum to her. The fleshy underside of her arms threaded with mine as river water squeezed out of her swimsuit and streamed down my stomach. She put her hand on the back of my neck, and her musky hair mixed with the green river swept across my nose and cheek. "Did you pull me out?" she whispered.

I knew who I was holding, but I could see that other hand reaching for me, see myself backing away. I imagined the river in winter, floes of ice colliding on upheaved rocks, bodies freighted downstream on some underwater railroad, snagging on dammed timber or snapped twigs. I buried my face in the warmth of her neck, then rolled around until my mouth was on hers. The boys whooped and whistled, but I didn't care. I want to say it was soft and gentle, a good first kiss. And it started that way, the foreign taste of Jolene's mouth, the flutter of her lips against mine. I had thoughts of sweet things I knew nothing about, like figs and pomegranates, and homemade brownie batter licked off someone else's finger. Smells went past my nose to my taste buds—the scent of tobacco leaf still in the field, barreled spices in the hull of a faraway boat, star-shaped flowers tucked behind an ear next to thick black hair. And then it wasn't enough. I lurched in, cramming my clumsy tongue down her throat, desperate to somehow take in this person who came alive after being dead in the water.

She pulled away, flushed, and ducked her head in embarrassment. "Stop." She touched three fingers to her lips.

Stung by her rejection, I stood up carefully and reached for her, but she refused my hand, getting to her feet on her own. "You're covered in dirt," she said, brushing tiny pebbles and sand off my back.

"Your knees, too," I said, and she brushed them off, never taking her eyes off me.

Kathryn's friend was in the crowd that had gathered. Her mouth was stunned open. This whole scene I knew would get back to Kathryn, but right then I could not have cared any less nor could I have known what it would set in motion.

Back at our bikes, Jolene leaned against the tree and, in the privacy, pulled me to her, and we made out there as if we needed each other to breathe.

My chest was alive with hummingbirds when we finally parted. It was the longest ride back to town. We stopped to put our feet in a ditch, to kiss more, took a detour so we could hide behind an abandoned farmhouse and press our mouths and bodies together, with only a feral cat as witness.

Back at her house, she rolled her bicycle into the freestanding garage that opened to the alley behind the house. I followed her in, laid my bike in the rutted gravel. She walked me back until I was against the rotting doorframe. She crossed her arms, leaned into me, and I wrapped her up. "I'm sorry," I said, "about the river."

She told me she was not sorry, not about one single thing.

I LEFT JOLENE ON A cloud that day, without asking her when or how I could see her again. Mush for legs, I took my time getting home, walking my bike through town past the newsstand, the pharmacy, the penny candy store. Suddenly, Loma wasn't so bad. Suddenly, Loma was a town where I could stay. When my father came for me, I would tell him we should find a house there, that it would be good for us both to be in a familiar place. I imagined introducing Jolene to him, how I'd put my arm around her in that way that says, "This is my girl."

I stopped in front of the thick plate glass window at the radio station. The afternoon disc jockey switched vinyl records on the dual turntables, spinning one on his finger before replacing it in the cardboard sleeve, a move practiced and perfected for passersby. I focused on my own reflection and saw, maybe for the first time, a ghost of my father—the same wavy hair, sloped posture, angled jaw. I could almost see stepping from his shadow and into his clothes and skin. I watched the reflection of me bring my right palm up to my left shoulder, push up the sleeve enough to see that his tattoo was not there. I knew next to nothing about him as a boy, only that he'd left his home in Utah young, a teenager. He'd said he was thrown out, disowned, and would say no more. I had no known grandparents from him, no uncles or aunts to speak of. As far as I knew, I was his only kin, yet still he could find it in him to keep his distance from me.

A bulbous black-and-yellow "B" on the poster in the window caught my eye, yanked me out of my reflection. Cartoon insects buzzed around the logo I'd seen all over the Barbosa Brothers midway that summer I spent with my father. The same outfit that brought him to town all those years before, when he first met my mother, would operate the midway at the county fair only a week away. The whole of me, still tingling from Jolene, now buzzed.

When I got home, I made straight for the kitchen, parched gray and yellow in the late-August sun. Surely Ruby had heard something from him with the carnival coming to town. Flies swarmed the sink, eager to light on a stray bit of hamburger meat dropped from the meatloaf baking in the oven. She listened to my familiar plea about my father while digging dirt and raw meat from under her fingernail with a jagged lower tooth. She spit into the sink. "Told you," she said. "Not a word." She undid the apron from around her waist and threw it at a fly greedily rubbing its legs together like a miser over money. "Goddamned pests."

"I can't believe he hasn't said anything. I thought for sure he'd have been back by now. It's almost fall. Maybe something happened to him."

"You're as bad as the flies." She flicked a plastic flyswatter with the swift arc of an arm wrestler, then shook the fly guts into the sink. "When was the last time he was even with the carnival, huh? Five, six years ago now? I don't know why I even bother to explain it to you, you're so dense about it."

"You'd tell me if he did call, though, right?"

She examined her nails, took another swipe along that tooth. "You ought to let it go. You knew back in January, just like we did, he wasn't coming back. I don't know why you keep on pretending he might." She sat down at the table and mopped her hand across her eyes, though no tears were there or coming. "You remind me of your mother, you know. She always thought she deserved something better. 'Better than what?' I'd ask her, but she didn't know. Take it from me, eat what's on the plate." She lifted her face and looked me flush in the eye.

"Ruby," I said, preparing to make another pass.

"No more," she said, raising her voice. "No more now. Why don't you go do whatever it is you do with that Rook girl."

I conjured a scene of me ending it with Kathryn, sped up so I wouldn't have to hear her rage. "We broke up," I said, sure that my saying it meant it was so.

Ruby leered and snorted, shaking her head. "Of course you did. Of course." Inevitability was in her every breath, like why would something good happen or last.

At the end of the next afternoon, Bull, Drew, and I were waiting in the barnyard for Lester to come in so we could quit for the day. A plume of baked dust rose between the fields as the yellow car barreled up the bumpy path.

"Shit," I said, turning my back to the road. Neither Bull nor Lester had said a thing to me about Jolene, which led me to believe she hadn't talked either. It honestly scared me, thinking she might have had second thoughts about the whole thing, embarrassed by me. I was keenly aware of our differences, of her brown skin and my white skin, of how our people might have specific ideas about the two of us together. I imagined the worst of what Gip and Ruby would say. It was hard to know about Mona and Troy, who seemed kind but cautious. And it crossed my mind, as Kathryn got out of the car and slammed the door, that Bull and Lester might just beat the shit out of me if Kathryn didn't do it first.

A flush blazed from her chest to her cheeks. I could see she was struggling with what to say, though I figured she surely rehearsed her tirade in the car.

"Kathryn—"

"Don't you dare. Don't you dare." Her hurt eyes narrowed as she pointed at me.

"Ah," said Bull. "Lovers' spat?"

I looked at him, willing him to go away so he wouldn't hear what was coming next.

"I don't get you, Wes," she said. "I really don't. An Indian? Seriously?" She shot a look at Bull and shook her head. "Sorry," she said to him, "it's just that—"

"What did I do?" Bull's eyes were wide open and amused. "Ballot, you been telling off-color barn stories? I swear, ma'am," he said, mocking Kathryn, "I only made him fuck that cow the once."

Kathryn cut off her rant, swiped her tears with her fingertips, calmer now. "Oh, you don't know, do you? Wes and your"—she grasped for the relationship, dismissing the importance with an elaborate hand flip and eye roll—"whatever. That Jolene. All hush-hush about it. First me, now her. Jeez, Wes," she said, pulling back as she prepared to launch her arrow. "I guess no girl wants to be seen with you in public. Not even an Indian. And don't think I'll take you back because I won't. We are broken up, you understand? I'm breaking up with you."

She stormed off, leaving me in a yellow cloud of dust to face Bull.

"Whoa, motherfucker. You're in the shit now," said Drew. "I would not want to mess with a girl like that."

"What the fuck do you know, Drew?" I asked. I tried to shrug it off. "Girls, man." I spit the last of the dirt from Kathryn's spinout and tried to get past Bull. He grabbed my arm.

"Mind telling me what that was about?"

"What?" I shook him loose and readied my fists. I wanted to punch him in the nose, the jaw. I wanted to pulverize someone. I wanted blood. "Nothing's going on. I saw her at the river, is all, and Kathryn's friends obviously made a big deal out of nothing."

"Ballot, man. You listen to me. That's not a girl you can trifle with. That thing with her mom fucked her up. Finally she's getting right. Last thing she needs is some guy messing with her head. Troy already had a talking-to with that one," Bull said, pointing his thumb at Lester, who was loping in from the field. "Panting over her like a fucking dog."

I let what he was saying settle in next to other things I thought I knew about men and girls and how a person gets broken. "I'd never hurt her. I couldn't."

"Yeah? Well, she said she took in a bunch of water at the river yesterday. You know something about that?"

"Yeah, maybe," I said, remembering her brown legs in the green water, her hair floating against my body, the frightening lifelessness of her in my arms, her rescued mouth on mine. Staying away wasn't going to work, and I told Bull as much when he and Lester dropped me back in town by the railroad tracks. Lester was still sulking that he'd missed the whole scene.

"You tell her I'll be by tomorrow. Tell her I asked after her and I hope she's feeling alright."

Bull shielded his eyes against the sun and squinted at me. "No way this ends well, Ballot."

"Tell her, Bull. Tell her I'll be by tomorrow."

"I swear. You do anything—"

I slapped the open window as Bull wrestled the stick into gear. The sun warm at my back, I followed my shadow down the tracks, back to the house.

CHAPTER 13

It was well and fine, I figured, for Bull to have a white friend, for Lester to hang around with me. It was another thing, me coming over for Jolene. So I was relieved when Mona opened the door to me. She smiled warm enough, though maybe with some curiosity, even distrust. Over her shoulder, I could see Jolene laid out on the long couch in the living room. The smile I got from her was delicate and careful and attached to her eyes and the memory of our bodies behind the old barn. Jolene rolled to the side, letting loose a cough that sounded like the bay of a hound. Mona winced and told me she and Troy worried Jolene might come down with pneumonia. "You can stay," she said, "but not for long."

I sat next to her on the ring-stained coffee table.

"Not a word about the river," she warned, after making sure Mona was out of earshot. "They don't know it was you." The story she told was that her foot got caught in a snag underwater and she'd gulped up half the river before jerking it clear, and that I was the one who got her safely to shore. "You're my hero," she said, sassing me more than teasing. I wanted to believe that story, how I'd heard her call for help, rescued her from drowning, diving deep down to free her foot, pulling her out with will and brute strength, breathing life back into her lifeless body.

I stayed longer than I should have, moved from the table to the couch when Jolene moved to sitting. Bull and Troy and Mariah got home, and all of them looked at me like I was some orphan dumped on their doorstep. As uncomfortable as I felt, I still didn't want to be anywhere else. I sat with Jolene and watched the Hightower household operate—shouts from room to room, the chasing and screaming and yelling that comes from having a little kid around, slamming doors, footsteps overhead. Lester walked in without knocking, saw me on the couch next to Jolene. His face twisted, and he rolled his head back. "Oh, you're kidding me, right? Troy," he shouted into the dining room. "You cannot be seriously letting this happen."

"Shut up, Lester," Troy said, exhaustion in his voice.

"Yeah, shut up, Lester," I mouthed so he could hear but Troy could not.

Lester glanced once at the dining room, then came at me, pulling me off the couch, taking my spot next to Jolene in one swift move. He put his arm over her shoulder, told her if she was ready for a boyfriend she could do better than me. I tried not to agree, seeing him next to her. Jolene hacked a soupy cough into Lester's face. He grimaced but pulled her closer still. She wiggled free and held her glass out to me.

"Would you mind getting me water? I need a minute alone with Lester."

"Yeah, Ballot, Jolene needs some water. You go on and fetch that."

I feared Lester was slick enough to talk her out of me and into him in the time it would take to fill a glass. "I'll be right back," I said, as much to Lester as to Jolene.

Mona batched chicken in a vat of oil while Mariah gnawed on a chicken liver and colored at the little kitchen table. "Fried chicken smells really good," I said. I made an awkward motion toward the sink, tried to come up with some small talk while I got water from the faucet. "We don't eat chicken at our house. Ruby doesn't want anything to do with them. Gets enough at work, I guess."

"You're welcome to join us," she said.

"Oh, that's alright. Ruby's probably expecting me for dinner," I said, though I knew it didn't matter to my grandparents where I ate. "I better get this to Jolene."

I passed Lester as he stormed into the dining room, clearly mad. He delivered a knuckled jab to my arm. He did it with a smile, like it was all in fun, but he put as much behind it as he could, message delivered. I dropped the plastic cup and, as water soaked the carpet, I prepared to take one on the jaw next. Troy set his book down on the table and stood next to the two of us. We were both taller than him, but he was somehow bigger than the both of us, maybe combined. Lester smiled and smoothed the spot where he'd hit me. "We're good, right, Ballot?"

"Yeah, yeah. Good." I bent to pick up the dropped cup, but before I could Troy grabbed each of us by the nape of the neck and brought our heads together for a knocking. We stared each other down while he talked, his voice a low rumble. "You two peckerheads will not make a match of this. That girl is not a prize. Either one of you makes her feel bad in any way and I will personally tear you ear to asshole, you understand?" He nodded our heads for us, up and down, so that with each dip our foreheads conked. "Lester, I'm guessing you're looking for Bull. He's upstairs. And you, you've outstayed your welcome. Out, now. Let's go."

I said goodbye to Jolene with Troy standing usher at the door.

"Will you come back tomorrow?"

I looked at Troy, who gave me tacit consent with a chin-up nod.

At the two-lane highway that cut through town, I saw the convoy's headlights. A long caravan of flatbeds with brightly painted equipment and colored bulbs and marquees and ticket booths strapped to the back and trucks pulling camping trailers rolled by, minding the speed limit, careful not to attract the wrong kind of attention. I checked each vehicle like it was a boxcar on a long train. Spot the driver, look for the cat on the dash. The blue Chevy stepside pickup, dented red Leer topper shell, was not there, at least not yet. The contract semis would come later, I knew, hauling the kiddie rides, the boxes full of Styrofoam-stuffed animals, crates of cooking oil, and boxed sugar for cotton candy. In a couple more days, the fair would open with livestock and apple pies, bingo and demolition derbies, the screaming and bell-ringing Barbosa midway, and maybe, just maybe, my father at the controls of the Dragon Boat casting back and forth in great green sweeps.

I ran the blocks back to the Hightowers' under lit streetlamps and halted at the front steps. I'd packed out of one place after the next with my parents, set up house in trailer parks and low-slung apartment buildings, in houses no bigger than sheds. Maybe the longest we stayed put was in the last two years before Bright Lake. Six months here, maybe a year there. I'd stopped counting schools, stopped keeping friends. My mother would say she wanted a place of her own, my father seemed to care less about that, not troubled like I was to wake up in the black of night with dark confusion about which way my head was pointing and whether that door led to a bathroom or closet. I stood in front of the Hightowers' crumbling house, shutters akimbo, a yard full of trash turned to treasure. My mother might have liked it here, the lived-in-ness of it, the way stuff piled up in a permanent way. Here was a home, but it wasn't mine. I jumped, enough to get air. Came down two-footed. Solid earth, uncracked. Yes, the carnival was in town and my father maybe with it. But the fissure of it hadn't spread from the highway to here quite yet. Jolene was on the couch still, blanket wrapped around her, a cup of something on the table. Troy was in the recliner next to her, Mariah on his lap. School would start after the weekend as the carnival left town, migrating south with better weather. September would bring cooler air, sweaters, and frost. After that, green would turn gold, red and brown leaves would give up the tree for ground, then fire, then earth.

By November, hats and gloves, snow and ice would return. Troy leaned over to Jolene, adjusted her blanket, threw Mariah over his shoulder. This could all be in my rear view. By the end of the weekend, Loma could be yesterday. I quaked, thinking about the impending cold. I did not know where I would or should be.

My grandparents were at each other when I got back home, the rent again, the bills again. Gip's hours would be cut back come November, when the seed and feed business hit the seasonal low. They were at the end of it when I'd come to live with them in January, and I hadn't heard much about the household bills during the summer months. My ears pricked up at the mention of Burt Rook, at the discussion of the cold shoulder he'd given Gip at the bank that morning after he'd let Gip know that late rent wouldn't be tolerated anymore. Ruby said there were no more hours to be had at the poultry farm. She spread her hexed fingers and her knuckles popped and snapped. How much longer she could work like that she didn't know and anyway, where was the taproom money, or did that all go to pay Gip's tab and was he drinking more than he was serving. I'd been giving them money each week from my paycheck, but that, too, would come to an end soon, and was the lure they used to reel me into their row. Silver-and-red empties were tumped and crushed on the table. They'd been at this awhile.

"You find a job for the school year yet?" Gip asked. "You're not freeloading again this winter."

"Carnival's in. I saw the trucks earlier."

"What? You planning on joining the circus now?"

"No, I thought maybe Dad . . ."

Ruby stood from the table at that. "I told you. Waste of time."

"I wish he would come for you. I do," Gip said. He poked a calloused fingertip into his nostril and dug around until he came up with something he could roll between his fingers. "Not likely, knowing that four-flusher, but still."

"Still you'd like me gone?"

He made an inspection of the glob, then wiped it on his trousers. "Thought you running with that Rook girl would grease the wheels for us maybe, but you must not be the shit after all. Ruby tells me that's done. Too much girl for you?" He glowered at me with sour eyes, but when I tried to match his stare, he rejected it and me, turning back to his beer, his cigarettes, the newspaper splotched with stew.

From my mother's bed, I stared at the ceiling, too low first by inches, then by feet, until I fell into a furtive sleep. I dreamed I was on a carnival ride, some great wheel that at first spun me around on the inside, a steely marble or ball bearing held in place by inertia. In that way of dreams, I was switched to the outside, became a cog to hook a chain on a bicycle. As it ground slowly to a near halt, it turned creaky and wooden like a waterwheel on a gristmill. Splinters barbed into my back and arms, and I was suddenly naked and strapped down in the well between the teeth with leather around my waist and wrists. In the ether of the dream, I chatted brightly with someone else on a factory floor. The voice drew nearer and nearer, and I knew it to be my mother, though the closer it got the more smoldery it sounded, until it became Jolene's and it was frantic as we realized that she, too, was on a great wheel but on the spike of it. She came into view, but the words we said to each other were lost in the crunching of skulls and bones.

I woke at dawn, dressed quickly. I slipped down the hall, past the bathroom door, the shower running, Gip getting ready for his shift. Ruby, bathrobed and slippered, was in the kitchen, already socked in by a cloud of cigarette smoke. Any sound I might have made leaving the house was masked by percolating coffee.

I sat at the counter of the café by the highway near the fairgrounds, coffee cup snugged in the palm of my hands. Shift workers, mostly men, came through the door. I watched the bell on the metal strap clang against the glass, watched the cashier poke the register keys with her long orange fingernail, watched the short-order cook spin the ticket wheel, which reminded me of the bone-crushed dream I'd had, watched for my father to make his first-morning-in-town breakfast appearance. The waitress topped off my cup, and I added cream and sugar until it was tolerable to me. Two cups later, stomach in knots, hands shaking, I gave up. If he was in town, he'd have come through those doors by now.

The carnival opened at dusk the night before the fair itself. To go with Jolene, I had to go with Mona and Troy and Mariah, too, all five of us in Mona's dented station wagon. We parked in a tamped-down grass field and walked toward the flashing lights and heavy metal music, the wafts of cooked sugar and popcorn and engine oil, the screams of the first kids on the first rides drowning out the rattling whir of generators keeping everything inflated and lit. My purposes were crossed and conflicted. On one hand, I wanted to focus on Jolene and what was feeling like a first date. My mind wandered to her hand in mine, my arm over her shoulder on the Ferris wheel, her leaning into me or gripping my leg on the roller coaster, to pulling her into the shadows and kissing her again. Then I would feel guilty, shake those thoughts out, and try to concentrate only on the Barbosas, on finding a familiar face, someone who would remember my father, maybe even me.

The Hightowers were the other in the parade of mostly white families heading through the gates. I imagined scornful eyes on us, imagined the whispers. "Stick with your own." Was I drawing dangerous attention to myself? Or worse, to Jolene and her family? Was this even allowed and by whose authority? Mariah said out loud what I feared Mona and

Troy thought, what I began to wonder myself. "I don't get why *he's* even here." Me the stranger, the castoff, me instead of Lester Two Kills. Mona shushed her and I smiled tight-lipped, gratefully, apologetically.

I protested when Troy paid my way with the rest of his family but made up for it with an offer to buy ride tickets. The seller was a fat man, bald, but with razor stubble down to his chest hair. He wasn't familiar to me and hardly looked up when he measured out a yard of tickets like a bolt of fabric. We made the exchange, money for tickets, wordlessly. I divided the line, giving half to Troy and pocketing the others. We made arrangements to meet them back at the gate at closing. I couldn't quite gauge what the look was I saw in Mona's eyes, but I could guess as they walked off.

"They don't like me," I said to Jolene.

"They like you fine."

"Then they don't trust me."

She didn't respond to that. Instead we walked quietly along the midway, already packed with wiggling toddlers and harried parents, with wild teenagers itching to make trouble. Boys were decked out in stiff dark jeans, new for school, desperate to be broken in. Girls the same, but with sweaters that seemed tighter since spring and blouse buttons undone one farther than when they left the house. Lust was in the air, along with fryer grease and the composted clover smell of manure coming out of the barns. Jolene grabbed my hand and I let her. "It's not that."

"It's not what?"

"Trust. I know what it is. What you saw. My mom. She dated white guys." Jolene paused then, and her hand drifted up to the scar on her face. Practically under her breath, she added, "She had a knack for finding the worst ones, too."

Happy tinkling music coming from flying elephants and swirling teacups was blotted out by acid rock as we entered the black triangle of rides meant to make you shit your pants. At the halfway point of the oval midway was the Dragon Boat, my father's ride.

"Let's go on," I said. "Before the line gets too long."

The hairy ride operator was as wide as he was tall. He wore a tight black T-shirt with a white skull on it that was made up entirely of contorted naked women. When we got to the front of the line, I asked if he knew a Moss Ballot. His thick red beard bobbed on his shirt collar when he spoke. "Don't know him. What's he done?"

"No, nothing like that. He used to operate this ride, is all."

"Been with Nicky three years. On this bitch the whole time." He shut the fur trap around his mouth and put his hand out for the tickets. Jolene scooted in next to me at the back of the ride. When the operator came by, he yanked the strap into our laps and acted like we'd never spoken.

The boat rocked back and forth, building momentum, the mouth of the dragon lurching toward the carnival lights and the rising moon. Jolene was joyful and thrilled, throwing her hands up, her head back as we swooped down on the dragon's tail. I clenched my teeth, gasping more than breathing. Somehow in that built-up pause between rising and falling, I thought I would die—that the strap would fail and I would be ejected or worse, sucked out, away, not thrown to the ground but disappeared into the colding fall air. Each sweep of the pendulum, I felt death swiping at me, like it had missed me by a claw in January, and here it had another chance. I squeezed my eyes shut and gripped the bar until my joints ached. It was only when I felt Jolene's hand on mine, prying my fingers up gently, that I opened my eyes. The waves subsided under the dragon boat as it slowed. Alive with relief, I knotted Jolene's arm with mine and kissed her hand, a silly gesture that made her laugh. "I think you'd have rather kissed the ground," she said. We unstrapped ourselves and moved quickly to the exit. It was then that I saw her: army jacket, black jeans, peroxide-blond spiked hair. She looked like a stalk of corn leaning against the junction box across the midway. Nicky Barbie, the Barbosa sister in the Barbosa family. Not a woman to forget, and I hadn't.

We caught up with Nicky, breathless from the ride, winded from the chase. I'd dragged Jolene by the hand, ignoring, for the most part, her questions. I touched Nicky's arm and she turned on me like she was ready for a run-in. "Yeah?"

"You probably don't remember me," I said. "I was little when you saw me last." And I was Little then, my dad's nickname for me as long as I could remember. "I'm Wes Ballot. My dad's Moss."

She sized me up, nodded. "You look like him."

"Do you remember I was with you guys for a while one summer, long time ago?" Jolene squeezed my hand then, and I knew she was with me. I gave her a quick smile but returned my attention to Nicky.

"Lots of kids come and go here. But sure, maybe." Someone hollered for her from a game booth and she gave a double-handed wave that said she'd get there when she was good and ready. Her eyes squinted with memory against the lights. "Boy, you sure look like him alright."

"I get that," I said, though it had been a while since the two of us were side by side for people to make any kind of comparison. "I'm wondering if you've seen him recently."

"Took off on you, huh?" The barker yelled for Nicky again, and she held up a finger. "I have to deal with this. It'll only take a minute."

We stood by while Nicky dealt with the man. Jolene slipped her arm behind my back and I put mine over her shoulder, pulling her into the crook, where she fit perfectly. I took it in then, the carnival, not through the eyes of a kid anymore. What I hadn't seen before, I saw now—the reckless boredom of a barker playing mumblety-peg with a balloon dart, dangling cigarettes glowing at every operator's stand, the distorted reflections paneling the House of Mirrors, everyone not quite what they seemed. I saw Kathryn then, standing in line for a ride, flanked by her friends from the river. I could tell by the look on her face that she'd been watching us, that we hadn't been spotted only then. She turned her head hard, away from me, and stiffened her back in a way that made me think she was holding her breath. Jolene saw her, too. "Kathryn."

"I know."

"You think you should go talk to her?"

But Nicky Barbie put herself in front of us. "Sorry about that. What's your name again?"

I repeated myself and introduced Jolene. I didn't feel the need to tell Nicky the whole story about my mother and the lake, about Gip and Ruby. I said I was staying with my grandparents and expected him to come around soon.

"All I can tell you is he's not with us. I don't think I've seen Moss Ballot for I'd say five years or more now."

I remembered what else was missing that had been there before. "Whatever happened with the Wandering Freaks?"

"Oh, you remember them, do you? Yeah, we had to shut that bit of the operation down. Started rubbing people the wrong way, I guess. Sorry to put those folks out of a job, I can tell you that."

"My dad had a friend. Topeka. Always wore a funny hat."

Nicky's face lit up. "Oh, Topeka's still with us. He's with Vince out west of here somewhere. Montana, South Dakota, Wyoming. Whole different crew. Only thing we share now is the winter warehouse."

"Montana?" My father had talked about Montana in the hospital. "Is there any way you could get a message to him, to Topeka? Maybe he'd know something."

Nicky shook her head, bunched up her red lips. "We don't really cross paths until about mid-October. He usually helps Vin with the haul out when we get everything squared away. Got a warehouse in South Dakota. Brookings. Couple weeks there maybe, doing a few repairs, dealing with inventory. That would be your best bet for finding him if you really want to." She dug a pen out of one of her coat pockets and wrote on a pack of matches. "Send a letter there. He'll get it. Otherwise, you can give me your information, and I'll try not to lose it."

I jotted down my name and address on a gum wrapper, exchanged it for the matches, and shook her hand.

"Listen, though, Wes, right? You may not quite get it, but sometimes people don't want to be found. Trust me. I seen a lot of what gets dished out. Folks go and they're gone and it's better that way. Life's not for everyone." The way she said it left it up for question whether she meant the carnival or something bigger. Was she saying it was okay, preferable even, to step out of your own spotlight or drop from the side of a building or let go of something solid, even if that solid thing was only a sheet of ice? Metal parachutes soared over Nicky's shoulder. Kathryn's hair bounced over the seat back as the ride arced upward. In its descent, I could see her better, slumped between consoling friends. I understood what it was to use a person but not love them, to walk away because something better came along. I didn't know then about leaving because something worse was coming, about leaving out of kindness.

"Here. You two take these," Nicky said, handing us a wad of tickets from yet another pocket. "Live it up."

I LEFT TOPEKA ON THE matchbook in my pocket and went on rides with Jolene—pants shitters like the Zipper, then gentle ups and downs on the carousel, Jolene gripped on the pole, swaying forward and arcing backward over the painted pony, teasing me until I thought I'd explode. I grabbed her off the horse as the ride slowed, and we jumped off it laughing, holding hands.

We spent the rest of that night huddled together in a trough of hay bales by the fairgrounds gate. I tried to kiss her in that darkness, but she pushed me off, telling me I had to wait, for what I didn't know. So we talked and talked, back and forth, trading stories with the rocking motion of a carnival ride. Her story about hitchhiking with Trudy led to mine about having a battery stolen right out of the car we were sleeping in at the time. Jolene learned how to roll joints and I watched my mother buy and sell them when she worked at the bowling alley. There were stories we'd heard whispered or yelled but were too young to remember, like when my mother came home one night to find me home alone, strapped into my crib with a belt. That was a story that came up again and again, one that my mother held over my father's head any time he accused her of neglect. "Least I took him with me," she'd say. "Least I didn't belt him into a crib." Jolene recalled coming home from school to a group of strangers—"white biker types, men and women"—sitting in the living room of her apartment, drinking beers, smoking hand-rolled cigarettes. They told her that her mother was gone, didn't want her anymore. Jolene turned to leave because she believed them, because it wasn't far-fetched, because it had happened before. They stopped her from going, laughing that no, Trudy would be back, that they would wait with her until then. "I spent the night on my mom's mattress on the bedroom floor, listening to them party." In the morning, Trudy was there, passed out in the hallway outside the locked door.

Jolene didn't smile much, not with her mouth at least. Her face would soften instead, she'd raise her eyebrows, which would draw up just one wry corner of her mouth. It was the prettiest thing to see, especially when she touched that scar, which she was doing while she talked. I couldn't know how long that one gesture would haunt me.

"You mind me asking about that?"

Her face darkened and she glanced away. "I got cut. Whiskey bottle."

"You don't have to talk about it."

She fidgeted, then moved across from me so we were face-to-face. "She had a boyfriend, when we were up in South Dakota. Everyone called him Freeman. I don't even know if it was his first or last name. Just

Freeman. Fat pig. I hated him. He was on something, crank maybe. He had her pinned on the floor. And he was right up in her face, screaming at her and calling her names—whore, slut, you name it. But this close." She put her hand up to her face. "He spit on her, big wads. I yelled at him to stop. He pointed at me and when he let go, my mom punched him in the throat. He rolled off her and grabbed a broken bottle."

"Stop," I said. "You don't need to. It's okay." With my thumb, I touched the arc of her scar, felt the ridges. "It's beautiful."

She grabbed my wrist and pulled it down. "It's not. It's ugly. He made her watch while he cut me. Then he said, 'You or her?' He dropped me but not the bottle. I ran. I left her there with him."

Without my permission, my imagination followed Freeman and Trudy into some dreadful bedroom, where I stood with my back to the wall until I couldn't stomach the worst of what I could figure happened there, picturing it was Jolene in there taking the abuse. "It's not your fault."

"She stayed with him. Even after that."

"Sorry" was all I could say.

"You don't have to apologize to me. I'm telling you so you know. I'm never taking that kind of shit off anyone."

"Is that what Mona and Troy think, that I might turn out like Freeman? Because I won't." I summoned all the conviction I could, but the truth was I didn't know what kind of man I would become. How do you convey you're someone to be trusted when you aren't sure whether you can trust yourself?

"What you are doesn't matter. I'm telling you what I am. I'm talking about me," she said, her hand on her chest swearing allegiance to herself.

"I know, Jo. I'm just telling you I would never hurt you."

"You're not listening to me, Wes. I will never let you hurt me. That's what I told Troy and Mona. And, yeah. They're not excited about you and me dating or whatever. They don't know you, but they know enough. Mona knew your mom. They know your grandparents some. They know how you wound up here. Mona watched white men heap loads of shit on her sister. Over and over. It was the same every single time."

I threw my hands up. "Well, fuck, Jolene. Why bother then?" I stood, kicked the hay bale. The lights came up on the midway. Crowds trickled toward the exit. I put out my hand to her. "Let's shake and be friends if that's okay. If I'm good enough to be friends with."

She took my hand and pulled herself up, wrapping herself around my waist so that she had to bend her head way back to look up at me. "You have a lot to learn, you know that, Ballot?" When we finally kissed again, I could feel her interlocking with me, her curves fitting into my hollows. It was all about coming together, like the gears in my factory dream.

We'd barely come up for air when we saw Mona and Troy approach the gate. Troy had Mariah over his shoulder, her face nestled deep into his neck. "Sugar poisoning," he said. Mona looked us over—my arm over Jolene's shoulder, hers around my waist, thumb hooked in my belt loop—took a breath in through her mouth, and let it out through lips just pursed. "Okay," she said. "Okay. Let's get out of here."

I SAW KATHRYN ONE MORE time at the fairgrounds that weekend. She was dashing into the home economics barn flanked not by friends but by her mother and father. The doorway was crowded with traffic trying to get in ahead of rain that had only begun to fall. I had Jolene's hand and was leading her through the crowd when I ran square into Mrs. Rook. I apologized before realizing who it was, and we all stood there stunned. I don't know what it was that I saw on Kathryn's face, but if she could have snapped her fingers and disappeared, I knew she would have.

"I'm so sorry. Are you okay?" I spoke to the mom but looked to Kathryn for clues as to what she wanted me to do or say. Her eyes were fixed on my hand holding Jolene's.

Burt Rook glared at me, starched as his new blue jeans. His face flushed, and he took Kathryn by the arm. She looked away, pissed and pained. "Watch where you're going, Ballot," gritted out from behind Burt Rook's teeth. He gathered himself like miffed royalty. Wife and daughter in tow, he pushed his way into the domestics barn, where tidy people had polite conversation and discussed the better nature of piecrust and embroidery. Jolene and I let ourselves be swept up in the roil of the fairgrounds, the mingling crowds, the nickering livestock, and the approaching storm.

CHAPTER 14

A kind of church was conducted in the Hightowers' crowded kitchen over strong coffee and sticky dough baptized in sizzling grease. Sunday mornings were for eating and talking and storytelling, for leaning up against counters and doorjambs if the chairs were taken, for bringing in the week's worth of groceries. Except for Sunday mornings, the television was almost always on in Jolene's house, tuned to a game or variety show with a live audience or a laugh track, background noise to the rest of the ruckus, Mariah's screeching, the constant ringing of the phone in the kitchen, Mona's telephone voice, which was louder than her loud speaking voice, and the tinkering racket from the shop in the garage, noise on top of noise. The outloudness of it was a stark contrast with my grandparents' contaminated house, where the only interruptions to murky silence were harsh fights erupting out of nowhere or sirens on televised crime shows.

I'd made myself a fixture at Jolene's house, so I was there in the kitchen eating warm fry bread doused in butter and clover honey the Sunday morning Bull announced that he'd joined the Coast Guard and would move to Oregon in a week. He said he'd had enough of the middle and was ready to see the edges and that he wanted out of Minnesota before another season of snow fell. "And I'd like to never see a cow on fire again. At least not one with its head still on it."

Troy patted down Bull with both hands, his sturdy son, pride and no shortage of love on both their faces. Mona pulled Bull to her, hand on the back of his bowed head. If they spoke words, I don't recall them, but what was unsaid lived between them and I felt it, too—an ending and a beginning and a sense that anything was possible and that it would all be one great adventure for Bull. Mariah squeezed Bull's legs and made him promise to bring back gifts from the ocean. Only Lester held back, before finally proclaiming it bullshit that Bull could leave but he had to stay and finish high school. "Don't see what the fuck it matters."

"Mouth," Mona said. Lester rolled his eyes.

"You'd wash out," Bull said, slapping Lester's back. "Stick around here, get tough like Bull. Maybe then your sister will let you go."

"Fuck you." Lester dropped his fry bread on the newspaper and wiped his hands on his jeans.

I knew Lester lived with his sister Agnes but not much more than that. He spent so much time with Bull that I almost forgot he wasn't really part of their family. "At least you only have one more year. I'm stuck—" I cut myself off, imagining Jolene graduating in the spring and what it would be like for me if I was still with Gip and Ruby and Jolene was gone.

"Agnes is right. You need to finish high school," Troy said.

Lester's anger sharpened on me. "Why are you even here, Ballot? I mean, who the fuck invited you to this powwow, huh?" He pointed at Jolene, taking a step closer to her. "You're an idiot, you know that?"

I made a move, too, thinking, I suppose, I would protect her honor, but Jolene put both her hands on Lester's chest and shoved him away. "Don't you dare," she warned.

Troy stood. "Alright, knock it off." He gripped Lester's shoulder enough to make him wince. "Let's you and me go outside and cool off."

The back door slammed shut, and through the window we could see Troy and Lester on the browning grass, Lester's hands gesturing wildly, Troy nodding, his hands raised in placation.

Mariah scrambled to the window, pressed her nose to the glass. "What's Lester so sore about?"

Mona grabbed her lightly by the scruff of her blouse. "Out, you," she said. "Leave them be now. Go play in the other room."

Mariah huffed but obliged, shoving one last piece of jam-smeared fry bread into her mouth, chomping it a time or two before showing it to me on her tongue on her way out of the kitchen.

"What *was* that all about?" Mona asked.

Bull wiped grease off his lips with the palm of his hand. "I knew he was pissed about the Coast Guard thing. I mean, other than Agnes, we're all he has. And now . . ." He waved his thumb at me like I was the turd in the pool.

Mona packed me off with fry bread to give to my grandparents. I couldn't tell her the truth, that I threw it away before I even got to the house. I'd brought home the grease-stained bag the first time Mona had given it to me, thinking my grandparents would appreciate something fresh-made like that. I'd set it on the kitchen table next to Gip, who sniffed the air.

"What's that smell?"

Ruby stuck her nose into the bag. "Smells like doughnuts."

"Fry bread. Friend's aunt made it." I hadn't told them about Jolene, though I was pretty sure Gip had seen the two of us walking down Main Street together. "She thought maybe you'd like it. Mona Hightower. You know her?"

Ruby picked up the bag, holding it away from her. "The Indian?"

I nodded. "My friend Jolene. That's her aunt. They live over there on Second Street."

"That the little thing I saw you with in town, hands on her and all?"

"Yes, sir."

"This Indian your girlfriend now?" Ruby asked.

"For a few weeks now, I guess. Yes, she is."

"Oh, how the mighty fall," Gip said. "Maybe you're not so stupid after all. Least the Indian will put out. They always do."

Ruby carried the bag between two fingers and dropped it in the trash. "You tell those Indians of yours they can keep their greasy bread and their greasy hair and their greasy ways. Mona Hightower. Mona High and Mighty, more like it. Sending us food like we need it. That girl is not welcome in this house, you hear?" She returned to tearing coupons at the kitchen table, to Green Stamps she would lick and paste into her little booklet. When I took out the trash days later, I saw the bag, crumpled and empty.

—

Mona and Troy put Bull on a westbound Greyhound a week later. With Bull gone, Jolene moved into the room at the front of the house with a west-facing window looking out over the porch. The two of us spent hours on the roof, watching the sun cast long-legged shadows under the early autumn leaves. We tucked up there, using our feet as brakes against the shingles, and let ourselves get wistful the way you do when the sun goes down, when you get above things far enough that you don't feel part of anything anymore. We talked and kissed until Jolene was called down for dinner or until our lips were sore and swollen plums. The slant of the roof made it so we couldn't collapse on each other and grope and explore, which is probably why Mona let me up those back stairs in the first place. We'd climb back in through the window, onto the bed, Jolene first then me. She never lingered there, though I longed to crawl under the striped wool blanket with her, to feel her naked next to me.

She hounded me about writing a letter to send to Topeka since I'd made such a big deal about finding him in the first place. It bothered her that here I had a solid lead in my hand, the kind of information about a father she would never get, and still I hesitated. Her frustration with me grew, but all that September, I kept Nicky Barbie's matchbook in my pocket. I did take it out once in front of Ruby, the first day of my junior year of high school, trying to bait her into yet another conversation on my father's whereabouts. She'd broken the chain of cigarettes and was searching for a light for her next one. I gave them to her but told her I needed the book back, that it had an important address.

"Same outfit my dad worked for," I said when she inspected the matchbook. "Same woman runs it, even."

"That right."

"She said a friend of my dad's is still in the business. Said he'd be in Brookings mid-October and I could write him if I wanted."

Gip's snort ruffled the newspaper he hid behind.

She lit her cigarette, pulled hard, and shook out the flame, dropping the spent stick into the ashtray. She took another long drag, the bones in her shoulders rising with breath then collapsing with exertion. She flicked the matchbook back to me. "What did I tell you?" She took a step toward me and rapped on my skull with her swollen knuckles. "You listen at all? You got a brain between those ears? You keep making excuses for him. He's not coming back. You want to think of him, you think of him as dead."

Gip slapped his newspaper shut and slammed it on the table, rattling coffee mugs, the sugar bowl, launching a mini cloud of snaked ashes. "Jesus Christ. The two of you. More breath has been wasted on that clown than I care to consider. He didn't show up. He's not going to show up. End of story. Not another word. Either one of you brings him up again, and I'll make sure it's the very last time. You can count on that."

Ruby turned her back. "Fine by me."

Lead or souvenir? Either way, I pocketed the matchbook.

"I COULD HELP YOU WITH that letter if you want. You still haven't mailed anything, right?" We were writing theme papers at Jolene's dining room table where, unlike my house, the overhead light had all its bulbs. In fact, every light in the house was on, enough that I thought maybe the house was warmer than my grandparents' from the heat of incandescent bulbs alone.

"I've been thinking about that. Maybe I'll wait awhile longer. See if Topeka gets in touch."

"But Nicky said she'd probably lose your address. You should definitely write."

It wasn't like I hadn't tried to write Topeka, despite my grandparents. I could get past the part that said I'd seen Nicky, that I remembered Topeka from way back when. I could even ask in a letter whether he'd seen my father. But then what? What did I want Topeka to tell me or to say to my father that would make up for the fact that he'd lied about coming back? The letter started to feel like that Ouija board in Jolene's closet. *Careful what you wish for,* they say. *Don't ask questions if you don't want the answers.* I worried about what would happen if I did get in touch with Topeka, if my father did come back, what that would mean for me and this girl I couldn't get enough of.

"Yeah, I think I should wait."

She picked up her pencil, rubbed the eraser against her scar. "What are you afraid of?"

"I'm not afraid. I think I should give him space, is all."

"Do you want to know or not? It's simple. I don't get why you wouldn't write the letter." She pushed her chair back from the table and stomped over to my side. "Here," she said, ripping a piece of white paper out of my spiral notebook. "Dear Topeka. It's me, Wes Ballot. You knew my dad, Moss Ballot. I met you one summer. I'm looking for him. Do you know where he is? If you do, call or write me. Love, Wes. There. Done." She pushed the paper to me. "Unless you're afraid."

I pushed it back to her. "Drop it, okay?"

"You don't think I understand, but I do. My mom—" Jolene zipped her mouth shut. "I got used to not knowing, then I started not caring. But in between I figured whatever she was hiding must be awful, like Satan awful, for her to keep it from me. Even if I change my mind, I don't get another chance. The truth died with her. And now here you are pissing away what might be your last chance. All because you're afraid."

"I'm not afraid. I don't want to get ahead of myself. I've got time. He has time."

"Forget it. Suit yourself." She shook her head, tapped her lip with the eraser before returning her attention to the table and her homework. Beneath the table, she kicked me in the shin. Under her breath, she added, "Chickenshit."

AND SO I FELL INTO a kind of contentment I hadn't known before. If I wasn't at school, I was out with Jolene or at her house, so I spent most of my time away from my grandparents. Even Lester and I regained our friendship. Without Bull around, he was at loose ends, so Jolene and I picked them up. The three of us were often together, Jolene in the passenger seat of Lester's Impala, me in the back, in the middle, poking my head through, making myself known. If me being with Kathryn Rook gave Gip and Ruby some sort of legitimacy, then it was a comedown for sure that suddenly it was two Indians picking me up in a noisy hot rod, music blaring from Lester's speakers.

I'm guessing Mona and Troy liked that Lester was with me and Jolene all the time, that it helped them believe we weren't getting closer than they'd like. We went to football games together, drove the loop, watched Lester run illegal quarter-mile races on a straight stretch out of town. We never went out without a case of beer, funded in part because Lester was old enough to buy for minors, a service he willingly provided for a fee. What Mona and Troy didn't know was how much time we were alone, when Lester would leave us in his car while he jumped in the back of another one to make a beer run. Not that we could keep our hands off each other when he was around.

With Kathryn, I'd always felt used up and weak with need, hers and mine both. But Jolene was all want, and that wanting was powerful to me. Jolene had no shits to give about what anyone else thought or said. She put her hand into the waistband of my jeans when we talked in the hallway at school, cupped the back of my neck when she kissed me, threw her legs over mine on the couch—never mind that her family was right there watching.

"What do you mean you can't drive stick?"

I'd been driving since I was barely a teenager, mostly at my mother's urging. She thought it was funny, watching me tiptoe the gas and brake pedals, craning my neck to see over the steering wheel of her banged-up, run-down Rambler. I can picture that boy driving like a man, her loose and mink, drinking beer from a bottle, eating white bread straight from the bag, leaning full against the passenger door. I'd sputter and barrel down lonesome back roads while she fiddled with the radio, turning it up to distraction when someone she liked—Roberta Flack or the Carpenters—came on so she could sing along, her meadowlark voice tuned in and sweet. Carefree memories like that one—tinged with gloss, lit by sunrays—they're fragile. I don't tamper with them much. The better I got at driving, the more often she'd call me to walk down to some bar to drive her drunk ass home. Had my father been a different man, I might have learned to work the clutch from him. The most he taught me was to shift the big stick when he said "when." Even that I hadn't done for years. I'd gotten my driver's license mostly to have something to carry around in my wallet. Ruby let me use her car for the test, figured it might save her trips to the store for smokes. *What's in it for me?* Like mother, like daughter.

"I mean I can't drive stick."

It seemed Lester had already bought beer for half the high school, and kickoff for the homecoming game was still an hour off. I was perched as usual in the back seat, leaning between him and Jolene.

He looked at me in the rearview. "How can you . . . oh, forget it. Ballot, you're hopeless," Lester said, pulling the tab on a can of beer, tucking it between his legs before shifting gears, slipping the Impala into third.

"Bull let me drive the farm truck once."

"This baby is no farm truck, Ballot. She requires a man's touch."

"Troy taught me, you can teach Wes," Jolene said. "Let him try."

"No way."

"Oh, come on!" She straight-arm shoved him against the door. "Just do it. Pull over right there in the bank parking lot."

How could he say no? The lot was mostly empty, so Lester parked diagonally across two spaces and left the motor running. Both doors opened and we all switched spots—Jolene in back, Lester in the passenger seat, me behind the wheel of Lester's precious car. He gave me the fundamentals, which I knew. Let up the clutch, give it a little gas. "Balance and timing, Ballot. That's all it is. Balance and timing. She's tight so you gotta go easy. You know what I mean, right?" The grin said it all.

Jolene's voice in my right ear, her eyes on mine in the mirror.

"Are you blushing? Did Lester make you blush?" she asked.

Lester shook his head. "Cut the flirting and let's get on with it already. You sit back," he said to Jolene. "Don't want you sticking your tongue in his ear or something."

I caught her eye again as she fell backward, smirking, satisfied.

I hiccupped my way through town, grinding gears, stalling at stop signs, at the only light, until I managed to make the transition from first, to a revved second, to a growling third, and back down. "Alright, Ballot. I've got whiplash and beer all over my shirt, so how about you pull back in there and let me take over?"

Jolene leaned forward as I made the turn into the parking lot. She put her hands over my eyes. "Bet you can't drive blindfolded!" It was only for a second, but Lester and I both panicked. I grabbed at her hand, Lester grabbed the wheel. The car died a spastic death.

"Jesus Christ, Jo!" Lester said. "Are you crazy?"

"Oh, lighten up! Nothing happened."

But something had. Someone had witnessed the whole thing. We flung the doors open, climbed out laughing, beer soaked. Sammy Hagar blasting from the radio. And there was Burt Rook. Lester and I saw him first, Jolene came up behind me, wrapped her arms around my waist, ducked like a swing dancer to get under my arm. We all tried to come to attention, though beer and the situation were making us silly. I tried to focus just on Kathryn's father's face, ignoring Lester, who seemed to be teeing something up.

"You mind telling me what you're doing?" He dipped his head toward a rusty sign. "No Loitering."

"You okay, there, Mr. Rook? You look shook," Lester said.

Jolene's hand popped to her mouth. I tried to unruffle Burt Rook. "Don't mind us. Switching drivers, is all. We won't be hanging around."

"But you are still around. Thought your father would have come to fetch you by now."

"Not yet," I said.

"Well, look at you. Making . . . friends."

Lester threw his big arm over my shoulder. "Friends, girlfriends. Isn't that right, Wes?"

Jolene gripped my other hand, pulled me back toward the car. "We should get going."

"You stay out of my parking lot. Stay away . . ." He hesitated. "Just stay away, you hear? I don't want to see you hanging around my . . . my property again."

We scolded each other, mocked Rook a little, popped open beers, and put the episode behind us as Lester peeled out of the parking lot, heading toward the lights of the football field.

Seemed the whole town of Loma came out for football weekends that fall. The lights on the field were new, so the games became a Friday-night social event. For the homecoming game, a rivalry, the excitement ticked up a notch. The booster club brewed hot cider and popped corn in the lean-to under the bleachers. The pep band led a throng of students on the march from the high school to the field, where a bonfire had been lit and the effigy of a hornet hung ready for torching.

The crowd of students circled the bonfire, which licked stories high. Kathryn was across from me, golden and glowing in the firelight. I caught her eye and smiled, hoping to tell her in that one gesture that there were no hard feelings, that I never meant to hurt her, that I hoped good things would come for her. And I did. She looked pretty there in that light. Her face softened, then seized up again. Jolene's arms encircled my waist, her mittened hands were on my belly.

"Hey, you," I said, pulling her around me. I put my lips on the part of her hair. She tilted her head up, let her chin rest on my shoulder.

"Kathryn's watching you."

"I know."

"Do you need to talk to her? She's really looking over here."

"There's nothing I need to say. She's fine. Look."

Like always, Kathryn was surrounded by friends, the two snide girls who'd first seen me with Jolene at the river, a few senior boys who would play basketball in the winter. Even Drew Fullerton was with her. They laughed about some shared joke, and Kathryn looked away from us, brightened for her friends. A boy and a girl broke away from the group and turned up behind me and Jolene.

"Hey, Jolene," the boy said. "We really need a win tonight. How about you do a war dance for us, you know, a little—" He put his hand against his mouth, baffling out a three-note whoop.

The girl raised her eyebrows and smiled, trying to keep a straight face.

"Put your hand down before I break it off," I said.

His head was shaped like a watermelon. I could smell liquor on his breath as he moved closer to me. "Yeah, you think?"

"Let's go," the girl said, pulling the boy by the arm.

He sneered, easing off the adrenaline. "Fucking Indian lover."

Lester stepped forward from the shadows as the boy turned. "Wanna repeat that, Robbie? What you just said there to my friends?"

Lester stood next to me and Jolene dropped my hand. The three of us, side by side, no one hiding, no one being a hero.

The girl tugged the boy's arm, pulling him away. "Robbie, let's go. Everyone's waiting."

"Yeah, I didn't think so, Robbie," Lester said. "Fucking punk."

We left the bonfire, downed a case of beer driving around in the boondocks, me holding Jolene's hand from the back seat. We made fun of the girl and that Robbie, who Lester said was a first-class asshole and drug dealer to boot, destined for jail time down the road. They ribbed me about Kathryn, what I ever saw in her. I was thankful Lester didn't go too far, though I wasn't sure whether he was protecting me or Jolene. The beer got me talking and I leaned in, put my arms around the two of them, kissed each on the temple, and declared my love. "I wish I could convert to Indian."

Jolene doubled over with laughter but not Lester.

"Sometimes you're so fucking ignorant it hurts, Ballot."

"Lighten up," Jolene said. "He's joking."

I let myself fall against the back seat. "I'm serious. I wish I was less me and more you."

Lester pulled up in front of Jolene's house and cut the ignition. "You know, just once it would be great if you at least acknowledged that you're just another interloping white man come into this family and taking it like it was already yours."

Jolene got out of the car and flipped the seat up for me to climb out. I put my head back in, one hand down on the warm leather where Jolene had been sitting, and extended my other hand to Lester. "I meant nothing by it," I said. But that wasn't true. I had never felt a part of anything that good and wanted more than anything to not be the thing I was. By day—with Jolene and her family, with Lester even—I let myself believe that my father's disappearance was on him and not me. But when I climbed into my mother's bed at night, when my fingertips touched that knife that I still stored in the bed rails, I couldn't help but think of myself as a person who didn't belong, a person who could be left behind.

How many times I've put my hand out to someone since that night on Bright Lake I can't even count now. But I wanted Lester to take it that night almost as much as I wanted my mother to the night she drowned. His contempt seemed to wither as I persisted. "Go, Ballot. Jesus. Your girlfriend is waiting."

I offered my hand again. "Take it."

He gripped my hand until the bones curled over on each other. "There. Happy?"

I was.

CHAPTER 15

By mid-October, I still hadn't heard from Topeka. The matchbook that lived in my pocket was worn from my handling of it. Jolene and I were sitting out on the porch roof watching a tangled flock of starlings murmur across the western sky, bursting black fireworks. They whiplashed, then descended on a red cedar like a great black cape, bending its boughs only to lift off as if they might pick up the tree and carry it away. I could hear Jolene's breathing change to gasps each time the shape shifted. I reached for her hand and wove my fingers through hers.

"It'll be winter soon," she said.

"No more porch roof."

A shadow passed over us and we heard a hundred wings beating. The flock briefly darkened the sky before settling in the trees.

Jolene climbed between my splayed legs. Her back to my chest, she tilted her head so her temple brushed my cheek. "Warm me up."

I wrapped myself around her, tight as I could. My hands drifted over her wool sweater, along her breasts, over her belly.

Her lips grazed my face, dragging on faint stubble. "Mariah's in a play tonight. There's a reception afterward."

"Do you want me to go with you?"

She looped her arm around my head, touching the velvet spot behind my ear. "I'm not going, Wes."

I SAID MY GOODBYES, MADE a show of leaving, but I didn't go home. Instead, I watched from a safe distance as Mariah flew out of the house dressed as a squirrel, Troy and Mona right behind her, then as the three of them piled into Mona's station wagon and pulled away from the house. The porch light flipped on. Our signal. I watched as, one by one, the other lights in the house went out like flames doused, though I was all fire. Only one light remained on, the one in the window above the front porch. I picked my way carefully through the dark house toward the dimmest light at the back stairs. I tiptoed past Mariah's bed as if she were sleeping there. Jolene was sitting on the end of hers, hands on her thighs, head down. She was still wearing the jeans and sweater I saw her in that afternoon. Her feet were bare. She had not heard me come in.

"Hey, you," I said.

Her head tilted up at an angle, and she smiled her barely smile.

I went to her, took her hands, and pressed them behind my back. I slipped my hands under her sweater and traced one by one the prayer bead bones on her back. She stepped away from me, crossed her arms at her waist to lift her sweater over her head. I stopped her, gently pulling her sweater back down. "Hold on," I said.

"You okay?"

It wasn't that I was stalling. It was more that I wanted to freeze that moment. If I could slow everything down, it wouldn't end, at least not so soon. And part of me felt like it couldn't possibly last, especially since it was so good. Nothing ever did.

I took a step toward the window, then turned back to her. "Want to sit on the roof for a minute?"

She touched the scar and shook her head. She took my jacket off and let it fall to the floor. Then my flannel shirt, then my T-shirt. "It's okay," she said. I was powerless.

Nothing went slowly after her lips touched mine—not kicking off my shoes, fumbling with buttons and flies. I melted when she peeled off her sweater, baring herself to me. I knew her body. I'd known it forever. We fell onto her soft bed in only our underwear. She threw a sheer scarf over the lamp so that every time we moved and shifted, purple and red and green danced around us like northern lights.

"You smell so good," I said, exhaling to make room for more of her while my hands swept the suede of her skin.

Her hand slowly moved down my stomach.

"You're sure?"

"Sure."

She took the band from her hair and lay back so it fell like feathers against her pillowcase. "God, you're beautiful," I said and she was. We rolled around on each other awhile more, touching curves, tensing muscles, tasting skin on fire, until there was nothing left to do. I went as slowly as I could and so did she, never taking our eyes off each other.

"Am I hurting you? I can stop."

"Nothing hurts," she said. "Nothing hurts."

I held on until I could do nothing but give in.

We lay together afterward, quiet, drifting in and out of shallow sleep. I felt a clutch of relief and guilt, knowing I'd taken something and had likely given little. Jolene's head was on my chest, her hand on my stomach. Her blanket was over us, and I was grateful for it, suddenly modest and self-conscious.

"Was that okay?" I asked, afraid of the answer.

"Mm-hmm."

"Did you, you know?"

She shook her head against my chest. "Don't worry about that right now."

My heart was pounding so hard I thought Jolene's head was moving to the rhythm. I wanted to tell her I loved her, that I wanted to be with her forever, that I would do anything for her, anything to make her happy. I wrestled with the words, phrasing and rephrasing, imagining her response.

"Wes, I want you to do something."

"Anything." I would have killed for her in that moment.

"Well, actually, two things." She tucked the bedsheet under her arms and sat up.

I leaned on my elbow. "Okay. Shoot."

"First. Will you go to the Sadie Hawkins dance with me? And before you even say it, I know I said I didn't give a shit about these things, but I actually really do. I want to go. It's my senior year, I've never gone to a high school dance. And—" She shrugged and let her eyes scan the mess we made of her bed.

"You don't have to convince me. I want to go with you, too. But the dress-up part, too?" It was a part of the fall tradition to wear corny costumes, like something out of *Hee Haw*. "I don't want to wear overalls."

"No dress up," she said, crossing her heart.

Her hair was tousled around her ears and her face was flushed. I pictured her in one of those *Hee Haw* Honey bandana tops and wondered if I could wear overalls after all. "Alright. So that's settled. What else?"

"I want you to go to Brookings. I want you to go find Topeka. I'm sure I can get Troy to let you borrow the Bronco. He trusts you. Just go down there, find out what he knows, come back here. The dance is a week from Friday. You don't hear from him by then, go the next day."

"What does it matter to you? He may not even be there. He may not know anything." I dropped my elbow and lay flat on my back, staring at the ceiling.

"You're always waiting for something to happen to you. You need to go make this happen so you know once and for all what the deal is. Otherwise, you're stuck. I don't want you to be stuck. And I won't be stuck with you."

"What if it's bad? What if something bad happened?" I didn't ask the other questions nagging at me. *What if I go and find him? What if he's there and I never come back here? What if finding him means losing you?*

"You can't live in the dark, Wes."

I thought of my mother, how she drew darkness to her, wrapped herself in it, right up to when she used her own body to punch a dark hole out of paper-white ice. I didn't want to be in that shadow, in that confusion of dim light anymore. "I know you're right."

She touched my face and lay back down so that we were side by side. She sniffed, and at first I thought she was crying. "What's that smell?"

A wisp of smoke rose from where the scarf—a black hole in the center now—had drooped down onto the bulb.

"Oh shit!" We sat bolt upright, aware of everything at once—the burning scarf, our naked bodies, the slamming car door. Jolene pulled the scarf off the lamp and jammed it into a glass of water on her bedside table.

I peeked out the window. The station wagon was there.

"It's Mona and Troy."

"You have to go. They'll kill me."

I was already up, hopping to get my pants on. Jolene shoved my socks into my coat pocket, her finger on her lips.

"Don't stomp! Get on the bed so they won't hear your feet."

She quickly slipped into pajama bottoms, pulled a T-shirt over her face.

Mona's voice drifted up the back stairs. "Jo, we're home." Then, "Is something burning?"

"I'll be right down." She shook her head, rolled her eyes, kissed me full on the lips. "Go out the window when the coast is clear. I'll see you tomorrow."

I pressed her open palm to my lips and kissed it. She flew out the door.

I waited agonizing minutes for Troy to finish his nightly cigarette under the streetlamp. When I heard the screen door shut below me, I jiggled the window open and climbed out onto the roof. The music of family played below me—Mariah's excited laughter, Troy's low voice more instrument than human, Mona's clapping, the uphill of Jolene's voice louder than usual as she peppered them with questions to cover the sound of me, newly made, sneaking out into the night.

THE NEXT MORNING WAS SUNDAY, and I showed up at Jolene's house as usual, walked through the door, and immediately flushed at the sight of her. Surely they knew from our stupid smiles, the fumbled way she greeted me. Troy didn't hesitate. "Let's talk for a minute," he said. "Man to man. Jolene, go help Mona." She glanced over her shoulder at me, mouthed, "It's okay." I feared the worst, that he knew what had gone on upstairs, and that this was the practical end of me. I imagined the gamut, from Troy insisting we marry on the spot to him running me out of town. Both scenarios involved a shotgun.

"Sit down," he said, pulling out a chair at the dining room table. "Jolene tells me you might need to borrow the truck."

"She told you about Topeka then," I said, relieved.

"She did."

I'd thought about the trip plenty, even before Jolene brought it up—how I'd get there, what it might look like, who I might find. "I could take a bus down, but once I'm there, I got to figure out where to go, and I can't afford to stay over. If I'm going, I want to go, ask my questions. Driving would make it easier."

"Quicker, too. Safer. Let me ask you something," Troy said. "Say you get there and you don't find him, this Topeka. What then?"

"I come back here. I'm down a tank of gas but I'm not worse off. I want to *know*, you know?"

"Okay. Let's say you find him. What if your dad happens to be running with Topeka? What then?"

The reunion played in my head, the manly hugs, the ruffled hair, pats on the back. I remembered the way Troy put his hands on Bull when he left and imagined my father's hands on me, how surprised he'd be about how I'd grown and filled out. But that was the homecoming of a prodigal son, not a missing father who knew where to find the boy he'd left behind. My brow furrowed on its own, tightening down on my eyes to keep the tears in. I shook my head. Shrugged.

"Listen to me, Wes. This isn't about my truck. You don't know what your dad might be mixed up in. Don't go running off with him if you find him. You call here if you need to and we'll help if we can." Troy pushed back his chair and I did, too, extending my hand to him in thanks.

"Will do."

"So a week from Saturday?"

"That's the plan. Unless something comes up in the meantime."

He put his left hand on my shoulder at the same time he shook my hand, the warmth of it pressing into bone. "Do not steal my truck."

"I swear I won't."

He patted my shoulder twice. "We better go on and get in the kitchen before Mona shuts down the operation."

If a boy can be in the glow of losing his virginity, then I was in it that week, unable to concentrate on much of anything except for Jolene and my daily rifling through the mail for any news that would make the trip to South Dakota unnecessary. I didn't want to be away from her for even a day. Since the night of Mariah's play, we hadn't had a single opportunity to be alone and suspected that Mona was on to us. Every day, she had a new chore for Jolene, one that required her to be home with the family or at least Mariah. That didn't mean I made myself scarce. If it was possible, I spent even more time that week at the Hightowers' house.

Come Friday, nothing in the mail, I made my plan with Troy to pick up the truck first thing the next morning. Jolene suggested I sleep on their couch after the barn dance to make it that much easier. Troy set his newspaper down on the kitchen table and laughed out loud. "No."

I CHOSE A DECENT SNAP shirt and my best jeans, fresh from the army-navy surplus and stiff as a corpse, to wear to the dance. Lester had offered to loan me an old pair of cowboy boots, but his feet were a size or more bigger than mine, and I figured if I had to clodhop around a dance floor I'd best do it in my own farm boots, worn but comfortable.

Lester honked from the street as I wolfed down one last bite of hamburger goop on rice. I told Gip and Ruby I was heading to the dance and had things to do the next day and wouldn't be around.

"Thought Gip told you to rake up the last of them leaves. Won't rake themselves."

"I'll do it Sunday," I said as I walked out the door. I couldn't know those leaves would not get raked at all.

WE SWUNG BY JOLENE'S HOUSE. She greeted me at the door, adorable in braids and cutoff shorts, a blue plaid shirt, and the cowboy boots she and Mona shared. "Hey! You said no dress up! You look cute alright," I said.

She shrugged. "I'm a little white farm girl. Whaddya think?"

I put my arms around the small of her back and pulled her to me. "You look right nice in them there shitkickers, girl," I teased.

"And you don't look too bad for a hayseed."

Lester laid on the horn. "Let's go!" A sophomore girl named Daphne, a waif of a thing with a perky figure-skater haircut, had asked him to be her date. He'd declined, preferring, he said, to go stag. "You watch. There'll be plenty of girls free to dance with Lester because their wrestler boyfriends will be in the toilet puking up Jack."

I sat in back, as usual, and Jolene sat up front. We cruised around town, chugging beers. By the time we got to the dance, we were all good and buzzed. Jolene was between me and Lester, arms hooked in ours. Kathryn and a cheerleader friend were selling tickets. The booster club chaperone was behind them both. We stood up straight and tried to look serious and sober.

"Hello, Wes," she said.

"Hello, Kathryn," I said, making the mistake of mocking her tone. Lester and Jolene snickered. "Two tickets."

"Okay. One," said Kathryn. "It's Sadie Hawkins. The girl is supposed to buy the ticket." She glared at Jolene. "If she can afford it. Two. This is a date dance. He can't come without a date." Another glare for Lester.

"Oh, you're wrong there," said Lester. He put his hands on the table and leaned into her. "I can come all by my lonesome. Unless you don't have a date. You can come with me."

Kathryn rolled her eyes and her friend whispered, "Gross."

Jolene put her hand on Lester's shoulder. "They're both with me. I have two dates and I can pay for all of our tickets." She laid the money down on the table.

"One date per person," the cheerleader said.

Jolene picked up the ticket, turned it over. "Nope. Says 'Admit One.' I'll take three." The cheerleader started to complain, but Kathryn turned suddenly sweet.

"Forget it. Let them in. More money for us. Besides, I have a favor to ask Jolene." She took the money and handed Jolene the tickets.

"There's a Halloween party tomorrow night at the Idle Hour. I was thinking of going as an Indian. Do you have anything I can borrow?"

"What the fuck is wrong with you?" I asked, not really looking for an answer.

The chaperone came to life momentarily. "Language there, young man."

"I take it that's a no?"

"Yeah," Jolene said. "It's a no."

We walked around her toward the gym. Lester called over his shoulder. "You can still come with me if you want."

Lester was right. There were plenty of girls interested in him. The girl Daphne wore overalls that made her look like a toddler. When she asked Lester to dance, he picked her up like a child and tossed her so high onto a pile of mats, her friends had to spot her when she jumped down. The band played Aerosmith, the Rolling Stones, and Styx, and Jolene and I leaned against the fold-up bleachers, sipping spiked punch, making out, dancing when she insisted. My dance skills were limited to swaying, so I was happier when the song was slow and I could match her rhythm, my hands on her hips, her head against my shoulder. I remember thirsting for her, imagining her turned to creek water, cold and fresh, water I could scoop with both hands, that would wet the dryness in me, that would keep me alive. I must have sighed at the thought of it. She lifted her head, rested her eyes on mine, touched my cheek, thumb to my mouth. I leaned in, kissed her hard like we weren't where we were.

We'd been at the dance maybe an hour when Lester tapped my shoulder, like he was trying to cut in. "I'm heading out. You two about done with the hillbilly ball?"

"No girl?" I asked.

"Nah, you got the best one, Ballot."

It was true.

"Yeah," Jolene said. "We should head out. Besides, you got a long day ahead of you tomorrow."

"What's going on?" Lester asked.

Jolene waved him off. "I'll tell you later."

CHAPTER 16

I HONORED TROY'S WISHES, SLEPT IN MY OWN BED BUT BARELY. TROY and Jolene and the dog, Sparky, met me outside their house with the keys. I was on the road at sunup. It was one of those red-barn, white-steeple autumn days. Leaves were just past peak gold and red, spiff and crisp against the impossible blue sky. Soon enough I would leave the overgrowth for farmland as I headed west toward Fargo, then due south, a straight flat shot down the state line to Brookings. Troy had gassed up the Bronco for me, just like him to be so kind. "If you wreck it," he said, winking, "don't even bother to come back. I want my truck back more than you."

Jolene kissed me hard like I was leaving for war. I was embarrassed by it since we never much did that in front of Mona and Troy. But it was good and nourishing. "Drive careful. And if you're tired, pull over. You don't have to come back tonight. Just come back in one piece."

In those hours driving alone, I let my thoughts wander. I shooed away my father and focused instead on Jolene, replaying our night together, the smell and feel of her. I thought about what our lives might look like, where we would live, the sex we would have, the babies, even thinking maybe she was pregnant already, a part of me putting down roots inside her. Though high wind warning signs ran the flatiron length of the Coteau des Prairies, the road seemed to propel me along like I was on a roller-coaster chain lift attached to the farmland, the cornfields crew cut for winter. The wind could not buffet me nor could I have veered even had I wanted to. I was heading toward an answer of some sort.

I got off the highway near the state university, stopped for gas and directions. The clerk said the warehouse was west of town, out by the little airport. I passed a series of trailer parks, all with hopeful names that included words like "estate" and "villa," and remembered staying with my mother one summer in a KOA campground where she'd rented out a room in a trailer that belonged to a couple desperate enough for money that they'd taken us in. I'd slept in the top bunk of a little girl's bedroom and my mom slept in the bottom. The girls, twins, were off with grandparents and a father who saw them only in the summer. I'd liked it there because the campground had a swimming pool and lots of kids around who didn't already have friends and were less inclined to be picky when it came to making new ones. We were tossed out before the end of summer. I can only guess at why now. The woman, her name I don't remember, watched us leave from the doorway, no smile on her face.

The warehouse was one of several in the area, corrugated metal, unmarked, and unremarkable. Two cars were parked next to the single white door, next to the single window. There were two overhead roller-style bays. Next to one of those, a red pickup truck with the familiar "B" logo. I was shaking, unsure my legs would hold me if I put my feet on the ground. "Okay, okay." I opened the cab door and was talking myself into getting out when a car pulled up next to me. A wiry man in a flannel shirt, gray work pants, and boots got out. His charcoal hair was combed back so the greasy tips curled along the nape of his neck. He was carrying several white bags that I imagined held lunch since it was around noon when I pulled up. He shifted one bag into his armpit to open the door.

He held it with his foot and stopped. "Help you with something?"

I made an eager jump for the door to hold it for him. "Yeah, let me get that for you."

He made no move to go inside. "You looking for a job?"

"No, I was looking for Nicky. Is she here?"

The man cocked his neck like a chicken. "Nicky's not here. She's gone already. Florida. What can I do for you?"

"Actually," I said, kicking the dirt, trying to get my nerves up. "I'm looking for a fella called Topeka."

"Which is it, buddy? Nicky or Topeka?"

"I'm sorry. It's Topeka. I'm looking for Topeka. Do you know him?"

His skin was weathered and his nose bent this way, then that. Up close I could see the gray whiskers on a face that had never grown a decent beard. When he was done looking me up and down, he nodded toward the inside for me to follow him.

The warehouse was vast and deep. Carnival equipment, booths, and rides were staggered in the back. Sparks flew from a welder's repair project in the center of the concrete floor. There was a little office near a side wall with a window to the shop floor. A man sat behind a desk there. It wasn't Topeka.

"Wait here," the man said. He disappeared behind the office door. Through the window, I could see a conversation being had, the glances my way. I stood still and tall, tried not to look around too much, to pass inspection if that's what this was. The longer I stood there, the more I felt cornered somehow, like a bandit was watching me from behind a rock. I imagined them huddled behind the equipment, trying to figure a way out.

Topeka strolled in, more tattoos than the last time I saw him, same fingers rising out of his collar brushing his jawbone, same porkpie hat. His blue eyes pierced me.

"So where is he?" I asked.

Topeka's head twitched, and he scratched the lobe of his ear. Confusion registered in his eyes. "Where's who?"

"My dad. Moss. I'm Wes Ballot. He's here, right? That's what took you so long."

"I was in the shitter, if you don't mind." He took the hat off and scratched his bald head. He squinted at me. Nodded slowly. "Yeah, yeah. I see it. You look like him. Nicky told me some kid was looking for Moss, said he was his son. I figured she had it wrong. Couldn't be, I told her."

"I remember you," I said. "You worked on the Fun House. You were his friend."

"Yeah, yeah. Wow. I can't get over this." He kept squinting at me, shaking his head. "Man, I'm sorry. He's not here. Hey, you want a sandwich? Phil brought enough for everyone."

So there would be no reunion. My stomach rumbled. "Yeah, okay."

"C'mon. Sit down and eat something."

Over tuna fish sandwiches, Topeka told me that he had seen my father in Sioux Falls the previous winter, how he'd come to Topeka's place there, crashed on the couch, the two of them getting shit-face drunk for days on end. "I knew something was wrong, but it wasn't like me to pry. I mean, man's got a right to his shit. Finally, one night, blotto drunk, he tells me about the accident, about . . ." He hesitated as if I didn't know the whole story. "You and your mom. About the ice."

Topeka looked away, took his hat off, and set it on the table. "Listen, now, I was pretty drunk, but I could have swore . . ." He licked his lips, huffed. "Swore Moss told me you both went into the lake. You both drowned. Hey, you want a cigarette?" He reached into his shirt pocket, drew out a pack, tapped twice against the table, then pointed the pack at me.

My stomach clenched, and I shook my head. I was on the lake, my mother reaching for me, pulling, clawing. Me backing away. The empty space. Dawn. My father in the hospital, accusing her of faking the whole thing. "No, it was only my mother who drowned."

Topeka exaggerated a shrug. "My mistake. Obviously. I mean, you're here, right?"

Had Topeka misunderstood, or was there something else? Something more grim. I glanced around the warehouse, at all the hiding places. I looked for a back door where my father could have snuck out unnoticed, gotten away from me like we were playing some sort of game. I looked again at Topeka, his cold eyes, the bony fingers on his neck. Had Topeka killed that man? Is that why he got that tattoo? I stood up, certain I couldn't sit for a second longer. "I don't believe you. You're lying to me."

"Believe me or don't. It is what it is."

I walked through the warehouse, opened the bathroom door. Empty. The welder stopped. Lifted his hood. It wasn't him. I turned back to Topeka. He was still sitting at the table, eating his sandwich. I was probably twenty feet away from the picnic table, alone on the concrete floor like I'd been alone on the ice. Dread was the nearest thing to me. It was all I was. "Where is he? Where is he?" I yelled it over and over, until Topeka ran to me, grabbed me, walked me outside.

The sun was high in the sky, bright and burning. I shielded my eyes against it, though I would have had it burn everything out of me at that moment.

"Look. He told me he was going straight. No more carnival. No more life on the road. He mentioned Wyoming. Montana. I haven't heard from him or seen him since."

"So he's dropped off the face of the earth, is that it? Or is that what he told you to say if I came looking for him? I don't get why he'd say I was dead. Where would that get him?"

"Listen. I probably shouldn't tell you this, but there was a woman by the name of Aveline Blue. I met her a couple of times some years back. I don't know nothing about her. Don't know if that's who he's with. Here's what I know. Face of an angel. Giant ass."

"What are you trying to say?"

"I don't know. But that's all I've got to tell you. I'm sorry you come all this way. If I see Moss . . ."

"Yeah, forget about it."

He had told me to wait, and I had. I was the living dead. I drove back to Loma in a daze. I felt part of nothing, not the land or the road. Not my grandparents. I had no family at all. Even my memories seemed to belong to someone else now. *Now that I'm dead,* I remember thinking, like the words could turn me to dust. I arrived back in Loma with no recollection of the drive. Nothing was different than when I'd left that morning, yet everything was changed.

Ruby was sitting in front of the television when I walked in. Gip was likely downtown, as usual.

"Don't you track in mud!"

"Where would I pick up mud, Ruby? It's bone dry outside."

She ignored me and took a swill from her beer can, her crab-apple face flickering blue and red with the changing image on the television.

"Is there anything to eat?"

"What? The Indians run out of government cheese?"

"I'm hungry, Ruby," I said. "I haven't eaten since lunch."

"Fend for yourself. You're not a cripple."

I got milk and leftover spaghetti, and Ruby hollered for me to grab her another beer. Some crime show was on the television, and instead of retreating to my room, I set Ruby's beer on her TV tray and plopped down on the couch. Two detectives were standing over a body that had washed up on a beach somewhere.

"Drove down to Brookings today."

"Turn up the volume for me, will you?"

I adjusted the volume and gave the side of the set a slap to stop the rolling picture. Ruby grunted, satisfied.

"Aren't you even going to ask why or whose car I drove or anything?"

"Got something to do with your Indian friend, I suspect, so I couldn't care less."

"Told you I heard about a friend of my dad's this summer. I went looking for him to see if he knew anything about where he is." The coroner arrived in a black car and zipped the body into a bag.

Her lower lip twisted around her cigarette. "And? Let me guess. He didn't know shit."

"Not exactly nothing. But not much. He had heard about Mom, though. Funny thing was, he thought I'd . . ." The medics kicked the wheels of the gurney and folded it into the back of the black car.

"He thought you what?"

I imagined her grip on my wrist, the ice beneath me cracking, the cold water seeping into my long johns for the moments before the ice gave and I launched face-first into the lake with my dying mother. I felt her hands and arms on my head, pushing me under. I saw my dad's slippers floating to the bottom, where the two of us, mother and son, would eventually sink. Two lives ending so tragically. *What a shame!* they would say.

"Nothing." The detectives talked about notifying next of kin.

"So that's that now? You done?"

"You think it's my fault, don't you, what happened to my mother."

Ruby's head cranked sideways so I couldn't see her eyes at all.

"That's why you're so mean, why you don't do anything for me. You can't even look at me."

"Who do you think you are? We never do nothing for you . . . put clothes on your back, food on your plate, roof over your head."

"You barely even know I'm alive. Half the time, I eat over at Jolene's anyway," I said.

"You feel free to take every meal over there."

"Maybe I will," I said. I purposefully blocked the television when I stood to leave. "I did everything I could. To save her. I did. I'm not sure she wanted to be saved."

She leaned back and crossed her arms, but I could see a kind of sorrow in her eyes as she stared me down. She blinked first.

"Go on, then. Move. I'm trying to watch this program."

I SLAMMED THE DOOR AS hard as I could, hoping it would knock some of the crap off the walls. Snow was in the forecast and the smell of it hung in the air. I wanted to go back in to get my coat, but I didn't want to give Ruby the satisfaction.

I parked Troy's Bronco out front and killed the engine. I felt safe there behind the wheel of a truck that had been my own for even those hours. I savored that freedom feeling and the quiet before I would go into Jolene's house, where I knew I would be bombarded with questions. Through the front window, I could see that the television was on and make out heads with black hair against the couch. I climbed the steps, knocked on the door, and opened it at the same time, like I always did.

They were there in the living room, my other family, the one that I thought cared about me, that asked how I was. The one that fed me and let me in. Troy in his recliner, Mona on the floor near his feet. Mariah sprawled out next to Mona, a bowl of popcorn in front of her. And next to Jolene was Lester Two Kills, his arm casually over her shoulder.

"Hey, Wes," said Mona. "C'mon in. You want something to eat?" She jumped up and headed for the kitchen.

I couldn't stop looking at Jolene and Lester on the couch.

"Come sit down," Jolene said, patting the spot next to her on the couch where Lester wasn't. "Tell us everything."

"Oh, you know . . ." I said. I fumbled with the keys in my hand, unable to take my eyes off Jolene and Lester next to each other like that. "Uh, Troy. Your keys. Thanks so much."

"Any time. It's a piece of shit but it gets the job done in a pinch."

"There's some chicken in here, Wes," said Mona from the kitchen.

My mouth was dry as a spent well. "No," I said, thinking what a fool I'd been. Here I'd let myself pretend I was part of something that I knew in reality I wasn't. No wonder she told me not to hurry back. Find your dad. Find your people. Your own people. People worthless as fallout ash. I would never be able to wipe them from my shoulders.

"No, no, thanks, Mona. Really. I just came—"

Jolene got up and headed toward me. I backed away. "To drop off the keys."

"What's the matter? Did something happen?" Jolene asked. "Come sit down."

Lester was on the couch still, feet up on the coffee table, eyebrows raised.

Every throb of my pounding heart jolted me. I was not wanted. Not here. Not anywhere. I couldn't hear it again. I stuttered a plan. "Gotta go. Meeting some people. Down at the Idle Hour. Shoot some pool."

"You're going to go shoot pool. What? With Kathryn Rook? Who else do you know hangs out down there?"

I lashed out. "Yeah, Jo, maybe Kathryn. Is that okay with you? Do I have to clear that with you before I go?"

"You sure you don't want something, Wes?" Mona asked, wiping her hands on the back of her pants as she came out of the kitchen.

"Really, thanks, but no. Thanks," I said, and headed back out the door. Jolene followed me onto the porch.

"Wes Ballot, what are you doing?"

"So you and Lester, huh?" I shoved my hands into my jeans pockets. *It will be easier this way. She deserves someone better than me.* "Makes sense, really. I mean, basketball stud, good-looking guy, plus he's got the whole Indian thing going for him."

"Oh, for shit sake, Wes! Don't be an idiot. I was waiting for you all day. Lester's hanging out. Like always."

Troy was at the screen door, Lester behind him.

"Don't worry, Troy. I won't bother y'all anymore," I said, and waved him off like none of this was a big deal. Like I had better places to be. I took off down the street into the darkness.

"Why are you being like this?"

I could hear Ruby's voice in my head telling me how I stuck out like a sore thumb with the Indians, how Mona Hightower probably figured she'd get a leg up around Loma having a white boy hanging around her rundown house, how, in the end, when those Indians had taken everything they wanted from us white folk, they'd discard me like their shitty cars and their shitty dogs and everything else in their shitty lives. I threw my arms up and laughed. I felt an urge to strip off my clothes and disappear into the waxing moonlight.

"Like what, Jo? Like what?" I said, and ran off. I could hear her calling my name, but she didn't say to come back, so I didn't.

CHAPTER 17

I DID GO TO THE IDLE HOUR AND I DID FIND KATHRYN ROOK THERE with her friends. I tucked Jolene away, promising myself to forget about her, and let Kathryn feel sorry for me. When she said they were leaving the pool hall and invited me to go with them, I did. I got in the back of someone's dad's car and sat next to Kathryn. When the beer was passed around, I took one. When Kathryn's hand crept up my thigh, I let it. We drove out of town, crossing that bridge over the same river I'd dragged Jolene out of the summer before. I tossed empty beer can after empty beer can out the window, silently damning that crying Indian with each one. Images of Jolene and Lester together became real in my drunken fog. I turned to Kathryn and her open mouth and her darting tongue. She tasted like beer and pepperoni and longing, and I devoured her. When the car stopped under a grove of trees, Kathryn was on me, her hands working quickly at the buttons on my jeans. I'd have been embarrassed, but the same sort of thing was going on in the front seat. I put my hand on the top of her head as she sank into my lap. I leaned back and closed my eyes and floated down a green river.

I was drunk as hell when they dropped me off. I fell out of the back seat onto the ground and Kathryn giggled, slouching over so her head was hanging out the door close to mine. The headlights came straight for the car, and I put my hand up to shield my drooping eyes. Gip's car jumped the curb and he cut the engine. I could see him behind the wheel, his head swirling in a figure eight.

"Oh shit," Kathryn said, pulling herself back into the car. "Come over tomorrow night. My parents won't be home. I'll pick you up."

"Go," I said. "Get out of here."

Gip picked me up off the sidewalk. We leaned into each other, struggled up the stairs, pushed through the front door. The two of us, wasted and worthless, stumbled down the long hallway. I collapsed into bed, splayed my arms to counter the spinning. The last thing I remember was Gip sitting on the end of the bed, his back to me, the mattress sloping toward the girth of him.

I ROLLED OUT OF BED at noon, head throbbing, bile surging up my throat. My jeans were wadded up on the floor, which reminded me that I'd had them down around my hips the night before, reminded me of what I'd done with Kathryn. What I'd done to Jolene. I pulled them on, slipped a T-shirt over my head, though lifting my arms made my head pulse. I walked into the kitchen, braced for the shit I'd catch from Gip for coming in drunk.

They were eating boiled hot dogs and beans at the table.

"That coffee still warm?" I asked.

"Should be," Ruby said.

"Boy was fucked up when he come home," Gip offered. "I waited up for him. Had to help him into the house."

What's the point, I thought. *Why does he even bother to make up a story when most nights he came in drunk anyway?* "Yeah, alright," I said.

"That the Rook girl you were with?" Gip asked.

I poured coffee into a stained mug and gulped it like it might flush the poison out of my system. "Yup."

"About time you wised up, got rid of that Indian. You play your cards right now."

"What's that supposed to mean?"

"Let me put it this way," he said. "Burt Rook don't give me the time of day. Barely knows my name despite the fact I been paying rent to him almost thirteen years. Always looking down his nose at people, that one. Quick to take what don't belong to him. Like this house here. We used to own it. I missed a few payments years back, hit a rough patch. Rook was still wet behind the ears then, not much older than Valerie. Him and his banker buddies, they seized it. Said it belonged to them. Yeah, you stick it to the daughter and we all stick it to Burt Rook."

Laughter wheezed out of him from some clamped-down place in his belly. "Can't wait to see Burt Rook's face when I tell him." He faked a boastful, earnest expression, puffing up his chest and tucking in his chin. "Well, hey there, Burt. Looks like our kids are something of an item again. Isn't that swell?" Gip could hardly contain himself as he continued. "Maybe I'll invite him and the missus and their girl over to the house for dinner. What you think about that, Ruby?"

"Keep your big mouth shut, is what I think. We don't want trouble. I don't like this one bit. Why's it so hard for you to find your own, Wes? Going between a whore and a squaw like that."

I slammed my cup on the counter. "Would you two shut up? None of this is your business. None of it. I don't know what sort of trailer trash you think would suit me, but I'll be sure to keep an eye out."

I shut myself in the bedroom, where everything closed in on me. I should have stayed in Brookings, should have gone with Topeka, should have sat down next to Jolene, shouldn't have gone to the Idle Hour. I shouldn't have gotten out of the cot at the cabin, should have stopped her from going out onto the ice in the first place. Shouldn't have let go of her hand, should never have let him leave my hospital room, shouldn't have come to Loma. I shouldn't have been so greedy to get with Kathryn in the first place, should have been more worthy of Jolene from the start. Should have told Lester I loved the girl. Should have told the girl. Shouldn't have started drinking. Should have been less like my father, less like my grandfather. Should have been more like . . . I had no one. All doors were shut. Before I knew it, the old knife was in my hand, the knobby bone rippling my palm when I gripped it. Nightfall swept across the ceiling while I stared at it and thought of ways I could make things right with that knife. What it could fix and what it could damage. I heard a familiar horn and remembered Kathryn saying she was coming to get me. I strapped the knife to my belt, threw on my jacket, and left the house in a trance. She was waiting behind the wheel. I got in.

The Rooks' house was in the center of town, off Main Street in the right direction. It was brick and square, solid, white door, white trim on the windows. Flimsy drapes drawn. Kathryn pulled the yellow car into the driveway around back. "Out," she'd said. "For the night. I told them I was staying in, watching television."

I nodded, followed her through the back door, through the mudroom where she hung her coat, kicked off her shoes, and made me do the same. We were in her kitchen, appliances that matched each other and the linoleum on the floor, wallpaper with vertical stripes pin straight and pattern matched, pictures of flowers and fruit perfect enough to smell and taste. "Sit down," she said. "You want something to eat?"

The light came on in the refrigerator. Milk, juice, eggs. Containers upon containers. Condiments in the door, multiple jars of jelly and preserves. The kitchen smelled clean, like grease never sizzled there, fish wasn't poached, nothing ever burned. "Whatever you're having," I said.

I'd never been in a kitchen so neat, like something out of a magazine. "Do you have servants?"

"Servants? What sort of people do you think we are, Wes? I mean, we have a housekeeper."

I ran my finger along the chair rail like I'd seen done in movies. It came up clean, but I wiped it on my jeans anyway. "She does a good job."

Kathryn cut the sandwich diagonally, then licked the mustard off her finger slowly, for me. "Here," she said, setting the plate on the table along with one of her father's bottled beers. "Eat."

My mother made her bologna sandwiches like that, lots of mayonnaise and mustard, a slice or two of meat, soft white bread that tacked to the roof of your mouth. She'd crush barbecue potato chips in with it, squash them into the bologna for crunch. Kathryn watched me eat, her elbows back against the counter so her chest burst forward out of her sweater. "You going to tell me what happened with you and Jolene Oliver?"

"What does it matter?" I said, as much to Kathryn as to myself. I swigged the beer and took another from the refrigerator. "You mind?"

"Be my guest."

She grabbed two more beers, then led me out of the kitchen, through a living room with tightly upholstered furniture—light colored because no one would spill, because no one would be allowed to eat in a room like that—up the carpeted stairs. I held onto the polished banister that didn't wobble or creak, watched Kathryn's ass sway like ripe fruit.

Her room was lavender and blue, soft and round like her. She turned on a lamp that shone on a cold painting above her bed of mountains and a blue stream. It reminded me of motel room paintings. Placeless and false.

I stood there, not sure what I was supposed to do next. Kathryn prowled up to me, pretending to be a woman who'd had a man before, pretending we were not still kids really.

"So . . ." she said. "Take off your jacket."

"Right."

"Don't be nervous. I'm ready. I have everything we need. Why don't you sit down," she said, pushing me gently onto the end of the bed. "I'm going to go slip out of these clothes. I'll be right back. You make yourself comfortable." She set the beers down. "Have another."

She disappeared into her own bathroom. I quickly drank another beer, fell back. The picture was upside down now, and I was trapped under ice or paint. I imagined my palms on the underside of the water, trying to push my way out. The bed spun like a whirlpool. I allowed myself to get sucked down, hoping there'd be a way out once I hit bottom.

"Are you ready?" Kathryn called from the bathroom.

I tried to block out the lake cabin, the hole in the ice, the sound of the loon's cry. *It's just sex,* I told myself. And then there was Jolene, emerging from the river, glowing like sunset followed her wherever she went. I opened my eyes and Kathryn was standing in front of me, backlit by the bathroom light. She was wearing a baby-blue bra and panties and nothing else.

"Ta-da!" she said as she spun around, obviously impressed with her ample, flawless body.

The thought of her in that bed—me naked with her and touching her body, climbing on top of her, then putting myself inside her—made me feel queasy and repulsed. I couldn't do what she wanted me to do. I pushed myself to standing, locked my knees.

Her hands flew to her hips.

"Wes Ballot! Get undressed! You're making me feel silly."

I rubbed my temples to clear my head. "I have to go," I said. "I can't do this. I really can't."

"What do you mean, you can't? Of course you can. You're just nervous. Here," she said, "let me help you." She moved closer, undid my belt buckle, and dropped my pants.

"Kathryn."

She shoved my chest lightly, enough to tangle me in my jeans so I'd fall back onto the bed. She straddled me, reached behind her back to unhook her bra, freeing white breasts to sway close to my face. I wormed out from under her and sat on the edge of her frilly bed.

"No," I said. "I . . . I don't want to."

"Don't be afraid," she said. I'd heard that sound in a voice before and I'd seen that look in pleading eyes. She had a plan and her plan included me. I shook my head, stood, and hoisted my pants up. She grabbed my wrists and tried to pull me down, but I yanked free.

"Let go of me!" The knife had fallen out of the sheath and was there on the floor. I grabbed it like I would use it to defend myself against attack, pointing it underhand to take quick, short jabs.

In the full-length mirror, I saw Kathryn cowered against her headboard, covering her bare breasts with her elbow. "I thought you'd want this. I thought you wanted me." Her hand flew to her mouth when she saw the knife. "Go!" she screamed. "Get out!"

In the reflection, I saw myself as she saw me, my people at their worst—a predator, a loser. A fatal mistake.

I dropped the knife, backed out of the room, hands up, all apology. I practically fell down the carpeted stairs, Kathryn's cries following me like a banshee. I took a bottle of good scotch from the open liquor cabinet, grabbed my shoes, and stumbled out the back door in my stocking feet. Headlights from the banker's car, green as money, blinded me. I shielded my eyes with the arm holding the bottle. The mother jumped out of the car first, her shellacked hair glowing white in the dark night.

"Oh my Lord!" Her hand went to her throat. I spun around to her side, figuring it was safer to run past her than risk a body check by Burt Rook. He was out next, palm slapping the roof of his car, demanding I return to the scene of the crime his shouting voice seemed certain I had committed.

When I was sure he wasn't following me, I stopped to get my shoes on. Clutching the scotch bottle by the neck, I walked past the Main Street Market and the little house behind it where Lester lived. The house was dark. Lester's car wasn't there. I drank my way through town, turned left onto Jolene's street. Mona's station wagon and the Bronco were parked by the garage. Lester's Impala was parked on the side street under a light, waxed and shiny like it was somehow better than every other car, like the light of God was shining down on it, protecting it, keeping it safe. I hated that car and I hated its owner. "Fuck you," I whispered, and leaned against it, purposefully rubbing the rivets on my back pockets against the paint. I took another drink, skimmed my belt for the missing knife, the pilled suede of the empty sheath coarse against my palm. I could see it like I'd been there when it happened. How he'd swooped in the second I left town. I imagined him maneuvering Jolene into the back seat of the Impala, or lying with her on the bed under the window. It was like a bloodletting—it felt good to think the worst, to wallow in the pain instead of always, always holding it away from me. It was Lester's throat I should slit. I imagined doing it, sneaking up on him, grabbing his long hair in my right hand. He'd beg me to stop, and grab at my hand that yanked his hair, not realizing the other one held a knife. Then, I'd speak his name so he'd know it was me and in one backhanded motion slice through his neck from ear to ear. His tendons unlashed in my hand. There'd be a gush of blood and I would smear it like war paint on my cheeks.

In my murderous thoughts, I was covered in the blood of my enemy. I could feel it trickling down my face, taste the mineral salt on my lips as I slowly scraped them clean with my teeth. I let my head drop on the hood of the Impala. Even victory felt like defeat. I kicked the fender of Lester's car, then kicked it again. I expected the porch light to come on, for Lester to come flying out to finish me off. Part of me welcomed it. Then I remembered. He always left the keys in the ignition.

I took another drink, threw the bottle on the passenger seat. I revved the engine enough that every house around would hear, boxing gloves on a speed bag, then laid a patch of tire on the asphalt as I tore off. My body prickled like I had been put to sleep and was waking. If I was going to fuck it up, I was going to fuck it up good.

The Impala's gas pedal was touchy and the gear shift tight. I was loose with whiskey and hopped it several times, gearing up and down. I swerved my way out of town like a tornado. I clipped a mailbox that flew over the car and into the road in my rearview. *Who cares?* I thought. *No one, that's who,* my thoughts answered.

I hadn't planned to go to the river but found myself there anyway. I killed the engine in the middle of the road on that bridge Jolene and I had jumped from months before. I closed my eyes, willed it to be summer again, wished that the billows of white in the headlights were fluff from a cottonwood tree instead of a snow flurry. I rolled down the window. Skunk and bark clung to the night air along with that smell of snow about to fall. I pressed my knuckles into my eyes until I thought I might crush them. I left the door open and leaned out over the guardrail. The river wound off into the distance, a gray-blue ribbon behind the night's dark dress. Dangling myself over the edge, I watched the water flow from behind me, to beneath me, and finally away from me. And I thought of Jolene and this river that belonged to her and me. I remember thinking, *If I could go back to that one moment when I kissed her. If I could go back to that spot or to the minutes before when we were under the green water together with the silver specks of mica and fish scales floating around us, catching in our hair, and sticking to our wet bodies.*

And I saw myself then on the riverbank far below, holding Jolene's face in my hands as if she was something new and precious brought to life. And her brown body was pressed into mine and she touched my hair and my cheek and it was all gone. I leaned over the rail, trying to see them, as if I could lure them out again from under the bridge or wherever it was they were hiding. I put one foot on the rail and then another. Little waves rippled over rocks, their fingers and hands beckoning me. But even that I couldn't do.

I stepped down, collapsed my back on the metal rail, raised my arms over my head in surrender. "I give," I said to no one. I'm not sure how long I sat there before the bridge let out a low rumble. Troy pulled up in Mona's station wagon and stopped behind the stolen Impala. He walked toward me, holding a twisted mailbox in his hand like the head of Medusa. Lester got out of the passenger's side and went to the aid of his precious hot rod.

"Looks like you went on quite the killing spree, Wes," Troy said. I lowered my head.

"Fucking A, Ballot," Lester said. His jaw was square and tight.

I lowered my head and charged him. He flew off his feet and we were both on the ground. An elbow to my throat, his ribs against my fist, his knee in my thigh, his hair in my hand. It happened quickly, the flip, the pin, my head slamming the pavement. Troy pulled Lester off me in a matter of seconds, though Lester had time to pound me good but didn't.

"Okay, there, tough guy." Troy's hand was out to keep Lester off me. "I said you could come along provided you could control yourself."

"Me! What about Ballot? He's the one that stole my car. He's the one that came after me." Lester raised his shoulders, puffed out his chest. I expected him to spit on me. Instead, "I thought we were friends."

"Yeah, I did, too." I ground my palms into roadside gravel laced with broken glass and rusted shrapnel to feel a pain someplace other than inside me. I got my knees, then my feet under me, brushed my hands against my jeans. "That why you stole Jolene from me? Because we're such good friends?" I touched the back of my throbbing head, checked for blood on my fingertips. "First chance you get . . . right in there."

"This is about Jolene? Christ, you're an even bigger idiot than I thought you were."

"Enough now, boys," Troy said. "Lester, you got your car back. Now go home."

Lester wiped his mouth, pushed his hair out of his face. "Just for the record, I would never horn in on a buddy. Not my style. You need to get your shit detector fixed." That night, I couldn't put it together, how knowing my father wasn't coming back made me want to sabotage everything, wreck it all, because hope was too heavy. It's easier to carry nothing. All I got at the time was that Lester was telling the truth and that I'd fucked up.

"Keys are in it." I couldn't even look him in the eyes.

He gunned the engine, turned the car around in the middle of the road, and was gone.

"C'mon, son. I'll take you home," Troy said.

"I don't wanna go home. I don't wanna go anywhere." I looked at the mailbox, watched the taillights of Lester's dented Impala disappear. "I'm in a heap of trouble, Troy."

"We'll deal with that tomorrow. Right now, you need to sleep this off. Go on and get in Mona's car."

I let Troy take me home. Once inside, I stumbled past my grandparents' bedroom door, collapsed onto the bed, the whiskey spinning me to dark sleep.

CHAPTER 18

I HEARD THE BANGING ON THE DOOR, RUBY YELLING FOR GIP TO answer it, Gip's heavy footsteps in the hallway. The sun was barely up, and it was unclear to me in the moment whether I was hungover or still drunk. My head throbbed and with each pulse, memories broke free like gumballs joggled out of a machine. Before I could piece it all together, Gip burst into the bedroom.

He kicked the bed, jostling me sideways. "Get up, Prince Charming. Get some clothes on."

I sat up slowly, like the flesh and bone of me had to drag my heavy soul up from the old sheets. I fingered the blinds apart, squinted at even the dim light. The green-as-money car was out front.

I took in air, blew it out. *Fuck me.*

Burt Rook was standing by the front door, dressed for work in a suit and tie, shoes clean enough, hair up straight, high and tight. Ruby was in a housecoat and slippers, Gip in his work overalls, though he only had a thermal shirt under them. I stung with sickness from gut to groin. I tried to drain expression from my face. What did he want? What did he know?

Coffee percolated in the kitchen. It was the only sound in the room. We stood there looking at each other longer than was natural until finally Ruby said, "So?" Rook spread his legs wide, to make himself look big, I suppose. "Your grandson stole something from me last night. A bottle of scotch."

"You're here over a missing bottle of booze?" Gip asked.

"It was an expensive bottle, Furniss."

"Seein' how the boy's hungover, I'm guessing that bottle's gone. How much you want for it? Give him money, Wes. Go on." Gip shoved me, but I stood my ground. Burt Rook was not there for my money.

"Mind telling me what you were doing in my home last night?" He put his head back, scrunched his lips to cover his nostrils, like there was a stench he wanted to block. "I distinctly remember telling you to stay off my property."

"What's he talking about, his property?" Ruby asked.

He turned his attention to Gip and Ruby. "The wife and I saw him sneaking out of our house like a common thief."

"Kathryn invited me over. We ate sandwiches."

"Seems you did more than that." Had they found Kathryn half-naked, curled around some stuffed animal? Had she told them some story to cover the truth?

"Less than she wanted."

I could see I'd struck a nerve with Burt Rook. He sagged and his eyes widened.

"You shut the hell up before I shut you up," Gip said to me. His voice simpered, cajoled. "I'm sorry about that. Boy's got no place. Now, your daughter. She's not hurt, is she? No real harm?"

The banker hiked up his pants by the belt loops and laughed. Laughed at me, laughed at Gip. "No harm done, Furniss. He took advantage of her kindness, is all. She never could resist a stray, no matter how mangy."

Ruby pulled her hands from the pockets of her housecoat, crossed her arms hard.

He pulled an envelope out of his breast pocket. "I'm going to speak frank with you all. We're selling this house. The bank is getting out of the property business. Goes on the market in a month, so we'll need you out by then." He hesitated before adding, "That is of course unless you have down payment money and want to take another run at home-ownership. Can't stop you from buying it outright."

Gip's voice was tight as a rubber band. "What are you talking about? You can't do this."

"I assure you, Furniss, I can do as I please."

"But we've paid you our rent. That ought to count for something."

"Even you know that's not how rent works. You couldn't make the payments and we repossessed the house. It doesn't matter if that was yesterday or twenty years ago. Now we're selling it." He handed the envelope to Gip, who took it without thinking. "Your eviction notice."

Gip let the envelope fall to the floor.

"You'll turn us out over this? A couple of kids horsing around?" Gip said, waving his arm. "Bank promised we could stay as long as we made the rent."

Burt Rook pushed back his jacket and pulled out my knife. "This familiar?"

Alarm flashed in Ruby's eyes, though she was cool not to implicate me directly. Gip took a step back, clutched at the pocket on the front of his overalls. His face drained to white. Ruby looked at him like she thought he might have a heart attack on the spot. I stepped forward to take what was coming.

"It's mine."

Gip's head swung my way. I met his stare as he sized me up.

"I put up with Kathryn's slumming. I knew she was just trying to get a rise out of me. But then he takes up with that Indian girl—everyone in town has seen them—and has the nerve to bring her filth into my house. No. I cannot abide that. I won't."

Electric rage locked every joint in my body.

Ruby stepped sideways to get between me and Rook. She put her chicken arm down, a crossing gate against a locomotive. "Jesus Christ," she said. "You are a son of a bitch."

"To be clear, this eviction business has been in the works awhile. But now seems as good a time as any to give you notice, don't you think?" He dropped his smile and, with a single flick, tried to stick the knife into the envelope. It flopped onto the mashed-pea carpeting. He shrugged off his failed attempt at drama. "Suppose it goes without saying, but you"—he swung his whole hand at me like an ax—"you stay away from my daughter." He opened the door and stepped out like all he'd done was drop off the mail. "You all have a good day, now."

We stood there long enough to realize he wasn't coming back. Gip slapped the door with his open hand. His breath caught in spurts, huffing out like steam from an old radiator, seething through his clenched jaw. "All over that filthy piece of tail. Got no more sense than Val, screwing all the wrong people all the damned time."

I pulled back to take a swing at him, but he caught my fist and pushed me back against the door. "Try that again and I'll knock your block off, boy."

Before I could get my footing back, Ruby stepped up to me, then got even closer so I could smell her foul breath piping right into my face. I tried to turn my head and not look at her. I wanted to duck away, but she'd gotten too close. "Good for nothing," she said, pushing on my chest with each word. I wished I had that knife in my hand, but I'm glad I didn't. She stepped away from me, shaking mad. She stamped around like fire ants were crawling all over her skin.

"And you!" she said, pointing at Gip. "You and your 'put it to her.' That all you ever think about, screwing girls? I should have known. Wasn't no way a girl like that was right to take up with the likes of him," she said, turning on me again. "Look at yourself. You? Gip? Me? We're nothing. What did I do to deserve this, anyhow? What did I ever goddamned do? Tell me that. You fix this, goddamn it." She screamed into Gip's face, her bony hands, veins inflated, flapping on the ends of her wrists. "You do whatever you got to do, you kowtow to that banker, but you fix this. This is all I got." She stormed down the hallway and slammed the bathroom door.

Gip kicked over an end table, sent a gold glass lamp crashing to the floor. "Shit. I never should have agreed to this, taking you in. Goddamn it! I don't even want to look at you." He stomped on the eviction notice, ignored the knife. "Goddamn it to hell, now I'm late for work." Blackness gathered around him and he raised his fist to me. "Where's mine? Where is mine?" He slammed the door, then opened it and slammed it again, then again until the whole house quaked.

I knew the cracks and warts of that house, the gurgles in the pipes, the droop and creak in the hallway outside the bathroom where leaking had warped the floorboards. I'd grown accustomed to heat that didn't always work in the winter and the damp, medicinal smell of mold in the summer. The freight train rattled my window twice a week, always on schedule. What did any of this matter to me? What was keeping me with these people? Wherever they went next, I didn't have to go with them. I didn't owe them anything. In that envelope on the floor, next to my mother's knife, was freedom or a coffin nail. I picked up the knife and left the envelope on the floor.

Ruby's voice shot down the hallway from inside the bathroom. "He gone?"

I nodded, though she couldn't see me. "He's gone," I yelled back.

She scuffed up to me, her slippers dragging more than usual. "Give that to me."

I bent to pick up the eviction notice.

"Not that, stupid. The knife. That don't belong to you. Give it to me."

The anger came back at me in a wave. I turned on her like she'd broken a twig in a still forest. I held the knife up, then pointed it at her. "What? This?"

Her eyes twitched back and forth, her lips puckered. She folded her arms across her chest.

"Who was she afraid of?"

"Don't you got school?"

"Not going. Who was she afraid of?"

Now it was her turn to push past me. I followed her to the kitchen. She reached into the refrigerator and pulled out two cans of beer. Every bone in my body quivered. I pulled out a chair, eased into it. I set the knife down in front of me, careful to line it up parallel to the edge of the table, to make it neat.

She sat next to me and popped open the beers, pushing one to me. It was nine o'clock in the morning. She tilted her cigarette pack toward me in question.

I shook my head. "Just tell me."

She lit up. "God, that girl." She sucked in a mouthful of air, scratching at years of exhaustion cracked into the flesh between her eyebrows.

"I told him to leave her be."

"Who, Ruby?" I knew. I needed to hear her say it.

She put her elbows on the table and looked at me straight, searched my face. Then she went back to her beer can, back to her cigarette. "Gip," she said. "That lemon smell of hers. All over him. Made me sick to my stomach." She rocked in the still chair, back and forth, a rhythm of confession rolling out of her.

Say he snuck in at night, while Ruby was asleep in the next room. Or maybe she was awake and watched him go. Maybe she sat in a dark kitchen lit only by a burning ash and watched the shadow at the end of the hall open and close the door. Say she tiptoed down that hall and opened the door a crack. Did she see the hulk of my grandfather mounting the bed? Did Ruby listen for grunts like the ones I heard through paper-thin walls? Did she hear protests, whimpers? Did she ever raise a finger to protect my mother? I set the beer can down on the table with shaking hands. Ruby's words buzzed in my ears. Gip's smell fouled the air. "Why didn't you stop him?"

She rocked away. "I tried to catch him. I did. Then I found out she was gonna have a baby. I thought Gip might have done it. 'Course she was running around with Moss by then. She swore up and down it was him got her pregnant and it was me who was disgusting for saying otherwise."

As much as I tried, I could not stop the tears. I picked up the knife, touched the tip to my palm, imagined running it through the bone gaps. "What's that got to do with this?"

"You seen the way he looked at it. I know you did. Like another hand was holding it. Oh, he knows that knife alright. I put two and two together, is all." She sucked down the rest of her beer and let her eyes rest on the long hallway. "She cooed at babies like they was puppies, even when she was a little girl. She'd stop ladies anywhere—the street, the market—and get right down into the stroller, real close. Made some of them uncomfortable, this stranger touching the little fingers and toes." Ruby's face shifted and crumbled. Her crying came out more like a gasp, a thing long denied. "I didn't want to lose her. I thought Gip might take her away and they'd both be gone."

I finished off my beer and got up from the table. "I have to get out of here."

Ruby grabbed me by the arm. "Don't go. Don't leave me."

A chill froze me in place and I knew for a heartbeat that feeling. I would not be dragged down.

"What kind of people are you, anyway? Who does that to a child?" I grabbed the weapon between us. "This belongs to me now." I was on the edge of something. If I had been up high somewhere—on a bridge, a cliff, a building—I would have jumped, been done with blankness for good. I stuck the knife in my back pocket and grabbed my coat from the hook.

I couldn't get away from her fast enough.

To no surprise, I found myself on the sidewalk in front of Jolene's house. Dry snow covered the ground in a pilled flannel sheet. Wind whipped the trees, clacking branch against branch like locking antlers. The sky was smoke gray. I stared at the house as if it were an apparition, conjured from a time before when I'd felt I almost belonged there. Now it looked shut off, cold as my bare hands. Troy appeared from around the side of the house.

"Wes. What are you doing here? Shouldn't you be in school?"

"Well, I wanted to apologize to you about last night. And to thank you. I also thought maybe I should talk to Jolene. Guess I kind of forgot it was a weekday. My head's not on straight."

He cinched his clay-colored canvas coat together and snapped it shut. "Come around back with me. Let's you and me talk."

The Bronco was backed into the garage, the hood propped up with a stick, an oily red rag lying over the edge of the fender. Troy pulled the stick out and let the hood slam down. He hopped up and sat, his long legs dangling near to the ground. He motioned to the spot next to him and we sat there together, watching the road go nowhere. He chewed on a larch twig he pulled from the gully between the hood and the windshield. I could tell he was trying to figure out what to say to me, so I tried to be patient. Birds were chirping all around us, preparing for migration. Their general cheeriness made me more aware of the unpleasant pounding in my head. I waited there for my punishment, not saying a word.

Finally he looked at me. "What the hell got into you, Wes?"

What could I say to him? It seemed impossible I'd been so stupid, yet that was exactly what I was. I also wanted to answer with something about my father, about Topeka, but still I couldn't see what one had to do with the other. I wanted to maybe tell him about what Ruby had said, about my knife, about Gip, but all that was salt in the wound. Maybe I could tell him I was about to become a bum along with my grandparents because my recklessness had lost them their home. Maybe he would feel sorry for me then. I felt sorry and pitiful.

"Got drunk, I guess."

"Don't much explain it, you ask me. I've seen lots of good people slip down the neck of that bottle until they're no better than the worm. It's poison. You don't want that in your blood."

I thought then about all of them, my whole family, and the poison they'd deposited in my blood that stained the person I was. It was like anyone looking at me could see what I'd amount to, and none of it was any good at all.

"Do you think I'm like them, my grandparents?" I asked.

He spat a plug of stick onto the ground. "I don't know them all that well, Wes, so it's not for me to say how you might be like them. But I know you. And I think you're better than what I've been seeing."

"Sometimes I feel like . . . I don't know. Like something ugly is growing inside me."

"Something inside you?" He grunted, bobbing his head, sizing me up. "No," he repeated, patting my leg. He took the twig out of his mouth. "I ever tell you I'm proud of you, Wes? All the grief with your mom going under the ice? Your dad taking off on you? Plus, you got those grandparents of yours? That's a lot for one person to take. But you've been nothing but decent here with my family and me."

"I'm not sure I can handle much more, you know?" I shook my head, turned away. "Feels like everything is closing in around me. Like I need to run or something."

"I know what you mean. Restlessness. Fear. Sometimes both. Make you crazy," he said, tapping his temple. "You need to think of it this way. Each new day is like a new life. More chances to make good and be honorable. That sun goes down, it can take sorrow with it, leave it on the other side if we let it. But you, you hold onto things." Troy clutched nothing in his big hand as he gently tapped his belly. "You keep looking for someone else to make you whole, make it better. So much yearning. So much fight."

I put my elbows on my knees, rested my stacked fists on my forehead, felt the throbbing hangover in my thumbs, heard it thumping on my eardrums.

Troy whistled, puffed breath into his cupped hands. "Getting to be winter for sure."

I sat back up. How long would this stalling go on? "Yup."

"Good time for a story. I got one for you."

I let out a pained sigh. Nothing Troy liked better on a Sunday morning than telling old stories about some poor guy shitting himself or getting a stick shoved into his butt. "Please tell me it's not another one of your rectum stories."

Troy laughed, slapped my back. "I do like a good snake-climbing-out-the-butt story, but no. This one is about an epic struggle for the heart of a woman. Listen now and I'll tell it to you."

His voice turned soft and he set his eyes on a spot down the road. "Ah-ah. So back in the beginning, before things were decided, a girl blossoms into a woman and her father knows, before long, the young men would come for her. He is right. All the boys in the village come to his lodge, tell the father how great they are. But none would do. Soon enough the village is overrun with hunters and warriors from the horizon and beyond, all of them come to prove themselves worthy. '*Gaawiin. Gaawiin. Gaawiin.* No. No. No,' the father would say.

"Then along comes this young man called Ziigwan. He doesn't come with feathers in his war bonnet, he has no weapons. He is gentle, handsome. Fistful of flowers of all colors in one hand, a basketful of fresh berries in the other. The girl falls for him right away. Everyone does. A date is set for the couple to wed, sew their garments together in unity. So, it's good, right? Everyone's happy, right? Not so fast.

"Along comes another man, a strong warrior with an impressive war bonnet. He'd heard about this clever, beautiful girl and traveled to see her even though she'd already made her match. Biboon, that was his name. He sees her and is in love, just like that." Troy snapped his fingers and, for a moment, the spell lifted.

I had a sinking feeling how this would end. "Yeah. So?"

"So Biboon, he challenges gentle Ziigwan, who didn't have much of a chance, let's be honest. Beats him to a pulp, leaves him to die."

"I get it," I said. "No chance."

"You going to let me finish? So Biboon goes back day in and day out, beats poor Ziigwan, until finally defeated, he slinks out of the village. He says to the girl, '*Giga-wabamin menawah.*' I shall see you again. Everyone laughs. How could he come back?

"Now Biboon is all full of himself, shows what a fierce warrior he is, what a skilled hunter, fights off war parties, kills partridges and deer, all sorts of game. Then one day he returns weary and hungry from a hunting expedition, and there's Ziigwan, brought back to life and full of vengeance. He attacks Biboon. Savages him, over and over."

I perked up.

"Now, the table is turned and it's Biboon who is begging for mercy, Biboon who leaves in shame. With him gone, Ziigwan is able to win the girl's affection again and there was warmth and beauty all around them. You're probably thinking, 'That's that.' But it's not. Biboon returns and the whole thing starts over. Back and forth, back and forth. The fighting, the exhaustion, the retreat. These warriors become so focused on beating each other, they forget what they are fighting for. They did not honor that maiden by fighting over her. You see, Wes? You see?"

Troy hadn't glanced over at me once while he spoke, choosing instead to focus on an invisible audience who sat quietly, rapt like I was. The words came out one at a time, like he was surprised when the next one appeared, like he hadn't heard or told the story before. But now he shifted, rested his hand on my shoulder.

"Troy, it wasn't just Jolene. It was a lot of things."

"You don't think I know that? Just listen. So, the poor girl, lonely and in despair, paddles out in a canoe to the middle of the lake, and she tosses herself in. Goes under. Her father calls for her. But nothing. She's gone. The next morning a water lily appears right where she went in, next to her drifting canoe."

Another girl lost to a lake. I looked to Troy for any good news. "What about the fighters, Biboon and Zeeg—"

"Ziigwan. Those doofuses keep fighting, year in and year out. Spring, winter. Spring, winter." He hopped down from the hood, stood up straight, so I did, too. He put his flat palm on my chest and I felt the heat of his knowing. The lines in his face were deep, weathered by sun and wind. "You can waste an awful lot of time fighting. End up hurting innocent people. End up punching yourself, right?"

He put his arm around my shoulder and I sunk into it. "You think she hates me?"

"She doesn't hate you. Give her time to cool off."

"You don't know. I've kind of fucked things up."

"That's true. Come clean with her. Then you got to fix things with Lester. You got a bone to pick with him, you pick it. Then be done with it."

"I'll talk to Lester. Make it right. These are my mistakes to answer for."

"Without winter, how would we know to welcome spring? No death, no rebirth. Accept the cycle of things. How about I'll talk to Jolene for you. You come around in a day or two."

Troy tossed the last of his twig into the alley. In some ways, Troy was like my father, full of himself, full of stories. But where Troy was steady and generous, my father had been mostly unmovable, stubborn even, stingy with affection. Always, my mother and I were trying to earn it. And here was Troy, pulling me into him, hugging me like I'd done nothing wrong. "Take courage," he said. "Things will work out."

I tried to hold on to that courage he gave me along with the good feeling of his embrace when I walked back into the house. Ruby was gone. The house was empty. I stood inside, closed my eyes, breathed in the smell of it, trying to suss what it was that made it smell the way it did. It wasn't animal or vegetable so it had to be mineral—some desiccated amalgam of spilled blood and wishes left for dead. I walked the plank of hallway, disappeared behind the door. I would sleep a day away and dream for hours and hours of spring flowers and girls at the bottom of lily-covered lakes.

THE NEWSPAPER WAS SPRAWLED ON the table in front of Gip the next morning. He was down to four days a week, his winter schedule at the feed mill, which meant he was taking on more shifts behind the bar to make up for the lost wages. And that meant more drinking, more late nights. No wonder my mother hated winter.

"What do you want me to do? I got no clout," he said. I'd walked into the middle of an argument. "You think I can waltz into that bank and insist they let us stay on? He sits in that office of his. I know he's there but his girl says I can't even make an appointment."

"Well, I'm not going anywhere." Ruby poured more coffee into her cup and planted herself next to him like she was stuck in cement.

He threw the classifieds at her. "Find someplace or we'll be out on the street."

She let it fall to the ground, then stomped it with her feet, over and over. "That's what I think of your classifieds."

"Don't just stand there," Gip said, turning his sights on me.

"What did I do?" I said.

Gip tossed his head side to side, mocking me. "'What did I do?' Nothing's what you did. You'll have no place either in a couple weeks unless you plan to move onto the reservation. Fat lot of good either of you are. I'm going downtown."

"It's eight in the morning," Ruby said.

"And it's my day off. I'll do as I please." He pushed past me and out the door.

Ruby wadded up the stomped paper and shoved it in the trash. "You heard him. We got to figure something out."

"I got school, Ruby."

She sat down at the kitchen table. Invisible strings seemed to pull her body up, but her head lolled around. "You have to stay with me."

It was my mother's face aged, her voice weakened. Those same words again, off the ice. Life on repeat. I wouldn't be dragged down. "My mother said that to me, the night she died," I said. Ruby got up and walked into the living room. "Where are you going? I'm saying this whether you like it or not."

"I don't want to hear it," she said, her voice weak and pale.

She was sitting on the sofa, staring at the front window. I sat down next to her and looked at it, too. *One more time,* I thought. *I will try one more time.*

"Ruby, what you said about Gip, what he did. Makes me think about a lot of things. Makes me think about her that night. She and my dad arguing. When she fell through, she kept saying something like 'He's coming.' I thought she was talking about my dad." Ruby covered her ears, shaking her head back and forth like a little girl. I tried to imagine what Troy would do, how he would be gentle. I touched her arm and she flinched like I'd scorched her. "Ruby. What if it wasn't my dad but hers? Maybe that's why she called for you before she went under."

"I tried! That was cruel what you said to me yesterday. About not helping her. I might could have done better. So could have you. You let her go, too, you know."

The air in the room felt colder by degrees. I sat back against the couch in surrender. Ruby got up, took a thin sweater off a chair, and wiggled into it. "May as well turn up the heat," she mumbled, twisting the thermostat knob. "See this picture?" She snatched the crooked one off the wall. "He's the one brought me up to this godforsaken place. I never wanted to come here. It's cold." She held the picture close to her face, staring down her nose at it, like she was examining the details under a magnifying glass. "He made me old." She stilled her body a second more, then flung the picture like a hatchet. The glass shattered against the wall, the metal frame hit the floor. Ruby dropped into Gip's recliner.

"Let me get something to clean that up," I said.

"You can leave it right where it is for all I care."

I got the trash can and dropped the shards of glass and twisted metal on top of the classified ads. The picture was punctured. I set it on the shelf. "I'll leave this right here."

"You think you know everything. You think you got it all figured out. You couldn't save her any better than I could. Nobody can save no one don't want to be saved, and that's for sure. Now get out. I'm done talking."

I WAITED ON THE STOOP of the little house behind the market until school was out. I stood when I heard the rumble of the Impala's engine as it rounded the corner. The front fender on the passenger side looked like it had been opened up by a dull can opener. Lester got out of the car, cocked his head. “What now, Ballot?”

I’d seen too much sick and tired, that weariness that pulled at the edges of Ruby’s eyes, wheezed out of Gip in his labored exhales. I’d seen it in my mother, the way she stared out windows like the world on the other side was against her. And I felt it in me, begging me to weigh myself down, stone by stone, and sink.

“I’m a lousy friend.”

“Fucking right you are.”

“I’ll help you with the car.”

“No shit. So, you believe me? About Jolene? ”

“Yeah, I believe you.” I offered my hand to Lester. “So, we’re good?”

He pushed it away. “No, Ballot. We’re not good.” He snuffed, hocked. We both watched the glob of spit hit the pavement, then Lester slugged me in the stomach, doubling me over. “Okay, now we’re good.” He slapped my back and bent over to smile at me as I grimaced. “See you around.”

I knew I had it coming and it felt honest for a change. I coughed to get my breath back, checked to make sure I wasn’t hacking up blood. Hands on my knees still, I caught Lester as he was heading into the house. “Hey. How about you and me take a road trip?”

CHAPTER 19

I SPENT THAT NIGHT ON THE COUCH IN LESTER'S LIVING ROOM, WRAPPED in an afghan and an old felt blanket. Come morning, we headed over to the Hightowers'. I knew I'd have to talk to Jolene before we left, plus the cold was coming in fast along with ice and maybe snow the farther north we got. We would need tire chains for the Impala.

"That car okay to drive?" Troy asked.

"Simple assault," Lester said. "Not homicide."

"I'll need to look for those chains. Road trip, huh? Where you boys headed?"

I glanced at Lester, thinking how glad I was not to be making this trip by myself. "Lester and me"—I knew saying it would make it true—"we're going up to Bright Lake. Got a ration of shit yesterday from Ruby. Looks like they're losing the house, by the way. Bank's selling it. Anyway, after, you know, the water lily stuff—"

"Water lily stuff?" Lester asked.

I shook him off. "That, and what Ruby said, I want to go back there and look around. Think about some stuff. Thought it would be better not to go alone."

"Any excuse to get out of school, am I right?" Lester said, grinning his idiot grin.

Troy bunched up his mouth and nodded his head back. "Let me grab my boots. Why don't you boys come inside for some breakfast."

The look he gave me told me that he'd talked to Jolene and that now it was my turn.

THE HOUSE SMELLED GOOD LIKE always, buttered toast and coffee, linked sausages sizzling in a pan. Lester and I ambled into the kitchen, me more careful than him. Mona and Mariah were dressed, but Jolene was still in her robe and slippers. She stood when she saw me. Her arms were folded and one foot was forward in a boxing stance. I hoped she wasn't planning on hitting me, too.

"What are you doing here? And since when are you two buddies again?"

"We made up. After I tackled him. And he punched me."

"Not in the 'nads, Jo. Don't worry," Lester added.

She shook her head, clearly disgusted.

Every part of me wanted to grab onto her and never let her go. But I knew I had too much to sort out and that I was bound to screw up what might be my only chance with her if I didn't at least face up to some things. "Can we maybe go into the other room and talk for a minute?"

Mona helped rescue me. "Lester, why don't you sit down there next to Mariah and I'll make you some scrambled eggs. Troy will be back down in a minute." She smiled, a soft, pitiful thing, like there was no way I was going to salvage this but good for me for trying.

I STARTED WITH AN APOLOGY and backtracked to my conversation with Topeka, to the story my father had told him. Being so close to her reminded me that it had only been just over a week since we were on her bed together. Now we were so far apart. Her face softened. I dug my hands deeper into my coat pockets to keep from touching her cheek, tracing her scar with my fingertip. I stared at the ground. "I need to tell you something else. It's about Kathryn." I said it all quick as I could, not wanting to dwell on any of it. I told her about everything except what Ruby said about Gip. That I didn't have words for yet. "Aren't you going to say something?" Blood rushed in my ears and chest as I waited.

"I'm sorry about your trip."

I released the breath I was holding. "He's not coming back for me. He killed me off."

"I think it will be good, you going back up to Bright Lake. It's time."

"What about the other stuff, with Kathryn?"

"Well, if you think I'm going to stomp out of here all broken up, you're wrong. But you should have known I wouldn't . . ." She took a step back so she could see the kitchen doorway. Her voice dropped to a whisper. "Wes, what we did . . ." Her face glowed crimson. "You know I've never done that before. What did you think? I was going to hop into bed with someone I didn't care about? Maybe while you're doing all that thinking about your mom and dad, you ought to spend some time thinking about what it would mean to trust a person."

Unbrushed hair slipped out of her ponytail and danced loosely around her face. I tucked a strand behind her ear and we were caught there, quiet though the laughter from the kitchen was all around us. "I'm so sorry."

She knocked my hand away. "You get one strike. That was it. You're not going to hurt me, Wes."

"I'm not." I shook my head. "I'm not."

"We can talk more when you two get back. Let's get breakfast now, though. One of us is still planning to go to school today."

Before she walked away, I took her hand, cupped it in mine like a bird. I turned it over, then intertwined my fingers in hers.

She took a step closer to me, so she could look up and I could look down. "Jesus," I said, overwhelmed by her closeness. I had to stop myself from blurting out that I loved her, that I'd always love her.

Troy helped us dig a set of tire chains out from under shovels and engine parts in the garage, asking questions the whole time about what was going on with Gip and Ruby and the bank. I told him about how they had nowhere to go and that I didn't know what I would do once they figured out where that nowhere was. Lester moved things around haphazardly and walked away from us, though not quite out of earshot. He was embarrassed for me, I could tell. He'd never been privy to the details of my home. Later in the car, after we warmed the air with boy talk and bullshitting about basketball and girls, after I'd told him about Kathryn and he'd given me a ribbing about not seeing it through, I told him about the knife, about the night Gip came into my bedroom.

"So you think he, you know . . . I can't even fucking say it."

"All I know is that he climbed in there looking for my mom. I don't know what was going on. It makes me sick even thinking about it."

Lester and I made our way into the gray-and-green woods of northern Minnesota. Aside from traffic lights in pass-through towns, the only color came from cardinals and blue jays flitting in the trees. The road was rutted like frozen corduroy from winter after winter of freeze and thaw and salt. We ate pemmican and red licorice and drank can after can of Mountain Dew, stinking up the lukewarm car with burps and farts. When we got close enough for me to realize I had no recollection of how to actually get to Bright Lake, we stopped for a map and put on the tire chains since the dirt road around the lake was unplowed. After a few wrong turns, things started to look more familiar. "That's it," I said. "Down there." The roof of the cabin was barely visible. The approach hadn't been cleared at all, so Lester popped the car into reverse. He pulled off into the pines about a hundred yards from where the long driveway down to the cabin cut off from the main road.

"Chains won't help with that," he said. "Guess we're hoofing it."

We picked our way down based on where the trees weren't instead of where the road was. When the cabin came into full view, it seemed smaller, more ragged than I'd remembered. Had it shrunk or had I grown? One window was broken. Snapped pine branches lay across the roof like thatching.

I cupped my hands around my eyes and looked in. The shock of seeing it again wrung my insides.

"Well?"

"There ought to be a key around the side. Hold on," I said. I rummaged for the key like my father had but came up empty-handed.

"Hey," Lester yelled.

"I can't find it."

"It's not locked, dumbass."

I stood there with my hands in the shallow snow and dug a little more for a key I didn't need. I stood up slowly and walked into the past.

Nothing with color remained. Not the red ticking-striped mattresses, not the torn calico cushion on the chair my mother had used. The couch was gone. No amber bottles were on the counter, no red-labeled cans, no hunting pictures on the wall. A shadow was all that was left of the trophy buck that had stared down at me from over the fireplace. Someone had cleared the place out.

"Homey," Lester said, flashing the dumb grin again, slapping my back. "Glad we brought sleeping bags." He closed the door and walked past me to the fireplace. He pulled a flashlight out of his bag and stuck his head up to check the flue. "Looks good," he said. "Let's get some wood."

I nodded like I'd go with him, but I couldn't seem to move.

"You okay?"

"Yeah," I said. "Just . . . Give me a minute, will you?"

"Sure, man. Sure. How about I'll get the wood. You . . ." He patted my arm once and left me.

I could barely allow myself farther inside. Some ghost had led me there, some remnant, an echo or ripple. Ruby had grabbed my arm, Jolene had held my hand. But it was another woman's touch I was thinking about. And just like that, the past seeped out of the logs and chinks, wormed its way out of the floorboards, and descended from the rafters. The door creaked and color flowed back in. Valerie kicked the threshold, cursing the cheap boots she wore that kept her feet neither warm nor dry. She dropped a single bag on the wood floor. Behind her, a boy shorter than I was now, thinner, stomped his feet and rubbed his bare hands together. Mattresses and wool blankets appeared on the cots. The windowpane became unbroken. There was my father, on his knees, blowing on bits of paper to get the fire started. I could see that night unfolding, this time as an outsider, watching my mother sit alone at the missing table, using what Ruby had told me to put words in her mouth and thoughts in her head.

Busted boughs and pine cones and critter sounds tapped on the roof.

"How can anyone stand being out here? Feels like there are eyes everywhere." Her own eyes darted around the room like she was dodging people on a crowded street.

She stood up to get the bag she'd brought in, then stopped. She seemed to watch her fire-baked shadow as it bent at the knees and climbed the log walls. She stretched her arms slowly, sending long shadow fingers crawling along the ceiling and over the barely realized image of my former self as if she might scoop that boy up and sweep him into the dark rafters.

I watched her from the safety of time. I could almost see the wheels turning, her mind racing. Could she have known or feared her life was nearly over? Was she recalling that lost child? I tried to picture my mother as a teenage girl, pregnant, afraid of so many things. How had she even told my father about that first pregnancy? What strength had she mustered to tell him after all that had happened to her? When he asked her if it was his, she would have burst with a raging anger I'd seen plenty. She would have said yes in a way that left no doubt, whether she believed it to be true or not. And before he could say otherwise, she would have told him she was keeping it and did he want to be a family with them or not.

The cabin was cold, but sweat glistened on Valerie's forehead. She cocked her head up into the rafters as if something might be dangling there, dripping on her. She touched her hair, put her hand to her face, and sniffed it. She let out a cry and jumped up, patting herself all over like a woman caught on fire.

Lester's voice called out from the woods, coming in through the broken window. Valerie and Moss and the boy stopped what they were doing. They locked eyes with me before disintegrating into the abandoned cabin. The embers snuffed and disappeared into the stirred-up dust. Rusted cot springs were exposed again with the mattresses gone. Scat littered the floor. The cabin returned to disrepair.

Lester poked his head through the door. "Hey, I found some wood. Come give me a hand."

I got up from my seat against the wall, brushed myself off, looked around the empty cabin. "Here I come."

I stepped out onto the porch. My breath clouded up in front of me and I bundled my coat against the cold. The lake was iced over, though open water rippled in spots. Ice would come in early this winter and stay late, they'd said on the radio. *Won't be long now,* I thought. A light came on in a house on the far shore. Was that house occupied last winter? Could I have made it there and back to my mother in time to save her? I conjured a different boy, happy and young, with his mother calmly walking past me, swinging hands held between them. They smiled like neighbors passing on the sidewalk and went about the business of crossing the ice. I watched until they made it safely to that light. Somewhere in the distance, a hawk screeched. A shiver rose in me, and I remembered a time my mother told me I had to put a coat on even though I didn't want to, even though I thought I'd be fine without it. "You'll catch your death of cold," she'd said, as if our death is a thing that belongs to us. Death, out there waiting for us to slip up, to drive too fast, to swallow too many pills, smoke too many cigarettes, to pick the wrong lover, or to forget to wear a coat on a cold day.

Lester came out from the side of the cabin. "Wood's around here. It's a little wet, but it should do the trick."

I nodded but turned my attention back to the lake. Lester came onto the porch.

"So, this is where it happened, huh?" He scratched his head vigorously, checked his nails, rubbed his nose. "Sorry, I mean, of course it is."

"Weird to be here, is all," I said. "Lots of memories. Let's get a fire going before we catch our death of cold," I said, immediately wishing I could take those old words back. The light across the way went out.

We patched the broken window with a piece of cardboard, lit a fire, warmed up cans of pork and beans and the foil-wrapped meat pies Mona forced on us as we left Loma. Then the two of us got drunk as hell on a bottle of Wild Turkey we'd picked up on the way. I told him about the weeks leading up to my mother drowning, about my father leaving me with Gip and Ruby. Lester told me how he'd lost his virginity when he was thirteen years old to a friend of his mother's while she was passed out on the couch not five feet away. He showed me places where one of her boyfriends burned him with cigarettes.

"Where is she now?"

"Sioux Falls. I see her every once in a while. Maybe around Christmastime we'll go. She's better on her own."

"My mom hated being alone." I imagined the strangers retrieving her bloated body from the lake, how embarrassed she'd have been. I could almost hear her saying she didn't want anyone to see her like that, without makeup, her hair a mess. No amount of talking kept the ghosts away. "I'm ashamed," I confessed. "I watched her die. I couldn't help her."

"But you stayed with her, man. Right out there. The last thing she saw was you alive. You didn't let her down, man. You lived. That's all. You lived."

We hopped around the empty cabin in a kind of a redemption dance, whooping and swigging from the whiskey bottle. When I tried to explain to Lester the difference between each of the loon's calls, wrapping my drunk mouth around sounds I couldn't make sober, flapping my arms like they were wings, Lester fell over laughing. I hurled the empty bottle into the fireplace, smashing it against the rock, and collapsed next to him on the floor. He grabbed me around the neck, pulled me over, then flattened me. The exertion tapped him out, and he flopped down next to me. We lay there on our backs, panting, the floor spinning under us. He patted me on the chest without lifting his head. "From now on, man, you and me are brothers. The brotherhood of crazy mothers."

I woke in the night still drunk, shivering. The fire had died way down. I threw the rest of the logs in, blew the embers until flames ignited, and crawled into my sleeping bag. As I was drifting off, I thought I heard the sound of a loon, but then my father's voice told me no, too close to winter for loons this far north.

Lester kicked me in the side to wake me. The cabin was ice cold but light was streaming in. "Get up. Something you got to see." He was fully dressed, but his sleeping bag was unzipped and around his shoulders. "Hurry. It's cold as fuck, but trust me, you are not going to want to miss this."

I scrambled to my feet, though my stomach and head would have liked a few more hours to sleep. I pulled on my boots and coat and followed Lester out the door and down the familiar trail. He'd already caught up with a figure bundled in a blanket-striped coat, a fur-trimmed hood covering the face completely. Lester looked over his shoulder and grinned, motioning me to hurry.

I hesitated, seeing someone else was there. A trail of footprints cut me off from the right and led right to Lester and this other person. Whoever it was had come out of the woods, west of the abandoned cabin. I lowered my head and steeled myself.

"Check it out." Lester pointed to the middle of the lake. A figure was hunched over the frozen surface a hundred yards or more offshore.

It was a woman standing next to Lester. "My crazy-assed boyfriend. Darin's a dummy, I swear. I love him, though." She pulled down her hood. Strands of black hair like twisted yarn dangled across her flabby face. She pushed them back along the skunk stripe of gray at the roots. "I couldn't stop him. His heart is so big. I'm Rhonda, by the way."

"What's he doing out there?"

Lester chimed in. "Rescuing a bird. He's walked all the way out there because a bird got stuck."

"Oh," the woman cried. "I think he's got it. I think he's got it." Excitement climbed up her voice and she bounced on the balls of her feet. She cupped her hands to her mouth. "Be careful, sugar. Be careful."

I squinted, trying to get a better look at the man making his way slowly back toward us.

The woman shouted now. "Darin! Are you bleeding? You're my hero, Darin. Do you need a blanket?"

We could make out his voice but not the words. He was carrying the bird like a football under his right arm. He dropped a fishing net and shovel on the ice. As he drew closer, he started talking. "Babe, I did it. I got it."

"Oh, honey, oh, sweetie!" she said, choking back tears. "I'm so proud of him." She put her arm around Lester and squeezed him close to her. Lester looked at me sideways and stifled a laugh.

"You did. You got it. Thank you, Jesus, for keeping him safe."

The black-and-white checkerboard bird stood out against the man's corn-colored canvas jacket. Its head extended forward, the long beak like black shears rested against his chest.

"Holy shit," I said. "It's a loon."

"Her beak's frozen," the man said as he approached. "She's in pretty bad shape, babe. We have to get her help."

"I want to hug you so bad right now," the woman said.

"Keep clear, Rhonda. I don't want her to peck at you. That beak of hers could do real damage."

"No shit," Lester said. "Look at that hell-diver."

"You should have seen her when I tried to grab her. She'd have run it right through my hand if I hadn't had gloves on. But she gave up and let me take her. Didn't make a peep."

My father had taught me all the loon's calls—the wail for separation from a chick or mate, the tremolo to warn that a predator was near, the yodel to signal aggression, and the hoot for curiosity or even happiness. But this loon was quiet. Was there a call for gratitude, for rescue from the verge of death? What was the call for surrender?

"Oh, babe. I'm so glad you're okay. You remember that fellow died trying to save his dog?" She turned to us. "Dog climbed right out of the ice over the guy's head. Been a few drownings here over the years."

"You got to be careful with a distressed animal. Even the tame ones can be unpredictable."

"These boys are checking out the old place," Rhonda said, gesturing toward the cabin.

"That right? Well, I bet you've never seen anything like this before."

I took a step closer to the loon and bent slightly to make eye contact. "What was she doing out there, you think?"

"I don't know exactly. Something about this lake. Every couple of years a loon gets stranded here. This one should be off having drinks on a beach somewhere in Mexico. Could be they're young or they lose their bearings. Some have injuries so bad their wings don't work. The back end here, that's where the baggage is," Darin said, lifting the bird slightly. "It's real heavy so they need a lot of running room to get going, like a cargo plane. Runway's too short, or iced in like this one, they can't take off."

"What happens then?" Lester asked.

"Honestly? They usually just disappear. Dive maybe, can't find the hole again. Hard to rescue once they're stranded, I know that for sure. They don't know what's good for them anymore. This one, she's lucky I got to her before a hawk or a coyote."

"We'd better be going if we're going to get her to a vet," Rhonda said. "You boys be careful around that cabin, you hear? Don't do nothing stupid."

They veered off along the other path, the excitement still raising their voices.

"Wow, that was crazy, huh?" Lester said. He scratched his neck when I didn't answer. Instead, he did what I did, which was to stay put and stare at the spot where the loon had been stuck. All the commotion of the rescue had settled, and other than the tools Darin had dropped, the ice was as it should be. No intruders, just a black scar where that bird had nearly died. Desperate and lost. Stuck in a jam.

"She tried to pull me in with her."

"What?"

"My mother. When I couldn't pull her out, she tried to pull me in."

I grabbed my own wrist, feeling the way she'd latched on, feeling the pull toward the hole, the ice collapsing, my elbows wet with advancing water. I stood still, watching it unfold out there, magnified by time. The boy, taking off his coat. Already he'd tried to go for help against her pleading but had turned back, knowing help couldn't come in time. Kneeling now, his hair silver in the moonlight. He looks like something sprouted in the freeze, a winter shoot. She tells him he looks like the moon. He tosses the coat. She doesn't even reach for it. Now he's on his belly, elbowing toward her. The ice shudders, bends. They grip each other's wrists. He yanks free, she disappears below the waterline, surfaces, sputters, gasps. All is quiet now. By dawn, I know they will be lost to each other.

"Are you kidding?" Lester asked. "That's fucked up, man."

"I keep trying to imagine what was going through her head. All I could ever figure is she didn't want to be alone."

"Pretty lousy way to get company, if you ask me."

I think about that, about the boy I was and my drowned mother. What did I know, really? Her love for me was deep and frantic. And the desperation of her dying the way she did was keen, sharp like the blade she left behind, like the loon's black bill. I was not able to put my thoughts together right then, not for years, that the ice had closed in on my mother long before she went out onto Bright Lake.

Darin and Rhonda, back from the veterinarian, knocked on the cabin door with news that the loon would be fine, that she wasn't injured so much as lost and lonely. Rhonda insisted we join them for stew, and given how hungover we both were, stew and a warm cabin and a fire sounded good. Their place was farther back in the woods, away from the lakeshore but with a nice view from a new deck. They'd lived on the other side for years, Rhonda said, and bought this place the previous spring. She and Darin picked at their stew, and the conversation came to an awkward stop.

"Lester told me this morning that was your mom they pulled from the lake last April. She was the one who went through the ice."

Lester scrunched his face. "Sorry, man. It kind of slipped out. She asked what we were doing here."

"It's alright," I said. "Yeah, we were staying here last winter. It was temporary. My dad's friend owns the place. Or owned it. Looks like it's been abandoned."

"Yeah, some fellers came up here early last summer. Cleared the place out. Was that your pop and his friend, maybe?" Darin asked.

I lowered my head, my appetite suddenly gone. "I haven't seen my dad since my mother died, so I wouldn't know."

Out the corner of my eye, I saw Rhonda give Darin a stern look, flicking her fingers and wrist to her throat, the knock-it-off signal. I pretended not to see it, quietly grateful the conversation was cut short. Darin changed the subject, returning to the safety of weather and the winter nearly upon us.

Darin and Rhonda said we could sack out in their living room, but I declined for the both of us. They insisted we take wood from their pile and their last rolled joint, so we did that and headed back to the old place and our other bottle of whiskey for one last night.

"You want to tell me what that was all about?" Lester asked. "You think your dad was up here?"

"I don't know what I think anymore. I mean, why would he come here? Unless he wanted to have a look around, I guess. Figure shit out."

"Sounds familiar."

"Doesn't it?"

"Let's get high," Lester said. "Unless you want to keep talking."

I had to admit that I'd never smoked pot before. Lester didn't mind. He lit the joint, took a toke, and passed it to me. He eked out his instructions. "Don't cough. Wastes good dope."

We sat on unsplit logs next to the fire, passing the bottle and the joint between us. I suspect Lester got a kick out of seeing me stoned, so he gave me more than my share. Between the pot and the whiskey, I was good and shit-faced before long. I closed my eyes in the bliss, imagining my father walking through the door, catching me stoned. When I opened them, Valerie was in the rocker next to me, smoking a joint of her own, staring calmly into the rafters, the fear gone. I almost asked Lester if he could see her, but I knew she wasn't really there. I let her drift away in the smoke and thought instead about Jolene.

"Do you like white people?"

"You're alright, I guess."

"Not me. I mean, white people. Like the white race."

"You're white."

"I know I'm white."

"Then what are you asking?"

"I'm asking if you would let Jolene marry me if you were Mona and Troy or if you wouldn't want her to be with a white guy."

"Why didn't you just say that then?"

"I just said it."

"Said what?"

The thread of the conversation got lost in the weed, and we watched the flames instead. "Man, Lester. I am so in love with that girl it hurts."

Lester took a melancholy breath and nodded. "Yeah. I loved a girl so much once my johnson hurt."

"I'm not talking about my johnson, I'm talking about my heart. My heart, man."

"You are so stoned, brother."

"I am that. But I'm in love. Crazy, crazy love."

"Love's good," Lester said, his words swaying out of him. "Until it's not."

I WAS UP AT DAYBREAK, listening to the quiet. Lester was curled asleep on his side in a position that said he'd gotten cold during the night. I tiptoed into the single bedroom, so different from the way I'd stormed into it the last time. I'd not given much thought to their argument, shut it out like all the others. The vulgarities. Him accusing her, saying she was a lousy mother. Her screaming at him to fuck her. I could picture myself on the opposite cot, the blankets wrapped around me, twisting myself around to not hear anymore. In that room again, I could barely remember it. Something about my sister. Something about family. Some family. I sat on the bare metal frame, the sagged springs poking my backside. Lester was right about love, how it could make you whole or pretty near leave you completely empty. What good had it done my parents? What had it done for me?

I left the cabin without waking Lester and went down to the lakeshore. A layer of fog hung above the surface. I fanned my cold hands out in front of me with my thumbs together, palms to the rising sun, firebirds in a mating dance. Then I folded my fingers, the wings and feathers, over each other. I blew into my thumbs, into the cave my hands created, the way my father had taught me, using one hand to baffle the lonely separation call. It skipped across the ice, trapped and back heavy like a winter loon.

LESTER WAS PACKING UP WHEN I came back in. "You about had enough?" he asked.

"Let's get out of here."

It was dusk by the time we got back to Loma, hungover and talked out. We stopped at Jolene's to drop off Troy's chains. Lester backed up to the garage, and we both got out of the Impala. I pulled open the door and Lester hauled the chains in and dropped them where we found them.

"You going in or you want a ride home?" he asked.

Plenty needed to be said to Jolene, but in that moment, it was someone else I wanted to talk to, someone I hadn't talked to in a long time.

"One more place I need to be. You got another half hour in you?"

LESTER WAITED FOR ME AT the iron gates, and I made my way down the bleak path alone. Skeletal trees, their branches stripped by the wind and cold, stood like sentries, arms raised to halt trespassers. I'd visited my mother's grave only once that summer, when grass on the mound was new and tender. Gip had told me to get in the car, that we were going to the cemetery. I'd stood there with him above the spot I imagined her feet must be. I pictured myself down there with her, so much so I could taste dirt in my mouth. Gip stared at her name on the headstone but didn't say a word.

The ground was already winter hard. Worms that tilled the soil in summer, that turned flesh to bone, had left behind frozen clumps of mud I could feel through the soles of my shoes.

"I couldn't go with you," I said to the name on the headstone. "I'm sorry you didn't make it." I laid myself down on top of the grave, my head beneath the stone that bore her name, not mine, the date she had died and I had lived. "I know what you were trying to do. I forgive you. You hear me, Mom? I forgive you." My grief and guilt soaked into the ground. I folded my arms over my chest like a dead man and watched the first star appear.

Lester pulled up to the house but didn't cut the engine. He got out of the car when I did and put his hand on the roof. "Something's on your front door."

I could just make out the official-looking seal on the cockeyed piece of yellow paper.

"My guess is that's an eviction notice."

"You okay?" he asked.

I shrugged. "This ought to be a lot of fun." I grabbed my bag from the back. "Sorry again about the car."

He cocked his head and swatted the top. He was done talking about it. He climbed in and revved the engine. I tapped on the window, and he rolled it down.

"What now?"

"Thanks, man," I said.

"No problem, brother."

CHAPTER 20

Both my grandparents were there when I walked in. The television was on, Ruby was at the kitchen table, Gip was in his recliner. The place smelled like cigarettes and dirty socks. I was straddling past and present, trying to get my balance.

Gip pushed down the footrest with his stocking feet. "Nice of you to show up."

Ruby looked over her shoulder, stood quickly. For a second I thought she was going to run over and hug me. She checked herself.

I handed Gip the eviction notice I'd torn off the house. "You don't have to leave this out there. He gave you thirty days. He posted this to humiliate us."

"I wanted to leave it so the neighbors would know what kind we're dealing with here. You should have left it. Where you been? We worried," Ruby said.

"You heard her. Let's have it. Some sort of prima donna coming and going when you like."

I walked past Ruby to the refrigerator, opened a beer, and took a drink before I spoke. "Went up to Bright Lake with Lester, that's where."

"Why would you want to go up there?"

"Wanted to have a look around, is all."

"Why now?" Gip asked. "What's so special that you had to go up there all of a sudden?"

I answered Gip but kept my eyes on Ruby. "Me and Ruby had a little conversation about my mom. Helped me see her in a new light."

Ruby's face clenched and her eyes widened. She twitched her head, begging me in an instant to say no more.

I turned to Gip. "Got me thinking. I had some things to sort out."

"Well, la-di-da," Gip said. "Don't suppose you've done any deep thinking to make this house mess right."

"That's your problem. Not mine. Wherever you two go is fine by me. Maybe I won't even go with you, seeing's how I've been nothing but a thorn in your side."

"You're serious about that?" Ruby asked.

I nodded. I had no idea what I was saying or where I would go, but it felt good to put the threat out there.

"Why's that surprise you?" Gip asked. "Valerie took off, now him. Get all they can from you, leave when it suits them. Ungrateful. That's what it is. But what do I care? Make it easier to find someplace without you in tow."

Ruby turned her back to me, a purposeful shunning. Her voice croaked out on a plume of smoke. "Glad you had some time to think. No one ought to be kept in the dark."

I slept soundly in my mother's bed that night. And I slept on my back, belly exposed, unafraid.

THE BRONCO PULLED INTO THE school parking lot the next morning. Jolene smiled at me from the passenger seat. Students were scampering from cars and buses, eager to get into the school and out of the falling snow. Troy waved at me and I waved back. I let the snow pile up on me while I waited for her. So much needed to be said between us, but I hoped it could wait. We met each other halfway.

"You look nice," I said, and she did. Her white stocking cap was pulled down low to her eyebrows and pressed her black hair against her cheeks. She favored woolen mittens over gloves, and the ones she wore were thick and red, most likely knit for her by Mona's hand.

"You look cold." She reached up and brushed a layer of snow off my head.

I bumped her with my side and she bumped me back. We fell into step, our heads lowered. I stole a glance. She was smiling.

"Principal's office?"

"Yeah. Truant."

"See you at lunch, then?"

"Sure thing."

Lester was leaning over the office counter, smooth-talking the school secretary, making eyes at her, giving her some elaborate story as to why the two of us had missed school. We would laugh about that years later when we heard she'd left her husband for the truant officer, who was also a woman.

"Mr. Ballot. Your friend Mr. Two Kills says you were indispensable to him as he dealt with an urgent family matter." She tucked her chin tightly like she was passing an apple, then slapped her hands on the counter. "Mr. Two Kills, please stand up straight."

The first bell rang. "We'll take the detention," I said.

Lester threw up his hands and groaned in disgust.

"Here you are, boys," she said, and handed us each a slip of paper.

"Why'd you go and do that? I had her right here, right here," he said, poking his palm.

"Sure you did."

He laughed and stuck the slip in his back pocket. "Heard a couple girls talking about you this morning. Something about a teeny, tiny penis. My money's on Kathryn."

I let my head fall back. "Great."

Lester slapped my back. "C'mon, pencil dick. Let's get to class."

ALL MORNING, GIRLS SWARMED ME, laughing, puckering their lips, mocking sympathy, waggling their little fingers. I imagined the story Kathryn might tell, rubbing her hands together, buzzing back and forth between her friends. It's no secret that there are no secrets in a small town. By the end of the day, it seemed like the whole school had heard some version of Kathryn's story that I'd either chickened out or petered out. Either way, it was a failure on my part and, despite the embarrassment, I was relieved. It was the dropped knife I didn't want to hear about, and I was oddly grateful to Kathryn that she focused her retaliation on my manhood, not my character.

THE MORNING FLURRIES ENDED, LEAVING no real snow on the ground by day's end. I'd made plans over lunch to walk to the library, then home with Jolene after serving detention. She marched up to me in the courtyard, arms loaded with books. "God, I cannot stand her."

"You have a run-in with Kathryn?"

"Oh, she was talking shit with one of her stupid friends. Totem poles and squaw stuff. The usual. I wish she'd find another dick to stick in that big mouth of hers."

I stifled a laugh, put my arm around her. "I'm so sorry. You want me to carry your books for you?"

She rolled her eyes. "Yes. Yes, I do. Here you go." She thrust the pile straight at me, but I pushed them gently back. Jolene followed my eyes. Kathryn was walking alone in the other direction.

"Listen. I need to talk to her. Meet you at the library?"

"What about? This is ridiculous, Wes."

"It's about the house. That's it. I need to make nice, at least a little bit. Maybe she can do something about the eviction."

"I don't trust her. She's like the rest of them. I'm sure it makes her sick to think you'd choose me over her."

"I choose you. I choose you. Every time."

She stood on her tiptoes, books to her chest, and kissed me. "Be careful. And no joke, don't make a fool of me for trusting you. I mean it," she added, warning in her voice.

I drew an X over my heart.

I CAUGHT UP WITH KATHRYN at a low cement wall near the edge of the parking lot. "Hey, can I talk to you a minute?"

Her guard went up in a way that was almost visible, like she'd stepped into a gunnysack and cinched it up around her. She stiffened, looked around for witnesses. "What do you want?"

"Just to talk for a second."

"So talk."

When you can have whatever you want, you look for things to want that you can't have. I'd always seen Kathryn as that kind of spoiled, someone who had everything, who wanted everything else. I was a novelty, something new in a town that didn't change much at all. I'd figured that's about the only reason she'd glommed onto me. I was too young then to understand much about girls and their cyclone thinking, but something inside me said she needed a win more than I did.

"The other night. I'm sorry if I hurt your feelings. I shouldn't have let it go that far."

She fumbled in her purse. "I can't find my—shit. What was I thinking?" Her face flushed and tears welled in her black-rimmed eyes. "He grounded me. No car for a week. I have to walk."

That fullness was there that I'd seen in her when I first got to town. She was a pretty girl for sure, and I hoped right then that she would be happy. I fast-forwarded years into the future, saw Kathryn with some go-along type like Drew Fullerton, no one with bluster like her dad. They'd have a passel of kids, all blond, all well fed. I mumbled again that I was sorry.

"Yeah, I'm sorry, too." She glanced back at the school, like the building itself had been spreading rumors about me all day.

"I can take it, what people say. It doesn't bother me. But lay off Jolene. I mean it."

She rolled her eyes, lifted her chin in bare-boned acknowledgment, like the highest bidder at an auction. "And for the record, evicting your grandparents? That was my dad, not me. He's not going back on it. I tried, believe it or not." She tightened her grip on her books, breathed in, and held it, let her words come out on that breath. "I wish he'd notice me for a change. Give a shit, you know?"

I knew exactly.

—

I MET JOLENE AT THE library, made out with her in the walnut stacks until the whiskered librarian marched over in sensible black shoes, reading glasses bobbing on the ends of a gold chain around her neck, and pointed to the door. "Out," she said.

Leftover daylight turned the darkening sky jewel blue as we walked home. We stopped across the street from Jolene's house, out of the white wedge from the streetlamp. Yellow lights flickered in the twilit windowpanes. Mona passed back and forth by the kitchen window. The bathroom window went dark. Troy emerged from the hallway, wiping his hands against his pant legs.

"I like looking into your house like this."

Jolene squeezed my hand. "We should pull more curtains."

"Did I ever tell you my father was a terrible hunter? He never came home with anything. Oh, sometimes he'd help a friend carve up a kill, and they'd send him home with some deer steaks. Never bagged anything of his own, as far as I can remember. Stopped duck hunting because he was too fidgety for the blind. You know the saying 'jump the gun'? That's my dad."

"Why are you telling me this now?"

I grabbed her hand and kissed it, then her neck, her mouth. I thought about what Lester had said, stoned but still sage. Love's good. Until it isn't.

"I don't want loving me to wreck you. I don't come from much good. But I'm going to try. I want you to know that. I want Troy and Mona, Bull, Mariah, Lester even. I want everyone to know that." I mimed placing a ring on her finger.

"Why don't you let me be the judge."

A car lurched up the street, its headlights wobbling. Gip's Plymouth.

"Christ," I said. "What now?"

The car stopped half in the street and Ruby climbed out. She didn't see us. Instead she walked right up to the front door and banged on it. Jolene held her finger up to her lip. We crept closer to hear.

Mona came to the door. Her voice sounded surprised, confused. "Ruby. Hi."

"I need to see Wes."

"He's not here."

I couldn't run off and leave Jolene's family to deal with whatever Ruby had in mind. What had I just said? I didn't come from much and that not-much was standing on the doorstep. Jolene and I walked hand in hand into the light.

"I'm right here, Ruby."

CHAPTER 21

In all the time I'd lived with Gip and Ruby, I'd never known either one of them to be in another person's house. But there she was, sitting at the table, in the same spot where Mona usually sat, smoking a cigarette in a kitchen where no one ever smoked at all. She dropped the ashes on a plate. We were all on edge.

"So what's this about?" I asked.

"The cops," Ruby said. Her eyes darted between Mona and Troy, to Jolene, then back to me. "Maybe we ought to go back home, you and me. I can't talk in front of them."

I was as uncomfortable as she was, our trouble on display that way. Still, I knew not to be alone with Ruby right then. Whatever brought her to this house was more than I could manage alone.

"It's okay, Ruby," I said. "Let us help."

She stuck her finger in her ear, twisted it violently. "They're looking for Gip."

Ruby told us the whole story, her lips tucked in around her gums like piecrust. Spittle was everywhere. Gip had apparently been running his mouth for hours at the bar, going on about Burt Rook and the eviction notice, about the bank and all. Maybe he was on his way over to the Rooks' house to set him straight when he saw Kathryn walking down the street. He'd stopped the car and gotten out, stumbling over to her, hoping to give her a lift home, or at least that's what she told the police. She'd declined nicely at first, but Gip insisted and grabbed her arm. Kathryn apparently told him to get his "filthy hands off her." He'd slapped her mouth, which stunned her long enough for him to drag her toward the car, telling her the whole time he didn't think her father was going to take kindly to Kathryn speaking like that to her elders. Kathryn got her wits about her and kicked Gip in the nuts. She ran the rest of the way home. Burt Rook called the police. And now Gip was missing. Ruby found his car parked downtown.

"What happened to your teeth?" I asked.

"The cops come to the door. I was so flustered. I told them he wasn't there, but they went ahead and searched the house for him anyways. Thought I was hiding him. I run into the bathroom to put my teeth in and dropped the plate. Busted it in half."

Mariah appeared next to Troy in the doorway.

"Is Wes in trouble?" she asked.

"You go to your room. This is for the adults, not you," Mona said. "Go on."

"What can we do for you, Ruby?" Troy asked.

"I need Wes to come home. I don't want to be there by myself when Gip shows up. I'm too old for this shit." Her face drooped. The knit sweater she wore over her housedress was buttoned lopsided. Her thick stockings sagged at the knees. She was dissolving into a puddle of old age.

"Let's get you home," I said.

"You two going to be okay?" Mona asked.

What could I say? I shook my head and shrugged.

"You sure you don't want some tea or coffee? I can put a pot on," Mona said.

Ruby looked like a kitten in a box. I could tell she didn't know what to make of this kindness. She was the center of attention, surrounded by people who would help her if she asked, despite the fact she'd never shown kindness to them. How long had it been since anyone showed her real concern?

"Don't want to be a burden on you all. Just want this over. Want to be in my own home." She stood up and handed me the keys. "I thank you for offering, though."

"I'll walk them out," Jolene said.

We got Ruby settled. I hugged Jolene and kissed her forehead. "Sorry about all this," I said.

"Don't be. It's okay. Call me when you hear anything."

As we pulled away, Jolene raised her hand and waved. Ruby stared at her. "They're good people, aren't they," she said.

"Yes. They are."

Ruby said to wake her up when Gip came home. I slept on the couch. My plan was to call the cops if Gip came in. He never showed.

The next night, Jolene came over with dinner Mona had made for the two of us. "I wanted to bring it by before Ruby got home from work. She probably doesn't want me here much."

"It's okay. Stay. She won't care."

I was right. Ruby walked in looking ten years older. She set her purse by the door, turned on the television, and sat down in the recliner.

"Jolene brought dinner by, Ruby. Mona made it."

"Not hungry. Tired, yes. Hungry, no. Any word from your grandfather?" She pushed backward. Her feet went up and her eyes closed like a doll's.

"Nothing," I said.

Ruby had been sleeping in the recliner for an hour when the phone rang. She bolted upright. "Don't you get that. I got it."

Our side of the conversation was only "yes" and "yup" until Ruby put the phone back in the cradle. "Gip was at the Covered Wagon. Bartender there said he was drunk as a skunk. I best go get him."

"Let me go with you."

"Fine. But I'm driving." The keys were already in her hand.

I rolled my eyes at Jolene.

"Should we call the police or something?" Jolene asked.

Ruby was already out the door.

"Would you tell Mona and Troy? I think we're going to need help."

When we got outside, all that was left of the Plymouth was taillights. Ruby was gone.

I WENT WITH JOLENE BACK to her house for reinforcements. Troy piled into the Bronco, and the three of us drove through town. Troy said we probably ought to go to the police station, but we never made it that far. The Plymouth was up on a curb on a side street, a tow truck maneuvering behind it. Two cop cars were stopped in the street, their blue lights strobing the drugstore and radio station windows. Ruby was standing head down next to an officer. An ambulance was pulling away.

"Wes, maybe you ought to let me deal with this," Troy said.

"No," I said. Ruby looked up and saw me. I expected to see panic. What I saw was calm.

"That's my grandson, officer. That's Wes," Ruby said. "The one I was telling you about."

The officer looked down at his notebook. "You're Wes?" he asked.

I couldn't imagine how I fit into this equation. How were Ruby and Gip blaming me for whatever it was that was happening here?

"It's your grandfather. There's been an accident. Your grandmother here has been asking for you."

"What happened, Ruby?"

"He got hit by a car," she said, motioning to the Plymouth, which was being pulled up by the tow winch.

"What?"

"I couldn't find him, then all of a sudden he steps out in front of the car. I thought I was hitting the brake, but I guess I hit the gas instead. He busted the windshield and rolled off. I sort of hit him again and pinned him up against that telephone pole."

"Wait. You're the one who hit him? Jesus, Ruby!"

She spit through her toothless gums, her voice childlike, frantic. "It was an accident! They wouldn't let me ride in the ambulance with him. They made me walk the line. Right here in front of everybody."

"I told your grandmother we'd take her over to St. Pat's. You probably ought to ride with her," the officer said.

I broke away from the officers and Ruby and went back over to the truck, head hung.

Jolene threw her arms around my neck. "What happened?"

I told them, trying to keep in check the shackled hopelessness I could hear in my own voice. "I have to go. To the hospital. I'll ride with Ruby."

"We can drive you, Wes," Troy said. "It's no problem."

"I want to go with you. I could help," Jolene said.

"No, you guys go home. I'll come by later, when I know more."

"Anytime you want," Troy said. "Day or night. I mean it." He spread his arms like wings, then enfolded me in an embarrassing hug. I fought off the urge to collapse there, to beg him not to lump me in with the mess that seemed to follow me.

I EXPECTED WE'D BE WAITING in the emergency room for hours while the doctors worked to pin and sew Gip back together. But when we arrived with the police, the desk nurse said they'd moved him to the ICU.

The air was sour, pungent from waste and blood and curatives. Gip was hooked up to wheezing machines and bags dripping and draining fluids. Tubes poked up his nose and out his mouth, and a yellowed crust had formed on his lips. His bulging eyes were closed and his brow, usually so prominent, seemed collapsed. A nurse was standing at his bedside, making notes on a clipboard.

I stood in the doorway, staring at the scene, trying to account for my indifference. Ruby gripped my arm. "What have I done?" she said.

The nurse looked up. "You're the family?"

I nodded. "So, is he in a coma or unconscious or what?" I asked.

"Let me go find the doctor," she said.

With the nurse gone, Ruby went to Gip's bedside. She tapped the sheet from his foot up the length of his body, like she was feeling for a hot spot. She rested her fingertips at his shoulder, then turned to me. "You think he can hear me?"

"Beats me, Ruby."

"I don't want to make him madder. He's probably awful mad at me."

"It's probably fine. Go on."

"You started this, you know." She seemed to be steeling herself for the argument. "He did," she said to me, before turning back. "You shouldn't have gone after that girl. You should have stayed away from her. Don't you tell me it was my fault. It wasn't. I did everything I was supposed to do. You couldn't keep it in your pants, was all, could you?"

"Ruby." Whispers from the other side of the curtain, another family in crisis. "Now's not the time." I walked over next to her, closer to Gip than I wanted to be. "No one said he tried anything with her," I whispered. "Don't make it worse than it already is."

She looked at me like it was a surprise I was there, then nodded silently.

The doctor walked in, wiping his hand over his bald head. "I'm so sorry. Crazy night. You're Mrs. Furniss?" Ruby nodded. "And is this your son?"

"Grandson. Wes Ballot."

"Yes, right. So, let's leave Mr. Furniss here for the moment and take a walk to the lounge. It's around the corner there."

"I don't need to go nowhere. Tell me what's wrong with him."

"Well." His voice was reverent, practiced. He pulled a swivel stool from behind the door, straddled it, and sat next to Ruby. "Mr. Furniss has suffered massive internal injuries. When they brought him in"—he paused to consult the chart—"well, as you know, when he made impact with the car, the trauma was severe."

"Does he need surgery?" I asked. I wondered how they would afford it, whether Gip's insurance would even cover this, since his own wife was the one who ran him down. "Are there broken bones?"

"I really must insist we step out of the room. Just for the moment. Please, Mrs. Furniss."

"C'mon, Ruby," I said, extending my hand to her. She batted it away.

"Oh fine! It's just words. Don't see why they can't be said in here."

We followed the doctor into the dim hallway.

"What's this all about?" I asked.

"Mr. Furniss's body has endured a cataclysmic event. His life is being sustained by these machines that keep his airway open and breathe for him. Despite our best effort, I'm afraid there's nothing more we can do for Mr. Furniss."

"You mean right now?"

"I'm sorry, no. We can give you the time you need to gather family, to say your goodbyes. There's clergy available here in the hospital or you can call your own minister if you choose. The night nurse has information you might need if you are considering organ donation."

Ruby folded her arms and pressed her lip out in an exaggerated pout, the corners of her mouth turning down as she nodded. "Well, then," she said. "So what? Do I take him home like this and wait for someone to donate new organs for him? How am I supposed to take care of him?"

"Ruby, I think he's saying Gip's not coming home," I said. "Is that right?"

"I'm afraid so. Once you're ready, we'll shut off these machines and Mr. Furniss will pass."

"So don't shut them off if it'll kill him!" Her iron voice roared down the hallway like a locomotive out of a mountain tunnel.

"I wish there was something we could do for him, but I'm afraid there's nothing. Again, I'm very sorry for your loss. The nurse will be right in to discuss your options."

"I can't have killed him. I didn't mean to kill him. Am I going to jail?"

She stressed the *kill* part as if her intent was only to maim. I was glad the police weren't listening in just then. The doctor touched Ruby's arm. "It was an accident, Mrs. Furniss. His blood alcohol level was sky high. If he was wandering around in the street, it's no wonder he was hit. You were at the wrong place at the wrong time, I'm afraid. Go back in. Spend all the time you need with him."

He dismissed us with a nod and a single word to me that held no meaning anymore. "Son."

Ruby spun on her worn heels, went back in the room, muttering about this being "some bullshit alright."

What malady or disease or accident brought the other patients to share the room with Gip, I wondered. A couple in the corner whispered gently to each other, the young woman touching the crippled hand of an old woman—maybe her mother—who was more corpse than human, approaching death drawing her skin into the bedsheets. The tenderness of the daughter's touch, of their hushed tones, was a curiosity to me. I found myself staring. The young man gave me that half smile that said, "Yup, we're in the same boat." But he was wrong. I had no tender feelings for Gip. I tried to summon a good memory I could cling to, anything to make me tear up so I wouldn't look heartless standing there next to my dying grandfather.

Ruby pulled the chair up to Gip's bedside. Trembles seemed to come from somewhere in her gut. Her whole body shook as she sat. "I don't know what I'm supposed to do now."

I sat next to her, watched the accordion folds of the respirator expand and contract. I wanted to cry for the losing of something important. I should have loved him despite it all, but I didn't. Any spark of it was snuffed out by the knowledge of what wasn't mine to remember. Had he ever been kind to me? Once maybe. But in hindsight, even that was tinged.

It was in the fall. I was ten years old. My mother and I were in Loma, probably so she could ask for money. She was in the house and had sent me outside while she and Ruby talked. Gip was standing on the sidewalk, a beer in his hand. He'd set fire to a pile of leaves and was watching it burn in the gutter. "Come over here, Wes," he said. "You wanna light the next one?"

What boy doesn't want to light stuff on fire? I walked over to him. He reached for my head, plucked a red leaf out of my hair, then held my chin in his hand, turning my head this way and that. "You look so much like her," he said. "'Course, you look like your father, too, but your mouth? Definitely Valerie. And her skin. You got that, alright."

He dropped his hand and turned back to the fire. "She is so pretty, your mother." The rest was lost in the smoke from that autumn fire. I couldn't even remember if he let me strike the match.

Sitting there waiting for him to die, I made up a happy house with flower boxes in every window and furniture that was more than moving boxes covered with tablecloths. I imagined a different Gip, helping my mother learn to ride a bike or showing her how to bait a hook. And

I finally felt sad enough to well up, not for Gip but for everything he didn't have and for what he couldn't give my mother or me and for the pain he caused instead. My tears were angry, but I hoped they might pass for grief.

"He said once I had my mom's mouth. You think I look like her at all?"

Ruby wrinkled her nose like she was trying to decide something. "Yes, you do, I guess."

"You think she's in heaven?"

She looked at me and laughed, not like I'd said something funny but like I'd said something stupid. "She wasn't no angel, that's for sure. She was probably better than I gave her credit for, though."

Buzzers sounded down the hall. Ruby was lost in some kind of reverie and seemed not to notice a commotion of blue scrubs and squeaking shoes that flew past the door. She smoothed the sheet that covered Gip's chest.

"When I was little, my daddy, he never believed I come from him. Said my mama'd taken up with some moonshiner. When I come out with the black hair, well, he said he knew right then. Time my mama died, he'd like to have tossed me in the ground with her. He'd sit on that porch skinning squirrels—used that knife you got—while my brothers, they'd take me out behind the shed and take turns on me. Daddy, he didn't give a lick. I'd scream and holler and scratch at them. They thought it was funny. Right up until that night I took a shovel to Jim and knocked the funny clean out of him. My daddy run me out for it. Never was much for cock after that."

"That's awful," I managed to say, though I would have liked to unhear my grandmother say "cock." "How old were you?"

"I's seventeen when I left, about the same as you," she said, before returning her gaze to the past.

"Glad to be gone, too. I hopped the train to Virginia, worked odd jobs, housekeeping and whatnot, for years. Started working one of those dance halls after the war broke out. There's a woman there, Maureen was her name. After the men left, Maureen and me would slow dance. Lots of the girls danced together. She was bigger than me, Maureen, real big, and she'd hold me close to her. Always liked the smell there on her chest. She'd been held close by men all night long, but she still had a touch of woman left right here," Ruby said, tapping the place on her own chest where cleavage might have been on someone bigger breasted. "Girls came and went in places like that. One day, Maureen wasn't there anymore. I missed dancing with her. Then I met Gip. Bet you didn't know none of that, did you?"

I shook my head. She kept watching the wall behind Gip's bed like a movie was playing there.

"Gip'd come in and pay for dances. He was stationed stateside, back from fighting the Nazis in France. He'd bring in hard candy sometimes or caramels. Brought me flowers once, even. He was nice to me mostly back then, not as rough as my brothers, that's for sure. We got married and Valerie come along after that. Moved up here to get away from the heat. Didn't know it would be so goddamned cold."

I tried to imagine this Ruby as the woman in the picture she'd busted against the dining room wall. I didn't know what to say. She sighed and sighed, shriveling like a leaky balloon.

"Lord, I am tired!" said Ruby. "Life is too goddamned long." I guess it was some kind of grief that made her come clean about all of it, like she had to purge her shame, confess in the face of death, even if it wasn't her own. "If God's real, he'll send this one to hell, I think."

"Ruby, I don't think this is the place for that kind of talk," I said.

"Why not? Maybe this is exactly the place. Maybe God's listening in, trying to decide. I'll witness to him. Here's what I'm thinking. I'm thinking Gip always liked little girls, scrawny girls, like me, like your mother. Maybe even that Rook girl, though she's awfully chubby. I think he got what was coming to him in this life. Any fairness at all and he'll get the brimstone, too."

"You said yourself you don't know any of that for certain."

"I know enough. Anyway, he goes to hell I hope I'm not going there with him. The devil scares me. And I'd like to see my baby again."

She blinked like the lights had come up in the theater. The couple in the corner was staring at us now, no longer able to hide their prying eyes. "What are you looking at?" she said, returning to her old self. "And where is that nurse? I don't have all night."

She patted the arms of her chair like that was that, then leaned into Gip. "You left me with nothing. You hear?" she said. "I got nothing left. Then again, maybe I never had nothing at all." She stood, pushed back the chair, and did something I had never seen her do. She pecked my grandfather's forehead with her thin lips.

"What are you doing?" I asked. "You can't just leave him here. Where are you going?"

"I'll fill out them papers and wait for you in the lobby."

"Ruby!"

"You do this for me, Wes. Don't let them take none of his organs, neither. Devil wants all of him. And get them to wipe that crust off his lips."

I spun around the room like I was trying to pin a tail on a paper donkey, then threw up my arms in surrender. "Unbelievable."

The couple whispered to each other again. "What?" I said, daring them to pass judgment.

The young man spoke. "Are you okay? Is there something we . . ." He looked at his wife, then back at me.

"No, I'm sorry. It's fine," I said. "It's always like this." What else could I do? I sat back down next to the hospital bed and the weary machines.

THE NURSE CAME IN AND drew the curtain around his bed. She told me Ruby said I'd stay while the machines were unplugged and that I was to come fetch her if Gip stayed alive anyway. I glanced at the nurse, then rested my hand on my grandfather's, wishing I didn't feel like such a fraud. She turned off the switches one by one and the respirator sank down. Machines whined from beyond the curtain, but in that space, there was no sound. Then a god-awful exhale seeped out Gip's mouth. I expect it was his fetid soul escaping on his dying breath. I shuddered, then burst into tears. It was the dying that got me, not the dead.

I found Ruby sitting in the lobby, holding a cup of coffee. And next to her was Jolene. The breath fell out of me. I dropped my head and walked to her.

"Thought you might need me. So I waited here. Ruby came out and sat down next to me. Hasn't said a word. What's going on?" She reached up and wiped my eye with her thumb.

I shook my head. "I'll tell you about it later. Can you take us home?"

"Sure," she said.

Ruby stood. "So?" she asked, substituting one word for what could have been an entire conversation.

I shrugged.

"Alright, then," she said.

"Why couldn't you wait with me, Ruby? You could have stayed with him. You could have stayed with me."

"Wouldn't have done any good. Lord, I need a cigarette. I want to go home. Take me home."

Blue lights from television sets flashed in front room windows as we drove by house after house of life going on. Gip's dying didn't matter to them any more than it mattered to me. Main Street was dark save for the neon bar lights flashing at Barney's Taproom. Jukebox music poured out as we drove past. Gip would not work that bar again. His money would never again be lost at the backroom poker table.

The house was dark when we pulled up. We all got out. I opened the door for Ruby and offered my hand. "I don't need help. I'm perfectly capable," she said, pushing past me.

"I'm sorry, Ruby," Jolene said. "For your loss."

Ruby was halfway up the walk. She stopped and came back to where we were standing. For a second, I was afraid of what she might say or do and thought to herd Jolene behind me, to protect her with my body.

She looked at each of us, then the two of us, judging us separately and together. She returned her gaze to just Jolene. "You're a pretty thing, aren't you? You tell your aunt and uncle I thank them." Then she turned and walked into the house, leaving me and Jolene too stunned to say anything.

"It's getting late. You ought to go home." I pulled her close to me, wrapping my arms around her waist. A light came on in the living room.

"Try to get some sleep. And we'll help you. You don't have to do this alone, you know."

I kissed her and wished we could drive off together and never look back.

"Talk to you tomorrow."

Ruby was sunk into Gip's recliner. The lines in her face were so deep her skinfolds cast shadows in the lamplight. She put her head back on the cushion. "His was always nicer than mine," she said, kicking off her shoes.

"You want to talk about what happened?" I asked.

Ruby seemed to wait until her eyes adjusted to the past. She sucked on her cigarette like it was fresh air, staring off into the middle distance, muttering "yup, yup," and shaking her head. She mashed the cigarette in an amber glass ashtray.

"Take that tablecloth off them boxes in the corner and bring me the one at the bottom," she said.

I set aside two smaller boxes and recognized right away the happy cartoon tomatoes dancing on the side of the last. "What is this, Ruby?"

"Just open it, for Christ's sake," she said, rocking back and forth, back and forth.

"You told me Gip threw this stuff out," I said.

"Thought he did. Apparently he kept a few things for himself. I told you, he was soft about her that way," she said. "She knew he favored her."

I pulled out a photo album and opened it delicately, like it was made of spun sugar. There were pictures of my mother as a little girl, some with Gip and Ruby. There was my mother in a sailor shirt sitting on top of a pony. There she was, holding me when I was a baby. There was my dad and me—I couldn't have been more than two—spooning on a couch, both of us asleep. There was a picture of me holding a kitten. "It's Elizabeth," I whispered. "Why wouldn't you leave this out?"

"Yeah, well, at first I thought Gip had tossed it all, like I told you. Turns out he saved this one box of things. I found him rummaging around in it, sobbing like a baby. I didn't want him pining like a pup over her. His grief never felt right to me."

I took out my mother's keepsakes one by one: a sparkling rock that used to sit on her bedside table, a jewelry box with only a spinning spring where a ballerina used to be, a half-empty bottle of Love's Fresh Lemon perfume.

"So it was Gip you were keeping this from? Not me?"

"You ever see that scar across Gip's belly?"

"Yeah. So?"

"He told me he got sliced at the feed store. I got to thinking about it, seeing that hunting knife again. I think that was around the time that knife went missing from my panty drawer. I was mad we got a bill for the stitches. Thought work ought to pay since he said it happened there. She sassed him about it, hands on her hips, mouthing off. You know, 'Yeah, why isn't work paying for it, huh?' I talked to him that way, he'd have kicked my teeth in. Maybe I know why now. Maybe it was her that opened him up."

"You think that's why that knife was there? That she attacked him?"

"If she'd been truthful with me, I might could have helped."

I could see the knife in her hand, how it might lash across that hard belly. I could see the blood on her sheet. "Maybe she thought you couldn't do anything to stop him."

"Well, I stopped him tonight now, didn't I?" She looked right at me and I saw it there in her eyes. She was satisfied.

"You said it was an accident. But it wasn't an accident, was it? You did it on purpose."

"Not what I set out to do. He was out in the street. He could barely stand up. I suppose that's what he was like stumbling into Val's room, like my brothers stumbled up on me. And I'll tell you what. He knew exactly what hit him. He knew it was me."

I sat down on the coffee table and let my head rest in my hands, picturing Gip in the headlights, seeing Ruby's face coming at him over the hood of his own car.

"No brakes?"

"Nope. Not even a tap. It was like I had the rapture in me. Don't remember deciding to do anything. Happened, is all."

The calmer she was, the more I quaked. The house was dead quiet but for the ringing in my ears. The shock of her confession kept me turning the album pages. There was a series of pictures of my mother walking along the snowy river bottom I knew so well. Most of them were of her walking away; in one she was glancing over her shoulder for one last look. I flipped the page and saw myself and my father with Topeka. Trampled grass, manure from the racetrack, the hay bale perimeter of the midway, my father's arms over my shoulders, his chest behind my head—I could feel it, smell it all, like some part of that boy was still inside me and that summer never really ended after all. The full moon over the midway was the same one over Bright Lake that could see everything. That moon knew where my father was, but I didn't. If Ruby was right, Gip had lurked at his daughter's bedroom door, waiting for the opportunity to turn the knob. My father had simply disappeared, the lesser of two evils. Gloom surrounded me like an old shed, gray and rickety and rotted. "Fathers should love their children right," I said. "Families shouldn't be like this one."

"Let me see that," Ruby said, sticking out her hand.

I lifted it from the brittle page and gave it to her. "I'd kind of forgotten what he even looked like," she said. "You're more and more like him every day. Here. You can have all of it. No reason for me to keep it now."

I returned the album back to the box, then got beers for the both of us. Ruby stretched out in Gip's recliner. The light bulb flickered and blew. We drank in the dark.

CHAPTER 22

We buried Gip near my mother. Aside from a few coworkers who held their John Deere hats in their hands, only Jolene, Mona, and Troy stood with me and Ruby graveside. Plus one face I would not have expected to see. Burt Rook stood apart, hands together, head bowed. It impressed me to no end that he would come, that he would put aside Gip's trespasses to pay his respects. I spent more time during the brief service thinking about the kind of man I wanted to be, the one who would not live in the past, who would let bygones be. I decided right there and then that I would shake Burt Rook's hand, apologize for all that had happened, thank him for being there. It made me stand up a little taller even as my grandfather was being lowered into the ground.

The Hightowers offered Ruby their sympathies and, after a quick hug, Jolene mouthed to me that she would see me later. The three of them walked away, Jolene in the middle holding Mona's hand, her head resting against Troy, who had his arm around her shoulder. I'd thought we were the same once, both living without our parents. How different her family turned out to be from mine.

Burt Rook was last in line to offer his condolences. Ruby stood rigid as he approached. I held out my hand. "Thank you for coming, Mr. Rook," I said. "We, my grandmother and me, we sincerely appreciate it. I hope Kathryn's alright after the incident and all."

"She's fine, Wes. Thank you for asking after her." He cupped my hand in his. "I'm sorry for your loss."

"Mrs. Furniss," he said as he moved on to Ruby. "What a thing to happen. I know this must be devastating." Ruby kept her head level and looked up at Burt Rook with just her eyes. "On behalf of the bank, I wanted to let you know we've extended your notice."

Ruby unhinged her head. "You mean I can stay on?"

"I'm sorry, Mrs. Furniss. No, we extended it. We can't revoke it. But we can give you an extra few weeks to recover."

So much for being the better man, I thought.

"You'll kick a widow woman out into the street. That's what you'll do?"

"Mr. Rook, is there any way she could stay, maybe until the summer?" I asked.

"I'm sorry, Wes."

"Here's what I think of you and your bank," Ruby said. She shifted her purse to her left arm, stepped back with one foot, and spat from her toothless mouth right on Burt Rook's shiny black shoes. "Better plan on dragging me out."

The banker closed up like a fern. He walked away because he could.

Church ladies brought lunch to the house. Ruby met them at the door and told them they could shove their goddamned ham.

THE POLICE CALLED THE HOUSE asking for Ruby. She hadn't left her bedroom since after the burial—not to eat, not to watch television, only to use the bathroom. I hadn't even been able to get her to drink coffee. She'd only yelled at me to leave her alone, said she wasn't hungry. I told the officer as much. "Maybe I could bring her down tomorrow or the next day to talk to you," I said, thinking for sure they'd figured out Ruby meant to run her own husband down.

"Sure," the man said. "We have some of Mr. Furniss's things here, is all. Won't take but a minute to sign for them. Plus you can take your car out of the impound lot. We're done with it. You're going to need to get the windshield fixed."

I was glad the police weren't at the door because knowing the truth was shaking me. But over the phone, I was able to conceal my nerves. "So that's it?" I asked. "Nothing else?"

Ruby came out after I hung up. Her hair was stringy and loose, her eyes sunken in along with her lips, but she was dressed, which I hadn't expected.

"I know what they're doing," she said. "Trying to trick me into coming down there so they can arrest me." She crumpled up a cigarette box and tossed it on the table. "Make yourself useful. Run down and pick me up some smokes. And matches, too. I'm out."

Our routine revolved around Gip's coming and going, one paycheck for bills, one for groceries, dinner when he asked for it, quiet when he demanded it. Would the shape of things change with him gone? It was a Saturday, so I walked to the little store next to Lester's house for Ruby's cigarettes. He was outside tossing a baseball with the red-haired kid who lived next door to him. Lester had a limber way with people. Though his edges were hard, the billow and sway that made him a good basketball player would eventually make him a good salesman. When he saw me, he lobbed the ball and told the kid to get lost, though he said it in a way that made the boy smile. He knew about my grandfather, but I'd only told Jolene about Ruby's confession. The fewer people who knew that truth, the better, I figured.

"Picking up smokes for Ruby. Thought I'd say hi."

"Man, I heard. Wild shit, your grandma running him over like that. You okay?"

"Yeah," I said. "Worse thing is, I keep imagining that moment when she hit him. Looking through the windshield at her. Grisly."

"What about Ruby? Jesus," he said. "Gives me the shivers thinking about it."

I told him how she'd spent her days since, closed up in her room. I'd heard sounds through the door and the wall at night. Not sniffling or crying. It was all exhale, nothing drawn in, only despair of some sort letting out. I told him, too, how she'd stood up to Burt Rook, though in my mind that had been the wrong thing to do. What it was, I would soon discover, was that she'd backed herself into a corner. Those exhales were Ruby exorcising her fear so she could lash out at all comers she suspected were lying in wait.

When I got home, the tomato box was next to the door. Ruby was sitting at the table, drinking a beer.

"Here you go," I said, handing her the cigarette carton. "What's that doing there?"

"You get matches? Told you I was out."

"Yeah, here. So what's with the box?"

"I want you to take your stuff and get out."

I pulled out the chair next to her and turned it around, straddling to face her. She looked away and fumbled with the red pull tab on the pack. "What now?"

"What took you so long, huh?" she asked. "You down at the bank? The police station?"

"I stopped to talk to Lester. What's got into you?"

"I want you out, is all. Take your shit, all of it. Take that box. And get out."

"Let's get you something to eat, Ruby. You're not thinking straight."

She slammed her hand down on the table, jiggling her coffee cup and the centerpiece basket of rubber fruit. "I don't want you here anymore. I don't trust you. I don't need your help. I don't need anything from you. And I got nothing left to give. I'm sick of you. I'm sick of your Indian friends. I'm sick of talking about Valerie. I'm sick of all of it. I want you gone. Today. Now. Don't leave anything here you want to see again. I won't let you back."

Her jaw locked behind her sunken lips. She stared at me, her eyes squinting, shifting. She went back to her beer without saying a word.

"So that's it?" I asked. "You're going to throw me out just like that. Where do you expect me to go?"

"Find a couch somewhere. Sleep on the sidewalk for all I care. You're not my problem anymore," she said, and emptied the can into her toothless mouth.

As much as I wanted away from that house, I was also scared of what would happen to me next. She steeled her mouth, blinked frantically. If it was a bluff, I would call it. I hit both my hands on the table, called Jolene while Ruby sat there, told her I was moving out and asked could she help me with my stuff. All the while I stared at Ruby. She looked like an animal capable of chewing off its own foot to escape a trap.

I knew the contortions of Ruby's face—so much of her was carved into those lines. She had a scowl cleft that extended from the bridge of her nose to the part in her hair. The cracks around her mouth, smoking fissures, puckered up to her nose. Bags of worry hung beneath her eyes. But right then, I saw her face at rest, cast in mud, as if any expression would crackle it to pieces.

I took the duffel from the back of the closet. I stuffed in the few things I needed, realizing it wasn't much. My mother's high school picture, books I wanted to keep, a newspaper photograph of me, Lester, Jolene, and a few other kids after a football game that I took down off the wall, folded into a square, and tucked in next to my clothes. Last, I retrieved the hunting knife from under the bed, feeling again that knobby handle rib the palm of my hand. After what Ruby told me, I'd put it back in the slats where I found it, a resting place of sorts. Fear and suspicion had been sweat into the bone first by that squirrel skinner, then by my grandmother, then my mother, finally by me. I considered for the briefest moment giving it back to Ruby but thought better of it. Was she capable of hurting herself or me? I tossed it in the bag along with the rest. The house rumbled like a pot set to boil as the freight train approached. I closed my eyes and let it pass, then looked at the clock. Right on time.

—

Ruby stood up from the table when I came down the hallway. She mashed out her cigarette. "You got everything you want, right? Because I mean it. I don't want you coming back."

"Yeah, Ruby. I got it."

"And you take that tomato box. You take it, hear?"

I flung the duffel over my shoulder. Ruby grabbed me as I was about to stoop for the box. She held onto me, squeezed me like a child clings to her mom. She pulled back and her calm face cracked wide open, a breached dam. Tears flowed out of her, down her cheeks, spring melt in a dry creek. She wiped her face with both hands. "Go on, now."

"Ruby."

"You heard me. Go. I want you out. And take that box."

—

Over dinner, Mona assured me that this was Ruby's way of grieving, that some people needed to be alone. The thing I couldn't understand was how Ruby could run Gip down on purpose and feel bad about it at the same time. How she could want him dead, but then grieve when she got what she wanted. Mona dragged out, "Can't live with 'em, can't live without 'em," then punched Troy in the arm when he said, "Apparently you can run 'em over, though."

I left most of my things, including the tomato box, with Jolene, then went to Lester's to sack out. I figured I'd give Ruby a few days to settle down, then go check on her again.

THE SIRENS SOUNDED IN THE middle of the night, a call to the volunteer firefighters to report to the station. Lester roused me from my sleep. "Wes," he said. "Radio has the fire at your house."

By the time the fire trucks arrived, the whole house was engulfed in flames. A barricade of furniture against the door made breaking it down a struggle for the firemen. Mona stayed back at their house with Mariah, and all we could do—me, Lester, Jolene, and Troy—was stand by and watch it burn. We covered our mouths and noses to keep out the stench, to hold in the disbelief. Our eyes watered and stung from the smoke and from knowing what was in the oven of those cinder block walls. Flecks of flaming debris rose in the heat like birds taking flight. The contents I'd inventoried—cans, bottles, medicine, knickknacks, photographs, newspaper and nail clippings, sheets and blankets, television and recliners—melted, exploded, disintegrated in that hotbox. My knees buckled and I crouched on the ground, arms over my head.

We stayed until we heard a fireman shouting, "Cap! We got someone," long after that someone could have survived. "Let's go on now, kids," Troy said. "It's over." And it was. The house was reduced to smoldering rubble. The fire, they said, started in the bedroom. They found Ruby's body burned to a crisp in the bed she'd shared with Gip. We went back to the Hightowers', the four of us. Mona had breakfast waiting.

I HAD NOT RECOGNIZED THAT Ruby's face smoothed out the same way my mother's had because Ruby was old and death had been coming for her for much longer than it had stalked my mother. But now I could see it. Ruby had thrown me out to save me. She had not once reached out to me and begged me to stay. She'd held on to me but she'd let me go. In her violet hour, she had found her shred of decency, long buried. I repeated over and over what she'd said, what she'd done, wondering at what point she knew how it was she would never give up her house, not to the bank, not to anyone. What a joke that I thought she could hurt herself with that knife. Ruby wasn't much for small gestures. Recalling her insistence that I take the tomato box was what made me open it again. Sure enough, the things I'd replaced had been rearranged. On top was an opened envelope addressed to me and postmarked from Montana a week before my sixteenth birthday. There was no return address.

The birthday card was ragged on the edges, handled over and over. I counted the money, all small bills, none crisp from the bank: $387. A small fortune. My father's spelling was poor, his handwriting so sloppy, to read it was like breaking code. Whole lines were crossed out. It was clear he'd struggled through each word. I imagined, too, that despite the errors he was not about to go out and buy another card. Or maybe he already had and this was the best he could do.

Dear Wes,

So your 16 now. A man. I hope this money is something you can use. I suspect there tight with you, your grandparents. Can't blame them. Its hard to keep food on a table. So look here. I have not been much of a dad to you. I been thinking about it a lot and you and I probably make each other worse not better. Probably we both should shoot for better. I will miss you but think its for the best you stay there. Maybe your ready to be on your own. I was at your age. Life is full of hard choices. This was one for me. I hope for your sake you can put me and your mom behind you and make a good life for yourself. It may not seem it but I do love you.

He'd struggled with the signature, writing Moss, striking it out in favor of Dad, though he put a line through that as well, deleting himself in all his incarnations. No mystery then. He didn't want me and that was that. Though that money. Ruby had left it in the envelope. I couldn't imagine she ever told Gip about it, since surely he would have pocketed it without a second thought. To hold that amount in my hand, to think of buying anything with it, felt like I was accepting a bribe. In return for your broken heart, in return for all you've lost, for all I've taken from you, here is a handful of money.

Along with my mother's keepsakes, Ruby included mementos of her own. A coloring book. A girl's sweater. A stuffed bear. A gold necklace with a tiny cross. A naked baby doll, her hair cropped short, plugholes exposed. At the very bottom of the box, flat against the cardboard, was the wedding photograph, the one she'd hurled against the wall. A puncture hole from the broken glass went right through Gip's chest. On top of it, a dark yellow packet of photographs with a receipt from the developer dated the day before Ruby ran Gip down.

So she'd gotten herself dressed and sent me out for cigarettes. Maybe she sat on the living room floor, these remnants around her, arranging them in the box in some order that made sense to her. Had she smelled the doll's hair, touched the gold cross with her stained fingertips, held the child's sweater to her face, hoping the scent of little girl still clung there somehow? And those photographs. Fresh fingerprints all over them. On the edges, swiped across the face of my mother holding a baby dressed in pink. Another with my father in profile holding the baby well on his shoulder. Maybe a month or two old, the baby is bulky, robust, a heavy brow over dark eyes. She took after my mother's side, that was clear. None of it was proof of anything. I knew that. Was giving them to me Ruby's way of justifying the punishment she had meted to

Gip? Or maybe she simply wanted me to see pictures of the long-dead sister my mother missed so much that Ruby could never bring herself to look at? And what did it matter anymore? They were all gone.

Each time I lifted the lid—and I did, over and over for days—it was like a dirge would play, organ strikes, minor keys. Sometimes Jolene sat with me and we'd rehash what we knew of death. Her mother had left her with few belongings, nothing of worth, though she slept with a stuffed bear that had survived countless upheavals. "I've got this," she said, touching the scar, a reminder, a warning. "And this." She rested her hand on her chin, glanced around the dining room, into the kitchen. It was a gesture at the very ceiling and walls that sheltered her, but I knew she meant more than that. She had a family. She had a home. I had what Ruby left me.

Despite her coarseness, for the life of me I couldn't imagine Ruby handling these items with anything but care, placing them gently, as if they were fragile crystal. She gave no explanation, leaving it to me to glean her intent. With the task complete, she would have had to get on all fours, using the box as leverage to push up, to get a foot under a knee, to press her bones to standing. Had she hoped I'd think of her kindly from time to time, that I would know she was a person fractured, that her sorrow was all over that box, that this was as much as she could do? What I knew was that when dying came for her, she wanted me at a safe distance, away from her thin spirit. That box was a kindness, the only true gift she ever gave me.

I'd gone over to the burned-down lot in the days after the fire, thinking I would pick through to look for any other clues—a piece of jewelry, a photograph with only the corner burned, a metal box full of answers. There was no police line, no signs warning me away. My boots sank into the wet ash like it was mossy loam. Heat-twisted metal frames slumped in the two bedrooms, coils of bedsprings all that remained of the mattress where Ruby had been found. Gip's recliner—charred and singed but somehow spared—was the only furniture that was recognizable. I thought of the years they'd lived there, the three of them, the two of them, then me. What the walls had seen, what was swept under the rugs, painted, or patched over, was reduced to coal.

We buried Ruby next to Gip, whose plot was still mounded soil. The funeral expenses, even a headstone for the both of them, were covered by an anonymous donation. At first I thought it was Mona and Troy, and I tried to pay them back with the money from the envelope. But they assured me they hadn't done it. Then I realized. Burt Rook. The day of Ruby's burial, a bank envelope arrived at the Hightowers' addressed to me. In it was a check, made out to me, and a letter telling me the bank would receive an insurance settlement, that while the fire was suspicious, it had been deemed an accident caused by an old woman smoking in bed. The check was meant to cover my losses, it said, though the human toll could never be compensated, that losing a loved one comes at too high a price.

"I keep thinking about that baby in the pictures," I said. Jolene was sitting on the end of her bed, I was still on my back, staring at the ceiling.

"Hurry up," Jolene said. "Get your pants on. They'll be home soon."

Mona and Troy thought it would be better if I stayed at their house until something more permanent could be worked out. Jolene and I had promised chastity but broke that promise every chance we got, sneaking up to her room whenever the house was empty. My intense want to be inside her, part of her, was more than a boy in heat or love. She was what I knew when everything else was in shadows. I could hold her in my arms, feel her with every part of me. She was whole when all else was lack. We screwed with abandon—quick, frantic, clumsy—as if each time was to be the last. No time was sacred. If Troy was in the shower and Mona was dropping off Mariah at school, I took the stairs two at a time to get to her before she dressed for school. She flopped on the bed, I stood next to it, not bothering to lie down, not bothering to step out of the jeans that shackled my ankles. She giggled and I worked up a selfish sweat. I left her mostly frustrated but tried to make it up to her, taking what time I could when a vacant house allowed.

"Seriously," I said, grabbing her hand, pulling her down next to me. "You think my dad knew what happened to my mom or suspected at least? And their fight at Bright Lake. I told you it was about having another baby."

"Wes, please." She kissed me and pushed me off her bed. "We've been over this. I don't know what you want me to say. Let it go. There's no way of knowing. You keep going over this and it's like living in the past. Now, get out before Mona gets home."

"Okay, okay," I said. I pulled on my jeans and T-shirt. "What do you think they'd do? It's not like they don't suspect."

"Well, it's one thing to think you know something and another to know it for sure."

It was true. The photos, that letter, the box itself had me dizzy with speculation and suspicion. I couldn't know everything but I could know more. To do that I'd have to find the person I'd given up on because he'd given up on me. I had tried to talk myself out of it, reasoning that if he cared at all, he knew where I was. But I kept going back to the letter and not so much to what was in it, but that Ruby had put it on top—and not to give me the money, of that I was sure. Those bills folded flat had not been touched. That had to be Ruby's doing. She could have pocketed the money, destroyed the envelope. Instead she'd left it for me, a bread crumb. I did not want to be in the dark anymore, like Ruby said. That was no way to live.

In my mind, it was clear. Jolene and I would get out of Loma together and head west into the sunset. I'd traced the route on a fold-out map. We'd cross Minnesota and North Dakota, through the head of the Badlands into Montana, then down through Billings and across the mountains to this postmarked town. "So about that." I pulled my boots on and took her hand. "I'm going to go look for my father. I want you to come with me."

WE MADE OUR WAY DOWNSTAIRS and into the kitchen, barely dodging getting caught by Mona. "It's not that I don't want to help you," Jolene said, pouring us each a glass of milk. "What about school?"

Mona was putting groceries away and chimed in. "Wes, maybe you should wait until spring or summer even. The information isn't moving."

"If you wait," Jolene said, "I'll go with you."

"Hold on, now. We need to talk this through. As a family. You don't get to take off as you please."

"I'll be eighteen," Jolene said.

"Yes, I know that. But I don't want you leaping before you look. There's a lot to consider. Let's slow down here. We can talk about it with Troy when he comes in later. No one's going anywhere right now."

MY GUARD WAS UP WHEN Troy took me aside that night, said he wanted to have a man-to-man with me. We sat in the dining room and I told him my plan.

He nodded slowly in that way of his, head bobbing and swaying to some natural rhythm. Then he stopped and looked right at me. "You can't take Jolene with you, Wes. Come on," he said, backhanding my arm. "Let's take a walk."

The leaves were long gone, piled up and burned in the gutters. Pickup trucks had plows attached, ready to combat the feet of snow that would fall. I caught an icy chill. I shoved my hands in my pockets and walked next to Troy, trying to form my argument.

I offered a compromise. "I could wait until Christmas, I suppose. More time off from school."

"Not good enough."

"No disrespect, but I think we're old enough we can decide for ourselves."

"I agree. But you need to decide not to take her. She needs to decide not to go."

We rounded the corner, out of sight of the house. Troy shoved me hard and I fell, pile driving my shoulder onto the frozen ground, wrenching my hand under me.

I stood up, flexing the sprained wrist, and stared him down. "What did you do that for? It's because I'm white, isn't it? You and Mona never thought I was good enough for her."

"Get up and stop acting like a boy, Wes. Take your hands out of your pockets." He kept walking and I had to step quick to catch up with him. "This is your journey to make. If your dad is out there somewhere, you need to see him as a man, your arms swinging free. Having Jolene with you, you'd put her in your pocket, check on her, make sure she was alright. You'd snuggle her and hold her," he said, sweetening his tone to tease me. "You'd be thinking with little Wes down there, wondering when you could tangle her up in the sheets again."

I dropped my head and flushed with the truth. The road trip I'd drawn for myself was one part domestic, one part pornographic, though I didn't admit that to Troy.

"You know I'm right. We set rules. You break them. We know what you two are up to. I'm telling you, Wes. You take her with you and you'll get sucker punched. You won't know what hit you. You'll fall back on her and you'll be needy and pathetic."

The picture he had of me, this sniveling kid, was as much a blow to me as his knocking me down. "That's really how you see me? A weakling?"

"To be honest, she is tougher than you. But you're not weak. I don't think that at all. You need to keep looking for your strength. You have to piece yourself together. That's the sort of thing a man has to do on his own. You've got to make yourself whole again. Solid," he said, raising his arms like a boxer. "You've heard me talk about Nanabozho before."

I nodded.

"His mother was human but his father was a *manitou*, a spirit. Right after Nanabozho was born, his mother, Winonah, died and his father left him. So Nanabozho was raised by his grandmother, like you. Maybe that grandmother was a little bit nicer. Anyway, when he got older and learned that he was a *waebinigun*, a castoff, he got so mad thinking maybe his father caused his mother's death, made him miss out on her love, that he goes to look for him, to get even with old Dad, heads west, since that's where his father is said to reside. Sound familiar?"

"You made that up."

"Now, you know I wouldn't do that, mess with the stories that way."

"So, what happens?"

"Too long to tell now and Mona's going to start to wonder. But here's what I want you to know: Being hateful won't get you anywhere. Wisdom is not gained through vengeance."

The sadness of it all swept over me. What was I getting myself into? "Will you tell me this? Does Nanabozho survive? Does he come back in one piece?"

"He does. Now let's go before my wife tans my hide."

"Who's getting pushed around by a woman now?" I asked.

"See, Wes? That's the thing. When you know yourself, you can rest. The strong need to rest, too. The strong need to be able to close their eyes, trust sleep."

We stood together, me and Troy, at the end of the sidewalk leading up to the house. Lights glowed gold in the windows, and I remembered the first time Jolene dragged me in to summon the ghosts of our dead mothers out of a game board. "I loved her from the moment I saw her," I said, not taking my eyes off the house where she lived.

"Plant your feet, Wes. Loosen your arms. It's going to come at you. You need to be ready." He shoved me again. This time I stepped right.

Ruby's murder weapon, the Plymouth, was turned over to me. But the groove Gip's backside made on the bench seat felt like quicksand, and when I gripped the rubbed ten-and-two spot where Ruby held the wheel, I felt the clench she had on it that night and the force with which she hit her own husband, then hit him again. Worst of all was looking out the windshield, seeing Gip's face there like a twisted hood ornament. Troy went with me and I traded it in for a mint-green sedan that had never run over a soul. "Better gas mileage," he said. "You'll be glad for that. Trust me."

I went over to the burned lot one last time to kick through the ashes, to walk inside the soot-stained blocks. What was there was gone. I rubbed my hands in the char, turned them black with everything destroyed in the fire. I was tempted to black my eyes, to prepare myself for battle as bright as the sun. Instead, I picked up a piece of coal by the front stoop and wrote on the last wall standing, "Wes Ballot Was Here."

I stopped by Lester's house the night before I left Loma. He was sitting in the Impala listening to the radio. I slid into the passenger seat.

"Heading out tomorrow," I said. "Thought I'd come over and say goodbye." I'd paid Lester off for the fender damage with the bank money, throwing in a little extra when he complained I wouldn't be around to help with the work.

"What about school?" he asked. "Listen to me. I sound like Troy."

"School will be there. This feels more important right now."

He shrugged. "Be careful out there in the big bad world, man. Sure you don't want old Lester to go along with you?"

"Going this one alone, I'm afraid. Thanks for the offer, though," I said.

Lester reached into the back seat and took a beer from a little cooler. "One more here. You want it?"

"Sure," I said.

He shook the can before handing it to me with a grin. I pulled the tab and the foam rolled out over the edge and onto my hand.

"You're an asshole," I said. "You know that, right?"

"I know. Don't get that on the seat."

"So Troy said you got a job?"

"Almost, man. Ray has a plow driver with a broken leg. Make me some bank this winter, son."

"Cool."

Three kids rode by on two bicycles, a boy and girl doubled up on one banana seat. The sun was low in the sky and their shadows were long and alien. "Remember being like that?" Lester asked. "No shits to give? No idea what time it was? Nobody wanting a goddamned thing from you? I'd ride my bike in the dead of winter to be out of the house. Freedom, man."

My childhood hadn't been like that and I felt it again, listening to Lester, watching the kids as they disappeared around a corner, bundled for winter but acting like it would always be summer for them. Something had been denied me, and I decided then it was that freedom

Lester saw. I'd been a fearful boy. Now, there I was, grown tall, filled out, shaving stubble on a face that looked like my father's.

"I gotta get going. Thanks for the beer." I dropped the can on the floor and got out of the car.

"Yeah, I guess I ought to go in, too, before I run the battery down."

Lester met me between our two cars.

"Do me a favor, will you?" I asked.

"Sure, man. You name it."

"Watch over Jolene for me. Not that she needs it. Just. Remind her every once in a while that I'm out there, that I'm coming back."

"You got it. But I'm curious. How long exactly does she have to wait around for you before I get to go in and pick up the pieces, work my Lester charm on her?" He grinned and ducked away, knowing a punch was coming.

"I mentioned that you are an asshole, right?"

We hugged, pounded each other's backs hard.

"Take care of yourself, Wes."

"You, too, man. You, too."

Jolene came to me quietly in the night. I woke with her hand on my mouth and her face next to mine. She led me to her bedroom, her finger to her lips as we snuck past Mariah, sound asleep. We didn't speak a word to each other, not a single one. In the darkness, my head buried in the fragrant curve of her neck, I prayed to a god I didn't trust. *Let this not be a mistake. Let me not lose her, too.*

CHAPTER 23

Goodbyes had been said the night before, so at dawn all that was left for me to do was to leave. It was the hardest thing I had ever done. Ghosts were all around me as I walked out that door with the screen Troy had finally fixed after Sparky crawled under the porch to die on his own terms. I'm sure Mona and Troy were in bed behind their closed door, smelling the bacon and eggs Jolene cooked for me, listening to our whispers, giving us space to let go of each other.

"I have to go."

"I know."

She walked me out in her slippers and watched as I threw my bag onto the seat next to the tomato box. I smoothed her mussed-up hair and took her face in my hands. She tucked her elbows in, entwined her fingers, and thumped my chest once, like she was jump-starting my stopped heart. Tears were streaming down her face into my hands. I wiped them away with my thumb.

"Don't go," she said, crying fully now.

I pulled her into me, hoping her tears would soak my shirt and that it would never dry.

"I have to. But I'm coming back, Jolene. I am." I could hear my own desperation as I tried to convince myself as much as her that I wasn't leaving for good. "It's not forever."

"I'm scared."

Somehow kissing her, embracing her, wasn't enough. I dropped to my knees and held her hands in mine.

She bent to me, sheltering my body with hers. "Maybe it's silly," she said, dropping my hands to reach into the pocket of her thick sweater. "But keep this with you. Keep me with you." She looped a leather string over my head and tucked a pouch into the collar of my shirt. She fingered a section of hair into her hand, showing me the blunt end, freshly shorn, then drew a matching pouch from her pocket, the drawstrings open.

From the tomato box, I pulled out Ruby's knife. With my left hand, I grabbed a tuft of my own hair and with my right, cut it for Jolene, dropped it into the pouch she held open. She handed it to me and bowed her head.

"I will see you again." She clutched the pouch around her neck with one hand and pressed her hand against my chest and the pouch she'd placed there with the other, sealing me to her.

I GASSED UP, BOUGHT A road map, beef jerky, red licorice, and a big bottle of Mountain Dew, and headed west. Mona left a crumbling old cooler full of meat pies and sandwiches in the back seat, enough to last me a week, though if all went as planned it would take me maybe two days to get where I was going.

With each mile I traveled, I felt the past slipping away from me and catching up at the same time, a leapfrogging memory game stuck in reverse. The radio crackled in and out, until finally I gave up and switched it off. With only my thoughts for company, I rewound and rewound, skipping over what made me happy, dwelling instead on the low points, turning snapshots into entire scenes, real or imagined, always settling down on one question. Would I find him? And in that question was buried another. What might have been? I crossed into

North Dakota, leaving Minnesota and Jolene in my rearview. The landscape flattened even more, and the sky opened up with miles and miles of nothing, not even a fence post, in between the horizons. The road disappeared into clouds piping up in the distance. I pressed the gas until the car shuddered. I imagined myself getting smaller with distance, disappearing into nothing. I wallowed in the emptiness of the vast prairie, gray and grim. Long-haul truckers whipped past, stirring up a thin layer of dust and dry snow. I felt my mother in the car with me and thought it strange that I was driving, not her. I put my hand on the tomato box from time to time, whether to keep the lid on or to draw some truth out, I don't know.

Somewhere after Bismarck, after crossing the big Missouri, a ground blizzard picked up, blowing early winter snow across the highway until the stripes whited out. I slowed to a crawl, not seeing a single car coming the other direction for long stretches of time. I considered pulling off but was afraid I'd get sideswiped or rear-ended by another lone traveler thinking no one else was on the road. Out of the whiteness behind me, high headlights flashed and an armored whirl of green pulled up next to me, then in front of me—one army truck, then another. A hand out, a wave to follow, then both trucks pulled in front of me. More headlights came up behind and I was in the cradle of a convoy, safer than I was before. When the wind died down, somewhere outside Medora, the full convoy went around me, another arm, a final wave. My eyes glazed over in the twilight, tired from fighting the disappearing highway. I didn't see the mule deer until she stepped out. I hit the brakes and skidded into a shallow ditch. She stood there, her head turned to me, neck and ears craned. We watched each other, that deer and me. Troy had shot one weeks before. It hung in their garage, black nose almost to the floor, its accusing eyes fixed. But this deer was alive and she seemed to have no opinion of me at all. She seemed not to know me. And I had not killed her. I had not killed her. She turned her head and trotted off into a break of trees. I drove as long as I could, holding my thoughts like a forked twig over that deer, trying to divine some meaning out of the guardian soldiers and a near miss. Though I was exhausted, I felt new and possible, like the future might be mine for the shaping.

The first motel I found after crossing the Little Missouri River was the same kind of long white single-decker place I'd stayed in so many times before. I paid the man at the desk an extra five dollars to stop asking me how old I was and what I was doing on my own. I knew without stepping foot in the room what it would look like. One double bed covered in a worn cloth, two pillows, a metal-framed chair tucked into a chipped veneer desk, bad art, stained brown carpet, half a roll of toilet paper with the end folded into a triangle to let me know that the maid had been in the bathroom, though she probably hadn't really cleaned it much. There would be a phone book but no map, pen but no paper, a Bible but no God. The difference was neither one of my parents would be there. I was truly on my own. Duffel bag over my shoulder, I turned the knob and walked in, alone but unafraid.

It was not the good sleep I needed. Instead, I dreamed as I still often do of deep and dark places, of things held tight and shut doors. In my dream, I crushed some small animal with my bare foot, its bones popping under my toes. Jolene was in my dreams, too, but at a distance. I called to her, but when she turned, her face was my mother's and her skin had turned blue. She told me she was cold, but it was my own chill that rescued me. It was barely daybreak when I woke up, stiff and shivering, thin blue blankets at my feet.

I stepped outside and stretched. Against the distant buttes, the sun was rising. Though the motel was close to the highway, there were no road sounds at all. Somewhere a prairie dog scolded. The vacancy sign was lit but the office seemed closed. Only one other car was in the motel lot. I felt like I was the only person anywhere. I pulled the collar of my jacket up and laid the map out on the hood of the car, tracing with my finger the miles I'd clocked. I was in the middle of the sage-and-sandstone Badlands, near the Montana line. I would cross the border, follow the highway, turn south with it, and follow the river coulee down through Billings and across the state. I punctuated my route with a tap on the town of Burden Falls. I had nothing to go by once I got there except a name and a postmark. He could be there. He could be gone. I let my eyes drift back to Minnesota, to Loma, where I hoped a more distant future would continue to wait for me.

CHAPTER 24

I turned on the radio, but the best signals came from Christian stations, with screaming preachers telling me what a sinner I was, what a failure. Day two on my own and already I felt hollowed out, my pumpkin innards scraped into a paper bag. I thought about calling Jolene, to let her know where I was and that I was fine, but who wants to know the details of loneliness, the way it sticks to the inside of your mouth, runs through you, a spit through a pig? Better to wait until there was something to report. I pulled out the pouch tucked into the layers of my shirts and held it tight in my hand as I steered my way onto the westward highway.

I passed town after town until finally the interstate downshifted into a two-lane highway winding through one-stoplight towns, past cutoffs to the foothills and the mountains that cropped up out of the empty prairie. Winter hay lay like rolling pins in fields dotted with cattle. Beyond the fields, thickets of cottonwoods and evergreens followed the highway's path, their roots sapping water from a hidden riverbank. The sky was blue and vast.

I kept driving, past a meatpacking house, a motorcycle and snowmobile shop, a concrete and gravel plant on the side of the hill. A dented guardrail skirted a bend in the road. White crosses lined the curve where the road turned into the river span. I crossed a silver trestle bridge over a rocky river into Burden Falls.

THE SMALL TOWN WAS LAID out in a neat grid with the highway running north and south and the river roughly following the same path around a center that included a grocery store at the east end of Main Street and a school at the west. I checked into an L-shaped motel next to a brick creamery. The room was rustic, more Western and homey than highway motels. The headboard was a wagon wheel and the pictures hanging on the walls were all of cowboys and Indians waging war. I stared at a woman adorned in fur and hides sitting next to a teepee. I remember thinking Jolene would hate it, Mona, too, for that matter. The way the animal skin fell off the brown shoulder, the feathers and vegetables and baskets scattered around her as if that's all Indian women ever did, lounge around waiting for a warrior to come home. She would only wait so long for me.

I didn't know where to begin, how to look for someone who didn't want to be found. I could hang around a coffee shop or bar. I knew he'd been at the post office but not whether he'd return. I could watch for the familiar pickup, the Minnesota plates. The loneliness struck me, and I understood why my dad took Elizabeth on those long trips. And I longed for my mother. The motel room smelled like her—not the lemon perfume but the rootlessness. It smelled like packing up.

There was no phone book in the room, so I went back down to the front desk, thinking I'd start my search there. I thumbed to the Bs, tracing down the column. No Ballot. The woman at the desk was flat chested and boy thin with a shock of frizzy hair the color of processed cheese. She watched me with buggy blue eyes while I searched. I slammed the book shut, stared out the office window.

"Didn't find who you're looking for?"

I shook my head. "You know anyone by the name of Moss Ballot?"

"What kind of name is Moss? That's not much of a name."

"So, no?"

She shrugged and shivered her body, crumpling up her whole face like even the name repulsed her.

I had another thought and went back to the phone book, back to the Bs. I let my finger rest on a color, no address, and spun the directory around. "Do you know these people?" I asked, pointing to the name.

"Blue. Arthur and Geneva." Her voice was twitchy, like each sentence came out after a shock from a cattle prod. "Can't say as I do. But I'm pretty new here myself." She let out a laugh like machine-gun fire. "I got to make more friends, I guess. What's your name?"

Deflated, I pushed the directory back to her without answering. "Anyplace around here I can get a good dinner cheap?"

"There's an A&W out on the highway. Or the Cozy Cup up the road here on the right."

"Thanks for your help."

"Any time! And, hey, if you go to the Cozy Cup you might want to ask if Aveline is working. Her last name's Blue. Maybe she knows that couple you was looking for."

I stopped with one foot out the door. "What was that?"

"Aveline Blue. She's a waitress. At the Cozy Cup."

According to the article framed by the cash register, the town was founded by a Jesuit named Father Burden. He raised chickens and doves behind his bark slab cabin and tended his flock, human and avian. Someone suggested that adding the word "Falls" would make Burden sound more appealing to settlers. So, being an honest man, Father Burden climbed up into the canyon, found a creek and named it Burden Creek, then christened the little spot where a pile of rocks dropped the creek down about seven feet or so Burden Falls. I liked the name. It seemed like a place a person could finally be at peace.

I passed the sepia-toned pictures of Father Burden, then took a seat at a booth in the back where no one could get past me. The waitress came over. She was low to the ground with bottle-black hair piled high on her head. She seemed too old for the tangerine-colored lipstick that snaked off in tiny tributaries around her mouth. She did not seem like my father's type. Her name tag, in the shape of a turkey, told me her name was not Aveline.

"What can I do you for?" she asked, pressing the coffeepot toward me.

I turned my cup over. "Burger, I guess. Fries."

The dining room was small, maybe a dozen or more tables, most occupied with men tanned to leather from working outdoors, plaid shirts rolled up to the elbows, cowboy hats—some set on the table, some not—old tattoos bled to death under curling arm hair. There was a frazzled woman about my mother's age in the booth opposite mine, cutting a whole sandwich into three for her kids to share. Her kids were young and fretful, a buzz-cut boy and two girls who might have been twins spun from a tornado. The mother slapped at their grabbing hands and pointed a warning finger at their jabbering mouths. That would have been my mom with kids who talked back, kids who acted up, instead of me, who never did fuss much.

I considered every waitress on the floor and behind the counter, looking for an angelic face and what Topeka had described as a giant ass. She wasn't there. My waitress waddled over, a burger piled on the plate in her hand. I heard a voice call from near the cash register, though I couldn't see the person. "Thanks again, hon! See you in the morning!"

"Happy to help!" the waitress called back, waving her free hand as she set the plate down in front of me. The bell on the door rang as it opened and closed. Out the window I saw a flip of blond hair in the light and a backside that was not at all small.

"Sorry about that. Switching shifts. Anything else I can get you?"

A car pulled out of the parking lot. The taillights disappeared down the street.

THE NEXT MORNING, I SAT at the Cozy Cup's bustling counter. The crowd was mostly men, mostly friendly. There was no sign of my father. Aveline, though, she was easy to spot. When I was in fifth grade, there was a kid in my class called Roper Powell. Roper said his dad had stacks of girlie magazines under his bed and that any kid could look at them for a quarter. Roper was scrawny and he'd sell the peep show by drawing these women with swoops of his hands and arms, great curving tops, teeny-tiny waists, blossoming bottoms. He was drawing Aveline. Even her hair was curvy. Even her voice. I kept my head down when I ordered, watching her in glances. I ate my omelet slowly, drank cup after cup of coffee to stay. The counter waitress called me "love" and "hun," and I tried to keep from drawing attention to myself, especially when Aveline came behind the counter for a coffeepot or to put an order in. I listened for clues. I listened for my father's name. She did hesitate once when I spoke, turned like she'd heard a familiar voice. The coffeepot was in her hand.

"You want a top off?" she asked. Her head was cocked slightly, so her ponytail rested on her shoulder.

"No, no. I'm done. Thanks. No." I fumbled my words, grabbed the bill, practically fell off the spinning stool trying to get to the cash register and out of the café. I was afraid her eyes were on me, so I didn't look back.

I drove around Burden Falls, looking at the faces of the men walking down the street. When I figured the lunch rush would be over and the early shift ending, I went back to the café. From my surveillance spot in the parking lot, I watched Aveline come out in her pale pink uniform, a down coat over it. She got into a little brown car and drove off. I tailed her down Main Street and turned behind her on Maple, where a pharmacy stood on one corner and a bank on the other.

The house on the corner was simple enough, small and white with a low fence around the yard. She pulled into the driveway and stayed in the car. I stopped a ways back and watched. Had my father cut the grass at this house? Was the last layer of paint one that he had put on? If the tomato box next to me did not connect to the house in front of me, what then?

The front door opened and a hunched woman stepped out onto the porch. She wore a blue checkered blouse tucked into pants pulled up high around her waist. Her glasses were thick and her hair was thin and gray. Aveline got out of the car, made her way to the woman quickly, taking her arm, stroking it. She glanced my way and I tried to make myself small like a detective on a stakeout. She held me in her sights for a second more, then turned her attention back to the woman, who she guided into the house. Seconds later, though, she was outside again, coming toward the car.

I started the engine, then cut it. Why had I come here if not to be seen, if not to show this woman the letter Ruby had left for me and to ask if she knew my father? I lifted the lid of the tomato box and took out the envelope Ruby had so carefully laid on top. I slapped it on the palm of my hand for courage but fumbled it when I heard the rap on my window glass. I leaned over and scooped up the envelope with one hand and she was there, making the roll-it-down motion.

"Excuse me," she said while I was still cranking down the window. "Who are you and why—"

Her tone changed and she said again, "Who are you?"

She took a couple of steps back from the car and I got out. "My name's Wes. Wes Ballot." I extended my hand and she took it, but she never stopped staring up at me. "I'm sorry to bother you," I said, glancing back to her house. "It's, well, I'm looking for Miss Aveline Blue. I'm wondering if that's you. If you're her, Aveline Blue, I mean."

We stood there in the street, two people locked in the past. Finally, she spoke again. "I know who you are. You look just like Moss." Her voice died down to a whisper. "It's like looking at a ghost."

"I know I take after him," I said, and she nodded.

"Maybe not the mouth but the eyes, my God."

I'd only felt my father's blood roiling in me. I'd never felt it do what it was doing then—thickening up and gurgling, blushing my face. She was the kind of person who stands a little closer than what's usually comfortable, and she was up close to me, looking me over. I'd have taken a step back, but in that way you let a dog sniff you first, I didn't want to cause suspicion. Her eyes had tiny lines in the corners that would have made her look cross if it hadn't been for the deep dimple in her right cheek. Her blue eyes flickered and her lower lip twisted up as she bit the corner. I'd had plenty of time to practice all I would say to this woman, but I was dumbstruck, imagining my father standing in the spot where I stood, maybe holding a beer or the brown wax duffel bag he took with him on the road.

She put her hand to her mouth, then dropped it again. "Let me look at you." I stood stock-still while she surveyed me. Her hand was back to her mouth. She read my face like it was a palm.

"Where'd you come from?"

"I've been living with my grandparents. Minnesota. It's, well, I got this letter and I—maybe I shouldn't have come. It's just . . ." I tried to organize my thoughts, but the miles I'd traveled logged in my veins and I could feel the tire treads rumbling the marrow like I was still driving. She rescued me from my bumbling.

"We don't need to stand out here. Come on up to the house so we can talk better."

I followed Aveline, watching her ample top and bottom crowd out the middle of her pale pink uniform with each twitch of her hips. The old woman stood in the doorway and squinted at me through her thick lenses. "Well, look what the cat drug in!" she said. "Where you been, Moss?"

"Mama, this is Wes, not Moss. Moss is—I'm sorry, Wes. This is my mom. Geneva."

I wanted to hear her say it: Moss is dead. "It's nice to meet you, ma'am."

"You sure you're not Moss?" the old woman asked.

"He's sure, Mama." Aveline's voice snapped with tension. She must have heard it, too, because she softened toward her mother and guided her into the house.

Blue-and-yellow bunches of wallpaper flowers plastered the sunlit walls. Little lace mats sat under every candy dish and lamp and on all the armrests. There was a faint smell of soap and roses. I imagined myself curled up on the davenport, blanketed beneath the crocheted afghan.

She snuck up on me, quiet as could be. I felt her first, pushing against my ankles, weaving through my legs. The mewing. Her fur, a gray-and-white watercolor, ruffed at the neck and fanned out like a feather along her tail. I bent to pick her up and she collapsed against me, mew turning to purr. "Elizabeth," I whispered, burying my head in the cloud of fur.

Mrs. Blue had settled into her rocker by the front window. "Even the cat thinks he's Moss."

"Mama, please. Wes, why don't you come with me into the kitchen and let me get you something. And you can bring Elizabeth. She probably wants something to eat anyway."

I followed her through the living room past an upright piano and into the yellow kitchen, Elizabeth safe in my arms for the first time since Bright Lake.

"Have a seat," she said. "Looks like Elizabeth missed you." There it was again, that tension, contempt even, in Aveline's voice.

"I'm sorry to drop in like this."

"You don't have to apologize. I'm glad to have you. I'm just, well, surprised isn't the half of it."

She handed me a glass of water and sat down in the chair across from me.

"Can you tell me how it is you knew to come here?"

I'd rehearsed the conversation, thinking I would go all the way back to Bright Lake. But I wasn't sure I was ready for that story quite yet. I took in the details of the kitchen—white stove, white cupboards, a rounded refrigerator covered with finger-paint art, flecked countertops, canning jars filled with beets and beans lining the shelves, the hanging plant with spidery offshoots dangling next to—

"What is that?" I asked, pointing to the corner as I got up from the table.

Aveline turned in her chair. "I'm sure you recognize it. Your dad made that for me."

Three willow branches stacked like rungs on a ladder turned gently on the end of fishing line hung from a hook on the ceiling. Stuffed sparrows and chickadees balanced on the ends, bobbing in a slow circle as I touched each branch of the homemade mobile. The birds' feathers were dusty, but the amateur taxidermy had held up pretty well.

"Elizabeth can't stop herself from killing birds," I said quietly.

I remembered my mother screaming at my father. She'd say, "Make her stop that!" and my dad would laugh and tell her he couldn't stop Elizabeth, that it was in her nature to go after the birds.

"You can't stop a thing from doing what it was meant to do, Val," he'd said, picking up the dead bird, which he then wrapped tightly with gauze and stuck in the freezer until he could get to the business of taking its innards out and stuffing it full of batting instead.

"Well, you can't keep it in the freezer. It's probably covered in germs. It'll get all over the food."

"What food? Nothing in there but ice. It's fine," he'd said, then tossed the bird in with the others and closed the freezer door, which ended my recollection.

I turned to Aveline. "He'd put them on a string or on the end of a stick and tease her with them. I've never seen anything like this before, though." I touched the birds and they bobbed around, one teetering while the other tottered. Then I remembered similar mangled remains I'd collected from the road years earlier.

She stood and was close enough to me now that I could smell her perfume and something else, something clean and mineral. I suspected she'd hung her clothes out to dry on the line and that I was smelling the sun and the air behind her house. She touched one of the branches, sending the birds around again. "He wanted me to have the birds so I could think about flying."

We watched the flight slowly come to a rest.

"He's dead, isn't he? I could tell by the way you were talking to your mom. My father's dead."

Aveline stepped to the sink and held onto it, pulling back like she was trying to settle a team of horses. She dropped her head between her outstretched arms, then stood up straight and turned her head to me.

"He's not dead. Not as far as I know. I'm gonna kill him, though." She filled a red kettle with water from the tap and put it on the stove to boil. "I'm sorry, but will you please tell me how you ended up here? I need to know."

"This came in the mail. Last summer. I only just got it, though." I handed Aveline the envelope, worn now from my handling of it. She took the letter out, and the folded money fell to the floor. She held it in her hand, leaned against the counter, and read the letter. She turned the paper over to the blank side, then seemed to read it again. She placed the money back in the letter, folded it, returned it to the envelope and the envelope to me. Her lips tightened, the dimple filled with fury and disappeared.

"What kind of a person . . ." Her voice trailed off. She walked out of the kitchen. The pot whistled on the stove. I turned the knob off and waited. I was bound to the knowing, to the finding out. I had no interest in running from it anymore.

I looked out the window into a backyard surrounded by a fence woven together like a basket. There was a small bare garden plot, an apple tree with a rope swing, flower beds filled with dirt. In the summer it would look like something from a picture book. Whose life was this?

She came back into the kitchen. "Can you stay for a while? Please?"

I nodded.

"Good," she said. "Good. I need to get changed. And the bus will be here soon." She hesitated on that thought, something in it brought both calm and sadness. She bunched her lips together and smiled at me. Her face was like a dimpled heart, and I imagined my father in this kitchen falling in love with that woman and that face.

CHAPTER 25

The bus horn beeped three times, followed by the sound of footsteps, small feet running up the walk, the front door opening and slamming shut. Mrs. Blue clapped and sang out, "There she is." I followed the voices and saw a girl, white-blond hair done up in braids like antennae on a bug, hugging the old woman's neck. "You'll squeeze the stuffing out of me," Mrs. Blue said.

"Oh, Gram! You're not stuffed."

Aveline came down the hall in a T-shirt and jeans. "Wes," she said. "I got someone I want you to meet."

I knew what was happening. I knew the moment I looked at that little girl who she was and who she was to me. I let Aveline lead me like I was a child, too.

"Hey, Mama," the little girl said, smiling like Aveline right down to the dimple. She caught sight of me a breath later and twisted her smile sideways and dropped her eyebrows. "Who's that?"

"This is Wes. Wes, this is my daughter, Annaclaire."

I put out my hand. "Real nice to meet you, Annaclaire. That's a pretty name."

She put one hand in mine, the other on her hip. "Who are you a friend of?"

I looked at Aveline, not sure how to answer the question.

"He's a new friend, miss."

She looked at me matter-of-factly. "Well, he looks like my dad, don't you think?" She took my breath away, this little thing.

Mrs. Blue banged the bottom of her water glass on the arm of her rocker. "See? I told you so. Moss Ballot."

IF YOU'VE EVER BEEN IN a house with a first grader, you know there's no such thing as an uninterrupted conversation. So it took a while before Aveline and I could get back to the one we both needed to have. The four of us eyeballed each other over a supper of meatloaf and mashed potatoes. Aveline managed the conversation like a switchboard operator, pulling the plug when talk got too difficult. While Aveline settled her mother in bed, Annaclaire gave me a tour of the dollhouse her grandfather had built for Aveline. "It used to have electricity but it doesn't anymore," she said, toggling the dead switch on and off. "Maybe you can fix it."

"Maybe."

"Or I can wait. My dad maybe could fix it."

She reminded me of Jolene in a way, that boldness that comes from wearing your skin well. "You see him, then? Your dad?"

"Sure, I see him." She took the doll I was tucking in out of my hand and put it in a different bed in a different room. "That's not her bed."

"Oh. I'm sorry."

"He'll be here soon."

I looked at the door to her tiny bedroom. "Soon? Like tonight?"

"No, silly. Soon like Thanksgiving." Only days away.

Aveline popped her head in. "Time to brush teeth, miss." She clapped her hands and Annaclaire made a production out of stomping to the bathroom.

"Fine. But don't let him mess anything up."

I held up my hands in surrender. "I won't touch a thing."

"I'll be out in a few minutes, Wes. Why don't you go sit down. Make yourself comfortable."

The living room was lamplit and tasteful, with matching furniture and oak side tables. There was a small television in the corner with rabbit ears wrapped in tinfoil. It seemed more her mother than Aveline. Had the tiny bedroom been Aveline's when she was a little girl? If so, Annaclaire was growing up like I had, sleeping in her mother's room in her grandparents' house. But how different this house was. I sat down on the floral sofa and waited for Aveline to take a seat next to me in the swivel rocker.

"Your house is nice. Did you grow up here?"

"I did. Annaclaire's bedroom was mine. I had my own apartment for a while, but after I got pregnant, I had to move back. Then my dad died. Didn't make sense to be anywhere else."

I spoke the obvious so I could hear the words come out. Here I thought it was way too late for me to have a sister who lived. "So Annaclaire, she's my half sister?"

Aveline nodded. "I had an older brother named Neil. He was killed in a motorcycle accident when I was fifteen. One of those crosses out by the bridge belongs to him. I thought I'd have a big family. At the very least I thought Annaclaire would have a brother. I mean, Moss told me about you," she said.

"Where is he? Annaclaire said he'd be here for Thanksgiving."

"That's what he told us. He's lucky he's not here right now, I can tell you that."

She didn't wear a ring on her wedding finger, but I'd inspected it for a white line, some indication there'd been a commitment. I saw nothing. "Are you married to him?"

"I wanted to be. But no. We never got married."

"Will you tell me what's happening here? Because I'm awfully confused. Annaclaire. She's, what, six?"

Aveline curled herself around a pillow, tucking her legs off to the side. "How about I tell you what I know, then you tell me what you know, and the two of us figure out together what sort of a pickle we're in?"

"That sounds good to me."

"First off, I think it's better that I start at the beginning so maybe we can sort out the end a little better. You be patient with me, okay?"

And so Aveline told me how she met my father, how he'd come into the Cozy Cup, flirted with her while she was working the morning shift. He told her to come over to the carnival and he'd give her free rides on the Shooting Star. She told the story wistfully, like she was alone and daydreaming. I could tell she was thinking of other things, things maybe she was unwilling to share. "You don't really want to hear this," she said.

But I did. More than anything I wanted to understand. "I'm a good listener," I said. "Go on."

"I still remember what I was wearing: my good denim skirt, black cowboy boots, and a pink lace top. Moss had on a Pink Floyd T-shirt and his tattoo was peeking out from under his sleeve. I can close my eyes, like this," she said, pausing to rock her head back and take a deep breath, "and still see it."

I closed my eyes then, too, remembering when he came home with that tattoo and how mad my mother was that he'd gotten birds tattooed on his arm instead of her name in a heart. I think she slapped him across the face, because I mostly remember that weepy ink, freshly wrapped around a bicep flexed to strike.

"I know I'm probably not supposed to ask, but how old were you?"

"Twenty. Spring chicken. Your dad was too old for me, at least I thought he was at first. I didn't know he was married when I took up with him, Wes. You have to believe that. It was something about the ride, the lights, the way he looked at me. It was a bad time for me. I wasn't doing shit with my life. My brother had just died. My parents were sad. And there I was on that ride, at that spot where it's almost straight up and down, when you feel like you don't weigh anything. I felt like I was leaving my body up there and something else was going back down. I felt like a bird." She spread her arms out and threw her head back. "When I got off the ride, there he was, looking at me in that way of his." She tried to imitate my father's glare, the one that punctured my thoughts when I was little, and knew when I was fibbing.

"It was all bigger than me. I was a stupid, restless girl and I fell hard for him. I sure hope Annaclaire will have better sense than I did."

I'm sure I blushed thinking all sorts of thoughts about what Aveline was capable of doing after hours on a carnival ride. "So when was this?" I asked. "I'm trying to think where we were. I did spend a summer with him, but this must have been after."

"Summer of 1971. I can't believe it's been that long."

I did some math, tried to recall the summer by calculating my own age. "I remember. They'd gotten in a fight, he and my mother," I said. "We moved into a tiny apartment. She said we didn't need room for him anymore. I remember because she had a broken arm and was trying to pack boxes with that cast. She hit him with it when he touched her things. So what happened when the carnival pulled out?" I asked. Did he stay here and live in this house? I wondered. Had he showered here, changed the sprinklers, repaired the fence, while my mother and I barely scraped by?

"I was saying I felt like I was leaving part of myself behind at the top of the ride? Well, I felt like I caught up with me, being with him. I left my job, my friends. I got in the truck with Moss and Elizabeth when the carnival pulled out. I believed everything he told me. I didn't mind the carnival at night, all the twinkling lights and music, but during the day I was bored as Elizabeth, batting at them little birds that went nowhere. I worried about what I'd gotten myself into.

"I was so young and I think maybe I got in over my head. Plus, I missed my folks. I knew I hadn't been fair to them. He begged me not to, told me he loved me. I cried and cried, but I caught a Greyhound and left.

"Got back here. No job. No Moss. My daddy was still alive. Then I found out I was pregnant. They did the best they could for me, but I felt like a real fuckup. I didn't know what to do. I was a terrible Catholic, but there was no way I would do anything other than have the baby."

Listening to her talk about that pregnancy, about telling her mom and dad who cried with her, who were afraid for her and her baby and what kind of life they would have, I couldn't help but think about my mother, about Daisy, about Ruby and Gip.

"So I tracked him down. Told him over the phone I was pregnant. That's when he told me about you and your mom, the family he already had. Broke my heart. Broke it." She stopped talking, wiped her eyes, though no tears were there. "He said he couldn't leave her, couldn't leave you."

He did, though, I thought. Over and over he left.

"Fast-forward three years. The carnival comes back to town and there's Moss. I hadn't heard from him, hadn't seen him since that phone call, and he shows up. My daddy had passed. Stroke. It was just us three girls here in the house. And he shows up on the porch. Blurts out to Annaclaire that he's her daddy. She falls for him. And I fall for him all over again. Like the idiot I am. He tells me he's getting a divorce. He was talking about the four of us—me, Annaclaire, him, and you—like we were a family. But he tells me I have to be patient. And I was. I took him in dribs and drabs. Welcomed him here whenever he came. I thought I was doing it for Annaclaire. I don't know who I was doing it for.

"He was here last Christmastime with presents. He told me he'd be back in the spring, back for good. I have to tell you, I'm scared now to hear your side of this."

I thought about a Christmas tree covered in lights with packages wrapped in bright paper underneath it. Did it sit in the living room near the piano? Did Mrs. Blue play Christmas carols while Aveline and my father sang along? "I'm trying to imagine him here with you," I said. "At Christmas. We waited for him, but he didn't show up. Finally decided we'd get the tree without him. The two of us drug it back on our own. When we got it home, we realized we'd broken the top pretty bad. It was the stupidest-looking tree, but we decorated it anyway. My mother laid the angel down on top like she was sleeping. When my dad saw it, he burst out laughing. We all did." I didn't tell Aveline, but that last Christmas morning, I found my parents passed out on the living room floor of that laundromat apartment. They were naked under a thin blanket, clothes down to the underwear strewn around them, that lousy tree, half the lights burned out, still plugged in though the sun was already up.

I tried to imagine my father taking me away from my mother, the scene it would have caused. The screaming and crying. Maybe I didn't have to imagine it at all. Maybe that was what the fight was about that night at Bright Lake. "So you think the plan was that he would take me away from her and leave her all alone?" I thought then about Daisy, the other child she'd lost.

"He told stories. He said he wanted to get you away from her."

"Well, he sure as hell did that. Then he left me."

She shook her head, gestured with her hands like she was trying to catch the answers swirling around her. Her voice ratcheted up a gear. "I hadn't had a single phone call from him in months. Then in March, right before Annaclaire's birthday, he shows up. He was a wreck. He told me about an accident on a lake." She tried to steady her voice, her breathing. "Oh my God, I'm so mad. This is why I need you to tell me what happened. Your dad told me that you and your mom . . . that she broke through a frozen lake and you'd drowned trying to save her."

She was crying now, her whole body shaking. "He told me you were dead. I thought you and your mom were dead. The way he was acting—withdrawn, angry, even—I thought it was grief. He said he felt awful he wasn't there to save you. All our plans got put on hold. And now here you are and the whole thing stinks to high heaven. He made it up, didn't he? Your mom, where is she? You said you've been living with your grandparents. Where is she?"

So that was the story he'd crafted. He'd tried it out on Topeka first. It was easier to have a dead son than a sad son with a long memory. "That part's true. He wasn't there. The lake. My mom did break through. She drowned, not me. I never went in." My hand rested on the pouch under my shirt, and I wished Jolene was with me. Was it a double life or half a life? Twice as much or never quite enough? "Promises, promises," my mother had said, more than once. His word was worth nothing. Not to me, not to my mother, not to Aveline.

I told her about Bright Lake, them fighting, him storming off. I even told her about my mother trying to pull me in with her and how I'd selfishly gotten away. Each word sobbed out of me, lumpy and thick. "Did you know they had another baby? Her name was Daisy." Aveline's brow furrowed and she shook her head. Sickness formed behind my teeth, squeezed at my throat. "She died in her crib before I was ever born." I falsified the story about my grandparents, allowing Gip's death to be an accident and Ruby's to be overwhelming grief. I couldn't tell Aveline about what Gip had done to my mother or my growing fear of what my father might have done if he'd discovered Daisy was not his after all.

Aveline put her hand to her mouth as the body count rose.

"I don't know what losing Daisy meant to her. But I know my mom loved me something fierce. I don't think she could lose another child. I think she'd just as soon I was dead right there with her."

CHAPTER 26

Three days I ate breakfast and lunch at the Cozy Cup, and dinner with my father's other family. Three nights I stayed in the rustic motel. I called Jolene collect from the phone in the lobby. Troy accepted the call but told me I had to make it fast, five minutes tops, or I'd run up their phone bill. Jolene got on the line and I pictured her in the kitchen, the long phone cord kinked over her elbow, the receiver tilted so Troy could hear, then relay to Mona about my father's whereabouts and this woman Aveline, about the girl Annaclaire, who I was falling for madly, and Mrs. Blue, who was by turns fascinated by me and angry at me when she mistook me for my missing father. When Troy got off the phone, I told Jolene the quieter things about how much I missed her, that I would see her soon. I had a hard time finding the right words when she wasn't in front of me. By the time I got comfortable talking, it was time to hang up. It gutted me to realize how much distance I'd put in between us. Worse, I scared myself when I realized it would probably be less painful after a while not to call at all. My father had done that to us and to Aveline. He was never much for a long goodbye.

The next day, the day before Thanksgiving, the frizzy redhead drew me a map and I drove into the canyon to the trailhead near Burden Creek and its piddly falls. Snow was due to fall that night, and I wondered how deep it might get in the cold shadows of the mountain. I climbed a rocky outcrop on all fours, more animal than human, until

I came to a spot where I could stand upright and see the town in the valley below. I circled a spot on the postcard I'd taken from my pocket. *I'm here,* I wrote, *waiting for my dad to show up. I miss you like crazy. Tell Troy I'm keeping my hands out of my pockets.*

Aveline asked if I would meet Annaclaire's bus since it would be early for the holiday and Mrs. Blue would still be at the senior center. I let myself in to the empty house. A woman's house. Even Elizabeth seemed to have an extra, more feminine sashay as she moved from one sun spot to the next. I wandered through, thinking about the first day I was alone at Gip and Ruby's and how different this house was from that one. There were no signs of men anywhere. Not in the flowery living room or kitchen, not in the bathroom with its lace-lined towels. And not in the back bedrooms. The doors were open and I looked from one to the next. I stood in the doorway of Mrs. Blue's bedroom. The bedspread was threadbare with faded blue flowers and yellow stripes that probably shimmered when the cover was new. There was a wooden dresser with bottles on top and a mirror speckled black where the glass had failed. The room smelled like Mrs. Blue, the dusty fragrance like dried roses that made me think of time passing. I turned away from the thought and found myself looking into Aveline's bedroom.

The bedspread was the sherbet color of sunset or a salmon rising, and the bed was covered with different shapes and sizes of white pillows. There was a white dresser and matching side table. On the wall in the corner was a bulletin board with a collage of photos. I listened for sounds from the front door—the twist of a knob or the slamming of a car door—then stepped in for a closer look.

One picture overlapped the next, each showing happy people, smiling, their arms around each other. Pictures of Aveline as a girl, dressed in Sunday clothes in one, running through sprinklers in a swimsuit in the next. Aveline and her dead brother sandwiched between her mom and dad. Then lots of Annaclaire. There was one picture of Aveline and my father. He was standing behind her with his arms wrapped around her waist. She was leaning back against him, her head on his chest, her weight back against him. There were no other boys or men. Just my father. Six years and no other man had come into her life for long enough that she would add him to her pin board.

I picked up the perfume bottles on the dresser and smelled each one, trying to pinpoint which was her favorite, which one she most smelled like. I pulled open the top drawer and saw a crumpled assortment of colorful underwear and bras. I put my hand in the drawer and felt around, touching the texture of the fabric and the lace, imagining her body underneath her jeans, her T-shirt, the uniform she wore to work each day. I looked up and saw myself in the mirror. I did look like my father. I could see it better in this house where he'd stood. Behind my reflection, I could see her bed. Had my father held her there, pulled the shirt over her head? I embarrassed myself, how far I could go with Aveline in my imagination, occupying my father's skin.

Annaclaire's bus dropped her off right when the snow began to fall. We played Candy Land and dolls until the squat senior shuttle delivered Mrs. Blue home. By the time Aveline arrived with bags of groceries and a turkey for Thanksgiving, several inches were on the ground and it was coming down hard. We ate spaghetti for dinner, and I took note that all three of them ate it differently. Mrs. Blue used a spoon to manage the twirl, Aveline spun her fork against her plate, and Annaclaire shoveled and slurped with such force that the ends whipped up and splatted against her nose, which caused eruptions of laughter around the table. *So she's a shoveler,* I thought, *like our father.* My mother used to cut her spaghetti with a knife just to spite him, to prove somehow that she was more cultured. Here, another kind of family—one that didn't put on airs. Me, a spectator again. I rolled my spaghetti like Aveline, though I was a shoveler, too.

By the time the dishes were done and put away, almost a foot of snow had fallen. Annaclaire kneeled in the sofa cushions under the front window and watched as thick snowflakes streaked the skirt of light from the streetlamps. Aveline sat next to her and turned to look out as well. The street wasn't plowed. There were no tire tracks. No sign of my father.

"At least let me shovel you out before I go," I offered.

Aveline answered, though she still faced the window and the falling snow. "You should sleep here tonight."

Annaclaire jumped up and down on the sofa. "Yes, yes, yes!" Aveline scolded her softly and she bounced down into a perfect sitting position.

"No sense you going back to that old motel tonight. I was going to invite you over here for breakfast tomorrow anyway. I can make up the sofa."

I accepted, glad to spend more time with them, glad to not be in the motel room where I missed Jolene even more. I put my boots and coat on, the worn gloves from my pocket. Annaclaire insisted on going outside with me. Aveline tried to tell her it was too late to play outside, but she made her case that my being there was a special occasion plus Thanksgiving was a holiday anyway.

"She has a point," I said.

Annaclaire held out her told-you-so hands.

"I guess, since Wes's going with you. Take off your coat so I can string your mittens." Aveline carefully laced both ends of a length of purple yarn through the hole in a safety pin, tied a knot, then secured each pin on the matching mittens that Mrs. Blue knit at the senior center. She stuck her arm down the sleeve of Annaclaire's coat and pulled the mitten through, then repeated the process on the other side. "That'll do for now."

Everything about that home seemed to be about kindness, and for the life of me, I couldn't imagine why my father wasn't there. I could see how he might choose Aveline over my mother, as painful as that silent admission was. I would think to myself it was Ruby's fault my mother was the way she was, Ruby who was nothing like Mrs. Blue at all. But then I'd remind myself that Ruby was brought up in a house full of no women at all and how the only comfort she'd known were those fleeting ones on a dark dance floor after the men had gone home, back to their wives or girlfriends.

I let Annaclaire lead me onto the tiny landing, mittened hand in mine. Every branch and line was draped white, even the moon that could see everything was shrouded. The blanket of snow muffled sound. All that was left was my breathing and Annaclaire's, and Mrs. Blue's piano playing floating out into the night. *I am holding my sister's hand,* I thought.

Without warning, it was Annaclaire who let go. She took two steps forward, swooned left, and collapsed into the snow. She put her arm straight up. "Do not take one step farther. I'm making a snow angel."

"I will too, then," I said, collapsing into the snow next to her. The two of us spread and closed our angel wings, scissored our angel dresses. I looked over at her. Her eyes were squinted shut and her mouth was open. I did the same. Snowflakes fell into my mouth and melted like tiny cathedrals of ice. I savored each one.

"Wes?" she said. The Montana sky was thick with falling snow.

"Yeah?" I turned my head so I could see her face. Her eyes were blinking hard like she was sending signals into the air.

"Nothing."

Snow melted against my back and neck, but there was no chance I'd move until she gave the sign. "Hey, Annaclaire?"

"Yeah?"

"Nothing," I said.

She laughed and laughed and I listened to the sound. My sister laughing. Beyond her, from the bright light of the house, Aveline looked on.

After Annaclaire was hustled off to bed, I sat in the quiet living room, trying to remember any time my life had been so ordered. What could Aveline see in my father? How could he be one person with me and my mother and another capable of deserving this life? It made no sense.

Aveline sank into the seat next to me. "Ah," she said. "I'm exhausted. That was fun, though, wasn't it? They sure love having you here."

"What are you going to do if he comes home tomorrow?"

She shrugged, then rested her head against the cushion. "I want to give him a chance to explain. But I don't understand. I'm not much of a fighter. And I don't want to hurt Annaclaire."

"He'll keep leaving you. Even if he comes back, he'll leave you again."

"I know that."

"So why? Why do you let him do this?"

"I do love him. And he gives me all he has when he's here. I thought it would be enough. I thought I could put up with anything for my daughter. This is a small town, Wes. A girl like me. I mean, I've got a kid. A mom who needs me. I'm not exactly a catch." She was on the verge of tears. "I don't think I deserve to be lied to, though. Not like this."

"You don't. I'm sorry he's done this to us. I'm sorry for my part in it."

"You have nothing to be sorry for. And who knows? Maybe things will change with you here. We should get some sleep. Could be a long day tomorrow." She pushed to standing, touched my shoulder in a way that made me think she was on my side, whatever that might mean.

I DREAMED ABOUT HOLDING HANDS with Aveline on the Shooting Star. I dreamed about her waiting tables at the Cozy Cup diner. I dreamed about the softness of her bedsheets and her underthings and her skin. I dreamed about her as a girl, I dreamed about swimming with her in the river. Her heart-shaped face replaced Jolene's and I replaced my father, and there was no one on earth but her and me and Annaclaire between us. In my dreams I fell asleep with her resting in my arms. I woke up in the dark house to the smell of brewing coffee. Mrs. Blue stared at me from her rocking recliner.

"Put a shirt on, Moss," she said. "We need to stuff the turkey."

Aveline's voice came from the kitchen. "Mama!"

"What?" Mrs. Blue said, still staring at me.

"Wes, Mama. *Wes*. Good God."

"Whatever you say!" she replied, giving me a wink. "Come on when you're dressed."

I smiled at her and pulled my clothes on once her back was turned. I padded to the bathroom barefooted, feeling strange and fresh from that dream, like the man of the house.

Aveline was at the stove, squeezing a tube of sausage into a frying pan. I imagined walking up behind her, wrapping my arms around her waist, burying my face in the white flesh of her neck. It felt like possession, ripe and sinful. What was my place in this house?

"Have a seat. I'll throw some breakfast together after we get the stuffing made. Could you tear that loaf up into bits? Mama will help. You want coffee?"

I nodded and sat down. There was a loaf of Wonder Bread on the table next to a shallow stainless steel bowl. Mrs. Blue plucked soft pieces off each slice, dropped them in the bowl. "Like this. Not too big, not too small."

Annaclaire came in, hair mussed, nightgown twisted, slippers scuffing along the cold floor. Soon, the three of us were tearing bread. Aveline let the sausage cool, sautéed celery and onions, which she added to the bread along with sage and pepper and raw eggs. Mrs. Blue stuck her long fingers in to the knuckles, squishing egg into bread. The sausage was last, crisp and greasy.

"This is my favorite part," Annaclaire said, dipping her fingers into the raw stuffing.

Aveline's eyes flashed, her dimple deepened. "Mine, too."

In unison, the four of us sat back, sighed together at the job well done. The rising sun lit the morning sky sapphire and streaked our little kitchen with Thanksgiving gold.

CHAPTER 27

Aveline was scraping stuffing from the turkey's cavity when Annaclaire, all dolled up in a corduroy jumper, ran down the hallway and bolted out the front door. Her voice, high and happy, came into the house clear. "Daddy!"

"You," Aveline said, pressing my arm. "You go sit in the living room with Mama. Do not go outside, you hear me?"

I nodded weakly and did as I was told.

She wiped her arm and hands on her apron and untied it in one motion, then followed Annaclaire outside. The little girl came back in holding a stuffed bear and a chocolate bar, her eyes bugged wide. "I'm to go to my room for a bit. Mama said to tell you two to stay put, so stay put."

"What's going on?" Mrs. Blue asked.

"Moss is here, I think."

"About time. Supper's almost ready," she said, then went back to her knitting.

From my seat on the couch, with my hands on my thighs, I measured distance. Me to the door, the door to the front steps. The sofa to the curtain, the curtain to the window. The shoreline to the hole in the ice, the body to the front of the cabin. Bright Lake to Loma, Loma to Burden Falls. Jolene to me. Me to my father. I stood and walked to the door. In the five strides it took to get there, I stuffed my hands in my pockets, remembered, and pulled them back out. Through the lace curtain on the door, through the tiny squares in the screen inches away, I saw Aveline sitting on her front steps next to a man hunched over. Her hand was on his back, rubbing gently, her head cocked in a careful way so she could see up into his face. He was much taller than her, even sitting down. The back of his neck was bared to me because his head was buried in his folded arms, his hands on top of his head, his fingers pointing backward toward me. Aveline wiped her cheek, put a hand on his thigh. He pushed her hand away. I felt betrayed by her kindness toward him. Their voices hummed through the glass, the notes low and minor. I refocused my eyes on the swirling lace, like cotton ice crystals, then the black cells of screen mesh, blurring Aveline and this man into a watercolor of flannel and wool, of gray branches and gray sky.

I put my hand on the doorknob. The cold brass of it slid in my sweaty palm. The layers between us were more than curtains and screen. A web of time and deception and sorrow and muck were there, too, and I imagined I'd have to buckle and cut through it all to get to him. We found each other's eyes and held on. Then he shook his head, grabbed his bag, and walked back to the familiar truck parked there. Aveline ran after him. I could hear her through the door. "Moss. Don't you do this. Moss!" I couldn't turn the knob. I could only watch as Aveline hit the side of his truck with her palm as he sped off.

"Give him time" is what she said to me.

Her calm aggravated me. I matched it with fury. "Time? I don't need to give him time! He takes it from me." *Just you wait,* he'd said to me. And I had waited. I was at the end of my ability to do that anymore, but I didn't know what came after the waiting was done. I pointed my finger at her, yelling, "What are you giving him, huh?"

She was firm when she faced me. Her voice was a whisper, but she stamped each letter of each word. "Don't you raise your voice at me again. You do not know me. Now, you are welcome to stay and to have dinner with us. Or you can leave, too. It doesn't matter to me which you choose. But you stay, and by God, you will be civil."

I could see in her face, hear in her voice. My father would face a reckoning.

We sat down to dinner without him. A place had never been set. Aveline had conditioned herself and Annaclaire to expect nothing. "We're here," she had said, "but we're not waiting here."

Annaclaire said grace, thanking God for the bounty. She eyeballed me, then added, "And thanks for sending Wes, I suppose."

"Annaclaire," Aveline scolded.

"Well . . ."

I could tell she blamed my being there for her father's abrupt exit. I bowed my head and prayed this would all come right somehow.

"Enough, you two," Mrs. Blue said. "I'm starving. Moss, get up there and carve the turkey already." Aveline sighed and I sliced the bird. "Was that so hard? Now let's eat," Mrs. Blue said, digging in.

And so we did, three of us in a stuffed silence, Mrs. Blue with abandon.

After the leftovers were put away, the dishes done, everyone else gone to bed, I lay awake, listening to the clock tick in the hallway, listening for the sound of tires crunching snow. How many nights had I gone to bed, wondering if he would be there in the morning? Then I heard the faintest click. A shadow stooped, moved across the room in my direction. I was still, like a hunter. I didn't want to spook him. He was bigger than my fingertip, bigger than the fist resting on my forehead. When he sat down in the soft blue rocker next to me, I closed my eyes and breathed in. He smelled like motor oil on pavement, exhaust backing up into a car, licorice snaps and tobacco, and something wild, flushed geese, prairie sage. He was close enough to me, I could feel the temperature change when he exhaled. It took every bit of courage I had to open my eyes. And he was there. His face glistening and bent toward mine.

"Dad."

On our knees, grovel and grope, men crawling out of mud, out of quicksand, desperate for relief and mercy. He held my face in his rough hands, turning it over like clay, checking for wounds, for blood, like I had been lost to war, not disappeared in a face-saving lie. It had been eleven months since I'd seen him, since he'd promised to return for me. "I'm so sorry," he said, over and over. The light switched on and Annaclaire barreled into us. We three were a sobbing dog pile when Aveline found us there on her living room floor.

CHAPTER 28

He had lost weight, fallen into the hollows between his bones. Aveline put Annaclaire back to bed, then closed the two of them in the little girl's room. She would not share a bed with my father. I couldn't sleep knowing he was on the other side of the living room wall, in that peach-and-white bed, in those sheets, sleeping off the seasons and miles that had kept us apart.

The house was quiet the next day, no piano playing, no back talk from Annaclaire. Aveline's shoulders were down and her head was up as she tidied the house around me. She'd emptied my father's duffel into a basket and taken it downstairs to launder. I heard footsteps, the bathroom door close, the shower curtain pulled along the rod, water spray. I waited. Before long, my father came down the hall, wearing thick work pants and nothing else. His hair was soaking wet. He rubbed it with a white towel where it brushed his neck. His beard was rough from weeks without a shave. Blue feathers had been added to the birds tattooed around his bicep. Three fluttered up to his shoulder, one fluttered down his chest, a last feather seemed to pierce the skin and embed in his heart. Sunshine had stained his body around short sleeves so his torso was lighter than the rest of him. His hands were darker still, cut and calloused.

"I wasn't sure you'd still be here," he said. He followed my eyes, pressed his right hand on his chest. He glanced up to where Aveline stood in the doorway. "They're new."

I couldn't believe she wasn't screaming, throwing things around the room, punching at my father for what he'd done to me, for how he'd lied to her.

"Annaclaire still sleeping?" my father asked.

"Let's let her be awhile," Aveline said.

He grabbed at the scruff of his neck. "You think you could cut my hair for me?"

"Yeah, okay," she said. When they had it out, I knew by the caution in her voice, it wouldn't be in front of me or anyone else.

My father wrapped the towel around his shoulders, followed her into the kitchen. His shaving kit was on the kitchen counter. So this was a ritual already established. I took the spot in the doorway that she vacated.

She cut his hair first, carpeting the newspaper she'd laid under the chair with slick S hooks. She clipped away at his overgrown beard, then told him to slide down. He stretched his legs and bent his head back over the chair. His arms dangled to his sides. He kept his eyes closed while Aveline slathered shaving cream on his cheeks, his lip and chin, and down his stubbly neck. She twisted a new blade into the razor and dipped it in hot water plugged up in the steaming sink. She touched his shoulder, the back of his head. One hand seemed to always be on him. He tried to reach for her, too, but she steered clear, brushed him off. "Stop it," she said quietly. Her long strokes plowed the foam away. I thought of that knife of Ruby's, still in the sheath, still in the tomato box. How clean a cut it would make.

"That's what you wanted, isn't it?" I said. "A fresh start."

Aveline pulled the razor away. My father sat up, wiped his face with the towel. He started to talk but I couldn't hear it. I dressed for the weather and walked out of the house.

Snow melted in the bright sun and clumps fell from the trees onto the street and shoveled walks. On Main Street, city workers wrapped poles with bell-shaped tinsel and blood-red bows. Colored lights were strung crisscross from streetlamp to streetlamp. I found a phone booth outside a saddle and boot tannery. My pocket was full of all the coins I had. I shoved them into the slot, dialed the familiar number, felt a rock form in my gut. The operator told me I'd bought myself five minutes of talking time. Troy answered the phone, and I realized instantly how much I missed them all. In that pause after his "yell-oh," I understood my father a little more, how you could be gone, miss a person. How too much time could pass, how time could become a river no bridge could span.

Is it snowing there? Has Jolene started talking about graduation yet? Lester eating you out of house and home? Is that fry bread I smell? Have you fixed that busted step on the porch? Will Bull make it back for Christmas? Will Mona be satisfied with the tree this year? Is she ever?

This is what happens when too much time passes. You end up with so many questions that need answers, but there's no time to ask. Wait much longer and they don't matter anymore. Then you're left with, *Do you miss me? Are you happy?* Wait too long and there's not even that left to say.

"Troy. It's me. Wes."

"Yeah, okay, good to hear your voice. Any news yet?"

"I'm still out here in Montana. And, well, he showed up. My dad."

Troy grunted low into the phone, the sound of a person taking a soft punch. "Are you in trouble? You need something?"

"No, nothing like that, but I'm wondering if maybe Jolene's there, if I could talk to her? I only have a few minutes."

"Sure, sure. Let me go find her. Hold on. And Wes?"

"Yeah."

"Watch yourself there."

"Will do."

It snowed here, big, wet flakes. The kind that glisten like crystals at daybreak. I think about you every single day. I wonder where you are, who you're talking to. I don't miss Loma but I miss the river. I miss your porch roof. I miss that turn off the highway, where the hardtop goes to gravel and sentinel trees lead to that abandoned farmhouse, our make-out spot where we talked about having a place of our own someday. I like being in the mountains. I feel sheltered. I saw a girl who looked like you walking a brindle pup. I knew it wasn't you, but I slowed down to watch her, to pretend she would look my way and I would see your face. I wear the pouch you gave me. My father showed up on Thanksgiving Day. This woman Aveline, I'm not sure what to make of her. On one hand, she seems to love him more than my mother ever did. On the other, I don't see her putting up with him the way my mother did. I had a dream about her. I thought I could be him instead of me.

I could hear Troy call her, imagined her running to the phone. She said my name in notes, like a song, drawn out to a question at the end, like I was already something long gone, that it would be some great surprise to us all if I ever returned.

"Hey," I said.

He was alone in Aveline's house when I returned. I carried the tomato box in from the car and set it down on the living room floor, daring him to not recognize what it was. *I'll confront him with all of it,* I thought. *March through my list of grievances one by one.* He folded down the page of the *Reader's Digest* he was thumbing through.

"So what, you're the keeper of the sacred tomato box now?" He watched me lift the lid like there might be worms or snakes inside. The letter addressed to me was still on top. I tossed it at him.

He set it on the glass-covered coffee table next to a white knobby vase of plastic flowers. “You want to do this now?” he asked. “Just jump right in?”

“Money’s still in it. I don’t want it.”

“My money’s no good? You independently wealthy now?”

He was a head taller than the back of Mrs. Blue’s swivel rocker. The old woman’s figurines crowded around him, her delicate watercolor paintings on the walls surrounding him. Even though he was clean, something about his ruggedness made him look dirty sitting there, like there was no way he wasn’t soiling what he touched.

I put the lid back on the box and pushed it into the corner with my foot. “No, I don’t want your payoff, is all.” I looked around. I had no place in Aveline’s house with him there. “I can’t believe you left me there with Gip and Ruby. I only just got that letter, you know. Up until, what? Not even a month ago, I had no idea what happened to you. You could have been dead for all I knew.”

“How was I supposed to know that?”

Jolene’s voice was in my head, telling me fighting with him wouldn’t do me any good, telling me to be patient. “You were supposed to know because you were supposed to come back for me. That’s what you told me you’d do.”

Elizabeth glided into the room, leapt into my father’s lap. He ran his fingers against the nap of her fur, making her arch her back. “Thought you’d be better off.”

“No, you thought *you’d* be better off. You took your cat but left your son behind.” I shook my head in disgust. “I don’t know what Aveline sees in you. I’m going back to the motel.” I picked up the box and rested it on my knee to open the door.

He stood, dropping Elizabeth unceremoniously to the floor. “Give me a chance to set things right. You’re welcome here in this house with the rest of us. You leave now and Aveline won’t forgive me. Do this for me, Little.”

"I'm not Little anymore."

"I'm sorry. I know that. Wait and see, Wes," he said, adding promises of better days ahead.

Answers. A way forward. Patience. I said I'd stay a few weeks, maybe until after Christmas, though my father was quick to remind me I had nowhere else to turn. I checked out of the motel, my few belongings in the bag over my shoulder. The redhead touched my fingertips when I pushed the plastic key to her. She told me she was sorry to see me go.

In those early weeks of December, Aveline worked day shifts while Annaclaire was in school and Mrs. Blue was at the senior center. That left me and my father alone. We worked alongside each other getting storm windows in, though it was late to be doing it, snaking the chronically clogged bathtub drain, then unskewering a Barbie gown tangled with Aveline's blond hair. "Not glamorous anymore, doll," he said. We rehung a cabinet in the kitchen that had come unmoored. Talk was small, even when the subject was serious. He knew about Gip and Ruby from Aveline, but neither of us seemed able to talk about the bigger things. Instead, we nodded and yupped at each other like a couple of sheep in a pasture.

He'd promised Mrs. Blue we'd try to fix a dead key on her piano and that was our task for the day. We removed the doilies from the top of the upright and flipped the lid open. "You know," he said. "I'm surprised Ruby and Gip didn't off each other sooner." He climbed on a stepladder. "Hand me a flashlight, will you?"

"There was more to it than that," I said.

"Yeah?" His voice knocked around inside the piano, against the wires and wood, playing flat notes like a dull mallet.

"Ruby got it in her head that Gip . . ."

"That Gip what?" The voice in the piano again.

I was glad the women weren't in the house. I couldn't have said it in front of them, didn't want them to even hear the words. "Well, that he'd molested Mom, I guess."

A hard knock, a curse, and his head popped out of the piano. "What?"

I tried to make it short, about Kathryn, the eviction, and finally, the hunting knife I'd found and kept.

"What knife? I don't know about any knife," he said. He let the lid drop with a thud that shook all the wires at once. He handed the flashlight back to me and stepped down. "I have no fucking idea how a piano works."

I got the knife from the box I stored in the front closet under the sheets and blankets I folded up and put away each morning. He unsheathed it, touched the blade and tang. No hint of recognition, no fear like I'd seen in my grandparents.

"Jesus Christ," he whispered, with a hint of admiration. "So Ruby thought Val used this to cut Gip, to keep him away from her? Fuck."

"There's more." I handed him the pack of photographs.

He took them out, handled each one, layering his fingerprints over mine, over Ruby's. He turned them over, looked at the date on the back, then to the images again. His eyebrows told the story—raising, twitching, knitting. "She won a camera playing bingo. We never could afford to get the film developed. That's Daisy alright." His voice hushed. Teeth raked across his lip. He raised his chin. "Never thought I'd see her again." He shuffled through the pictures again. "You found the film in that box of hers?"

"No," I said. "Ruby must have had it the whole time. Got it developed right before the fire."

He sat down on the top step of the ladder, dropped his head into his hands, lifted it again. His face was anguished. "Why are you doing this? Why bring this up again?" He probed me with that look of his, and I tried to give it back so I wouldn't have to speak. "Oh Christ," he said, his backbone collapsing.

"Did you know?" I asked.

He stood, shook his head, handed the pictures back to me. His voice balled up like a fist. "Clean up. Geneva's going to be here soon. And put that fucking box away." He grabbed his coat from the open closet and walked out, leaving me with the stepladder and tools, the photographs and the past.

He was back an hour later, sober, which was something of a relief to me. After dinner, Mrs. Blue tapped the dead key. "I tried," he said, his eyes on me. "I couldn't fix it."

My father's wakefulness began to run opposite to the length of days. We shifted sleeping arrangements to get me off the couch. "Too much bustle in the morning," Aveline said, using her worry I wasn't getting the rest I needed as cover for the fact that my father wasn't sleeping much. He woke up early and stayed up later and later, well into the night. Annaclaire moved across the hall to share Mrs. Blue's soft bed, though she told me privately she hated it because her grandmother farted in her sleep. I moved into Annaclaire's little room and little bed, where my feet hung off the end. She took one look at me under her princess bedspread and decided to call me Gulliver. My father and Aveline seemed to be reconciling. She was sharing her bed with him again when he went to bed at all.

When I wasn't watching him, I could feel him watching me. Could he get over the sight of me? I'm guessing no. His dead son who refused to stop haunting him. He lingered in a way he hadn't before, holding still as if he lived in the pause between actions, as if between those moments of plenty, he gathered up something he would need for the times of none.

Razor stubble appeared in the bathroom sink, the toilet seat was left up. He often went without a shirt in the house, especially in the mornings, baring himself, always touching Aveline, though some frost between them remained. I did my own laundry. He left his for Aveline to do. When men's clothes piled with the lady things Aveline folded while watching television, I couldn't help but think of my mother and the lousy jobs she always had. I offered to help fold, which Aveline refused, smiling in a way that said I couldn't possibly do it to her liking. I felt his eyes on me.

THE SATURDAY BEFORE CHRISTMAS, AVELINE and Mrs. Blue took Annaclaire shopping. My father was outside, trying to solve the mystery of a ticking sound the truck's engine was making. I took advantage of a quiet house to call Jolene. I'd talked to Aveline about her some, getting advice on what to do with so much distance between us. "Don't let too much time pass," she offered, adding I could make calls from the house phone as long as I reimbursed her when the bill came. I'd only just gotten past Jolene's opening gauntlet of questions, when my dad popped his head through the front door. He had an ax in his hand.

"Come take a ride with me," he said.

I motioned to the phone. "I'm a little busy."

"That can wait. Come on. Now."

"I have to go," I said to Jolene, promising I'd call back when I could. It was the worst part of every call, saying goodbye, bad enough it made me not want to call at all.

He was in the truck, revving the tick-free engine. I climbed into the passenger seat. "Where are we going?"

"Getting a tree."

We had planned to go to the tree lot that night, all of us together. They'd argued the night before—fresh cut or a tree from the lot in the center of town? "We always get a tree from the lot," Aveline said. "Why go up into the mountains when there are perfectly good trees right handy?"

"What's more perfect than nature?" my father asked. "It'll be fun. We can get our boots on, make a day of it."

"Mama can't go up into the woods, Moss," Aveline said. "End of discussion."

A ribcage of bone-colored clouds streaked the sky as we headed south on the highway out of town. He told me he knew just the place.

"But Aveline said."

"Listen to you. 'Aveline said.' You don't always have to do what you're told. You don't always have to cave to a woman. I know what I'm doing."

The logging road narrowed and the curves became tighter as we climbed. A sign said we were on forest service land. "Do we need a permit or something?" I asked.

"You really are a mama's boy. Speaking of that, I wanted to talk to you about something. It's that box of hers. When we get home today, I want you to get rid of it."

The snow was deeper and the road more narrow the higher we climbed. Ponderosa pines blocked out the sun. We skidded on icy patches. My father geared down but hit the gas.

"What's it to you? It's just a box."

The bed of the truck fishtailed and the back tire edged into a shallow ditch. He pumped the gas, pulled hard on the steering wheel, shifted again. We slid back onto the road. "I don't need some big discussion. I want it gone. I'm sick of looking at it."

"Is this about Daisy? About those pictures?"

He slammed hard on the brake and the truck slid sideways. "This is good enough. Get out. Grab the ax from the back." He left the truck in the middle of the road. "There," he said, pointing to a tree bigger than we could fit in the house. "That one."

The snow was almost to our knees when we stepped off the road. "It's too big," I said.

"Too big for you, maybe." He took the ax from me, unsnapped the rawhide blade cover, and took a swing, then another one, at the center of the tree. The blade bounced, hardly making a notch. He checked it against his palm, took another whack. "Fuck," he said, swinging more wildly now, taking inconsistent bites out of the trunk with each try. We heard the low engine roar at the same time. A logging truck was on the ridge above us, coming down the road with a full load. My father looked at his sideways pickup, then back to the half-chopped tree. "Fuck it. We'll get one at the lot. Let's go."

The shallow creek slalomed over rocks, raced us down the foothill until the gravel road turned to pavement and it disappeared into a culvert. My father was quiet.

"What did you and Mom fight about? That night at the lake. She wanted another baby, didn't she? She wanted to. You wouldn't." What I remembered wasn't that gentle, but I thought I had the gist of it.

His tongue rolled into his cheek and he let out a scornful snort. "You have a lot to learn about where babies come from. Any woman wants a baby can have a baby. Your mom didn't want any more kids. What she wanted was to keep me where I was. You may as well know. I told her I was leaving her. I told her about Aveline and your sister. That set her off. She said you only would ever have the one sister." He said it like he couldn't bring himself to say her name.

"What really happened to Daisy?"

He pushed in the lighter, took a pack of cigarettes out of his coat pocket, shook it until one slid free. He dropped the pack on the seat between us and lit the one in his mouth.

"I came in. Valerie was on the floor." He shook his head violently, to scatter the recollection, it seemed. "She wouldn't let her go. Hours she sat like that. Holding her against her pregnant belly." He turned to me. "Against you." He shrugged. "Crib death, they called it. Nothing we could do."

"What about a funeral? I don't even know where she's buried."

"Oh, she was dead set against a funeral. It was only her and me. Guy at the mortuary there in Wisconsin talked her into cremation. I was against that. I thought the baby deserved a proper burial. Should have stuck to my guns on that one." He sucked on the cigarette until the embers flared out, then rolled down the window, dropped the butt into the cold. "Your mom wanted to keep Daisy with her."

I had no memory of an urn, anything sacred my mother kept close. "So where is it, the container or whatever?"

Dug-up pain spread across his face. His knuckles turned white on the steering wheel. He kept his eyes on the road. "I took some boxes to the dump. Kept the wrong one. When I realized what I'd done, I went back for it." His hands were on his head, fingers in his hair, that familiar frustration of his. The truck pulled left into the oncoming lane. A car swerved and honked.

"Dad."

Hands back on the wheel, he was still talking. "Time I got there—I picked through pounds of rubbish—everything inside was out. She'd packed it with the baby's clothes. Little pink dresses, lambs and flowers on them, little things I'd seen her in, all crapped up and filthy. The top was off it. Thing was crushed." His voice cracked. "Fucking tomatoes smiling at me. I tried to scoop her up . . ."

He went quiet again and I did, too. I suppose we were both picturing him hands and knees on a garbage heap, trying to rescue the spilled remains of a dead child.

"She said I did it on purpose. Why would I do it on purpose? Maybe those pictures are why. Maybe she knew something I didn't. That's when she divorced me. She took me back but she *never* let me forget."

"Oh fuck," I said. "The tomato box." How wrecked and broken we were, all of us, a clattering boneyard of broken souls.

He pulled into the tree lot and bought the first one he saw—a blue spruce as big as a whale. I tried to talk him out of it, but he wouldn't hear it. Annaclaire flew out of the house when she saw us with the tree. My father manufactured a big smile for her. "Surprise!" he said.

"It's perfect," she squealed.

Mrs. Blue was less impressed. "It will never fit in this house. It's too big," she declared, pointing her finger at the ceiling like a politician.

"Help me get this in," he said to me. "I want it up when Aveline gets home."

I was still reeling from his confession. "Don't you think we ought to wait for her?"

His face was empty, drained. "Do as I say."

We righted it together, Mrs. Blue as our guide. He sent Annaclaire up the pull-down attic ladder to gather and lower the flame-shaped string lights and decorations. We had just finished winding the lights around the tree when Aveline came home from work. Annaclaire ran from the house, told her mother we had a surprise, insisted she close her eyes before coming in.

"Okay," Annaclaire said. "Open."

Aveline's face dropped. "I thought we were going tonight. You all went without me."

"Not all of us," Mrs. Blue said. "Those two. I told them it was too big. But no one listens to me."

"It's okay, Mama. No one listens to me either."

I wanted to defend myself but my father cut me off. "Thought we could use some father-son time. We cut it down ourselves."

Aveline took her coat off and hung it on a hanger in the closet. "May I talk to you in the kitchen, please?"

"Looks like I'm in trouble," he said, winking at me. That grin. Like when I was a kid. My mother would be angry and he would tease her to make her even more mad. Always with the same smirking look on his face like "Watch this."

Mrs. Blue knitted while Annaclaire and I quietly replaced the burned-out bulbs, an ear to the argument in the other room. We heard Aveline's voice, hushed but clear. It was not his decision to make. Yes, they were his children. No, it was not his house, too. No, that's not how it was going to work. No, he could not. No. No.

"He's getting in trouble," Annaclaire whispered, taking some glee in it.

"I think so."

Annaclaire scrunched her face, huddled against me. I put my finger to my lips.

They returned and we finished decorating the tree in measured politeness. Aveline cupped her hand around her daughter's ear, and Annaclaire ran out of the room only to burst back in carrying an open shoebox with a shiny gold star inside. My father picked her up and swung her toward the treetop, but she squirmed away from him. "No," she said. "I want Wes to do it."

He shrugged and smiled at her, but I saw hurt in his eyes.

"Okay, boss. Here you go." I scooped her up onto my shoulder and she stretched her arms, pulling the tip down, then releasing the branch. The star wobbled to a stop, a little cockeyed.

"Perfect," she said, satisfied that everything was the way she wanted it. Elizabeth scooted around my father's legs, purring up at him. Mrs. Blue stood next to me and patted my hand.

"Merry Christmas, Wes," she said. The colored lights shimmered in her thick glasses. I couldn't see her eyes at all.

I learned to dance the waltz that night. My father and Aveline both had a couple of beers with dinner. The mood was lighter than it had been. The tree lights helped. Annaclaire was splayed out on the floor, folding down the pages of a toy catalog to make some sort of angel decoration. Aveline went to turn on the television and my father grabbed her hand as she walked by, pulled her onto his lap in a smooth motion. He wrapped his arms around her so one of his hands was on her shoulder and the other around her waist. "Wes, we ought to take our girls dancing."

Aveline nudged his chest, gently enough I could see she didn't really want him to let her go. "We're not going out now," she said.

"Who said anything about going out? Geneva, why don't you play that song you like so much. What's it?" He snapped his fingers. "'The Black Hawk Waltz.'"

"Oh," she said, setting her knitting down. "I do like that one."

"Little miss, why don't you push those things off our dance floor."

"Only if I get to dance with Wes."

"Looks like you got yourself an admirer," my father said.

Mrs. Blue played the piano and sang aloud the sounds she played—"brrring dum dum brrring dum dum brrring dum dum dum." I watched my father with Aveline, the way he held his arm out and she laid her hand in his, his other hand on the small of her back, stroking the channel of her spine, the way her spread of hips pressed into him. I picked up Annaclaire and clowned with her, though I couldn't stop watching him, how assured he was, how in control. Only hours earlier he had been so lost. Aveline's hand drifted onto the back of his neck, her thumb going into the wave of hair. He didn't take his eyes off her, not for a second. And I knew that look, that way he rounded his shoulders toward her, made himself into shelter. I knew it because I'd felt it in the slope of my own shoulders and in the unflinching way I'd tried to tell Jolene by just looking at her how I was feeling. I was my father's son.

"You're a terrible dancer, Wes," Aveline said. "C'mon now. Let's switch so Annaclaire can dance with her daddy and I can teach you a thing or two."

Then Aveline was in my arms and, despite my best efforts, I was on her feet, much to Annaclaire's delight. Aveline and her mother switched places, and I danced with Mrs. Blue while Annaclaire sat between her parents on the piano bench. I spun her around and she said, "Oh, Moss!" to me and I said, "Oh, Geneva!" Annaclaire tossed her head back and laughed like it was the silliest thing she'd ever seen. Mrs. Blue unpinned her gray hair and let it fall in light wisps around her face. I imagined her as a young woman and tried to hold her in a way that would take her back to that time. Annaclaire cut in on her grandmother. I bowed princely and swept her off her feet, spinning her around with no method or form until we were both too dizzy to stand.

I heard my father whispering to Aveline about California, about the sun. How nice it would be there. A record on repeat. *Salmon as big as goats,* he'd said. There was always somewhere better where the fish jumped higher, pies were juicier, where money sprouted in the money garden, and happiness fell from the happy trees.

CHAPTER 29

It was that night that my father told Aveline he was putting down roots, that he wanted me to stay in Burden Falls, too, that he wanted us to be a family. It was like the demons had been vanquished in his confession to me. He was rebuilding. The next morning, she laid down the law about the house, school for me and a full-time job for him, about helping with Mrs. Blue and Annaclaire. I was swept up by the idea. We agreed with all of it. Even Annaclaire was willing to let us replace her bed with one that would fit me better, though by day that room would remain hers. I would again be sleeping in someone else's space, but for the first time in my life the mattress would be new.

Two days before Christmas, I placed a collect call and Mona accepted it. Her voice made me more than homesick. I felt a hunger, home craving. I imagined it like a loaf of bread fresh from the oven, warm berry juice sluicing from fork holes in a pie, or the slow, steady sounds of a meal coming together, a table being set, a family gathering. I wanted to use the ingredients that made Mona's kitchen so good to create its equal in the kitchen I was in. Mona wasn't much for measuring. She always seemed to know how much of anything to use and how to adjust if it didn't seem like the right amount. How much love would you need to put in to make a family, and what would happen if it was added too late? She would know that by heart.

I'd been away more than a month. It would be months and months before I could go back to Loma. The words I was forming while Mona found Jolene sounded false and dangerous, like the ones my father had said to me. "Just you wait. Come spring." I swore to myself when I heard her voice that I would not make promises I couldn't keep.

"I knew you weren't coming back." She didn't sound hurt or angry. Only sure.

"I'd regret it if I didn't stay. I at least have to try. I wish I could be in both places."

"If wishes were horses . . ."

Beggars would ride. I was done begging.

"So I'm going back to school. You and Lester will graduate. I'll come visit when school's out. Or you'll come here."

"Yeah."

"And we can write to each other. I'll give you the address. We can talk on the phone once in a while."

"That sounds good."

What more was there to say? I closed my eyes, listened to the distance, static on the line. The void reminded me of the closet in the corner of the upstairs bedroom.

"Jo, remember the séance?"

"Sure."

"I was afraid of what I'd find in there. Ghosts. My own shadow. But I'm not afraid anymore. I'm not afraid because you made it okay when I was. Does that make sense?"

Her voice was choked. "Mm-hmm."

"Don't cry, Jo."

"This is too hard," she said.

"We'll get through this winter. See how things go. Then I'll see you in the summertime. Promise."

I'd never had a Christmas morning like that. Snow was falling, cars were off the street so it piled up like we lived in the woods. Annaclaire pulled me out of bed at sunup, declaring it time for presents. She could hardly contain herself but was forced by her mother to wait until at least the coffee was made. The moment we gathered in the living room, she was pulling wrapping paper off her gifts. Aveline got her a swimming pool for Barbie and my dad gave her a doll with hair that could be pulled straight out of her head to make it long instead of short. Mrs. Blue knit her a sweater with matching mittens. And I gave her the most exotic thing I could find and afford in that mountain town—a stuffed octopus.

"What on earth?" she said, pulling it out of the box. "Look at all those legs!" She jumped up and wrapped her two arms around me. "That's the best octopus anyone has ever given me."

"Tell the truth. It's the only one."

"Still the best."

I got Aveline a hat and scarf set. She gave me a striped wool blanket that reminded me of the one on Jolene's bed. I gave Mrs. Blue a kaleidoscope with an open lens to form patterns from things outside the scope. "You hold it up like this," I said, pointing it to the lit tree. "Everything gets jumbled around. It's pretty."

She looked through it, spun it around a few times. "Oh, I like that. I'll keep it." She slipped it into the pocket of her red housecoat.

My father gave me a pair of lined leather work gloves. I gave him a diary and a pen.

"What's this for?" he asked.

"I thought maybe you'd want to write down some things. You read and all. Maybe you have a story to tell."

He nodded like maybe he did. "Thank you."

He started drinking at noon, well ahead of dinner. Aveline didn't have whiskey in the house, only beer and the pink jug wine she kept in the refrigerator. She'd sent him out on Christmas Eve for something bubbly to go with dinner. My guess is he got a little something extra for himself. From Mrs. Blue's plush rocker, he sipped whiskey and watched Annaclaire play with her toys. I filled her doll's swimming pool with water so Barbie could have a Christmas pool party. She and I tried to get my father on the floor with us, but he waved us off with a loaded smile. "Swimming dolls? Sinking dolls, more like it. She's got nice legs, though."

The table was set with ham and sliced potatoes, green bean casserole, and Jell-O salad. My father uncorked the cheap champagne and poured it for the four of us into Mrs. Blue's special flutes. Aveline stood, smoothed her dress nervously, then clinked her bubbling glass with her spoon. "I want to say how special it is to have the Ballot men here together. This is your home, both of you," she said. "To family." We all touched glasses, my father and I last.

Dishes were passed and the conversation was easy, focused mostly on Annaclaire. I misread my father's quiet for contentment. Leave it to Mrs. Blue. She stuck her fork into a piece of ham on the platter. "So which of you two takes off again?"

"Mama. Please."

"What?" she said. She held her hand out to Annaclaire. "Pass the potatoes, would you?" Then to Aveline, she said, "I get confused, is all. Don't you?"

The rest of us kept our heads down, spooning dinner into our mouths, chewing to cover the silence.

"It's me," my father said. "I'm the one who leaves, Geneva. I'm the one."

"There," said Mrs. Blue. "Now everyone's clear. See how easy that was?"

"Nobody's going anywhere anymore, Mama. Isn't that right?"

My father nodded. "That's right." He motioned for me to pass the casserole.

He and I leaned against the kitchen counter after the dishes were dried and put away. I tapped the birds dangling from the twig. He poured whiskey into a highball glass. "You remember giving me a mobile like this one? Mom threw it into the road."

"Yeah, I remember."

"I tried to fix it. Couldn't figure it out."

"Yeah," he said. "Sometimes it's easier to build something new than it is to fix something broken."

He flicked a bird with his middle finger. It bobbed awkwardly on the filament, bumping into another bird before settling into a flat spin.

EPILOGUE

In my life, I'd gotten used to the sounds walls let through. The pad of feet in the hallway, the click of a carefully closed door, the sorrow of tears cried into a pillow, an engine turning over, winter birds mourning on the wire.

He took the work boots Aveline gave him and the wool blanket she gave to me. He took the diary and pen, which surprised me. He took back the work gloves he'd given to me, which didn't. He took Elizabeth but left behind her soiled litter box. The mobile was busted up and crammed into the full garbage can. There was one last thing my father took from me—the photographs of Daisy. No matter what, she belonged to him.

When Annaclaire woke up, Aveline told her he was gone. She dropped the doll he'd given her and folded herself into a ball on the floor, screaming at me that it was all my fault, that I'd wrecked everything. Aveline tried to explain that some people are natural givers, some are takers, that my being there hadn't changed what Moss was. "He never wanted anything and he never had anything to give."

Mrs. Blue was in her chair, one eye closed, the other fixed in the kaleidoscope. She pointed it at Annaclaire. "Your mom needs a hug. Go on now."

Annaclaire climbed into her mother's lap, buried her head. The sobbing was unbearable. I turned away to keep from doing the same.

"This is so pretty," Mrs. Blue said, tilting her head back and forth into the kaleidoscope. "You don't have to look at a thing the way it is at all."

I left them in the living room with their sadness, took my blame with me to pack my things. I listened to Annaclaire's asking, asking, to Aveline's soft there, there. I'd seen firsthand how to love a hurt child, not from my wounded parents, not from Gip and Ruby, whose decisions were cast from failure and despair, but from Mona and Troy, who'd taken Jolene in, who gave her love that was a constant, steady drumbeat. That drum was beating in my ears and chest. I stepped over my duffel, went back to the living room to ask Aveline if I could stay. I made solemn and careful promises. I would stay as long as she would have me, abide by the rules she'd already laid out. I would do more than she asked.

Over that next week, only Annaclaire talked about Moss, mostly wondering if he would ever come back. At first, I thought she was hoping he would, then I began to think she feared he might. That was a crushing thing, to see her fear. For me and Aveline, it was simple honesty to tell her he wouldn't be back. Something about this leaving was final. We would never see him again. Mrs. Blue never mentioned his name, not once. It was clear to her who I was and who I was not. It would take me time to be so sure.

Jolene and I talked on the phone on New Year's Day. We agreed that calls wouldn't make sense anymore, that the time and distance would mean letter writing instead since neither of us could afford the bill. I had sent her a filigreed locket that Christmas. She sent me a picture of her wearing it, which I put in a frame so I could look at her face, talk to her as I struggled to write letters good enough to keep her writing back.

Maybe we were too young or maybe distance makes the heart break. We fought several times—mostly because I kept falling into my own traps, making promises I couldn't keep. Then I would turn on her. Why couldn't she look at colleges in Montana or, better yet, skip college altogether? We could get married. Start our own lives together. Why wasn't I enough? And she'd snap back that I didn't listen to her, that I did not consider her dreams, only mine.

The local high school where I enrolled was small and I kept to myself. I had no interest in joining and looked with some wonder at the way we humans fall into types. I saw Kathryn and her friends, the Drew Fullertons, even the Lester, who at this school was an affable wrestler and the oldest kid in a family that owned a car dealership. I did not find a Jolene, though I wasn't looking. For me, that person could not be replicated or replaced.

Mostly I spent my time with Annaclaire. I played all the roles she would allow me—big brother, prince, carriage driver, pony, coach. I learned how much I loved reading out loud, a thing I had never done in my life and no one had ever done for me. It was the best part of most of my days, sitting with Annaclaire, reading whatever book she'd brought home from the library. I liked the weight and weave of the covers, the colorful pictures. I liked the sound of my own voice and could hear my own affection when Annaclaire's hand rested on mine or on the page. She was a loved child, and her ease lifted me even when the letters from Jolene dwindled to almost none.

LATE THAT FIRST SUMMER, LESTER passed through Burden Falls on his way to Oregon, where he would follow Bull into the Coast Guard. We drove up into the canyon, drank beers, shot off bottle rockets. He told me Jolene was good, same with Mona and Troy and Mariah. He handed me an envelope with my name written on it in Jolene's round script, then asked if Aveline had a boyfriend and whether I thought he had a chance with her.

I did not need to break the seal to see what was on the inside. "So this is it?"

Lester chucked a stone into the creek. "What did you expect, Ballot? I mean, really. You thought she'd come live here with you in that old white lady's house while you finish high school? You thought she'd want to, what, clean up bedpans in a hospital or something? Take the letter, man. Take what you get. Be grateful for what you had. Now let's get going. I need to be over that pass before nightfall."

After one last cold one for the road, Lester dropped me off in front of the little house.

"See you around, Ballot." He put both his hands on my chest, then punched my arm.

"Keep your head low, Lester."

"It's the Coast Guard, Ballot, not the goddamned Marines. I need to keep my head above water." He peeled out in the Impala, which bore no signs of the damage I'd inflicted, his arm waving from the window in a high salute.

Daylight stretched long into that summer night. Somehow I couldn't get myself into the house. It was as if opening that door would mean closing the door on the past that I'd wanted for my future. I sat on the steps, the unopened envelope in my hand, and watched the corner where the Impala had disappeared. Aveline came out, sat down next to me, handed me a glass of lemonade.

"What you got there?"

"This?" I asked, holding up the white envelope. I tried to say it matter-of-factly. "This is a Dear John letter. This is Jolene finally giving up on me." I pursed my lips together, nodded, knowing.

"You planning on reading it?"

"Suppose I ought to."

Streetlights flickered on. A neighbor's bug zapper flashed purple as the mosquitoes came out to feast.

"Can I make a suggestion, since you haven't opened it yet?"

I FOLLOWED AVELINE'S ADVICE, SET the envelope next to Jolene's picture, and wrote a letter, one that was not a response to hers, one that would maybe be the last letter I ever sent to her, the last words I would ever say to this girl who lived so deeply in my heart. "Time to be a man now, Wes," Aveline had said. "Time to be a man who can give this woman the gift of honesty and of good wishes. A man of courage who can love and let go. Be that man. For her and for yourself. Be kind." I wrote long into the quiet night. When I was finished, I slipped out of the house while the others slept and walked the letter to the mailbox, the man in the moon watching my every step as I put the past in the past.

AFTER HIGH SCHOOL, I WENT to work pouring concrete. I liked driving the heavy truck, the way concrete flows and hardens, becomes permanent and solid, something you can build on. Eventually I moved into an apartment of my own close enough to Aveline and Annaclaire and Mrs. Blue that I could walk over for dinner a couple nights a week. I was Annaclaire's date to every father-daughter banquet and dance, though she was quick and sharp to point out to the adults who plan such things that some kids don't have fathers and ask why is it that they insist on making kids feel bad who don't have that kind of family. I accompanied Mrs. Blue and Aveline to every recital and play that Annaclaire was in, to every art show at her school. And when Aveline started dating the new music teacher at the high school, I was the babysitter of choice, though Annaclaire hated the term. "You're my brother who is staying home with me. How does that make me a baby?"

Over the years, I dated some nice girls, though none made me feel like that other girl had—the girl on the seesaw with the waning moon scar, the girl on a porch roof, skin like felt, who glistens in my memory like some mythical being, a kelpie in river water. Aveline warned me not to build her up so much that she became a wall between me and happiness. I did have to put away that photo of her wearing the locket for fear that my handling of it would ruin the image forever. Now I keep it, along with the pouch she'd made for me, in the tomato box with everything else. I thought about replacing that box with something plain but decided against it. In a way, it was all I had left to remind me of those people, dead or gone.

Aveline's stoop is still one of my favorite places to sit after work, to take a load off. Last October, on those same steps where Aveline confronted my father, where Annaclaire and I have watched rain turn to hail and back to rain again, and Mrs. Blue sips her lemonade, I opened a lumpy package addressed to me in a familiar, loopy script. In it was a heart-shaped talisman, a memory I could hold in my hand.

Seems Jolene had gone to the upstairs closet in search of a beaded dress that Mona swore was in the house somewhere. The dress had slipped from its hanger, lay crumpled and stiff in the forgotten corner. Jolene found it there with a thin slice of slivered wood caught in the hem. She unsnagged it, turned it over, and saw the engraved "O" and "U." She remembered. The séance, the desperate call to Trudy and Valerie. How I'd broken the planchette from the Ouija board while fleeing the ghosts of our dead mothers. Jolene crawled back into the closet and felt around until she found the other half.

Had that call gone through after all? Had Trudy and Valerie gotten together in the Great Beyond and decided it was about damned time? Maybe our grandmothers, too, and theirs and back and back. Generations of hurt women watching me and Jolene stitch ourselves whole again, then lighting the way back to each other, wish granted.

She took the pieces out to Troy's shop, dug wood glue from one of his bins. She fitted the snapped heart back together, the broken hole at the point made into a circle again, and thought of the boy who'd never really left her thoughts at all. She wrapped our wishful séance in layers of tissue, wrote me a letter telling me facts of her life, and waited.

The planchette rested on my palm. I remembered her body next to mine in the frost of fall. For Jolene, sending me this heart repaired was her fingertips guiding her to a *maybe*, a *perhaps*. Could it be? Could we try? With or without the Ouija planchette, for me the answer was yes, always yes. I wrote her back, and waited.

We got caught in a whirlpool of memory and swam down, recalling the ways we'd been battered, storm after storm. Over weeks and months, we shared a decade's worth of want and wound, of battles won and lost, like lovers separated by war. Then somehow, the waters calmed, became more peaceful. Through words that fell like feathers into my outstretched hand, I was let back into the Hightower house and lives I missed so much. I came to know Jolene as a social worker advocating for Native women, pulling up those who'd fallen, standing with those who stood up, while the ornery roots of her own scars tangled with her independent streak and her ache for company. I shared stories of the Blue women, my Montana family, and the way I'd come to realize that all my life I'd been sheltered and shaped for the better by women who'd had to fight for every last thing and who'd done their best, even my mother, even Ruby, in her way. I wrote about Big Tom Small Concrete, the father-and-son team I work for, how sometimes their easy way with each other made me miss the idea of my father but not the man himself, how understanding that the blame of his leaving was squarely on him had made me stronger, more able to withstand the blows.

Jolene sent me a stack of snapshots—the two of us, me with Bull and Lester, of Mona, Troy, and Mariah, their house, and a recent one of her with her one-eyed rescue pup, Apple Pie. That one cut a hole in me at the same time it filled me up. Jolene. She was always so beautiful to me. When I took a closer look at the photograph, I could see she was wearing the locket I'd given her that first Christmas. On the back of the photograph were the words *A time of innocence*. In the envelope was a tape with only one Simon & Garfunkel song on it.

Nine months' worth of letters live on my kitchen table, the heart-shaped planchette on top of the pile, a flimsy paperweight. I will confess to reading them over and over, decoding, memorizing the layers of stories upon stories, like hands over hands. The cassette tape I keep in my pickup, the photograph in my wallet.

Not long ago Aveline got a call from the county sheriff for Index, Washington. Local fishermen found a drifter by the name of Moss Ballot dead on the banks of the Skykomish River. There were no signs of struggle, only whiskey in his blood and traces of river in his lungs, likely from having fallen face-first and taken his last breaths underwater. He'd set up camp in the trees under a tarp. It seemed he'd been there for a while, living off fish and canned beans. There wasn't much worth keeping, according to the sheriff. He did say that inside the wax duffel bag there was a diary, the one I'd given to him, it turns out. Inside it were written the words *For my children Wes and Annaclaire in care of Aveline Blue, Burden Falls, Montana*. There was one sentence, the start of a story never written but told nonetheless: *I lose everything*. The rest of the pages were blank.

ANNACLAIRE AND I DROVE OVER to Washington, picked up what was left of our father. We put him and his things in an unmarked cardboard box and rested it on the seat between us. It was her idea to scatter his ashes in Burden Canyon near the falls. She's sixteen now—tough, feisty, the kind of girl who scares the boys in a good way. I'd had unkind thoughts about dropping him in a dumpster or leaving him by the side of the road or getting drunk enough to completely forget where I'd left him. She said we owed it to ourselves to be rid of him properly. We've hiked the canyon trail plenty over the ten years I've lived there and knew it well in almost any weather.

"Suppose we ought to say something," I offered. Insects swarmed us in the heat.

Annaclaire slapped her leg, wiped the dead bug on her shorts. She took the can from me and held it out in front of her like an offering to the gods. She yelled the first words into the canyon, so they banked off the walls. "Moss Ballot was a selfish prick, a burden to all who knew him," she said. "He got one thing right, though, and that's you and me. So thanks, old man, for making us family."

It's been years since Troy told me the story of Nanabozho. In that time, I learned the rest, how he'd fought his father, how they'd reconciled. How Ae-pungishimook had offered the peace pipe to his son. But there had been no peace between me and Moss. I carried my father around my sagged shoulders like some burdensome hide. How he bore me or Annaclaire in his life I would never know. When it was my turn to scatter the ashes, the hide of him slid off my shoulders, down my back, fell with his weightless body to the granite, the weeds, and wildflowers at my feet.

Coming down out of the canyon, I thought about my father's songbird mobile, about connection and motion, how a tap on one wing set the other end of the branch in flight. One bird dipped, the other soared.

When I got home, I composed one last letter to Jolene, dropped it in the mailbox. I wouldn't wait for her reply. I headed east, gliding on faith and a mended heart.

—

I've been trespassing here on the shore of Bright Lake for days, sleeping in the back of my pickup under a sky full of stars, tugging on these memories like taffy, losing myself in heat and sugar. I swam out to the spot where my mother drowned, floated belly up, arms splayed and free. Ruby's hunting knife is sunk to the bottom of the lake now, along with my father's slippers. The log cabin is gone, same with Darin and Rhonda, same with the little boy who saw the diving loon, and the version of me who watched his mother drown. What's left is this man waiting for Jolene, who came back around gently, a bird on filament. I have what we need for now—blankets, pillows, food to last us, time. At dusk, a pair of silent loons will ripple the thick water, bob the lilies, and Bright Lake will blur into its own reflection. Into summertime.

ACKNOWLEDGMENTS

Sincere thanks and gratitude to these fine people who deserve so much more:

My agent, Mark Gottlieb, for his passionate support and for changing his Facebook cover to a loon. My editor, Hafizah Geter, who embraced a bit of bleakness and whose careful touches helped bring out poetry in the manuscript. To everyone at Amazon Publishing and Little A who believed in this book and helped launch it into the world.

Michael Olmert, who told me to read the *New Yorker* and believed I could be a writer long before I did. William Kittredge, who sat with me one afternoon years ago and taught me about authenticity. Becky Tuch, Ben Winters, and Daphne Kalotay, who guided me through the messy middle. Elinor Lipman, who thrilled me by loving my first page and encouraged me to not kill off everyone. Alexi Zentner and Gail Hochman, who gave me critical feedback that made the novel so much better. Ben Percy, who encouraged me to value sentiment over sentimentality. Michelle Hoover, who helped me take the whole thing apart and put it back together again and saw me through to The End.

Maine artist R. Keith Rendall, whose haunted painting of a diving loon became my muse. Sherry Newell at Midwest Dairy Association, who helped me with the lay of the farmland. Ron Thomas for writing a lovely essay about being a teenage boy doing farmwork in the Bitterroot

Valley. Walter Piper, scientist with the Loon Project, for explaining how and why loons get iced in. Anton Treuer, who put me in touch with Sean Fahrlander, who then critiqued the manuscript. Sean gave me thorough and heartfelt advice as I incorporated traditional Ojibwe stories into this novel. I feel fortunate to have met and worked with Sean. My deepest condolences to his family and friends.

My fellow Four Points writers—Michele Ferrari, Kathy Sherbrooke, and Jessie Manchester Lubitz—who always and truly listen, pull me up when despair is deep, and spark my creativity and joy for the process. Lissa Franz and Louise Miller—dear friends, dear writers—for sticking with me and this novel, pushing me when I didn't want to budge, and sending love when I needed it most. The entire and awesome Novel Incubator family of die-hard cheerleaders, generous readers, and beautiful writers.

Dan Blask and the Massachusetts Cultural Council for hearing the loon and validating this writer. *Solstice Literary Magazine* for publishing an early excerpt and giving me hope. Eve Bridburg, Chris Castellani, and everyone at GrubStreet for creating space and opportunity, sharing wisdom, and championing expression. I started writing again thanks to Jumpstart, found a novel through continuing courses, and completed a working manuscript in the Incubator. Along the way, I have made so many Grubbie friends whom I sincerely cherish, too many to mention here. What an incredible place to call my writing home!

My Book Groupies—Ann Horwitz, Lynn Gallagher, Jen Rothenberg, Beth Girioni, Sarita Bhagwat, Sally Chvany, Eliza Jacob-Dolan, Sara Galantowiz, and Amy Hubbard—who read an early draft like it was a real book and had the good sense to hold back enough criticism so that I would keep writing. My dear friend Nancy Rhoads, who literally walked with me through this novel and inspired me by way of family taxidermy stories and a bird-killing cat named Elizabeth.

The FamSquad—my husband, Ben, and my children, Olivia and Miles, for putting up with lousy meals, lost weekends, and me crying about it, crying about it, crying about it. Thanks for your encouragement and support, for letting me read to you, for hugs and laughter. I and Love and You. Much. And thanks to Pippin for keeping my feet warm.

And finally, love and thanks to my long-gone dad, who I know would have been proud, and to my sweet mom, a great reader and book lover, who sure would have been tickled. Wish you'd both lived to see the day.

ABOUT THE AUTHOR

Photo © 2017 Miles Bernhard

Susan Bernhard is a Massachusetts Cultural Council Fellowship recipient and a graduate of the GrubStreet Novel Incubator program. She was born and raised in the Bitterroot Valley of western Montana, is a graduate of the University of Maryland, and lives with her husband and two children near Boston. *Winter Loon* is her first novel. Visit her at www.susanbernhard.com.